THE CORPS

The *New York Times* bestselling saga—a stunningly authentic portrait of the Marine Corps, the brave men and women who fought, and loved, in the sweeping turmoil of World War II . . .

"THE CORPS combines the best elements of military history and the war story—the telling detail and political tangle of one mated to the energy and sweep of another."
—*Publishers Weekly*

"W.E.B. Griffin has done it again. This is one writer who can spin and weave some of the most fascinating military characters in today's market."
—*Rave Reviews*

"This man has really done his homework . . . I confess to impatiently awaiting the appearance of succeeding books in the series."
—*The Washington Post*

"Packed with all the love, action, and excitement Griffin fans have come to expect."
—*Forecast*

BROTHERHOOD OF WAR

The magnificent *New York Times* bestselling saga that made Griffin a superstar of military fiction—the epic story of the U.S. Army, from the privates to the generals, in the world's most harrowing wars . . .

"Griffin is a storyteller in the grand tradition, probably the best man around for describing the military community. BROTHERHOOD OF WAR . . . is an American epic."
—bestselling author Tom Clancy

"Extremely well-done . . . First-rate."
—*The Washington Post*

"Absorbing . . . fascinating descriptions of weapons, tactics, Army life and battle."
—*The New York Times*

"A major work . . . magnificent . . . powerful."
—William Bradford Huie, author of *The Execution of Private Slovik*

"A crackling good story. It gets into the hearts and minds of those who . . . fight our nation's wars."
—William R. Corson, Lt. Col. (Ret.) U.S.M.C., author of *The Betrayal* and *The Armies of Ignorance*

W.E.B. GRIFFIN

MEN IN BLUE

Originally published under the pseudonym John Kevin Dugan

JOVE BOOKS, NEW YORK

This Jove book contains the complete
text of the original edition.
It has been completely reset in a typeface
designed for easy reading and was printed
from new film.

BADGE OF HONOR: MEN IN BLUE

A Jove Book / published by arrangement with
the author

PRINTING HISTORY
First published October 1988
Jove edition / March 1991

ISBN: 0-515-09750-0

Jove Books are published by The Berkley Publishing Group,
200 Madison Avenue, New York, New York 10016.
The name "JOVE" and the "J" logo
are trademarks belonging to Jove Publications, Inc.

PRINTED IN THE UNITED STATES OF AMERICA

20 19

For Sergeant Zebulon V. Casey
Internal Affairs Division
Police Department, Retired, the City of Philadelphia.
He knows why.

MEN IN BLUE

ONE

I think I am, the long-haired, long-legged blonde thought, torn between excitement and alarm, *about to have my first affair with a married man.*

Her name was Louise Dutton, and she pursed her lips thoughtfully and cocked her head unconsciously to one side as she considered that improbable likelihood.

She was at the wheel of a yellow, six-year-old, 1967 Cadillac convertible, the roof down, moving fifteen miles over the posted forty-five-miles-per-hour speed limit northward in the center lane of Roosevelt Boulevard, which runs through the center of Northeast Philadelphia, from Broad Street to the Bucks County line.

Louise Dutton was twenty-five years old, weighed 115 pounds, and her blond hair was real—a genetic gift from her father. She had graduated three years before (BA, English) from the University of Chicago. She had worked a year as a general-assignment reporter on the Cedar Rapids, Iowa, *Clarion;* six months as a newswriter for KLOS-

1

TV (Channel 10), Los Angeles, California; and for eleven months as an on-camera reporter for WNOG-TV (Channel 7), New Orleans, Louisiana. For the past five weeks Louise Dutton had been co-anchor of "Nine's News," over WCBL-TV (Channel 9), Philadelphia: thirty minutes of local news telecast at six P.M., preceding the 6:30 national news, and again at 11 P.M.

A crazy scenario entered her mind.

She would get arrested for speeding. Preferably by one of the hotshot Highway Patrolmen. He would swagger over to the car, in his shiny leather jacket and his gun and holster with all the bullets showing.

"Where's the fire, honey?" Mr. Macho, with a gun and a badge, would demand.

"Actually," she would say, batting her eyelashes at him, "I'm on my way to meet Captain Moffitt."

Captain Richard C. "Dutch" Moffitt was the commanding officer of the Philadelphia Highway Patrol.

And the cop who stopped her for speeding would either believe her, and leave her properly awed, or he would not believe her, and ask her where she was supposed to meet the captain, and she would tell him, and maybe he would follow her there to see if she was telling the truth. That would be even better. Maybe it would embarrass Dutch Moffitt to have one of his men learn that he was meeting a blonde in a restaurant.

It would not, she decided. He'd love it. The cop would wink at Captain Big Dutch Moffitt and Dutch would modestly shrug his shoulders. Dutch expected to have blond young women running after him.

I am losing my mind.

Is this what happened to my mother? One day my father appeared, and she went crazy?

Is that why I'm going where I'm going, and in this circumstance? Because Dutch Moffitt reminds me of my father?

Is it true that all little girls harbor a shameful secret desire to go to bed with their fathers? Is that what this is, "Dutch Moffitt, in loco parentis"?

Ahead, on the left, she spotted the site of their rendez-vous. Or was it assignation?

The Waikiki Diner, to judge from the outside decor, was not going to be the Philadelphia equivalent of Arnaud's, or for that matter, even Brennan's; more like the Golden Kettle in Cedar Rapids.

She turned into the U-turn lane, jammed the accelerator to the floor to move her ahead of an oncoming wave of traffic, and then turned off Roosevelt Boulevard, too fast. Louise winced when she felt the Cadillac bottom going over the curb.

The Cadillac was her college graduation gift. Or one of them. Her father had handed her a check and told her to pick herself out a car.

"I'd rather have yours," she said. "If I could."

He had looked at her, confused, for a moment, and then understood. "The yellow convertible? It's three years old. I was about to get rid of it."

"Then I can have it?" she'd said. "It's hardly used."

He had looked at her for a moment, understanding, she thought, before replying.

"Of course," he said. "I'll have someone bring it here."

She had leaned forward and kissed him and said, "Thank you, Daddy," and he'd hugged her.

Louise Dutton's father was not, and never had been, married to her mother. She was illegitimate, a bastard; but the reality hadn't been—wasn't—as bad as most people, when they heard the facts, presumed it was.

She had been presented with the facts when she was a little girl, matter-of-factly told there were reasons her father and mother could not be married, that he could not live with them, or see her as often as he would like. That was the way things were, and it wasn't going to change. She didn't even hate her father's wife, or her half-brothers and -sisters.

It wasn't as if her father considered her an embarrass-ment, wished she had never happened. The older she got, the more she saw of him. He spent his Christmases with his family, and she spent hers with her mother and her mother's husband, and she called both men "Daddy." So far as she knew, they had never met, and she had never seen her father's family, even across a room.

Her father had always, from the time she was nine or ten, found a couple of days to spend with her before or after Christmas, and he sent for her several times during the year, and she spent several days or a week with him, and he always introduced her as "my daughter."

She had been a freshman in college when he'd taken her deep-sea fishing for ten days in Baja, California. She'd flown to Los Angeles, and spent the night in his beach house in Malibu, and then driven, in the yellow convertible, to Baja. A wonderful ten days. And he knew why she wanted the convertible.

She had wondered what his wife, and her half-brothers and -sisters thought about her, and finally realized they were in the same position she was. Stanford Fortner Wells III, chairman of the board of Wells Newspapers, Inc., did what he damned well pleased. They were just lucky that what he damned well pleased to do was almost invariably kind, and thoughtful, and ethical.

Maybe that was easier if you had inherited that kind of money, and maybe he wouldn't have been so kind, thoughtful, or ethical if he was a life insurance salesman or an automobile dealer, *but he wasn't.* He had inherited seventeen newspapers and three radio stations from his father, and turned that into thirty-one newspapers, four television stations, and four (larger) radio stations.

The only thing that Louise could discover that her father had done wrong was, as a married man, impregnate a woman to whom he was not married. He had sown *her* seed in a forbidden field. But even then, he had done the decent thing. He had not abandoned his wife and children for the greener fields of a much younger woman, and he had not abandoned *her.* He could very easily have made "appropriate financial arrangements" and never shown his face.

She loved and admired her father, and if people didn't understand that, fuck 'em.

Louise found a place to park the yellow convertible, and then walked to the Waikiki Diner. There were no cars in the parking lot that looked like unmarked police cars, which meant that he had either come in his own car, or that he wasn't here yet.

She pushed open the door to the Waikiki Diner and stepped inside. It was larger inside than it looked to be from the outside. It was shaped like an L. The shorter leg, which was what she had seen from the street, held a counter, with padded seats on stools, and one row of banquettes against the wall. Beside the door, which was at the juncture of the legs, was the cashier's glass counter and a bar with a couple of stools, but obviously primarily a service bar. The longer leg was also wider, and was a dining room. There were probably forty tables in there, Louise judged, plus banquettes against the walls.

He wasn't in there.

She thought: *Captain Richard C. "Dutch" Moffitt, commanding officer of the Philadelphia Police Department's Highway Patrol, has not yet found time to grace the Waikiki Diner with his patronage.*

"Help you, doll?" a waitress asked. She was slight, had orange hair, too much makeup, and was pushing sixty.

"I'm supposed to meet someone here," Louise said.

"Why'ncha take a table?" the waitress asked, and led Louise into the dining room. Lousie saw that one of the banquettes against the wall, in a position where she could see the door beside the cash register, was empty, and she slipped into it. The waitress went thirty feet farther before she realized that she wasn't being followed.

Then she turned and, obviously miffed, laid an enormous menu in front of Louise.

"You want a cocktail or something while you're waiting?" she asked.

"Coffee, please, black," Louise said.

She didn't want alcohol to cloud her reasoning any more than it was already clouded.

She looked around the dining room. It was arguably, she decided, the ugliest dining room she had ever been in. Fake Tiffany lamps, with enormous rotating fans hanging from them, in turn hung from plastic replicas of wooden ceiling beams. The banquettes were upholstered in diamond-embossed purple vinyl. The wall across the room was a really awful mural of lasses in flowing dresses and lads in what looked like diapers dancing around what was probably supposed to be the Parthenon.

The coffee was delivered in a thick china mug decorated with a pair of leaning palm trees and the legend, *"Waikiki Diner Roosevelt Blvd Phila Penna."*

Captain Richard C. "Dutch" Moffitt came in as Louise had removed, in shock and surprise, the scalding hot mug from her burned lips.

He had no sooner come through the door by the cashier than a small, slight man with a large mustache, wearing a tight, prominently pin-striped suit, came up to him and offered his hand, his smile revealing a lot of goldwork.

Dutch smiled back at him, revealing his own mouthful of large, white, even teeth. And then he saw Louise, and the smile brightened, and his eyebrows rose and he headed toward the table.

"Hello," Dutch said to her, sliding into the chair facing her.

"Hi!" Louise said.

"This is our host," Dutch said, nodding at the mustached man. "Teddy Galanapoulos."

"A pleasure, I'm sure. Any friend of Captain Moffitt's . . ."

"Hello," Louise said. There was a slight Greek accent, and the gowned lasses and the lads in diapers dancing around the Parthenon were now explained.

"You're beautiful," Dutch said.

"Thank you," Louise said, mortified when she felt her face flush. She stood up. "Will you excuse me, please?"

When she came back from the ladies' room, where she had, furious with herself, checked her hair and her lipstick, Dutch had changed places. He was now sitting on the purple vinyl banquette seat. His left hand, which was enormous, was curled around a squat glass of whiskey. There was a wide gold wedding band on the proper finger.

He started to get up when he saw her.

It was the first time she had ever seen him in civilian clothing. He was wearing a blue blazer over a yellow knit shirt. The shirt was tight against his large chest, and there wasn't, she thought, a lot of excess room in the shoulders of the blazer either.

"Keep your seat," Louise said, "since you seem to like that one better."

"I'm a cop," he said. "Cops don't like to sit with their backs to the door."

"Really?" she asked, not sure if he was pulling her leg or not.

"Really," he said, then added: "I didn't know what you drink."

"I'm surprised," she said.

She had first met him two days before.

His Honor, Mayor Jerry Carlucci, who never passed up an opportunity to get his face in the newspapers or on television, reopened a repaired stretch of the Schuylkill Expressway with a ribbon-cutting ceremony. Louise, having nothing better to do at the time, had gone along with the regular crew of cameraman/producer and reporter, originally intending to do the on-camera bit herself.

But when she got there, and saw what it was, much ado about nothing, she had decided not to usurp the reporter. But instead of leaving, she decided to hang around in case the mayor ran off at the mouth again. Mayor Carlucci had a tendency to do that (in the most recent incident, he had referred to a city councilman as "an ignorant coon") and *that* would make a story.

She told the cameraman to shoot the mayor from the time he arrived until he left.

The mayor usually moved around the city in style, in a black Cadillac limousine, preceded by two unmarked police cars carrying his plainclothes bodyguards.

A third car had stopped right where Louise had been

standing. The driver's door had opened, and Captain Richard C. "Dutch" Moffitt had erupted from it. He was a large man, and he had been in uniform. The Highway Patrol wore different uniforms than the rest of the Philadelphia Police Department.

The Highway Patrol had begun, years before, as a traffic-control force, and had been mounted on motorcycles. They had kept their motorcyclist outfits—leather jackets and breeches and black leather puttees—even though, except for mostly ceremonial occasions, they had given up their motorcycles for patrol cars; and had, in fact become an elite force within the police department, deployed city-wide in high-crime areas.

In the Channel 9 newsroom, the Philadelphia Highway Patrol was referred to as "Carlucci's Commandos." But, not, Louise had noticed, without a not-insignificant tone of respect, however grudging.

Louise Dutton had found herself standing so close to Captain Richard C. Moffitt that she could smell his leather jacket, and that he had been chewing Sen-Sen. Her eyes were on the level of his badge, above which was pinned a blue, gold-striped ribbon, on which were half a dozen stars. It was, Louise correctly guessed, some kind of a citation. Citations, plural, with the stars representing multiple awards.

He winked at her, and then, putting his hand on the car door, rose on his toes to look back at Mayor Carlucci's limousine. Louise saw that he wore a wedding ring, and then turned to see what he was looking at. Two plain-clothesmen were shouldering a path for His Honor the Mayor through the crowd to the flag-bedecked sawhorses where the ribbon would be cut.

Then he looked down at her.

"I've seen you on the tube," he said. "I'm Dutch Moffitt."

She gave him her hand and her name.

"You look better in real life, Louise Dutton," he said.

"May I ask you a question, Captain Moffitt?" she had said.

"Sure."

"Some of the people I know refer to the Highway Patrol as 'Carlucci's Commandos.' What's your reaction to that?"

"Fuck 'em," he said immediately, matter-of-factly.

"Can I quote you?" she flared.

"You can, but I don't think you could say that on TV," he said, smiling down at her.

"You arrogant bastard!"

"I'd be happy, since you just came to town, to explain what the Highway Patrol does," he said. "And why that annoys the punks and the faggots."

She gave him what she hoped was her most disdainful look.

"I'll even throw in a couple of drinks and dinner," he said.

"Why don't you call me?" Louise had asked, flashing him her most dazzling smile. "At home, of course. I wouldn't want it to get around the station that I was having drinks and dinner with one of Carlucci's Commandos. Especially a married one. So *nice* to talk to you, Captain."

She did not get the response she expected.

"You're really full of piss and vinegar, aren't you?" he said, approvingly.

She had stormed furiously away. She first decided that he was arrogant enough to call her, even if her sarcasm had flown six feet over his head. She took what she later recognized was childish solace in the telephone arrangements at the studios. With all the kooks and nuts out there in TV Land, you just couldn't call Channel 9 and get put through to Louise Dutton. But they might put a police captain through, and then what?

When she went back to the studio, she went to the head telephone operator and told her that for reasons she couldn't go into, if a police captain named Moffitt called, she didn't want to talk to him; tell him she was out.

The arrogant bastard would sooner or later get the message.

And there was no way he could call her at home. The

studio wouldn't tell him where she lived, and the number was unlisted.

Today, three hours before, the telephone had rung in her apartment, just as she had stepped into the shower.

She knew it wasn't her father; he had called at ten, waking her up, asking her how it was going. Anybody else could wait. If they'd dropped the atomic bomb, she would have heard it go off.

The phone had not stopped ringing, and finally, torn between gross annoyance and a growing concern that some big story had developed, she walked, dripping water, to the telephone beside her bed.

"Hello?"

"Are you all right?"

There was genuine concern in Captain Dutch Moffitt's voice, but she realized this only after she had snapped at him.

"Why shouldn't I be all right?"

"People have been robbed, and worse, in there before," he said.

"How did you get this number?" Louise demanded, and then thought of another question. "How did you know I was home?"

"I sent a car by," he said. "They told me the yellow convertible was in the garage."

She raised her eyes and saw the reflection of her starkers body in the mirror doors of her closet. She wondered what Captain Dutch Moffitt would think if he could see her.

She shook her head, and felt her face flush.

"What do you want?" she asked.

"I want to see you," he said.

"That's absurd," she said.

"Yeah, I know," he said. "I can take off early at four. There's a diner on Roosevelt Boulevard, at Harbison, called the Waikiki. Meet me there, say four-fifteen."

"Impossible," she said.

"Why impossible?"

"I have to work," she said.

"No, you don't. Don't lie to me, Louise."

"Oh, hell, Dutch!"

"Four-fifteen," he said, and hung up.

And she had looked at her naked body in the mirror again and known that at four o'clock, she would be in the Waikiki Diner.

And here she was, looking into this married man's eyes and suddenly aware that the last thing she wanted in the world was to get involved with him, in bed, or in any other way.

What the hell was I thinking of? I was absolutely out of my mind to come here!

"I'm a cop," he said. "Finding out where you lived and getting your phone number wasn't hard."

"I think I will have a scotch and soda," Louise said. "Johnnie Walker Black."

He pushed his glass to her.

"I'll get another," he said.

It was rude and certainly unsanitary but she picked it up and sipped from it as he gestured toward the bar for another.

Why the hell did I do that? she wondered, and then the answer came to her: *Because I don't know what to do to keep myself from making more of a fool of myself than I already have. How am I going to get out of this?*

The mustached Greek proprietor delivered the drink immediately himself.

"We seem to have at least one thing in common," Dutch Moffitt said.

"Wow!" she said.

"Relax, Louise," he said. "I'm not going to hurt you."

She looked at him again, met his eyes for a moment, and then looked away.

"I don't know why I came here," she said. "But just to clear the air, I now realize it was a mistake."

Dutch Moffitt opened his mouth to reply, but before the words came out, he was interrupted by a male voice.

"Good afternoon, Captain Moffitt, nice to see you."

The sleeve of a glen-plaid suit passed in front of Louise's face.

"Hello, Angelo," Moffitt said.

Louise, once the arm was withdrawn, looked up. A pleasant-looking, olive-skinned man—Italian to judge by the "Angelo"—well barbered, smelling of some expensive cologne, was standing by the table.

"My father was asking about you just this morning," the man said.

"How's your mother, Angelo?" Moffitt asked.

"Very well, thank you," Angelo said.

"Give her my regards," Moffitt said.

Angelo smiled at Louise, and then looked at Moffitt.

"Are you going to introduce me to this charming lady?"

"Nice to see you, Angelo," Moffitt said.

Angelo colored, and then walked away.

"What was that," Louise demanded. "Simply bad manners? Or—"

"That was Angelo Turpino," Moffitt said. "You don't want to know him."

"Why?"

"He's a thug," Moffitt said. "No. Correction. He's a made man. Their standards are slipping. A couple of years ago, that slimy little turd wouldn't have made a pimple on a made man's ass."

"What's a 'made man'?"

He looked at her, into her eyes again.

"When one commences on a career in organized crime, one's highest aspiration is to become a made man," Moffitt said, mockingly. "A made man, so to speak, is one who is accepted, one who enjoys all the rights and privileges of acknowledged master craftsmanship in his chosen trade. Analogous, one might say, to the designation of an individual as a doctor of medicine."

"You're saying that he's in the Mafia?"

"The 'family,' we call it," Moffitt said.

"What did he do to become 'made'?"

"About six weeks ago, Vito Poltaro, sometimes known—from his initials, you see—as 'the vice president,' was found in the trunk of his car in a parking garage downtown, behind the Bellevue-Stratford Hotel. Poor Vito had two .22 holes in the back of his head. Five-dollar bills were found in his mouth, his ears, his nostrils, and other body orifices. This signifies greed. I think that Angelo did it. A week after Organized Crime found Vito, they heard that Angelo had been to New York and had come back a made man.''

There was no question in Louise's mind that what he was telling her was true.

''What about Organized Crime finding the body?'' she asked. ''I didn't understand that.''

''There's a unit, called Organized Crime, because what it does is try to keep tabs on people like Angelo,'' he said.

They were looking into each other's eyes again. Louise averted hers.

''You don't really want to talk about the mob, do you?'' he asked.

''No,'' she said. ''I don't.''

''Then what shall we talk about?''

''What about your wife?'' Louise blurted.

He lowered his head, and shrugged and then looked at her.

And then he said, ''Oh, *shit!*''

He was, she saw, looking over her shoulder.

She started to turn around.

''Don't turn around!'' he said, quietly but very firmly.

He slipped off the banquette and started toward the door, moving on the balls of his feet, like a cat.

She wanted desperately to look, and started to turn, and then couldn't, because he had said not to. And then she could see him, faintly, in the mirrored side surface of a service table. She saw him brush the flap of his blazer aside with his hand, and then she saw that he had a gun.

Then she turned, chilled.

He was holding the gun with the muzzle pointed down, beside his leg. And he was walking to the cash register.

There was a young man at the cash register, skinny, with long blond hair. He was wearing a zipper jacket, and he had a brown paper bag in his hand, extended toward the cashier as if he was handing it to her.

And then Dutch Moffitt was five feet away from him, and the pistol came up.

She could hear him, even over the sounds of the Waikiki Diner.

"Lay the gun on the counter, son," Dutch said. "I'm a police officer. I don't want to have to kill you."

The kid looked at him, his face turned even more pale. He licked his lips, and he seemed to be lowering the paper bag.

And then there were pops, one after the other, five or six of them, sounding like Chinese firecrackers.

"Oh, shit!" Dutch Moffitt said, more sadly than angrily.

The glass front of the cashier's stand slid with a crash to the floor, and there was an eruption of liquid and falling glass in the rows of liquor bottles in the service bar.

Dutch grabbed the skinny blond kid by the collar of his zipper jacket and threw him violently across the room. Then he took three steps to the door of the diner. He pushed it open with his shoulder, and went through it; and then he was holding his pistol in both hands, taking aim; and then he fired, and again and again.

The noise from his pistol was deafening, shocking, and Louise heard a woman yelp, and someone swore.

The skinny blond boy came running down the aisle. She got a good look at his face. He looked sick.

Louise pushed herself off her chair and ran down the aisle to the cash register.

Dutch was outside, on his knees beside a form on the ground. Louise thought it was another blond boy, but then Dutch turned the body over on its back and she saw lipstick and red, round-framed women's eyeglasses.

"He ran into the restaurant," Louise screamed. When there was no response from Dutch she screamed his name, and got his attention, and, pointing, repeated, "He ran into the restaurant. The blond boy."

He got up and walked quickly past her. She followed him.

The Greek proprietor came up.

"He ran through the kitchen, the sonofabitch," he reported.

Dutch nodded.

He put his pistol back in its holster and fished the cashier's telephone from where it had fallen, onto the cigars
and foil-wrapped chocolates, when the glass counter had
shattered.

He dialed a number.

"This is Captain Moffitt, Highway Patrol," he said.
"I'm at Harbison and the Boulevard, the Waikiki Diner.
Give me an assist. I have a robbery and a police shooting
and a hospital case. I'm hit. One male fled on foot, direction unknown, white, in his twenties. Long blond hair,
brown zipper jacket. No! God*damn* it. *Harbison* and the
Boulevard."

He put the phone back in the cradle, smiled reassuringly
at Louise, and raised his voice.

"It's all over, folks," he said. "Nothing else to worry
about. You just sit there and finish your meals."

He turned and looked at Louise again.

"Dutch, are you all right?" Louise asked.

"Fine," he said. "I'm fine."

And then he staggered, moving backward until he encountered the wall.

His face was now very white.

"It was a goddamned girl!" he said, surprised, barely
audibly.

And then he just crumpled to the floor.

"Dutch!" Louise cried, and went to him.

He's fainted! That's all it is, he's fainted!

And then she saw his eyes, and there was no life in
them.

"Oh, Dutch!" Louise wailed. "Oh, damn you, Dutch!"

Philadelphia, in 1973 the fourth largest city of the United
States, lies in the center of the New York–Washington corridor, one of the most densely populated areas in the country.

A one-hundred-mile-radius circle drawn from William

Penn's statue atop City Hall at Broad and Market Streets in downtown Philadelphia takes in Harrisburg to the west; skirts Washington, D.C., to the south; takes in almost all of Delaware and the New Jersey shore to the southeast and east; touches the tip of Manhattan Island to the northeast; and just misses Scranton, Pennsylvania to the north.

Within that one-hundred-mile-radius circle are major cities: Baltimore, Maryland; Camden, Trenton, Elizabeth, Newark, and Jersey City, New Jersey; plus a long list of somewhat smaller cities, such as Atlantic City, New Jersey; Wilkes-Barre, Pennsylvania; Wilmington, Delaware, and New Brunswick, New Jersey; York, Lancaster, Reading, Allentown, Bethlehem, and Hazleton, Pennsylvania; plus the boroughs of Manhattan, Brooklyn, and Richmond (Staten Island) of New York City.

There are more than four million people in the "standard metropolitan statistical area" of Philadelphia and its environs, and something over two million people within the city limits, which covers 129 square miles. In 1973, there were approximately eight thousand policemen keeping the peace in the City of Brotherly Love.

The Police Administration Building on Vine Street in downtown Philadelphia is what in another city would be called "police headquarters." In Philadelphia it is known to the police and public as "the Roundhouse."

The architect who envisioned the building managed to pass on his enthusiasm for the curve to those city officials charged with approving its design. There are no straight corridors; the interior and exterior walls, even those of the elevators, are curved.

The Radio Room of the Philadelphia Police Department is on the second floor of the Roundhouse. Within the Radio Room are rows of civilian employees, leavened with a few sworn police officers, who sit at telephone and radio consoles receiving calls from the public, and from police vehicles "on the street" and relaying official orders to police vehicles.

There are twenty-two police districts in Philadelphia, each charged with maintaining the peace in its area. Each has its complement of radio-equipped police cars and vans. Additionally, there are seven divisions of detectives, occupying office space in district buildings, but answering to a detective hierarchy, rather than to the district commander. They have their own, radio-equipped, police cars.

Radio communication is also maintained with the vehicles of the Philadelphia Highway Patrol, which has its own headquarters; with the vehicles of the Traffic, Accident, and Juvenile divisions; with the fleet of police tow trucks; and with the vehicles of the various special-purpose units, such as the K-9 Unit, the Marine Unit, the Vice, Narcotics, Organized Crime units, and others.

And on top of this, of course, is the necessity to maintain communications with the vehicles of the senior command hierarchy of the police department, the commissioner, and his staff; the deputy commissioners and their staffs; the chief inspectors and their staffs; and a plethora of other senior police officers.

With more than a thousand police vehicles "on the street" at any one time, it was necessary to develop, both by careful planning and by trial and error, a system permitting instant contact with the right vehicle at the right time. The police commissioner is not really interested to learn instantly of every automobile accident in Philadelphia, nor is a request from the airport police for a paddy wagon to haul off three drunks from the airport of much interest to a detective looking for a murder suspect in an alley off North Broad Street.

So far as the police were concerned, Philadelphia was broken down into seven geographical divisions, each headed by an inspector. Each division contained from two to four districts, each headed by a captain. Each division was assigned its own radio frequency. Detectives' cars and those assigned to other investigative units (Narcotics, Intelligence, Organized Crime, et cetera) had radios operating on the H-Band. *All* police car radios could be switched to an all-purpose emergency and utility frequency called the J-Band.

For example, a police car in the Sixteenth District would

routinely have his switch set to F-1, which would permit him to communicate with his (the West) division. Switching to F-2 would put him on the universal J-Band. A car assigned to South Philadelphia with his switch set to F-1 would be in contact with the South Division. A detective operating anywhere with his switch set to F-1 would be on the (Detectives') H-Band, but he too, by switching to F-2, would be on the J-Band.

Senior police brass are able to communicate with other senior police brass, and most often on the detective frequency or on the frequency of some other service in which he has a personal interest. Ordinary police cars are required to communicate through the dispatcher, and forbidden to talk car-to-car. Car-to-car communication is authorized on the J- and H-bands.

"Communications discipline" is strictly enforced. Otherwise, there would be communications chaos.

By throwing the appropriate switch, a Radio Room dispatcher may send a radio message to every radio-equipped vehicle, from a police boat making its way against the current of the Delaware River, through the hundreds of police cars on patrol, to the commissioner's car.

It happens when a light flashes on a console and an operator throws a switch and says, "Police Radio," and the party calling says, "Officer needs assistance. Shots fired."

Not every call making such an announcement is legitimate. The wise guys have watched cop movies on television, and know the cant; and ten or twelve times every day they decide that watching a flock of police cars, lights flashing and sirens screaming, descend on a particular street corner would be a good way to liven up an otherwise dull afternoon.

The people who answer the telephones didn't come to work yesterday, however, and sometimes they *know,* by the timbre of the caller's voice possibly, or the assurance with which the caller raises the alarm, that *this* call is legitimate.

The dispatcher who took Captain Richard C. "Dutch"

Moffitt's call from the Waikiki Diner was Mrs. Leander Polk, forty-eight, a more than pleasantly plump black lady who had been on the job for nineteen years.

"Lieutenant!" she called, raising her voice, just to get his attention, not to ask his permission. Then she threw the appropriate switch.

Two beeps, signifying an emergency message, were broadcast to every police radio in Philadelphia.

"Roosevelt Boulevard and Harbison," Mrs. Polk said clearly. "The Waikiki Diner. Assist officer. Police by phone."

She repeated that message once again, and then went on: "Report of a robbery, shooting, and hospital case." She repeated that, and then, quickly, to the lieutenant who had come to her station: "Captain Moffitt called it in."

And then she broadcast: "All cars going in on the assist, Harbison and the Boulevard, flash information on a robbery at that location. Be on the lookout for white male, long blond hair, brown jacket, direction taken unknown, armed with a gun."

And then she repeated that.

TWO

Highway Two-B was a Philadelphia Highway Patrol vehicle moving southward on Roosevelt Boulevard, just entering Oxford Circle. It was occupied by Sergeant Alexander W. Dannelly, and driven by Police Officer David N. Waldron. Sergeant Dannelly and Officer Waldron had moments before seen Captain Dutch Moffitt going into the Waikiki Diner, dressed to kill in civvies.

It was four in the afternoon, and Captain Dutch Moffitt usually worked until half-past five, and often longer. And in uniform.

"The captain is obviously engaged in a very secret undercover investigation," Sergeant Dannelly said.

"Under-the-covers, you said, Sergeant?" Officer Waldron asked, grinning.

"You have an evil mind, Officer Waldron," Sergeant Dannelly said, grinning back. "Shame on you!"

"How about a cup of coffee, Sergeant?" Waldron asked. "The Waikiki serves a fine cup of coffee."

"You also have a suicidal tendency," Sergeant Dannelly said. "I ever tell you that?"

Two beeps on the radio cut off the conversation.

"Roosevelt Boulevard and Harbison," the dispatcher's voice said. "The Waikiki Diner. Assist officer. Police by phone. Roosevelt Boulevard and Harbison. The Waikiki Diner. Assist officer. Police by phone."

"Jesus Christ!" Officer Waldron said.

"That's got to be the captain," Dannelly said.

"Report of a robbery, shooting, and hospital case," the dispatcher said. "All cars going in on the assist, Harbison and the Boulevard, flash information on a robbery at that location. Be on the lookout for Caucasian male, long blond hair, brown jacket, direction taken unknown, armed with a gun."

As Sergeant Dannelly reached for the microphone, without waiting for orders, Officer Waldron had dropped the transmission shift lever into D-2, and flipped the switches activating the flashing light assembly and the siren, and then shoved his foot to the floor.

"Highway Two-B in on that," Sergeant Dannelly said into the microphone.

The Ford, its engine screaming in protest, tires squealing, accelerated the rest of the way around Oxford Circle and back down Roosevelt Boulevard toward the Waikiki Diner.

The second response came on the heels of Highway Two B's: "Two-Oh-One in on that Waikiki Diner."

It was not the truth, the whole truth, and nothing but the truth. Two-Oh-One was not that *instant* responding to the call.

The Waikiki Diner was in the territory of the Second Police District. Two-Oh-One was a Second Police District patrol wagon, a Ford van.

Philadelphia police, unlike those of every other major city, respond to all calls for any kind of assistance.

If you break a leg, *call the cops!* If Uncle Harry has a heart attack, *call the cops!* If you get your fingers in the Waring blender, *call the cops!*

A paddy wagon will respond, and haul you to the hospital. Not in great comfort, for the back of the van holds only a stretcher, and there is no array of high-tech lifesaving apparatus. But it will cart you to the hospital as fast as humanly possible.

Paddy wagons are police vehicles, driven by armed sworn police officers, normally young muscular officers without much time on the job. Young muscles are often needed to carry large citizens down three flights of stairs, and to restrain bellicose drunks, for the paddy wagon also still performs the function it did when it was pulled by horses, and "paddy" was a pejorative term for those of Irish heritage. Paddy wagon duty is recognized to be a good way to introduce young police officers to what it's really like on the streets.

When the "assist officer" call came over the radio, Two-Oh-One was parked outside Sid's Steak Sandwiches & Hamburgers on the corner of Cottman and Summerdale avenues, across from Northeast High School. Officer Francis Mason was at the wheel and Officer Patrick Foley was inside Sid's, where he had ordered a couple of cheese steaks and two large Cokes to go, and then visited the gentlemen's rest facility. He and Francis had attended a function of the Fraternal Order of Police the night before, and he had taken advantage of the free beer bar. He'd had the runs all day.

Officer Mason, when he got the call, picked up the microphone and said Two-Oh-One was responding, flicked up the siren and lights, and reached over and pushed open the passenger side door. It was ninety seconds, but seemed much longer, before Officer Foley appeared, on the run, a pained look on his face, fastening his gun belt, and jumped in the van.

Officer Mason made a U-turn on Summerdale Avenue; skidded to a stop at Cottman; waited until there was a break in the traffic; and then turned onto Cottman, running on the left side of the avenue, against oncoming traffic, until he was finally able to force himself into the inside right lane.

"I think I shit my pants," Officer Foley said.

The broadcast was also received by a vehicle parked in the parking lot of LaSalle College at Twentieth Street and Olney Avenue, where a crew from WCBL-TV had just finished taping yet another student protest over yet another tuition increase. After a moment's indecision, Miss Penny Bakersfield, the reporter, told the driver that there might be something in the car for "Nine's News," if he thought he could get there in a hurry.

Highway Two-B made a wide sweeping U-turn, its tires screeching, from the northbound center lane of Roosevelt Boulevard into the southbound right lane and then into the parking lot of the Waikiki Diner.

There were no police cars evident in the parking lot; that made it almost certain that the "assist officer, shots fired" call had come from Captain Dutch Moffitt, who had either been in his unmarked car, or his own car.

Sergeant Dannelly had the door open before Highway Two-B lurched to a stop in front of the diner. Pistol drawn, he ran into the building, with Waldron on his heels.

A blond woman was on her knees beside Dutch Moffitt, who seemed to be sitting on the floor with his back against the wall. Dannelly pushed her out of the way, saw the blank look in Moffitt's eyes, and then felt for a pulse.

"He ran out the back," the woman said, very softly.

"Go after him!" Dannelly ordered Waldron. "I'll go around outside."

He pushed himself to his feet and ran back out of the diner. He recognized the signs of fury in himself—*some miserable fucking pissant shit had shot Dutch, the best goddamn captain in the department*—and told himself to take it easy.

He stopped and took two deep breaths and then started to run around the diner building. Then he changed his mind. He ran to the car, whose doors were still open, switched the radio to the J-Band, and picked up the microphone.

"Highway Two-B to radio. Will you have all Highway cars switch to J-Band, please."

He waited a moment, to give radio time to relay the message, and to give everybody time to switch frequencies, and then put the mike to his lips again.

"Highway Two-B to all Highway cars. We have a police shooting at Boulevard and Harbison involving Highway One. All Highway units respond and survey the area for suspect. Radio, will you rebroadcast the description of the suspect?"

He threw the microphone on the seat and started to run to the rear of the Waikiki Diner. He knew that all over the city, every Highway Patrol car had turned on its siren and flashing lights and was heading for the Waikiki Diner.

"Highway takes care of its own," Sergeant Dannelly said firmly, although there was nobody around to hear him.

The third response to the "assist officer, shots fired" call came from a new, light tan 1973 Ford LTD Brougham, which was proceeding northward on Roosevelt Boulevard, just past Adams Avenue and the huge, red brick regional offices of Sears, Roebuck & Company.

There was nothing to indicate the LTD was a police vehicle. It even had whitewall tires. When the driver, Peter F. Wohl, a tall man in his very early thirties, wearing a well-cut glen-plaid suit, decided to respond, he had to lean over and open the glove compartment to take the microphone out.

"Isaac Twenty-three," he said to the microphone, "put me in on that assist."

He pushed in the button on the steering wheel that caused all the lights on the LTD to flash on and off (what Ford called "the emergency flasher system") and started methodically sounding his horn. The LTD had neither a siren nor a flashing light.

"Isaac" was the call sign for "Inspector." Peter F. Wohl was a Staff Inspector. On those very rare occasions when he wore a uniform, it carried a gold leaf insignia, identical to the U.S. military's insignia for a major.

A Staff Inspector ranked immediately above a captain, and immediately below an inspector, who wore the rank insignia of a lieutenant colonel. There were eighteen of them, and Peter F. Wohl was the youngest. Staff inspectors thought of themselves as, and were generally regarded, by those who knew what they really did, to be, some of the best cops around.

They were charged with investigating police corruption, but that was not all they did, and they didn't even do that the way most people thought they did. They were not interested in some cop taking an Easter ham from a butcher, but their ears did pick up when the word started going around that a captain somewhere had taken a blonde not his wife to Jersey to play the horses in a new Buick.

As they thought of it, they investigated corruption in the city administration; fraud against the city; bribery and extortion; crimes with a political connection; the more interesting endeavors of organized crime; a number of other interesting things; and only way down at the bottom of the list, crooked cops.

Peter (no one had ever called him "Pete," not even as a kid; even then he had had a quiet dignity) Wohl did not look much the popular image of a cop. People would guess that he was a stockbroker, or maybe an engineer or lawyer. A *professional*, in other words. But he was a cop. He'd done his time walking a beat, and he'd even been a corporal in the Highway Patrol. But when he'd made sergeant, young, not quite six years on the force, they'd assigned him to the Civil Disobedience Squad, in plain clothes, and he'd been in plain clothes ever since.

It was said that Peter Wohl would certainly make it up toward the top, maybe all the way. He had the smarts and he worked hard, and he seldom made mistakes. Equally important, he came from a long line of cops. His father had retired as a Chief Inspector, and the line went back far behind him.

The roots of the Wohl family were in Hesse. Friedrich Wohl had been a farmer from a small village near Kassel, pressed into service as a Grenadier in the Landgrave of Hesse-Kassel's Regiment of Light Foot. Primarily to finance a university he had founded (and named after himself) in buildings he confiscated from the Roman Catholic

Church at Marburg an der Lahn, Landgrave Philip had rented out his soldiers to His Most Britannic Majesty, George III of England, who had a rebellion on his hands in his North American colonies.

Some predecessor of William Casey (some say it was Baron von Steuben, others think it was the Marquis de Lafayette) pointed out to the founding fathers that the Landgrave of Hesse-Kassel's Regiment of Light Foot (known, because of their uniforms, as "the Redcoats") were first-class soldiers, sure to cause the Continental Army a good deal of trouble. But they also pointed out that many of them were conscripted, and not very fond of the Landgrave for conscripting them. And, further, that a number of them were Roman Catholic, who considered the Landgrave's expulsion of the Church and his confiscation of Church property an unspeakable outrage against Holy Mother Church.

It was theorized that an offer of 160 acres of land, a small amount of gold, and a horse might induce a number of the Redcoats to desert. The theory was put into practice and at least one hundred Redcoats took advantage of the offer. Among them, although he was not a Roman Catholic and had entered the service of the Landgrave voluntarily, was Grenadier Friedrich Wohl.

Friedrich Wohl's farm, near what is now Media, prospered. When the War of 1812 came along, he borrowed heavily against it, and used the money to invest in a privateer, which would prey upon British shipping and make him a fortune. The *Determination* sailed down the Delaware with all flags flying and was never heard from again.

Wohl lost his farm and was reduced to hiring himself and his sons out as farm laborers.

The sons moved to Philadelphia, where they practiced, without notable success, various trades and opened several small businesses, all of which failed. In 1854, following the Act of Consolidation, which saw the area of Philadelphia grow from 360 acres to 83,000 by the consolidation of all the tiny political entities in the area into a city, Karl-Heinz Wohl, Friedrich Wohl's youngest grandson, managed to have himself appointed to the new police department.

There had been at least one Wohl on the rolls of the Philadelphia Police Department ever since. When Peter Wohl graduated from the police academy, a captain, two lieutenants, and a detective who were either his uncles or cousins sat with Chief Inspector August Wohl on folding chairs in the auditorium watching Peter take the oath.

There was a long line of cars slowing to enter Oxford Circle ahead of him, a line that was not likely to make room for him, no matter how his lights flashed, or he sounded the horn. He fumed until his path was cleared, then floored the accelerator, racing through the circle, and leaving in his wake a half dozen citizens wondering where the cops were when they were needed to protect people from idiots like the one in the tan Ford.

He reached the intersection on Roosevelt Boulevard, at the 6600 block, where Harbison and Magee come together to cross it, and then separate again on the other side. The light was orange and then red, but he thought he could beat the first car starting up, and floored it and got across to the far lane, and then had to brake hard to keep from getting broadsided by a paddy wagon that had come down Bustleton Avenue.

The cop at the wheel of the wagon gave him a look of absolute contempt and fury as it raced past him.

Wohl followed it into the Waikiki Diner parking lot, and stopped behind it.

There was a Highway Patrol car, both doors open, nose against the entrance; and Wohl caught a glimpse of a Highway Patrolman running like hell, pistol pointing to the sky next to his ear, obviously headed for the rear of the building.

Wohl got out of his car and started toward the diner.

"Hey, you!" a voice called.

It was the driver of the wagon. He had his pistol out, too, with the muzzle pointed to the sky.

"Police officer," Wohl said, and then, when he saw a

faint glimmer of disbelief on the young cop's face, added, "Inspector Wohl."

The cop nodded.

Wohl started again toward the diner entrance and almost stepped on the body of a young person lying in a growing pool of blood. Wohl quickly felt for a pulse, and as he decided there was none, became aware that the body was that of a young woman.

He stood up and took his pistol, a Smith & Wesson "Chief's Special" snub-nosed .38 Special, from its shoulder holster. There was no question now that shots had been fired.

"In here, Officer!" a voice called, and when Wohl saw that it was Teddy Galanapoulos, who owned the Waikiki, he pushed his jacket out of the way, and reholstered his pistol. Whatever had happened here was over.   .

Teddy hadn't been calling to him, and when he ran up looked at him curiously, even suspiciously, until he recognized him.

"Lieutenant Wohl," he said.

It was not the right place or time to correct him.

"Hello, Mr. Galanapoulos," Wohl said. "What's going on?"

"Fucking kid killed Captain Moffitt," Teddy said, and pointed.

Dutch Moffitt, in civilian clothes, was slumped against the wall. A woman was kneeling beside him. She was sobbing, and as Wohl watched, she put a hand out very gingerly and very tenderly and pulled Dutch's eyelids closed.

Wohl turned to the door. The cop from the paddy wagon was coming in, and the parking lot was filling with police cars, which screeched to a halt and from which uniformed police erupted.

"Put your gun away," Wohl ordered, "and go get your stretcher. The woman in the parking lot is dead."

A look of disappointment on his face, the young cop did as he was ordered.

A Highway Patrol sergeant, one Wohl didn't recognize,

walked quickly through the restaurant, holstering his pistol. He looked curiously at Wohl.

"I'm Inspector Wohl," Wohl said.

"Yes, sir," Sergeant Alex Dannelly said. "There was two of them, sir. Dutch got the one that shot him. The other one, a white male twenty to twenty-five years old, blond hair, ran through the restaurant and out the kitchen."

"You get it on the air?"

"No, sir," Dannelly said.

"Do it, then," Wohl ordered. "And then seal this place up, make sure nobody leaves, keep the people in their seats, make sure nothing gets disturbed . . ."

"Got it," the Highway Patrol sergeant said, and went to the door and waved three policemen inside.

Wohl dropped to his knees beside the woman, and laid a gentle hand on her back.

"My name is Wohl," he said. "I'm a police officer."

She turned to look at him. There was horror in her eyes, and tears running down her cheeks had left a path through her face powder. She looked familiar. And she was not Mrs. Richard C. Moffitt.

"Let me help you to your feet," Wohl said, gently.

"Get a blanket or something," Louise Dutton said, in nearly a whisper. "Cover him up, Goddamn it!"

"Teddy," Wohl ordered. "Get a tablecloth or something."

He helped the woman to her feet.

Officer Francis Mason and Officer Patrick Foley ran in, with the stretcher from the back of Two-Oh-One. They quickly snapped the stretcher open and unceremoniously heaved Dutch Moffitt onto it. Wohl started for the door to open it for them, but a uniform beat him to it.

The sound of sirens outside was now deafening. He looked through the plate-glass door of the diner and saw there were police cars all over it. As he watched, a white van with WCBL-TV CHANNEL 9 painted on its side pulled to the curb, a sliding door opened, and a man with a camera resting on his shoulders jumped out.

Wohl turned to the blonde. "You were a friend of Captain Moffitt's?"

She nodded.

Where the hell do I know her from? What was she up to with Dutch?

"Why are they doing that?" she asked. "He's dead, isn't he?"

I don't know why they're doing that, Wohl thought. *The dead are left where they have fallen, for the convenience of the Homicide Detectives. But, I guess maybe no one wants to admit that a fellow cop is really dead.*

"Yes, I'm afraid he is," Wohl said. "Can you tell me what happened?"

"He was trying to stop a holdup," Louise said. "And somebody shot him. A girl, he said."

A portly, red-faced policeman in a white shirt with captain's bars pinned to the epaulets of his white shirt came into the Waikiki.

His name was Jack McGovern, and he was the commanding officer of the Second District. He had been a lieutenant in Highway Patrol when Peter Wohl had been a corporal. He had made captain on the promotion list before Peter Wohl had made captain, and they had sat across the room from each other when they'd sat for the Staff Inspector's examination. Peter Wohl had been first on the list; Jack McGovern hadn't made it.

McGovern's eyebrows rose when he saw Wohl.

"What the hell happened?" he asked. "Was that Dutch Moffitt they just carried out of here?" he asked.

"That was Dutch," Wohl confirmed. "He walked in on a holdup."

McGovern's eyebrows rose in question.

"He's gone, Jack," Wohl said.

"Jesus," McGovern said, and crossed himself.

"I think it would be better if you took care of the parking lot," Wohl said. "You're in uniform. You see the woman's body?"

McGovern shook his head. "A woman? A woman shot Dutch?"

"There were two of them," Wohl said. "One ran. Dutch got the other one. I don't know who shot Dutch."

"He said it was a woman," Louise Dutton said, softly.

Captain McGovern looked at her, his eyebrows raising, and then at Wohl.

"This lady was with Captain Moffitt at the time," Wohl said, evenly. He turned to Louise. "I've got to make a telephone call," he said. "It won't take a moment."

She nodded.

Wohl looked around for a telephone, saw the cashier's phone lying on the floor off the hook, and went to a pay phone on the wall. He dropped a dime in it and dialed a number from memory.

"Commissioner's office, Sergeant Jankowitz."

"Peter Wohl, Jank. Let me talk to him. It's important."

"Peter?" Commissioner Taddeus Czernick said when he came on the line a moment later. "What's up?"

"Commissioner, Dutch Moffitt walked into a holdup at the Waikiki Diner on Roosevelt Boulevard. He was shot to death. He put down one of them; the other got away."

"Jesus H. Christ!" Commissioner Czernick replied. "The one he got is dead?"

"Yes, sir. It's a woman, and a witness says she's the one that shot him. She said Dutch said a woman got him. I just got here."

"Who else is there?"

"Captain McGovern."

"Jesus Christ, Dutch's brother got himself killed too," the commissioner said. "You remember that?"

"I heard that, sir." And then, delicately, he added: "Commissioner, the witness, a woman, was with Dutch."

There was a perceptible pause.

"So?" Commissioner Czernick asked.

"I don't know, sir," Wohl said.

"That was the other phone, Peter. We just got notification from radio," Commissioner Czernick said. "Who's the woman?"

"I don't know. She looks familiar. Young, blond, good-looking."

"Goddamn!"

"I thought I had better call, sir."

"You stay there, Peter," the commissioner ordered. "I'll call the mayor, and get out there as soon as I can. Do what you think has to be done about the woman."

"Yes, sir," Wohl said.

The commissioner hung up without saying anything else.

Wohl put the phone back in its cradle, and without thinking about it, ran his fingers in the coin return slot. He was surprised when his fingers touched coins. He took them out and looked at them, and then went to Louise Dutton.

"Are you all right?"

Louise shrugged.

"A real tragedy," Wohl said. "He has three young children."

"I know he was married," Louise said, coldly.

"Would you mind telling me how you happened to be here with him?" Wohl asked.

"I'm with WCBL-TV," she said.

"I knew your face was familiar," Wohl said.

"He was going to tell me what he thinks about people calling the Highway Patrol 'Carlucci's Commandos,'" Louise said, carefully.

That's bullshit, Wohl decided. *There was something between them.*

As if that was a cue, the Channel 9 cameraman appeared at the door. A policeman blocked his way.

"Christ, if she's in there, why can't I go in?" the cameraman protested.

Wohl stepped to the door, spotted McGovern, and raised his voice. "Jack, would you get up some barricades, please? And keep people out of our way?"

He saw from the look on McGovern's face that the television cameraman had slipped around the policemen McGovern had already put in place.

"Get that guy out of there," McGovern said, sharply, to a sergeant. "The TV guy."

Wohl turned back to Louise.

"It would be very unpleasant for Mrs. Moffitt, or the children," he said, "if they heard about this over the television, or the radio."

Louise looked at him without real comprehension for a minute.

"I don't know about Philadelphia," she said. "But most places, there's an unwritten rule that nothing, no names anyway, about something like this gets on the air until the next of kin are notified."

"That's true here, too," Wohl said. "But I always like to be double sure."

"Okay," she said. "I suppose I could call."

"That would be very much appreciated," Wohl said. He extended his hand to her, palm upward, offering her change for the telephone.

Louise dialed the "Nine's News" newsroom, and Leonard Cohen, the news director, answered.

"Leonard, this is Louise Dutton. A policeman has been killed—"

"At the Waikiki Diner on Roosevelt Boulevard?" Cohen interrupted. "You there?"

"Yes," Louise said. "Leonard, the police don't want his wife to hear about it over the air."

"You know who it was?"

"I was with him," Louise said.

"You saw it?"

"I don't want his wife to find out over the air," Louise said.

"Hey, no problem. Of course not. Have the public affairs guy call us when we can use it, like usual."

"All right," Louise said.

"Tell the crew to get what they can, at an absolute minimum, some location shots, and then you come in, and we can put it together here," Cohen said. "We'll probably use it for the lead-in and the major piece. Nothing else much has happened. And you *saw* it?"

"I saw it," Louise said. "I'll be in."

She hung up the phone.

"I just spoke with the news director," she said. "He

said he won't use it until your public affairs officer clears it. He wants him to call."

"I'll take care of it," Wohl said. "Thank you very much, Miss Dutton."

She shrugged, bitterly. "For what?" she asked, and then: "How will she find out? Who tells her?"

Wohl hesitated a moment, and then told her: "There's a routine, a procedure, we follow in a situation like this. The captain in charge of the district where Captain Moffitt lived was notified right away. He will go to Captain Moffitt's house and drive Mrs. Moffitt to the hospital. By the time they get there, the mayor, and probably the commissioner and the chief of Special Patrol, will be there. And probably Captain Moffitt's parish priest, or the department Catholic chaplain. They will tell her. They're friends. Captain Moffitt is from an old police family."

She nodded.

"While that's been going on," Wohl said, wondering why, since he hadn't been asked, he was telling her all this, "radio will have notified Homicide, and the Crime Lab, and the Northeast Detectives. They'll be here in a few minutes. Probably, since Captain Moffitt was a senior police officer, the chief inspector in charge of homicide will roll on this, too."

"And she gets to ride to the hospital, while the police radio is talking about what happened here, right? God that's brutal!"

"The police radio in the car will be turned off," Wohl said.

She looked at him.

"We learn from our mistakes," Wohl said. "Policemen get killed. Captain Moffitt's brother was killed in the line of duty, too."

She met his eyes, and her eyebrows rose questioningly, but she didn't say anything.

"The homicide detectives will want to interview you," Wohl said. "I suppose you understand that you're a sort of special witness, a trained observer. The way that's ordinarily done is to transport you downtown, to the Homicide Division in the Roundhouse . . .''

"Oh, God!" Louise Dutton said. "Do I have to go through that?"

"I said 'ordinarily,' " Wohl said. "There's always an exception."

"Because I was with him? Or because I'm with WCBL-TV?"

"How about a little bit of both?" Wohl replied evenly. "In this case, what I'm going to do is have an officer drive you home."

I have the authority to let her get away from here, to send her away, Wohl thought. *The commissioner said, "Do what you have to do about the woman," but I didn't have to. I wonder why I did?*

"I'm not going home," she said. "I'm going to the studio."

"Yes, of course," he said. "Then to the studio, and then home. Then, in an hour or so, when things have settled down a little, I'll arrange to have some officers come to the station, or your house, and take you to the Roundhouse for your statement."

"I don't need anybody to drive me anywhere," Louise said, almost defiantly.

"I think maybe you do," Wohl said. "You've gone through an awful experience, and I really don't think you should be driving. And we owe you one, anyway."

She looked at him, *as if she's seeing me for the first time,* Wohl thought.

"I didn't get your name," she said.

"Wohl, Peter Wohl," he said.

"And you're a policeman?"

"I'm a Staff Inspector," he said.

"I don't know what that is," she said. "But I saw you ordering that captain around."

"I didn't mean to do that," he said. "But right now, I'm the senior officer on the scene."

She exhaled audibly.

"All right," she said. "Thank you. All of a sudden I feel a little woozy. Maybe I shouldn't be driving."

"It always pays to be careful," Wohl said, and took her arm and went to the door and caught Captain McGovern's attention and motioned him over.

"Jack, this is Miss Louise Dutton, of Channel 9. She's been very cooperative. Can you get me a couple of officers and a car, to drive her to the studio, drive her car, too, and then take her home?"

"I recognize Miss Dutton, now," McGovern said. "Sure, Inspector. No problem. You got it. Glad to be able to be of help, Miss Dutton."

"Have you caught the other one, the boy?" Louise asked.

"Not yet," Captain McGovern said. "But we'll get him."

"And the other one, the one who shot Captain Moffitt, was it a girl?"

"Yes, ma'am, it was a girl," Captain McGovern said, and nodded with his head.

Louise followed the nod. A man in civilian clothing, but with a pistol on his hip, and therefore certainly a cop, was stepping around the body, taking pictures of it from all angles. And then he finished. When he did, another policeman (a *detective*, Louise corrected herself) bent over and with a thick chunk of yellow chalk, outlined the body on the parking lot's macadam.

"Where's your car, Miss Dutton?" Wohl asked.

Louise could not remember where she had left it. She looked around until she found it, and then pointed to it.

"Over there," she said, "the yellow one."

"Would you like to ride in your car, or in the police car?" Wohl asked.

Louise thought that over for a moment before replying, "I think my car."

"These officers will take you to the studio and then home, Miss Dutton," Wohl said. "Please don't go anywhere else until we've taken care of your interview with Homicide. Thank you very much for your cooperation."

He offered his hand, and she took it.

The first thing Wohl thought was professional. Her hand was a little clammy, often a symptom of stress. Getting a cop to drive her had been a good idea, beyond hoping that it would make her think well of the police department. Then he thought that it was a very nice hand, indeed. Soft and smooth skinned.

There was little question what Dutch saw in her, he thought. But what did she see in him? This was a tough, well-educated young woman, not some secretary likely to be awed by a big, strong policeman.

A black Oldsmobile with red lights flashing from behind the grille pulled into the parking lot as Louise Dutton's yellow convertible, following a blue-and-white, turned onto Roosevelt Boulevard.

Chief Inspector of Detectives Matt Lowenstein, a large, florid-faced, silver-haired man in his fifties, got out the passenger side and walked purposefully over to McGovern and Wohl.

"Goddamned shame," he said. "Goddamned shame. They pick up the one that got away?"

"Not yet, sir," McGovern said. "But we will."

"Every male east of Broad Street with a zipper jacket and blond hair has been stopped for questioning," Wohl said, dryly. Lowenstein looked at him, waiting for an explanation. "A Highway Patrol sergeant went on the J-Band and ordered every Highway vehicle to respond."

Lowenstein shook his head. He agreed with Wohl that had been unnecessary, even unwise. But the Highway Patrol was the Highway Patrol, and when one of their own was involved in a police shooting, they could be expected to act that way. And, anyway, it was too late now, water under the dam, to change anything.

"I understand we got an eyewitness," he said.

"I just sent her home," Wohl said.

"They interviewed her here? Already?"

"No. I told her that someone would pick her up for the interview at her home in about an hour," Wohl said.

Captain McGovern's eyes grew wide. Wohl had overstepped his authority, and it was clear to him that he was about to get his ass eaten out by Chief Inspector Lowenstein.

But Chief Inspector Lowenstein didn't even comment.

"Jank Jankowitz tried to reach you on the radio, Peter," he said. "When he couldn't, he got on the horn to me. The commissioner thinks it would be a good idea for you to go by the hospital. . . . Where did they take him?"

"I don't know, Chief. I can find out," Wohl replied.

Lowenstein nodded. "If you miss him there, he's going by the Moffitt house. Meet him there."

"Yes, sir," Peter said.

THREE

Leonard Cohen, before he had become the news director of WCBL-TV, had been what he thought of as a bona fide journalist. That is, he had worked for newspapers before they were somewhat condescendingly referred to as "the print media."

He privately thought that the trouble with most of the people he knew in "electronic journalism" was that few of them had started out working for a newspaper, and consequently were incapable of recognizing the iceberg tip of a genuine story, unless they happened to fall over it on their way to the mirror to touch up their makeup, and sometimes not then.

The phone wasn't even back in its cradle after Louise Dutton had called to make sure they wouldn't put the name of the cop who got himself shot on the air before the cops could inform his widow when he sensed there was more to what was going on than Louise Dutton had told him.

He was a little embarrassed that he hadn't picked up on it while he had her on the telephone.

He went quickly to the engineering room.

"Are we in touch with the van at the Waikiki Diner?" he asked.

"I dunno," the technician said. "Sometimes it works, and sometimes it don't."

"Find out, Goddamn it!"

Penny Bakersfield's voice, clipped and metallic because of the shortwave radio's modulation limitations, came clearly over the loudspeaker.

"Yes, Leonard?"

"Penny, can you see what Louise Dutton is doing out there?"

"At the moment, she's walking toward her car. There are a couple of cops with her."

"Tell Whatsisname—"

"Ned," she furnished.

"Tell Ned to shoot it," he ordered. "Tell him to shoot whatever he can of her out there. If you can get the cops in the shot, so much the better."

"May I ask why?"

"Goddamn it, Penny, do what you're told. And then the two of you get back here as soon as you can."

"You don't have to snip at me, Leonard!" Penny said.

Officer Mason, once he and Officer Foley had slid the stretcher with Captain Richard C. Moffitt on it into the back of Two-Oh-One, had been faced with the decision of which hospital the "wounded" Highway Patrol officer should be transported to.

There had been really no doubt in his mind that Moffitt was dead; in the year and a half he'd been assigned to wagon duty, he'd seen enough dead and nearly dead people to tell the difference. But Moffitt was a cop, and no matter what, "wounded" and "injured" cops were hauled to a hospital.

"Tell Radio Nazareth," Officer Mason had said to Officer Foley as he flicked on the siren and lights.

Nazareth Hospital, at Roosevelt Boulevard and Penny-pack Circle, was not the nearest hospital, but it was, in Officer Mason's opinion, the best choice of the several available to him. Maybe Dutch Moffitt *wasn't* dead.

They had been waiting for him at Nazareth Emergency, nurses and doctors and everything else, but Dutch Moffitt was dead, period.

Police Commissioner Taddeus Czernick had arrived a few minutes later, and on his heels came cars bearing Mayor Jerry Carlucci, Chief Inspector Dennis V. Coughlin, and Captain Charley Gaft of the Civil Disobedience Squad. Officer Mason heard Captain Gaft explain his presence to Chief Inspector Coughlin: Until last month, he had been Dutch Moffitt's home district commander, and he thought he should come; he knew Jeannie Moffitt pretty good.

And then Captain Paul Mowery, Dutch Moffitt's new home district commander, appeared. He held open the glass door from the Emergency parking lot for Jeannie Moffitt. She was a tall, healthy-looking, white-skinned woman with reddish brown hair. She was wearing a faded cotton housedress and a gray, unbuttoned cardigan.

"Be strong, Jeannie," Chief Inspector Coughlin said. "Dutch's gone."

"I knew it," Jean Moffitt said, almost matter-of-factly. "I knew it." And then she fumbled in her purse for a handkerchief, and then started to sob. "Oh, God, Denny! What am I going to tell the kids?"

Coughlin wrapped his arms around her, and Mayor Carlucci and Commissioner Czernick stepped close to the two of them, their faces mirroring their emotions. They desperately wanted to do something, anything, to help, and there was nothing in their power that could.

Jean Moffitt got control of herself, in a faint voice asked if she could see him, and the three of them led her into the curtained-off cubicle where the doctors had officially decreed that Dutch Moffitt was dead.

A moment later, Jean Moffitt was led out of the cubicle,

and out of the Emergency Room by Commissioner Czernick and Captain Mowery.

Chief Inspector Coughlin and the mayor, who was blowing his nose, watched her leave.

"Get the sonofabitch who did this, Denny," the mayor said.

"Yes, sir," Coughlin said, almost fervently. "We'll get him."

The mayor and Chief Inspector Coughlin waited until Captain Mowery's car had gone, and then left the Emergency Room.

As the mayor's Cadillac left the parking lot, it had to brake abruptly twice, as first a plain and battered Chevrolet, and then moments later a police car festooned with lights and sirens, turned off the street. Homicide, in the person of Lieutenant Louis Natali, and the Highway Patrol, in the person of Lieutenant Mike Sabara, had arrived.

When Staff Inspector Peter Wohl drove into the Emergency entrance at Nazareth, five minutes later, he was not surprised to find three other police cars there, plus the Second District wagon. One of the cars, except that it was light blue, was identical to his. One was a well-worn green Chevrolet, and one was a black Ford.

When he went inside, it was easy to assign the cars to the people there. The blue LTD belonged to Captain Charley Gaft of the Civil Disobedience Squad. New, unmarked cars worked their way down the hierarchy of the police department, first assigned to officers in the grades of inspector and above, and then turned over, when newer cars came in, to captains, who turned their cars over to lieutenants. Exceptions were made for staff inspectors and for some captains with unusual jobs, like Gaft's assignment, who got new cars.

Wohl wasn't sure what the exact function of the Civil Disobedience Squad was. It was new, one of Taddeus Czernick's ideas, and Gaft had been named as its first commander. Wohl thought that whatever it did, it was inaptly named (everything, from murder to spitting on the sidewalk, was really "civil disobedience") and he wasn't sure whether Gaft had been given the job because he was a bright officer, or whether it had been a tactful way of getting him out of his district.

The well-worn, unmarked Chevrolet belonged to Lieutenant Louis Natali of Homicide, and the black Ford with the outsized high-speed tires and two extra shortwave antennae sticking up from the trunk deck was obviously that of Lieutenant Mike Sabara of the Highway Patrol. Now that Dutch was dead, Sabara, the ranking officer on the Highway Patrol, was, at least until a permanent decision was made, its commanding officer.

Lieutenant Sabara's face showed that he was surprised and not particularly happy to see Staff Inspector Wohl. He was a Lebanese with dark, acne-scarred skin. He was heavy, and short, a smart, tough cop. He was in uniform, and the leather jacket and puttees added to his menacing appearance.

"Hello, Peter," Captain Gaft said.

"Charley," Wohl said, and smiled at the others. "Mike. Lou."

They nodded and murmured, "Inspector."

"You just missed the mayor, the commissioner, and Chief Coughlin," Captain Gaft said. "Plus, of course, poor Jeannie Moffitt."

The conversation was interrupted as Officers Foley and Mason rolled a cart with a sheet-covered body toward them.

"Just a minute please," Wohl said. "Where are Captain Moffitt's personal things? And his pistol?"

Natali tapped his briefcase.

"What's on your mind, Inspector?" Lieutenant Sabara asked.

"Natali," Wohl asked. "May I have a look, please?"

"What does that mean?" Sabara asked.

"It means I want me to have a look at what Dutch had in his pockets," Wohl said.

"Why?" Sabara pursued.

"Because I want to, Lieutenant," Wohl said.

"It sounds as if you're looking for something wrong,"
Sabara said.

"I don't care what it sounds like, Mike," Wohl said.
"What it *means* is that I want to see what Dutch had in
his pockets. Dutch and I were friends. I want to make
sure he had nothing in his wallet that his wife shouldn't
see. Let me have it, Natali."

Natali opened the briefcase, took out several plastic envelopes, and laid them on a narrow table against the wall.
Wohl picked up one of them, which held a wallet, keys,
change, and other small items, dumped the contents on
the table and went through them carefully. He found nothing that made a connection with Miss Louise Dutton.
There were three phone numbers without names, one written on the back of a Strawbridge & Clothier furniture
salesman's business card, and two inside matchbooks.

Wohl handed the card and the matchbooks to Natali.

"I don't suppose you've had the time to check those
numbers out, Natali?" he said.

"I was going to turn them over to the assigned detective," Natali said. "But it wouldn't be any trouble to do
it now."

"Would you, please?" Wohl asked.

Natali nodded and went looking for a phone.

Wohl met Sabara's eyes.

"What about the bimbo, Peter?" he asked. "Is that
what this is all about?"

"What 'bimbo,' Mike?" Wohl replied, a hint of ice in
his voice.

And then he felt a cramp. He urgently had to move his
bowels.

"Excuse me," he said, and went looking for a men's
room.

He wondered if it was something he had eaten, or
whether he had caught another goddamned flu bug, and
then realized it was most probably a reaction to what had
happened to Dutch at the Waikiki Diner.

When he returned to the corridor, Lieutenant Natali was
there, but the cart with Dutch Moffitt's body on it was

gone. Through the plate-glass door Wohl saw the wagon men loading it into the wagon.

"The furniture salesman's number is his home phone," Lieutenant Natali reported. "One of the others is the rectory of St. Aloysius, and the last one is a pay phone in 30th Street Station."

Wohl nodded and picked up another of the plastic bags. In it was a Smith & Wesson Model 36, five-shot "Chief's Special." There were also four fired cartridge casings in the bag.

"Just four casings?" Wohl asked.

Natali looked at Captain Gaft before replying.

"That's all that was in it, Inspector," he said. "I removed those from Captain Moffitt's weapon at the scene."

Wohl met his eyes.

There was no question in Wohl's mind that he was lying. There had been a fifth, unfired cartridge, and it was probably in Natali's pocket, or Mike Sabara's. Thirty minutes from now, if it wasn't already, it would be in the Delaware, or the Schuylkill.

The Philadelphia Police Department prescribed the weaponry with which its officers would be armed. Uniformed personnel were issued Smith & Wesson Model 10 "Military & Police" six-shot revolvers, chambered to fire the .38 Special cartridge through a four-inch barrel. Detectives were issued Colt "Detective Special" six-shot revolvers, also chambered for the .38 Special cartridge, which have two-inch barrels. They are smaller, and thus more readily concealable, weapons.

Senior officers, officers on plainclothes duty, and off-duty policemen were permitted to carry whatever pistol they wished, either their issue weapon, or one they had purchased with their own money, provided it was chambered for the .38 Special cartridge. Those who purchased their own weapons usually bought the Colt "Detective Special" or the Smith & Wesson Model 36 "Chief's Special," a five-shot, two-inch-barrel revolver, or the Smith & Wesson Model 37, which was an aluminum-framed version of the Chief's Special. There were some Model 38's around, "the Bodyguard," a variation of the Chief's Special which encloses the hammer in a shroud.

All the Smith & Wesson snub-noses were slightly smaller, and thus slightly more concealable, than the Colts. Aside from that, Colt revolvers for all practical purposes differed from the Smith & Wessons only in that their cylinders revolved clockwise and the S&W's counterclockwise. And there were some Ruger revolvers coming into use, and even recently, some Colt and S&W copies made in Brazil.

The regulation gave policemen no choice of ammunition. On duty or off, they would load their pistols with issue ammunition. The prescribed ammunition was the standard .38 Special cartridge, firing a round-nose lead bullet weighing 158 grains. Fired through a four-inch barrel at approximately 850 feet per second, it produces approximately 250 foot pounds of energy at the muzzle.

The .38 Special cartridges made by Remington, Winchester, and Federal are virtually identical, and what brand of cartridges are issued by the Philadelphia Police Department depends on who among the three major manufacturers offered the best price when the annual bids were let.

That particular cartridge is as old as the .38 Special pistol itself, dating back to the turn of the century. The U.S. Army found .38 Special cartridges inadequate to kill or immobilize the enemy, and turned to the .45 caliber automatic Colt pistol and cartridge long before the First World War.

In 1937, the .357 Magnum cartridge was developed. Despite the name, the .38 barrel has a diameter of .357 inch, and the new round fired the same bullet as the .38 Special. The difference was that the .357 cartridge case was a few thousandths of an inch longer, so that it would not fit into a .38 Special chamber, and that it fired the same 158-grain bullet at about fourteen hundred feet per second, and produced about 845 foot pounds of energy, or more than three times that of the .38 Special.

There was some hyperbole. The .357 Magnum would go through an automobile engine block as through a sheet of paper. It would fell an elephant with one shot. It would not; but it was, literally, three times as effective as a .38 Special in immobilizing people who were shot with it. It was, many policemen decided, the ideal police cartridge. There was only one thing wrong with it, as far as they were concerned: The heat generated when firing a lead bullet at the higher velocity was such that the outer surface of the bullet actually melted going down the barrel, leaving a thin coating of lead against the grooves and rifling.

It was a bitch to get out, and unless you promptly got it out after firing, not only would it adversely affect accuracy, but it would cause the barrel to become rusted and pitted. That problem was solved with the introduction of the jacketed bullet, which encased a quarter of an inch at the rear of the bullet in a copper alloy cup. This essentially eliminated "leading," and had another, bonus, characteristic. When the bullet hit something, the jacket kept the rear of the bullet together, which made the front of the bullet expand, causing a larger wound.

The .357 Magnum cartridge was, as many civil libertarians promptly decided, far too awesome a tool of death to be put into the hands of the police. Ideally, the civil libertarians reasoned, firearms should be used only as a last resort, and then to *wound* the malefactor, preferably in the arm or shoulder, so that he could be brought to trial, and then sent to prison to be rehabilitated for return to society. If a societal misfit, venting his frustration at his inability to cope with a cruel world by robbing a bank, were shot in the shoulder with a .357, capable of felling an elephant with one shot, it would blow the shoulder off, and the societal misfit's Constitutional entitlement to rehabilitation would be denied him.

The civil libertarians of Philadelphia prevailed. Philadelphia police were flatly forbidden to arm themselves with the .357 Magnum, or any cartridge but the issued, 158-grain round-nose bullet .38 Special. To insure compliance, Philadelphia police were flatly forbidden to carry a pistol that would even chamber the .357 Magnum. Doing so was cause for disciplinary action.

But it was possible for a skilled reloader to make, using .38 Special casings, cartridges that produced velocity and foot pounds of energy very close to those of the .357 Magnum, using jacketed .357 bullets. The trick was to put the right amount of gunpowder (Bull's-eye powder was the usual choice) into the case, enough to increase velocity, but not too much, so that the cylinder would not let go when it was fired. The cartridges were tough on small ("J" Frame) Smith & Wesson snub noses, but you weren't going to put a couple of hundred rounds through one.

Just a cylinderful, when it was important.

Captain Richard C. Moffitt was not only a skilled reloader, but he had given Staff Inspector Peter Wohl a box of such cartridges.

"Don't tell anybody where you got these, Peter."

There was no question in Peter Wohl's mind now that—when it was important, when the left ventrical of his aorta was already ruptured and his life's blood was pumping away—Dutch Moffitt had fired four homemade hot .38's at his assailant, and put her down.

Neither was there any question in his mind that, when Lieutenant Natali had examined Dutch's Chief's Special at the Waikiki Diner, there had been one unfired cartridge in the cylinder, and that the bullet in that cartridge had been jacketed and hollow-pointed, as had been the bullets in the cartridges Dutch had given him, as were the cartridges in his own Smith & Wesson "Bodyguard."

It was possible that no one "would notice" that the bullets that would be removed from the body of Unknown White Female Suspect were jacketed. It was unlikely that anyone could have missed the hollow-nosed jacketed bullet in the unfired casing. There would have been trouble.

"What about the female suspect?" Wohl asked. He could almost hear Natali's relief that he hadn't pressed him about a fifth cartridge.

"She's a junkie, Inspector," Natali said. "I talked to Sergeant Hobbs, who's at the Medical Examiner's. He said they found needle marks all over her. I called Narcotics and they're going to run people by over there, to see if they can identify her.''

"Well, I don't suppose there's any point in hanging around here,'' Wohl said.

Both Lieutenant Sabara and Captain Gaft shook hands with him formally. They had been worried, Wohl knew. He had a reputation for being a straight arrow, and sometimes a prick. Lieutenant Natali just nodded at him.

The van with Penny Bakersfield and the tape reached WCBL-TV fifteen minutes after Louise Dutton had walked in, trailed by two cops. There was time enough for News Director Leonard Cohen to get the story out of her, and to decide what he was going to do about it, before they put the tape up on a monitor, and he got a good look at it. It was even better than he hoped. There was a sequence, just long enough, thirty-odd seconds, for what he wanted. It showed Louise being put into her car, driven by a cop, and then following a police car out of the Waikiki Diner parking lot.

Cohen edited it himself, down to twenty seconds exactly, and then he sat down at his typewriter and wrote the voice-over himself for Penny to read.

"This is a special 'Nine's News' bulletin. A Philadelphia police captain gave his life this afternoon foiling a holdup. 'Nine's News' co-anchor Louise Dutton was an eyewitness. Full details on 'Nine's News' at six.''

He got the station manager into the control room, ran the tape for him, and with less trouble than he thought he would have, got him to agree to run the thirty-second spot during every hourly and half-hourly break until six. They would lose some advertising revenue, but what they had was what, in the olden days, was called a "scoop," or an "exclusive.''

And then he went to help Louise prepare her segment for the six o'clock news. He thought he would have to write that, too, but she had already written it, and handed it to him when he walked up to her. It was good stuff. She had looked kind of flaky, which was understandable, considering the cop had been killed in front of her, but she was apparently tougher than she looked.

And when they made her up, and lit the set and put her on camera, she got it right the first time. Perfect. Her voice had started to break twice, but she hadn't lost it, and the teary eyes were perfect.

"You want me to do that again?" she asked. "I broke up."

"It's fine the way it is," Leonard Cohen said; and he went to her, and repeated that she had done fine, and that what he wanted—what he *insisted*—was for her to go home and have a stiff drink, and if she needed anything to call.

Then he sat down at the typewriter again, and personally wrote what he was going to have Barton Ellison open with, fading to a shot of Louise getting into her car with the cop to go home.

"Louise Dutton isn't here with me tonight," Barton Ellison would solemnly intone. "She wanted to be. But she was an eyewitness to the gun-battle in which Philadelphia Highway Patrol Captain Richard C. Moffitt gave his life this afternoon. She knows the face of the bandit that is, at this moment, still free. Louise Dutton is under police protection. Full details, and exclusive 'Nine's News at Six' film after these messages."

What I should have done, Leonard Cohen thought, *was go to Hollywood and be a press agent for the movies*.

Stanford Fortner Wells III did not own either a newspaper or a radio or television station in Philadelphia, Pennsylvania. It might be closed on Sunday, as the comedian had quipped, but it was the nation's fourth largest city. It was also a "good market," in media parlance, which meant that newspapers and radio and television stations were making a lot of money. Since Wells had been in a position to be interested, none of the City of Brotherly Love's five newspapers (the *Bulletin,* the *Ledger,* the *Herald,* the *Inquirer,* and the *Daily News*) had come on the market, and only one of its five television stations had. The price they wanted for that didn't seem worth it.

When Louise called and told him she had accepted an offer to go with WCBL-TV in Philadelphia, therefore, there was not one of his people instantly available on the scene to deliver a report on what his daughter would encounter when she got there.

In his neat, methodical hand, "Fort" Wells prepared a list of the questions he wished answered, and handed it to his secretary to be telexed to the publisher of the Binghamton, New York, *Call-Chronicle,* not because it was the newspaper he owned closest to Philadelphia (it was not) but because he knew that Karl Kruger knew his relationship to Louise Dutton. Karl would handle the last question on the list *("Availability adequate, convenient to WCBL-TV,* safe, *apartment for single, 25-year-old female")* with both discretion and awareness of that question's especial importance to the chairman of the board and chief executive officer of Wells Newspapers, Inc.

Karl Kruger's report on Philadelphia, telexed three days later, would not have pleased the Greater Philadelphia and Delaware Valley Chamber of Commerce. Mr. Kruger suspected, correctly, that Stanford Fortner Wells III wanted to know what was wrong with Philadelphia, not get a listing of its many cultural and industrial assets.

Mr. Wells's first reaction to the report would not have pleased the chamber of commerce either. He judged, from what he read, that Philadelphia was no worse, certainly not as bad as New York City, than other major American cities, and a lot better than most. But in people's minds, it was something like Phoenix, Arizona, or Saint Louis, Missouri, not the Cradle of the American Republic and the nation's fourth largest city. Mr. Wells thought that if he was in Philadelphia (that is, if he owned a newspaper or a television station there), the first thing he would do would be clean out the chamber of commerce from the executive director downward, and hire some people who knew how to blow a city's horn properly.

Mr. Kruger's report had nothing to say about an apartment. Mr. Wells instructed his secretary to get Mr. Kruger on the horn.

"I thought maybe you'd be calling, Fort," Mr. Kruger said. "How've you been?"

"You didn't mention anything about housing, Kurt. Still working on that, are you?"

"I found, I think, just the place, but I thought it would be easier to talk about it than write it down," Mr. Kruger said. "You got a minute?"

"Sure. Shoot."

"How well do you know Philadelphia?"

"I went there to chase girls when I was at Princeton; I know it."

"It's changed a lot, I would suppose, from your time," Kruger said. "You know the area near Market Street from City Hall to the bridge over the Delaware?"

"Around Independence Hall?"

"Right. Well, that whole section, which they call 'Society Hill,' is pretty much a slum. Been going downhill since Ben Franklin moved away, so to speak."

"Can you get to the point of this anytime soon?"

"It's being rehabilitated; they're gutting buildings to the exterior walls, if necessary, and doing them over. Luxuriously. Among the people doing this, you might be interested to know, is the Daye-Nelson Corporation."

The Daye-Nelson Corporation was something like Wells Newspapers, Inc. Stanford Fortner Wells III was aware that in Philadelphia, Daye-Nelson owned the *Philadelphia Ledger,* WGHA-TV, and, he thought he remembered, a couple of suburban weeklies.

"Come on, Kurt," Fort Wells said, impatiently.

"They put together a couple of blocks of Society Hill," Kruger explained. "Knocked all the interior walls out, and made apartments. It looks like a row of Revolutionary-era houses, but they are now divided horizontally, instead of vertically. Three one-floor apartments, instead of narrow three-floor houses. You follow me?"

"Keep going," Wells said.

"Both sides of this street, twelve houses on a side, are all redone that way. And their title people did their homework, and found out that the street between the blocks had never been deeded to the city. It's a private street, in other words. It's more of an alley, actually, but they can, and do, bar the public. They hung a chain across it, and they've got a rent-a-cop there that lowers it only if you live, or have business, there. If you live there, they give you a sticker for your windshield; no sticker and the rent-a-cop won't let you in without you proving you've got business, or are expected. Sort of a doorman on the street.''

"Secure, in other words?"

"Yeah," Kruger went on. "And they leveled an old warehouse, and made a park out of it, and made a drive-way into what used to be the basement for a garage. It's ten, twelve blocks from WCBL, Fort. It would be ideal for your—"

"*Daughter*'s the word, Kurt," Wells said. "How much?"

"Not how much, but who," Kruger said. "What Daye-Nelson wants is long-term leases. And I don't think they would want to lease one to a single female."

"So?"

"The real estate guy told me they've leased a dozen of them to corporations, where the bosses can spend the night when they have to stay in the city, where they can put up important customers . . . there's maid service, and a cou-ple of restaurants nearby that deliver."

"How much, Kurt?"

"Nine hundred a month, on a five-year lease, with an annual increase tied to inflation. That includes two spaces in the garage."

"You've seen them I guess?"

"Very nice, Fort. There's one on a third floor available, that's really nice. You can see the river out the front win-dow, and Independence Hall, at least the roof, out the back."

"Call the real estate man, Kurt; tell him Wells News-papers will take it. I'll have Charley Davis handle it from there. Do it now."

"And what if Louise doesn't like it?"

"She's a dutiful daughter, Kurt," Wells said, and

laughed, "who will recognize a bargain when she sees one."

The barrier to Stockton Place consisted of a black-painted aluminum pole, hinged at one end. A neatly lettered sign reading STOCKTON PLACE—PRIVATE PROPERTY—NO THOROUGHFARE hung on short lengths of chain from the pole. A switch in the Colonial-style red-brick guard shack caused electric motors to raise and lower it.

The Wackenhut Private Security officer flipped the switch when he saw the yellow Cadillac convertible coming. It was too far away to see the Stockton Place bumper sticker, but there weren't all that many yellow Cadillac convertibles, and he was reasonably certain this had to be the good-looking blonde from the TV, whom he thought of as "6-A."

The barrier rose smoothly into the air. It was only when the car passed him, moving onto the carefully relaid cobblestones of Stockton Place, that he saw she was not driving, but that a cop was. And that the convertible was being followed by a police car.

He was retired from the Philadelphia Police Department, and it automatically registered on him that the numbers on the car identified it as being from the Second District, way the hell and gone across town, in the northeast.

The first thing he thought was that they'd busted her for driving under the influence, and the lieutenant or whoever had decided it was good public relations, her being on the TV, to warn her and let her go, have her driven home, instead of writing her up and sending her to the Roundhouse to make bail.

But when the convertible stopped in front of Number Six and she got out, she didn't look drunk, and she walked back to the police car and shook hands with the cop driving it. And 6-A didn't look like the kind of girl who would get drunk, anyway.

He stepped out of the guard shack and stood by the curb, hoping that when the police car came back out, they would stop and say hello, and he could ask what was going on.

But the cops just waved at him, and didn't stop.

Louise Dutton closed the door of 6-A behind her by bumping it with her rear end, and sighed, and then went into her bedroom, and to the bathroom. She saw her brassiere and panties where she'd tossed them on the bed. A plain and ordinary cotton *underwear* bra and panties, she thought, which she'd taken off to replace with black, filmy, damned-near transparent *lingerie* bra and panties after Captain Dutch Moffitt had called and she had gone to meet him.

She leaned close to the mirror. She had not removed her makeup before leaving the studio, and there were streaks on her face, where tears had marred the makeup. She dipped a Kleenex into a jar of cold cream and started wiping at the makeup.

The door chimes sounded, and she swore.

Who the hell can that be?

It was 6-B, who occupied the apartment immediately beneath hers.

Six-B was male, at least anatomically. He was in his middle twenties, stood about five feet seven, weighed no more than 120 pounds. He paid a great deal of attention to his appearance, and wore, she suspected, Chanel Number Five. His name was Jerome Nelson.

"I was going to bark," Jerome Nelson said, waving a bottle of Beefeater's gin and one of Johnnie Walker Black Label scotch at her. "It's your friendly neighborhood Saint Bernard on a mission of mercy."

Louise didn't want to see anyone, but it was impossible for her to cut Jerome Nelson off rudely. He wasn't much of a Saint Bernard, Louise thought, but had puppylike eyes, and you don't kick puppies.

"Hello, Jerome," she said. "Come on in."

"Gin or scotch?" he asked.

"I would like a stiff scotch," she said. "Thank you very much. Straight up."

"You don't have to tell me, of course," he called over

his shoulder as he made for her bar. "And I wouldn't think of prying. I will just expire right here on your carpet of terminal curiosity."

She had to smile.

"I gather you saw the cops bringing me home?" she asked. "Let me finish getting this crap off my face."

He came into the bathroom as she was cleaning off what she thought was the last of the makeup, and leaned on the doorjamb.

"You missed some on your ear," he said, delicately setting two glasses down. "Jerome will fix it."

He dipped a Kleenex in cold cream and wiped at her ear.

"There!" he said. "Now tell Mother everything!"

She smiled her thanks at him and picked up her drink and took a good swallow.

"Whatever it was, it was better than the alternative," Jerome said.

"What?"

"The cops come and haul you off, rather than vice versa," he said.

"I was a witness to a shooting," Louise said. "A policeman tried to stop a holdup, and was shot. And killed."

"How *awful* for you!" Jerome Nelson said.

"Worse for him," Louise said. "And for his wife and kids."

"You sound as if you knew him?"

"Yes," Louise said, "I knew him."

She took another swallow of her drink, and felt the warmth in her belly.

He waited for her to go on.

Fuck him!

She pushed past him and went into the living room, and leaned on the wall beside a window looking toward the river.

He floated into the room.

"Actually, I was going to come calling anyway," he said.

"Anyway?" she asked, not particularly pleasantly.

"To tell you that I have discovered we have something in common," he said.

What, that we both like men? she thought, and was ashamed of herself.

"Actually," Jerome said. "I'm just a teensy-bit ashamed of myself."

"Oh?" She wished he would go away.

"It will probably come as a surprise to you, but I am what could be called the neighborhood busybody," Jerome said.

The reason I can't get, or at least, stay, mad at him is because he's always putting himself down; he arouses the maternal instinct in me.

"Really?" Louise said, mockingly.

"I'm afraid so," he said. "And I really thought I was onto something with you, when you moved in, I mean."

"Why was that, Jerome?"

"Because I know this apartment is leased to Wells Newspapers, Inc.," he said. "And because you are really a beautiful woman."

I've had enough of this guy.

"Get to the point," Louise said, coldly.

"So I went to Daddy, and I said, 'Daddy, guess what? Stanford F. Wells has an absolutely gorgeous blonde stashed in 6-A.' "

"What the hell is this all about, Jerome?" Louise demanded, angrily.

"And Daddy asked me to describe you, and I did, and he told me," Jerome said.

"Told you what?"

"What we have in common," Jerome said.

"Which is?"

"That both our daddies own newspapers, and television stations, and are legends in their own times, et cetera et cetera," Jerome said. "My daddy, in case I didn't get to that, is Arthur J. Nelson, as in Daye hyphen Nelson."

She looked at him, but said nothing.

"The difference, of course, is that your daddy is very proud of you, and mine is just the opposite," Jerome said.

"Why do you say that?"

"Why do you think? *My* daddy knows the odds are rather long against his becoming a grandfather."

"Oh, Christ, Jerome," Louise said.

"I haven't, and won't, of course, say a word to anyone," Jerome said. "But I thought it might give us a basis to be friends. But I can tell by the look on your face that you are not pleased, and I have offended, so now I will take my tent and steal away, with appropriate apologies."

"I wish you wouldn't," Louise heard herself say.

"Pissed off I can take," Jerome said. "Pity is something else."

"I knew the cop who got shot," Louise blurted. "More than just knew him."

"You were *very good friends,* in other words?" Jerome said, sympathetically.

"Yes," she said, then immediately corrected herself. "No. But I went there, to meet him, thinking that something like that could happen."

"Oh, my," Jerome said. "Oh, my darling girl, how awful for you!"

"Please don't go," Louise said. "Right now, I need a friend."

FOUR

Brewster C. (for Cortland) Payne II, a senior partner in the Philadelphia law firm of Mawson, Payne, Stockton, McAdoo & Lester, had raised his family, now nearly all grown and gone, in a large house on four acres on Providence Road in Wallingford.

Wallingford is a small Philadelphia suburb, between Media (through which U.S. 1, known locally as the "Baltimore Pike," runs) and Chester, which is on the Delaware River. It is not large enough to be placed on most road maps, although it has its own post office and railroad station. It is a residential community, housing families whom sociologists would categorize as upper-middle income, upper-income, and wealthy, in separate dwellings, some very old and some designed to look that way.

What was now the kitchen and the sewing room had been the whole house, when it had been built of fieldstone before the Revolution. Additions and modifications over two centuries had turned it into a large rambling structure which fit no specific architectural category, although a real estate saleswoman had once remarked in the hearing of Patricia (Mrs. Brewster C.) Payne that "the Payne place just *looked* like old, old money."

The house was comfortable, even luxurious, but not ostentatious. There was neither a swimming pool nor a tennis court, but there was, in what a century before had been a stable, a four-car garage. The Payne family swam, as well as rode, at the Rose Tree Hunt Club. They had a summer house in Cape May, New Jersey, which did have a tennis court, as well as a berth for their boat, a 38-foot Hatteras, called *Final Tort IV*.

When Mrs. Payne, at the wheel of a Mercury station wagon, came down Pennsylvania Route 252 and approached her driveway, she looked carefully in the rearview mirror before applying the brake. Two-Fifty-Two was lined with large, old pine trees on that stretch, and the drives leading off it were not readily visible. She did not want to be rear-ended; there had been many close calls.

She made it safely into the drive, and saw, as she approached the house, that the yard men were there, early for once. The back of the station wagon was piled high with large plastic-wrapped packages of peat moss.

She smiled at the yard man and his two sons, pointed out the peatmoss to them, and said she would be with them in a minute.

Patricia Payne was older than she looked at first glance. She was trim, for one thing, despite four children (the youngest just turned eighteen and a senior at Dartmouth); and she had a luxuriant head of dark brown, almost reddish hair. There were chicken tracks on her face, and she thought her skin looked old; but she was aware that she looked much better, if younger meant better, than her peers the same age.

The housekeeper—the new one, a tall, dignified Jamaican—was on the telephone as Patricia Payne entered her kitchen and headed directly and quickly for the small toilet off the passageway to the dining room.

"There is no one at this number by that name, madam," the new housekeeper said. "I am sorry."

Ordinarily Pat Payne would have stopped and asked, but incredibly there had been *no* peat moss in Media, and she'd had to drive into Swarthmore to get some and her back teeth were floating.

But she asked when she came out.

"What was that call, Mrs. Newman?"

"It was the wrong number, madam. The party was looking for a Mrs. Moffitt."

"Oh, hell," Patricia Payne said. "Did she leave her name?"

"No, she did not," Mrs. Newman said.

"Mrs. Newman, I should have told you," Patricia Payne said, "before I married Mr. Payne, I was a widow. I was once Mrs. Moffitt—"

The phone rang again. Patricia Payne answered it.

"Hello?"

"Mrs. John Moffitt, please," a familiar voice asked.

"This is Patricia, Mother Moffitt," Pat Payne said. "How are you?"

"My son Richard was shot and killed an hour ago," the woman said.

"Oh, my *God!*" Patricia said. "I'm so sorry. How did it happen?"

"In the line of duty," Gertrude Moffitt said. "Like his brother, God rest his soul, before him. He came up on a robbery in progress."

"I'm so terribly sorry," Pat Payne said. "Is there anything I can do?"

"I can't think of a thing, thank you," Gertrude Moffitt said. "I simply thought you should know, and that Matthew should hear it from you, rather than the newspapers or the TV."

"I'll tell him right away, of course," Patricia said. "Poor Jeannie. Oh, my God, that's just awful."

"He'll be given a departmental funeral, of course, and at Saint Dominic's. We hope the cardinal will be free to offer the mass. You would be welcome to come, of course.''

''Come? Of course, I'll come.''

''I thought I had the duty to tell you,'' Gertrude Moffitt said, and hung up.

Patricia Payne, her eyes full of tears, pushed the handset against her mouth.

''You old *bitch!*'' she said bitterly, her voice on the edge of breaking.

Mrs. Newman's eyebrows rose, but she said nothing.

When Karl and Christina Mauhfehrt, of Kreis Braunfels, Hesse-Kassel, debarked from the North German Lloyd Steamer *Hanover* in New York in the spring of 1876, Christina was heavy with child. They were processed through Ellis Island, where Karl told the Immigration and Naturalization officer, one Sean O'Mallory, that his name was Mauhfehrt and that he was an *uhrmacher* by trade. Inspector O'Mallory had been on the job long enough to know that an *uhrmacher* was a watchmaker, and he wrote that in the appropriate blank on the form. He had considerably more trouble with Mauhfehrt, and after a moment's indecision entered ''Moffitt'' as the surname on the form, and ''Charles'' as the given name.

Charles and Christina Moffitt spent the next three days on the Lower East Side of New York, in a room in a dark, cold, and filthy ''railroad'' flat. On their fourth morning in the United States, they took the ferry across the Hudson River to Hoboken, New Jersey, where they boarded a train of the Pennsylvania Railroad. Three hours later they emerged from the Pennsylvania Station at Fifteenth and Market Streets in Philadelphia.

An enormous building was under construction before their eyes. Within a few days, Charles Moffitt was to learn that it would be the City Hall, and that it was intended to top it off with a statue of William Penn, an Englishman, for whom the state of Pennsylvania was named. Many years later, he was to learn that the design was patterned after a wing of the Louvre Palace in Paris, France.

He and Christina walked the cobblestone streets, and within a matter of hours found a room down by the river. He spent the next six days walking the streets, finding clock- and watchmakers and offering his services and being rejected. Finally, hired because he was young and large and strong, he found work at the City Hall construction site, as a carpenter's helper, building and then tearing down and then building again the scaffolding up which the granite blocks for the City Hall were hauled.

Their first child, Anna, was born when they had been in Philadelphia two months. Their first son, Charles, Jr., was born almost to the day a year later. By then, he had enough English to converse in what probably should be called pidgin English with his Italian, Polish, and Irish co-workers, and had been promoted to a position which was de facto, but not de jure, foreman. He made, in other words, no more money than the men he supervised, and he was hired by the day, which meant that if he didn't work, he didn't get paid.

It was steady work, however, and it was enough for him to rent a flat in an old building on what was called Society Hill, not far from the run-down building in which the Constitution of the United States had been written.

And he picked up a little extra money fixing clocks for people he worked with, and in the neighborhood, but he came to understand that his dream of becoming a watchmaker with his own store in the United States just wasn't going to happen.

When Charles, Jr. turned sixteen, in 1893, he was able to find work with his father, who by then was officially a foreman in the employ of Jos. Sullivan & Sons, Building Contractors. But by then, the job was coming to an end. The City Hall building itself was up, needing only interior completion. Italian master masons and stonecutters had that trade pretty well sewn up, and the Charles Moffitts, *pere et fils*, were construction carpenters, not stonemasons.

When Charles, Jr. was twenty-two, in 1899, he went off to the Spanish-American War, arriving in Cuba just before hostilities were over, and returning to Philadelphia a corporal of cavalry, and just in time to take advantage of the politicians' fervor to do something for Philadelphia's Heroic Soldier Boys.

Specifically, he was appointed to the police department, and assigned to the ninety-three-horse-strong mounted patrol, which had been formed just ten years previously. Officer Moffitt was on crowd-control duty on his horse when the City Hall was officially opened in 1901.

He had been a policeman four years when his father fell to his death from a wharf under construction into the Delaware River in 1903. He was at that time still living at home, and with his father gone, he had little choice but to continue to do so; there was not enough money to maintain two houses.

Nor did he take a wife, so long as his mother was alive, partly because of economics and partly because no woman would take him with his mother part of the bargain. Consequently, Charles Moffitt, Jr. married late in life, eighteen months after his mother had gone to her final reward.

He married a German Catholic woman, Gertrude Haffner, who some people said, although she was nearly twenty years younger than her husband, bore a remarkable resemblance to his mother, and certainly manifested the same kind of devout, strong-willed character.

He and Gertrude had two sons, John Xavier, born in 1924, and, as something of a surprise to both of them, Richard Charles, who came along eight years later in 1932.

Charles Moffitt was a sergeant when he retired from the mounted patrol of the police department in 1937 at the age of sixty. He lived to be seventy-two, despite at least two packages of cigarettes and at least two quarts of beer a day, finally passing of a cerebral hemorrhage in 1949. By then his son John was on the police force, and his son Richard about to graduate from high school.

Patricia Payne leaned her head against the wall and put her hand on the hook of the wall-mounted telephone, without realizing what she was doing.

A moment later, the phone rang again. Pat Payne handed the handset to Mrs. Newman.

"The Payne residence," Mrs. Newman said, and then a moment later: "I'm not sure if Mrs. Payne is at home. I will inquire."

She covered the mouthpiece with her hand.

"A gentleman who says he is Chief Inspector Coughlin of the Philadelphia Police Department," Mrs. Newman said.

Patricia Payne finished blowing her nose, and then reached for the telephone.

"Hello, Denny," Patricia Payne said. "I think I know why you're calling."

"Who called?"

"Who else? Mother Moffitt. She called out here and asked for Mrs. Moffitt, and told me Dutch is dead, and then she said I would be welcome at the funeral."

"I'm sorry, Patty," Dennis V. Coughlin said. "I'm not surprised, but I'm sorry."

She was trying not to cry and didn't reply.

"Patty, people would understand if you didn't go to the funeral," he said.

"Of course, I'll go to the funeral," Patricia Payne said, furiously. "*And* the wake. Dutch didn't think I'm a godless whore, and I don't think Jeannie does either."

"Nobody thinks that of you," he said, comfortingly. "Come on, Patty!"

"That old bitch does, and she lets me know it whenever she has the chance," she said.

Now Dennis V. Coughlin couldn't think of anything to say.

"I'm sorry, Denny," Patricia Payne said, contritely. "I shouldn't have said that. The poor woman has just lost her second, her remaining son."

Dennis V. Coughlin and John X. Moffitt had gone through the police academy together. Patricia Payne still had the photograph somewhere, of all those bright young men in their brand-new uniforms, intending to give it to Matt someday.

There was another photograph of John X. Moffitt around. It and his badge hung on a wall in the Roundhouse lobby. Under the photograph there was a now somewhat faded typewritten line that said "Sergeant John X. Moffitt, Killed in the Line of Duty, November 10, 1952."

Staff Sergeant John Moffitt, USMCR, had survived Inchon and the Yalu and come home only to be shot down in a West Philadelphia gas station, answering a silent burglar alarm.

They'd buried him in Holy Sepulchre Cemetery, following a high mass of requiem celebrated by the cardinal archbishop of Philadelphia at Saint Dominic's. Sergeant Dennis V. Coughlin had been one of the pallbearers. Three months later, John Xavier Moffitt's first, and only, child had been born, a son, christened Matthew Mark after his father's wishes, in Saint Dominic's.

"Patty?" Chief Inspector Coughlin asked. "You all right, dear?"

"I was thinking," she said, "of Johnny."

"It'll be on the TV at six," Denny Coughlin said. "Worst luck, there was a Channel 9 woman in the Waikiki Diner."

"Is that where it happened? A *diner?*"

"On Roosevelt Boulevard. He walked up on a stick-up. There was two of them. Dutch got one of them, the one that shot him, a woman. Patty, what I'm saying is that I wouldn't like Matt to hear it over the TV. You say the word, and I'll go up there and tell him for you."

"You're a good man, Denny," Patricia said. "But no, I'll tell him."

"Whatever you say, dear."

"But would you do something else for me? If you don't want to, just say so."

"You tell me," he said.

"Meet me at Matt's fraternity house—"

"And be with you, sure," he interrupted.

"And go with me when I, when Matt and I, go see Jeannie."

"Sure," he said.

"I'll leave right now," she said. "It'll take me twenty-five, thirty minutes."

"I'll be waiting for you," Chief Inspector Coughlin said.

Patricia hung up, and then dialed the number of Matt's fraternity house. She told the kid who answered, and who said Matt was in class, to tell him that something important had come up and he was to wait for her there, period, no excuses, until she got there.

Then she went upstairs and stripped out of her skirt and sweater and put on a black slip and a black dress, and a simple strand of pearls. She looked at the telephone and considered calling her husband, and decided against it, although he would be hurt. Brewster Payne was a good man, and she didn't want to run him up against Mother Moffitt if it could be avoided.

After ten months of widowhood, Patricia Stevens Moffitt had arranged with her sister Dorothy to care for the baby during the day and went to work as a typist, with the intention eventually of becoming a legal secretary, for the law firm of Lowerie, Tant, Foster, Pedigill and Payne, which occupied an entire floor in the Philadelphia Savings Fund Society Building on Market Street.

Two months after entering Lowerie, Tant, Foster, Pedigill and Payne's employ, while pushing Matthew Mark Moffitt near the Franklin Institute in a stroller, Patricia Moffitt ran into Brewster Payne II, grandson of one of the founding partners, and son of a senior partner, who was then in his seventh year with the firm and about to be named a partner himself.

Young Mr. Brewster, as he was then known, was pushing a stroller himself, in which sat a two-year-old boy, and holding a four-and-a-half-year-old girl at the end of a leash, connected to a leather harness. They walked along together. Within the hour, she learned that Mrs. Brewster Payne II had eight months before skidded out of control coming down into Stroudsburg from their cabin in the Poconos, leaving him, as he put it, "in rather much the same position as yourself, Mrs. Moffitt."

Patricia Stevens Moffitt and Brewster Payne II were united in matrimony three months later. The simple ceremony was performed by the Hon. J. Edward Davison, judge of the Court of Common Pleas in his chambers. Mr. Payne, Senior, did not attend the ceremony, although his wife did. Mr. Gerald Stevens, Patricia's father, was there, but her mother was not.

There was no wedding trip, and the day after the wedding, Brewster Payne II resigned from Lowerie, Tant, Foster, Pedigill and Payne, although, through a bequest from his grandfather, he owned a substantial block of its common stock.

Shortly thereafter, the legal partnership of Mawson & Payne was formed.

John D. Mawson had been two years ahead of Brewster Payne II at the University of Pennsylvania Law School. They had been acquaintances but not friends. Mawson was a veteran (he had been an air corps captain, a fighter pilot) and Brew Payne had not been in the service. Further, Payne thought Mawson was a little pushy. It was Jack Mawson's announced intention to become a professor of law at Pennsylvania, specializing in Constitutional law. Jack Mawson was not, as Brewster Payne II thought of it, the sort of fellow you cultivated.

Mawson had exchanged his air corps lapel pins for those of the judge advocate general's corps reserve when he passed his bar examination, and three months later had gone off to the Korean War as a major. He had returned as Lieutenant Colonel J. Dunlop Mawson, with a war bride (a White Russian girl he had met in Tokyo) and slightly less lofty, if more practical, plans for the resumption of his civilian law practice.

He had earned the approval of his superiors in the army with his skill as a prosecutor of military offenders. He had liked what he had been doing, but was honest enough with himself to realize that his success was in large part due to the ineptitude of opposing counsel. Very often, he was very much aware that if he had been defending the ac-

cused, the accused would have walked out of the courtroom a free man.

Odette Mawson had already shown that she had expensive tastes, which ruled out his staying in the army. He
would have been reduced in grade in the peacetime army
to captain, and captains did not make much money. About,
J. Dunlop Mawson thought, what a district attorney in
Philadelphia made. District attorneys do not grow rich
honestly.

That ruled out transferring his prosecutorial skills to
civilian practice.

But it did not rule out a career in criminal law. While
ordinary criminal lawyers, dealing as they generally do
with the lower strata of society, seldom make large
amounts of money, extraordinary criminal lawyers sometimes do. And they increase their earning potential as the
socioeconomic class of their clientele rises. An attorney
representing someone accused of embezzling two hundred
thousand dollars from a bank can expect to be compen-
sated for his services more generously than if he defended
someone accused of stealing that much money from the
same bank at the point of a gun.

When J. Dunlop Mawson, who had made it subtly if
quickly plain that he liked to be addressed as "Colonel,"
heard that Brewster Payne had had a falling-out with his
father over his having married a Roman Catholic cop's
widow with a baby, a girl who had been a typist for the
firm, he thought he saw in him the perfect partner.

First of all, of course, Brewster Payne II was a good
lawyer, and he had acquired seven years' experience with
a law firm that was good as well as prestigious. And he
was also Episcopal Academy and Princeton, Rose Tree
Hunt Club and the Merion Country Club—without question a member of the Philadelphia Establishment.

Brewster Payne II was not a fool. He knew exactly what
Jack Mawson wanted from him. And he had no desire
whatever to practice criminal law. But Mawson's arguments made sense. Times had changed. Perfectly respect-

able people were getting divorced. And the division of the property of the affluent that went with a divorce was worthy, in direct ratio to the value and complexity of the property involved, of the talents of a skilled trust and estate lawyer. He would handle the crooks, Jack Mawson told Brewster Payne, and Payne would handle the cuckolded.

Payne added one nonnegotiable caveat: Jack could handle anything from embezzlers to ax murderers, so long as they were, so to speak, amateurs. There would be no connection, however indirect, with Organized Crime. If they were to become partners, Payne would have to have the privilege of client rejection, and they had better write that down, so there would be no possibility of misunderstanding, down the pike.

Five months after Mawson & Payne opened offices for the practice of law in the First National Bank Building, across from the Bellevue-Stratford Hotel and the Union League on South Broad Street, Patricia Stevens Payne found herself with child.

Brew Payne, ever the lawyer, first asked if she was sure, and when she said there was no question, nodded his head as if she had just given him the time of day.

"Well, then," he said, "we'll have to do something about Matthew."

"I don't know what you mean, honey," Patricia said, uneasily.

"I'd planned to bring it up before," he said. "But there hasn't seemed to be the right moment. I don't at all like the notion of his growing up with any question in his mind of not being one of us. What I would like to do, if you're agreeable, is enter a plea for adoption. And if you're agreeable, Patricia, to enter the appropriate pleas in your behalf with regard to Amelia and Foster."

When she didn't immediately respond, Brewster Payne misunderstood her silence for reluctance.

"Well, please don't say no with any finality now," he said. "I'm afraid you're going to have to face the fact that both Amy and Foster do think of you as their mother."

"Brewster," Patricia said, finding her voice, "sometimes you're a damned fool."

"So I have been told," he said. "As recently as this afternoon, by the colonel."

"But you are warm and kind and I love you very much," she said.

"I hear that sort of thing rather less than the other," he said. "I take it you're agreeable?"

"Why did Jack Mawson say you were a damned fool?"

"I told him I thought we should decline a certain client," he said. "You haven't answered my question."

"Would you like a sworn deposition? *'Now comes Patricia Payne who being duly sworn states that the only thing she loves more than her unborn child, and her husband's children, and her son, is her husband'?"*

"A simple yes will suffice," Brew Payne said, and put his arms around her. "Thank you very much."

That was her sin, which had made her a godless whore, in the eyes of Gertrude Moffitt: marrying outside the church, living in sin, bearing Brewster's child, and allowing that good man to give his name and his love to a fatherless boy.

Patricia was worried about her son. There had been, over the past two or three weeks, something wrong. Brewster sensed it too, and suggested that Matt was suffering from the Bee Syndrome, which was rampant among young men Matt's age. Matt was driven, Brewster said, to spread pollen, and sometimes there just was not an adequate number, or even one, Philadelphia blossom on which to spread it.

Brewster was probably right—he usually was—but Patricia wasn't sure. From what she had reliably heard about what took place on the University of Pennsylvania campus, and particularly along Fraternity Row, there was a large garden of flowering blossoms just waiting to be pollinated. Matt could be in love, of course, with some girl immune to his charms, which would explain a good deal about his behavior, but Patricia had a gut feeling that it was something else.

And whatever was bothering him, the murder of his uncle Dutch was going to make things worse.

The traffic into Philadelphia was heavy, and it took Patricia Payne longer than thirty minutes to get into town, and then when she got to the University of Pennsylvania campus, there was a tie-up on Walnut Street by the Delta Phi Omicron house, an old and stately brownstone mansion. A car had broken down, against the curb, forcing the cars in the other lane to merge with those in the inner; they were backed up for two blocks, waiting their turn.

And then she drew close and saw that the car blocking the outside lane, directly in front of the fraternity house, was a black Oldsmobile. There was an extra radio antenna, a short one, mounted on the inside shelf by the rear window. It was Denny Coughlin's car.

When you are a chief inspector of the Philadelphia Police Department, Patricia Payne thought wryly, *you park any place you damned well please.*

She pulled in behind the Oldsmobile, slid across the seat, and got out the passenger side. Denny was already out of the Oldsmobile, and another man got out of the driver's side and stepped onto the sidewalk.

She kissed Denny, noticing both that he was picking up some girth, and that he still apparently bought his cologne depending on what was cheapest when he walked into Walgreen's Drugstore.

"By God, you're a good-looking woman," Denny said. "Patty, you remember Sergeant Tom Lenihan?"

"Yes, of course," Pat said. "How are you, Sergeant?"

"Tom, you think you remember how to direct traffic?" Coughlin said, pointing at the backed-up cars.

"Yes, sir," Lenihan said.

"We won't be long in here," Coughlin said, and took Pat's arm in his large hand and walked her up the steep, wide stone stairs to the fraternity house.

"Can I help you?" a young man asked, when they had pushed open the heavy oak door with frosted glass inserts and were in the foyer of the building.

"I'm Mrs. Payne," Pat said. "I'm looking for my son."

The young man went to the foot of the curving staircase.

"Mr. Payne, sir," he called. "You have visitors, sir. It's your *mommy!*"

Denny Coughlin gave him a frosty glance.

Matthew Mark Payne appeared a moment later at the head of the stairs. He was a tall, lithe young man, with dark, thick hair. He was twenty-one, and he would graduate next month, and follow his father into the marines. He had taken the Platoon Leader's Course, and was going to be a distinguished graduate, which meant that he could have a regular marine commission, if he wanted it, and another of Patricia Payne's worries was that he would take it.

His eyes were dark and intelligent, and they flashed between his mother and Coughlin. Then he started down the stairs, not smiling. He was wearing gray flannel slacks, a button-down collared blue shirt, open, and a light gray sweater.

Coughlin turned his back to him, and said, softly. "He's a ringer for Johnny, isn't he?"

"And as hardheaded," Pat Payne said.

Matt Payne kissed his mother without embarrassment, and offered his hand to Coughlin.

"Uncle Denny," he said. "What's all this? Has something happened? Is it Dad?"

"It's your uncle Dick," Patricia Payne told her son, watching his face carefully. "Dutch is dead, Matt."

"What happened?" he asked, tightly.

"He walked up on a holdup," Denny Coughlin said. "He was shot."

"Oh, *shit!*" Matt Payne said. His lips worked, and then he put his arms around his mother.

I don't know, she thought, *whether he's seeking comfort or trying to give it.*

"Goddamn it," Matt said, letting his mother go.

"I'm sorry, son," Denny Coughlin said.

"Did they get who did it?" Matt asked. Now, Coughlin saw, he was angry.

"Dutch put the one who shot him down," Coughlin said. "The other one got away. They'll find him, Matt."

"Did he kill the one who shot him?" Matt asked.

"Yes," Coughlin said. "It was a woman, Matt, a girl."

"Jesus!"

"We're going to see your aunt Jean," Patricia Payne said. "I thought you might want to come along."

"Let me get a coat and tie," he said, and then, "Jesus! The kids!"

"It's a bitch, all right," Coughlin said.

Matt turned and went up the stairway, taking the steps two at a time.

"He's a nice boy," Denny Coughlin said.

"He's about to go off to that damned war," Patricia Payne said.

"What would you rather, Patty? That he go to Canada and dodge the draft?"

"But as a *marine.*"

"I wouldn't worry about him; that boy can take care of himself," Coughlin said.

"Like Dutch, right? Like his father?"

"Come on, Patty," Coughlin said, and put his arm around her shoulder and hugged her.

"Oh, *hell,* Denny," Patricia Payne said.

When Matt Payne came down the stairs, he was wearing a gray flannel suit.

Denny's right, Patricia Payne thought, *he looks just like Johnny.*

They went down the stairs. Matt got behind the wheel of the Mercury station wagon.

"It must be nice to be a cop," Matt said. "Park where you damned well please. A guy in the house stopped here last week, left the motor running, ran in to get some books. By the time he came out, the tow truck was hauling his car off. Cost him forty bucks for the tow truck, after he'd paid a twenty-five-dollar fine for double parking."

She looked at him, but didn't reply.

The Oldsmobile moved off.

"Here we go," Matt said, as he stepped on the accelerator. "Want to bet whether or not we break the speed limit?"

"I'm not in the mood for your wit, Matt," Patricia said.

"Just trying to brighten up an otherwise lousy afternoon," Matt said.

Sergeant Lenihan turned right onto North Thirty-third Street, cut over to North Thirty-fourth at Mantua, and led the Mercury past the Philadelphia Zoological Gardens; turned left again onto Girard for a block, and finally right onto the Schuylkill Expressway, which parallels the West Bank of the river. He drove fast, well over the posted speed limit, but not recklessly. Matt had no trouble keeping up with him. He glanced at the speedometer from time to time, but did not mention the speed to his mother.

When they crossed the Schuylkill on the Twin Bridges their pace slowed, but not much. Going past Fern Hill Park, Matt saw a police car parked off the road, watching traffic. And he saw the eyes of the policeman driving follow him as they zipped past. But the car didn't move.

Lenihan slowed the Oldsmobile then, to a precise forty-five miles an hour. They had to stop for the red light at Ninth Street, but for no others. The lights were supposed to be set, Matt recalled, for forty-five. That they didn't have to stop seemed to prove it.

"There it is," his mother said.

"There what is?"

"The Waikiki Diner," she replied. "That's where Denny said it happened."

He turned to look, but couldn't see what she was talking about.

Lenihan turned to the right at Pennypack Circle, onto Holme Avenue, and into the Torresdale section of Philadelphia.

There was a traffic jam, complete to a cop directing traffic, at the intersection of Academy Road and Outlook

Avenue. The cop waved the Oldsmobile through, but then gestured vigorously for the Mercury to keep going down Academy.

Matt stopped and shook his head, and pointed down Outlook. The white-capped traffic cop walked up to the car. Matt lowered the window.

"Captain Moffitt was my uncle," Matt said.

"Sorry," the cop said, and waved him through.

There were more cars than Matt could easily count before the house overlooking the fenced-in fairway of the Torresdale Golf Course. Among them was His Honor the Mayor Jerry Carlucci's Cadillac limousine.

Matt saw that there was at least one TV camera crew set up on the golf course, on the other side of the fence that separated it from Outlook Avenue. And there were people with still cameras.

"Park the car, Tom, please," Chief Inspector Coughlin said to his aide, "and then come back and take care of their car, too."

He got out of the Oldsmobile and stood in the street, waiting for Matt and Patty to drive up.

Staff Inspector Peter Wohl walked up to him.

"Can't we run those fucking ghouls off, Peter?" Coughlin said, nodding toward the press behind the golf course fence.

"I wish we could, sir," Wohl said. "If you've got a minute, Chief?"

Matt stopped the Mercury at Coughlin's signal. Patty lowered the window, and Coughlin leaned down to it.

"Just leave the keys, Matt," he said. "Lenihan will park it, and then catch up with us." He opened Patty's door, and she got out. "I'll be with you in just a minute, dear. I gotta talk to a guy."

He walked Wohl twenty feet down the sidewalk.

"Shoot," he said. "I gotta get inside. That's Dutch's sister-in-law. *Ex*-sister-in-law. And his nephew."

"The commissioner said if I saw you before he did, I should tell you what's going on."

"He here?"

"Yes, sir," Wohl said. "There was an eyewitness, Chief, Miss Louise Dutton, of Channel Nine."

"The blonde?" Coughlin asked.

"Right," Wohl said. "She was with Captain Moffitt at the time of the shooting," he added, evenly.

"Doing what?"

"I don't know, sir," Wohl said.

"You don't know?" Coughlin asked, on the edge of sarcasm.

"She said that she was meeting him to get his reaction to people calling the Highway Patrol 'Carlucci's Commandos,' " Wohl said. "She was very upset, sir, when I got there. She was kneeling over Captain Moffitt, weeping."

"Where is she?" Coughlin asked.

"She went from the diner to Channel Nine—"

"They didn't take her to the Roundhouse?" Coughlin interrupted. "Who let her go?"

"The commissioner . . . I was a couple of blocks from the Waikiki Diner, and responded to the call, and I was the first supervisor on the scene, and I called him. The commissioner said I should do what had to be done. I didn't think sending her to the Roundhouse was the thing to do. So I borrowed two uniforms from the Second District, and sent them with her. I told them to stay with her, to see that she got home safely. Homicide will send somebody to talk to her at her apartment."

Coughlin grunted. "McGovern say anything to her?" he asked.

"I don't think Mac saw the situation as I did, Chief."

"Probably just as well," Coughlin said. "Mac is not too big on tact. Is there anything I should be doing?"

"I don't think so, sir. The commissioner knows how close you were to Dutch . . ."

"Is there . . . is this going to develop into something awkward, Peter?"

"I hope not," Wohl said. "I don't think so."

"Jesus H. Christ," Coughlin said. "This is going to be tough enough on Jeannie without it being all over the papers and on the TV that Dutch was fooling around with some bimbo . . .''

''I think we can keep that from happening, Chief,'' Wohl said; and then surprised himself by adding, ''She's not a bimbo. I like her. And she seems to understand the situation.''

Coughlin looked at him with his eyebrows raised.

''The commissioner asked me to make sure nothing awkward develops, Chief,'' Wohl said. ''To find out for sure what Captain Moffitt's relationship with Miss Dutton was . . .''

''I went through the academy with Dutch's brother,'' Coughlin interrupted. ''Dutch was then, what, sixteen, seventeen, and he was screwing his way through the cheerleaders at Northeast High. He never, as long as I knew him, gave his pecker a rest. I've got a damned good idea what his *relationship* with Miss—whatsername?—was.''

''Dutton, Chief,'' Wohl furnished, and then added: ''We don't *know* that, Chief.''

''You want to give me odds, Peter?'' Coughlin asked.

Mrs. Patricia Payne and Matthew Payne walked up to them.

''Patty, do you know Inspector Wohl?'' Coughlin asked.

''No, I don't think so,'' Patricia Payne said, and offered her hand. ''This is my son Matt, Inspector. Dutch's nephew.''

''I'm very sorry about this, Mrs. Payne,'' Wohl said. ''Dutch and I were old friends.'' He offered his hand to Matt Payne.

''*Inspector* Wohl, did he say?'' Matt asked.

''*Staff Inspector* Wohl,'' Coughlin furnished, understanding Matt's surprise that Wohl, who didn't look much older than Matt, held such a high rank. ''He's a very good cop, Matt. He went up very quickly; the brass found out that when they gave him a difficult job, they could count on him to handle it.''

There's something behind that remark, Patricia Payne thought. *I wonder what?*

''It was nice to meet you, Mrs. Payne, Matt,'' Wohl

said. "I just regret the circumstances. I've got to get back
on the job."

Chief Inspector Coughlin nodded, and then turned and
took Mrs. Patricia Payne's arm and led her to Dutch Moffitt's front door.

FIVE

FIVE

With some difficulty, Staff Inspector Peter Wohl extricated his car from the cars jammed together on the streets, driveways, and alleys near the residence of Captain Richard C. Moffitt. He turned onto Holme Avenue, in the direction of Pennypack Circle.

When he was safely into the flow of traffic, he leaned over and took the microphone from the glove compartment.

"Isaac Twenty-three," he said into it, and when they came back at him, he said he needed a location on Two-Eleven, which was the Second District blue-and-white he'd commandeered from Mac McGovern to escort Miss Louise Dutton.

"I have him out of service at WCBL-TV at Seventeenth and Locust, Inspector," the radio operator finally told him. "Thirty-five minutes ago."

"Thank you," Wohl said, and put the microphone back inside the glove compartment and slammed the door.

There would be time, he decided, to see what the medical examiner had turned up about the female doer. There was no question that there would be other questions directed at him by his boss, Chief Inspector Coughlin, and very possibly by Commissioner Czernick or even the mayor. Peter Wohl believed the Boy Scouts were right; it paid to be prepared.

A battered Ford van pulled to a stop in the parking lot of the medical examiner's office at Civic Center Boulevard and University Avenue. The faded yellow van had a cracked windshield. On the sides were still legible vestiges of a BUDGET RENT-A-CAR logotype. The chrome grille was missing, as was the right headlight and its housing. The passenger-side door had apparently encountered something hard and sharp enough to slice the door skin like a knife. There was a deep, but not penetrating, dent on the body on the same side. The body was rusted through at the bottom of the doors, and above the left-rear fender well.

The vehicle had forty-two unanswered traffic citations against it, most for illegal parking, but including a half dozen or so for the missing headlight, the cracked windshield, an illegible license plate, and similar misdemeanor violations of the Motor Vehicle Code.

Two men got out of the van. One of them was young, very large, and bearded. He was wearing greasy blue jeans, and a leather band around his forehead to keep his long, unkempt hair out of his eyes. After he got out of the passenger's side, the driver, a small, smooth-shaven, somewhat weasel-faced individual wearing a battered gray sweatshirt with the legend SUPPORT YOUR LOCAL SHERIFF printed on it slid over and got out after him. They walked into the building.

Staff Inspector Peter Wohl and Sergeant Zachary Hobbs of Homicide were standing by a coffee vending machine in the basement, drinking from Styrofoam cups. Wohl shook his head when he saw them.

"Hello, Inspector," the weasel-faced small man, who was Lieutenant David Pekach of the Narcotics Squad, said.

"Pekach, does your mother know what you do for a living?" Wohl replied, offering his hand.

Pekach chuckled. "God, I hope not." He looked at Hobbs. "You're Sergeant Hobbs?"

"Yes, sir," Hobbs said.

"You know Officer McFadden?" Pekach asked, and both Wohl and Hobbs shook their heads, no.

"Charley, this is Staff Inspector Wohl," the weasel-faced man said, "And Sergeant Hobbs. Officer Charley McFadden."

"How do you do, sir?" Officer McFadden asked, respectfully, to Wohl and Hobbs each in turn.

"Where is she?" Pekach asked.

"In there," Wohl said, nodding at double metal doors. "He's not through with her."

"Don't tell me you have a queasy stomach, Inspector?" Pekach asked, innocently.

"You bet your ass, I do," Wohl said.

Pekach walked in. McFadden followed him.

Unidentified White Female Suspect was on a stainless steel table. She was naked, her legs spread, one arm lying beside her, the other over her head. Body fluids dripped from a corner drain on the table into a stainless steel bucket on the tile floor.

A bald-headed man wearing a plastic apron over surgical blues stopped what he was doing and looked up curiously and unpleasantly at Pekach and McFadden. What he was doing was removing Unidentified White Female Suspect's heart from the opening he had made in her chest.

"I'm Lieutenant Pekach, Doctor," Pekach said. "We just want to get a look at her face."

The medical examiner shrugged, and went on with what he was doing.

"Jesus," Pekach said. "What did he shoot her with?"

"I presume," the medical examiner said dryly, not looking up, "that the weapon used was the standard service revolver."

Pekach snorted.

"She shot Captain Moffitt the way she was shot up like that?" Pekach asked.

"Before," the medical examiner replied. "What I think happened is that she shot Moffitt before he shot her."

"I don't understand," Pekach said.

The medical examiner pointed with his scalpel at a small plastic bag. Pekach picked it up.

It held a misshapen piece of lead, thinner than a pencil and about a quarter of an inch long.

"Twenty-two," the medical examiner said. "Probably a long rifle. It entered his chest just below the armpit." He took Unidentified White Female Suspect's hand, raised it in the air, and pointed. "From the side, almost from the back. The bullet hit the left ventricle of the aorta. Then he bled to death, internally. The heart just kept pumping, and when he ran out of blood, he died."

"Jesus Christ!" Pekach said.

The medical examiner let Unidentified White Female Suspect's arm fall, and then pointed to another plastic envelope.

"Show these to Peter Wohl," he said. "I think it's what he's looking for. I just took those out of her."

The envelope contained three misshapen pieces of lead. Each was larger and thicker than the .22 projectile removed from the body of Captain Moffitt. The ends of all the bullets had expanded, "mushroomed," on striking something hard, so that they actually looked something like mushrooms. The other end of each bullet was covered by a quarter-inch-high copper-colored cup. There were clear rifling marks on the cups; it would not be at all difficult to match these jacketed bullets to the pistol that had fired them.

The very large young man looked carefully at the face of Unidentified White Female Suspect and changed her status.

"Schmeltzer, Dorothy Ann," he said. "Twenty-four, five feet five, one-hundred twenty-five pounds. Last known

address . . . somewhere on Vine, just east of Broad. I'd
have to check.''

"You're sure?''

"That's Dorothy Ann," McFadden said. "I thought she
was still in jail.''

"What was she in for?''

"Solicitation for prostitution," McFadden said. "I think
the judge put her in to see if they couldn't dry her out.''

"She's got needle marks all over," the medical examiner said, "in places you wouldn't believe. No identification on her? Is that what this is all about?''

"Lieutenant Natali told me all she had on her was a
joint and a .22 pistol," Pekach said. "And the needle
marks. He thought we might be able to make her as a
junkie. Thank you, Doctor.''

He left the room.

Wohl and Hobbs were no longer alone. Lieutenant Natali and Lieutenant Sabara of the Highway Patrol had come
to the medical examiner's office. Sabara looked askance at
the Narcotics Division officers.

Natali saw it. "*I* like your sweatshirt, Pekach," he said
dryly.

"Could you identify her?" Hobbs asked.

"Officer McFadden was able to identify her, Sergeant,"
Pekach said, formally. "Her name was Schmeltzer, Dor-
othy Ann Schmeltzer. A known drug addict, who Mc-
Fadden thinks was only recently released from prison.''

"Any known associates, McFadden?" Hobbs asked.

"Sir, I can't recall any names. It'd be on her record.''

"If I can borrow him for a while, I'd like to take
McFadden with me to the Roundhouse," Hobbs said.

"Sure," Pekach said.

"I guess you can call off the rest of your people, then,"
Hobbs said. "And thank you, Lieutenant.''

"Now that I've got her name, maybe I can find out
something," Pekach said. "I'll get on the radio.''

"Appreciate it," Hobbs said. "If you do come up with
something, give me or Lieutenant Natali a call.''

"Sure," Pekach said. "Inspector, the medical examiner

said to show you these. He said he thought that's what you were waiting for."

Wohl took the bag Pekach handed him and held it up to the light. He was not surprised to see that the bullets were jacketed, and from the way they had mushroomed, almost certainly had been hollow pointed.

"What's that? The projectiles?" Sergeant Hobbs asked.

Wohl handed the envelope to Sergeant Hobbs. They met each other's eyes, but Hobbs didn't say anything.

"Don't lose those," Wohl said.

"What do you think they are, Inspector?" Hobbs asked, in transparent innocence.

"I'm not a firearms expert," Wohl said. "What I see is four bullets removed from the body of the woman suspected of shooting Captain Moffitt. They're what they call evidence, Sergeant, in the chain of evidence."

"They're jacketed hollow points," Hobbs said. "Is that what this is all about?"

"What the hell is the difference?" Pekach said. "Dutch is dead. The Department can't do anything to him now for using prohibited ammunition."

"And maybe we'll get lucky," Hobbs said, "and get an assistant DA six months out of law school who thinks bullets are bullets are bullets."

"Yeah, and maybe we won't," Wohl said. "Maybe we'll get some assistant DA six months out of law school who knows the difference, and would like to get his name in the newspapers as the guy who caught the cops using illegal ammunition, again, in yet another example of police brutality."

"Jesus," Pekach said, disgustedly. "And I know just the prick who would do that." He paused and added. "Two or three pricks, now that I think about it."

"Get those to Firearms Identification, Hobbs," Wohl said. "Get a match. Keep your fingers crossed. Maybe we will be lucky."

"Yes, Sir," Hobbs said.

"I don't think there is anything else to be done here,"

Wohl said. "Or am I missing something?" He looked at Sabara as he spoke.

"I thought I'd escort the hearse to the funeral home," Sabara said. "You know, what the hell. It seems little enough . . ."

"I think Dutch would like that," Wohl said.

"Well, I expect I had better pay my respects to Chief Lowenstein," Wohl said. "I'll probably see you fellows in the Roundhouse."

"If you don't mind my asking, Inspector," Hobbs said. "Are you going to be in on this?"

"No," Wohl said. "Not the way you mean. But the eyewitness is that blonde from Channel 9. That could cause problems. The commissioner asked me to make sure it doesn't. I want to explain that to Chief Lowenstein. That's all."

"Good luck, Inspector," Hobbs said, chuckling. Chief Inspector of Detectives Matt Lowenstein, a heavyset, cigar chewing man in his fifties, had a legendary temper, which was frequently triggered when he suspected someone was treading on sacred Detective Turf.

"Why do I think I'll need it?" Wohl said, also chuckling, and left.

There was a Cadillac hearse with a casket in it in the parking lot. The driver was leaning on the fender. Chrome-plated letters outside the frosted glass read MARSHUTZ & SONS.

Dutch was apparently going to be buried from a funeral home three blocks from his house. As soon as the medical examiner released the body, it would be put in the casket, and in the hearse, and taken there.

Wohl thought that Sabara showing up here, just so he could lead the hearse to Marshutz & Sons, was a rather touching gesture. It wasn't called for by regulations, and he hadn't thought that Dutch and Sabara had been that close. But probably, he decided, he was wrong. Sabara wasn't really as tough as he acted (and looked), and he probably had been, in his way, fond of Dutch.

He got in the LTD and got on the radio.

"Isaac Twenty-Three. Have Two-Eleven contact me on the J-Band."

Two-Eleven was the Second District car he had sent with Louise Dutton.

He had to wait a moment before Two-Eleven called him.

"Two-Eleven to Isaac Twenty-Three."

"What's your location, Two-Eleven?"

"We just dropped the lady at Six Stockton Place."

Where the hell is that? The only Stockton Place I can think of is a slum down by the river.

"Where?"

"Isaac Twenty-Three, that's Apartment A, Six Stockton Place."

"Two-Eleven, where does that come in?"

"It's off Arch Street in the one-hundred block."

"Okay. Two-Eleven, thank you," he said, and put the microphone back in the glove box.

He was surprised. That was really a crummy address, not one where you would expect a classy blonde like Louise Dutton to live. Then he remembered that there had been conversion, renovation, whatever it was called, of the old buildings in that area.

When Lieutenant David Pekach came out of the medical examiner's office, he found a white-cap Traffic Division officer standing next to the battered van, writing out a ticket.

"Is there some trouble, Officer?" Pekach asked, innocently.

The Traffic Division officer, who had intended to ticket the van only for a missing headlight, took a look at the legend on Pekach's T-shirt, and with an effort, restrained himself from commenting.

What he would have *liked* to have done is kick the fucking hippie queer junkie's ass from there to the river, and there drown the sonofabitch, and in the old days, when he'd first come on the job, he could have done just that. But things had changed, and he was coming up on his twenty years for retirement, and it wasn't worth risking his pension, even if somebody walking around with something insulting to the police like that—*Support Your Local Sheriff* my ass, that *wasn't* what it meant—printed on his sweatshirt and walking around on the streets really deserved to get his ass kicked.

Instead, he cited the vehicle for a number of additional offenses against the Motor Vehicle Code: cracked windshield, smooth tires, non-functioning turn indicators, and illegible license plate, which was all he could think of. He was disappointed when the fucking hippy had a valid driver's license.

Half a block from the medical examiner's office, Lieutenant Pekach put his copy of the citation between his teeth, ripped it in half, and then threw both halves out the van's window.

When Wohl got to the Roundhouse, he parked in the space reserved for Chief Inspector Coughlin. Coughlin was very close to the Moffitt family; more than likely he would be at the Moffitt house for a while. As he walked into the building, he saw Hobbs's car turn into the parking lot.

He was not surprised to find Chief Inspector of Detectives Matt Lowenstein in Homicide. Lowenstein was in the main room, sitting on a desk, a fresh, very large cigar in the corner of his mouth.

"Well, Inspector Wohl," Lowenstein greeted him with mock cordiality, "I was hoping I'd run into you. How are you, Peter?"

"Good afternoon, Chief," Wohl said.

"Do you think you could find a moment for me?" Lowenstein asked. "I've got a little something on my mind."

"My time is your time, Chief," Wohl said.

"Why don't we just go in here a moment?" Lowenstein said, gesturing toward the door of an office on whose door was lettered CAPTAIN HENRY C. QUAIRE COMMANDING OFFICER.

Chief Inspector Lowenstein opened the door without knocking. Captain Quaire, a stocky, balding man in his late forties, was sitting in his shirtsleeves at his desk, talking on the telephone. When he saw Lowenstein, he covered the mouthpiece with his hand.

"Henry, why don't you get a cup of coffee or something?" Lowenstein suggested.

Captain Quaire, as he rose to his feet, said "I'll call you right back" to the telephone and hung it up. When he passed Peter Wohl, he shook his head. Wohl wasn't sure if it was a gesture of sympathy, or whether it meant that Quaire too was shocked, and pissed, by what he had done.

"Peter," Lowenstein said, as he closed the door after Quaire, "it's not that I don't think that you are one of the brightest young officers in the department, a credit to the department and your father, but when I want your assistance, the way I would prefer to do that is to call Denny Coughlin and ask for it. Not have you shoved down my throat by the Polack."

"Frankly, Chief," Wohl said, smiling, "I sort of expected you would ask me in here, thank me for my services, and tell me not to let the doorknob hit me in the ass on my way out."

"Don't be a wiseass, Peter," Lowenstein said.

"Chief, I hope you understand that what I did at the diner was at the commissioner's orders," Wohl said. He saw that Lowenstein was still angry.

"The implication, of course, is that everybody in Homicide is a fucking barbarian, too dumb to figure out for themselves how to handle a woman like that," Lowenstein said.

"I don't think he meant that, Chief," Wohl said. "I think what it was was just that I was the senior supervisor at the Waikiki Diner. I think he would have given the same orders, would have preferred to give the same orders, to anyone from Homicide."

"The difference, Peter, is that nobody from Homicide would have called the Polack. They would have followed procedure. Why did you call him?"

"A couple of reasons," Wohl said, deciding to stand his ground. "Primarily because he and Dutch were close."

"And the woman?"

"And the woman," Peter said. "I'm sorry if you're angry, but I don't see where what I did was wrong."

"Was Dutch fucking her?"

"I don't know," Peter said. "I thought it was possible when I called the commissioner, and that if they had something going on between them, what I should do was try to keep anybody from finding out."

"Maybe the Polack was already onto it," Lowenstein said.

"Excuse me?"

"Just before you came in, Peter, I talked with the Polack," Lowenstein said. "I was going to call him anyway, but he called me. And what he told me was that he wants you in on this, to deal with the Dutton woman from here on in."

"I don't understand," Wohl said.

"It's simple English," Lowenstein said. "Whatever Homicide has to do with that woman, they'll do it through you. I told the Polack I didn't like that one damned bit, and he said he was sorry, but it wasn't a suggestion. He also said that I shouldn't bother complaining to the mayor, the mayor thought it was a good idea, too. I guess that Wop sonofabitch is as afraid of the goddamned TV as the Polack is."

"Well, it wasn't my idea," Wohl said, aware that he was embarrassed. "I went to Nazareth, and went through Dutch's personal possessions, and then I went to the medical examiner's office. I was going to come here to tell you what I found—which is nothing—and then I was going to call the commissioner and tell him."

Lowenstein looked intently at him for a moment.

"And go back to where I belong," Peter added.

"Yeah, well, that's not going to happen," Lowenstein said. "I was going to give you a little talk, Peter, to make it clear that *all* you're authorized to do is keep the TV lady happy; that you're *not* to get involved in the investigation itself. But I don't think I have to do that, do I?"

"No, sir," Wohl said. "Of course you don't."

"And I don't think I have to ask you to make sure that I hear anything the Polack hears, do I?"

"No, sir."

"The trouble with you, Peter, you sonofabitch, is that I can't stay mad at you," Lowenstein said.

"I'm glad to hear that," Wohl said, smiling. "What do you think I should do now?"

"I suspect that just maybe the assigned detective would like to talk to the witness," Lowenstein said. "Why don't you find him and ask him? Where's the dame?"

"At her apartment," Peter said. "Who's got the job?"

"Jason Washington," Chief Inspector Lowenstein said. "I expect you'll find him outside, just atitter with excitement that he'll now be able to work real close to a real staff inspector."

"There's a rumor going around, Chief," Wohl said, "that some people think staff inspectors are real cops."

"Get your ass out of here, Peter," Lowenstein said, but he was smiling.

There were twenty-one active homicide investigations underway by the Homicide Division of the Philadelphia Police Department, including that of Captain Richard C. Moffitt. An active homicide investigation being defined unofficially as one where there was a reasonable chance to determine who had unlawfully caused the death of another human being, and to develop sufficient evidence to convince the Philadelphia district attorney that he would not be wasting his time and the taxpayers' money by seeking a grand jury indictment and ultimately bringing the accused to trial.

Very nearly at the bottom of the priority list to expend investigatory resources (the time and overtime of the homicide detectives, primarily, but also including certain forensic techniques, some of which were very expensive) were the cases, sometimes occurring once or twice a week, involving vagrants or junkies done to death by beating, or stabbing. The perpetrator of these types of murders often had no motive beyond taking possession of the victim's alcohol or narcotics, and if questioned about it eight hours later might really have no memory of what had taken place.

There were finite resources. Decisions have to be made as to where they can best be spent in protecting the public, generally, or sometimes an individual. Most murders involve people who know each other, and many involve close relatives, and most murders are not hard to solve. The perpetrator of a murder is often on the scene when the police arrive, or if he has fled the scene, is immediately identified by witnesses who also have a pretty good idea where he or she might be found.

What many homicide detectives privately (certainly not for public consumption) think of as a *good* case is a death illegally caused during the execution of a felony. A holdup man shoots a convenience-store cashier, for example, or a bank messenger is shot and killed while being held up.

That sort of a perpetrator is not going to be found sitting in the toilet, head between his hands, sick to his stomach with remorse, asking to see his parish priest. The sonofabitch is going to run, and if run to earth is going to deny ever having been near the scene of the crime in his life.

It is necessary to make the case against him. Find his gun, wherever he hid it or threw it, and have the crime lab make it as the murder weapon. Find witnesses who saw him at the scene of the crime, or with the loot. Break the stories of witnesses who at first are willing to swear on a stack of Bibles that the accused was twenty miles from the scene of the crime.

This is proper detective work, worthy of homicide detectives, who believe they are the best detectives in the department. It requires brains and skills in a dozen facets of the investigative profession.

And every once in a great while, there is a case just like cop stories on the TV, where some dame does in her husband, or some guy does in his business partner, on purpose, planning it carefully, so that it looks as if he fell down the cellar stairs, or that the partner got done in by a burglar, or a mugger, or a hit-and-run driver.

But something about it smells, and a good homicide

detective starts nosing around, finding out if the done-in husband had a girl on the side, or a lot of insurance, or had a lot of insurance and the *wife* was running around.

Very near the top of the priority list are the homicides of children, and other sorts of specially protected individuals, such as nuns, or priests.

And at the absolute top of the priority list is the murder of a police officer. There are a number of reasons for this, some visceral *(that could be me lying there with a hole in the back of my head)* and some very practical: *You can't enforce the law if the bad guys think they can shoot a cop and get away with it. If the bad guys can laugh at the cops, they win.*

Technically, the investigation of the murder of Captain Richard C. Moffitt would be handled exactly like the murder of any other citizen. The case would be assigned to a homicide detective. It would be his case. He would conduct the investigation, asking for whatever assistance he needed. He would be supervised by his sergeant, who would keep himself advised on where the investigation was leading. And the sergeant's lieutenant would keep an eye on the investigation through the sergeant. Both would provide any assistance to the homicide detective who had the case that he asked for.

That was the procedure, and it would be followed in the case of Captain Richard C. Moffitt.

Captain Henry C. Quaire, commanding officer of the Homicide Division, had assigned the investigation of the murder of Captain Richard C. Moffitt to Detective Jason F. Washington, Sr., almost immediately upon learning that Captain Moffitt had been shot to death.

Detective Washington was thirty-nine years old, a large, heavyset Afro-American who had been a police officer for sixteen years, a detective for eleven, and assigned to Homicide for five. Washington had a reputation as a highly skilled interrogator, a self-taught master psychologist who seemed to know not only when someone being interviewed was lying, but how to get the person being interviewed to tell the truth. He was quite an actor, doing this,

being able convincingly to portray any one of a number
of characters, from the kindly understanding father figure
who fully understood how something tragic like this could
happen to the meanest sonofabitch east of the Mississippi
River.

Washington had a fine mind, an eagle's eye when dis-
covering minor discrepancies in a story, and a skill rare
among his peers. He was a fine typist. He could type with
great accuracy at about eighty words per minute. This
skill, coupled with Detective Washington's flair for writing, made his official reports the standard to which his
peers aspired. Detective Washington was never summoned
to the captain's office to be asked, "What the hell is this
supposed to mean?"

Detective Washington and Captain Moffitt had been
friends, too. Washington had been (briefly, until he had
been injured in a serious wreck, during a high-speed pursuit) then-Sergeant Moffitt's partner in the Highway Patrol.

None of this had anything to with the case of Captain
Richard C. Moffitt being assigned to Detective Jason F.
Washington, Sr. He was given the job because he was "up
on the wheel." The wheel (which was actually a sheet of
cardboard) was the device by which jobs were assigned to
the detectives of the Homicide Division. Each shift had its
own wheel. When a job came in, the detective whose name
was at the head of list was given the assignment, whereupon his name went to the bottom of the wheel. He would
not be given another job until every other homicide detective, in turn, had been given one.

The system was not unlike that used in automobile
showrooms, where to keep a prospective customer, an
"up," from being swarmed over by a dozen commission-
hungry salesmen, they were forced to take their turn.

Jason F. Washington, Sr., knew, however, as did everybody else in Homicide, that while Dutch's shooting might
be his job, he was going to be given a higher level of
supervision and assistance than he would have gotten had
Richard C. Moffitt been a civilian when he stopped the
bullet in the Waikiki Diner.

There was no suggestion at all that there was any question in anyone's mind that Washington could not handle the job. What it was was that the commissioner was going to keep an eye on the case through Chief Inspector of Detectives Matt Lowenstein, who was going to lean on Captain Quaire to make sure everything possible was being done, who was going to lean on Lieutenant Lou Natali who was going to lean on Sergeant Zachary Hobbs, who was going to lean on Detective Jason F. Washington, Sr.

And now Peter Wohl had been added to the equation, and Jason Washington wasn't sure what that would mean. He had found that out when he'd asked Captain Quaire why the witness hadn't been brought to the Roundhouse. Quaire had told him, off the record, that Wohl had stuck his nose in where it didn't belong, and that Lowenstein was about to chop it off for him. But an hour after that, Quaire had come out of his office to tell him that was changed. He was not to do anything about the witness at all, without checking with Staff Inspector Wohl. Staff Inspector Wohl was presently at the medical examiner's office and might, and then again might not, soon grace Homicide with his exalted presence.

Quaire had thrown up his hands.

"Don't look at me, Jason. I just work here. We are now involved in bullshit among the upper-level brass."

Detective Jason Washington had seen Staff Inspector Peter Wohl come into Homicide, and had seen Matt Lowenstein take him into Captain Quaire's office, throwing Quaire out as he did so. He was not surprised when Wohl appeared at his desk, five minutes later, although he had not seen, or sensed, him walking over.

"Hello, Jason," Wohl said.

Washington stood up and offered his hand.

"Inspector," he said. "How goes it?"

"I'm all right," Wohl said. "How've you been?"

"Aside from the normal ravages of middle age, no real complaints. Something on your mind?"

"I've been assigned to stroke WCBL-TV generally and

Miss Louise Dutton specifically," Wohl said. "I guess you heard?"

Washington smiled. "I heard about that." He pointed at the wooden chair beside his desk.

Wohl smiled his thanks and sat down and stretched his legs out.

"You ever read *Animal Farm?*" Wohl asked.

Washington chuckled.

"I wouldn't compare a pretty lady like that with a pig," he said.

"Let's just say then that she's more equal than some other pretty lady," Wohl said. "If you're ready for her, I'll go get her."

"Anytime it's convenient," Washington said. "But an hour ago would be better than tomorrow."

"Jason, all I'm going to do is stroke her feathers," Wohl said. "Did I have to tell you that?"

"No, but I'm glad you did," Washington said. "Thank you."

"But for personal curiosity, has anything turned up?" Wohl asked.

"Not yet, but if I was a white boy with long hair and a zipper jacket, I don't think I would leave the house today. I guess you heard what the Highway Patrol is up to?"

"I'm not sure how effective that will be, but you can't blame them. They liked Dutch."

"So did I. We were partners, once. Hell, Highway may even catch him."

"What's your gut feeling, Jason?"

"Well, he's either under a rock somewhere in Philadelphia, or he's long gone. But gut feeling? He's either here or in Atlantic City."

Wohl nodded and made a little grunting noise.

"An undercover guy from Narcotics thinks he identified the woman—"

"Sergeant Hobbs called me," Washington interrupted him. "If they can come up with a name . . ."

"I have a feeling they will," Wohl said. "Okay. So

long as you understand where I fit in this, Jason, I'll go fetch the eyewitness.''

He stood up.

Detective Jason F. Washington, Sr., extended something to Staff Inspector Peter Wohl.

''What's that?''

''Miracle of modern medicine,'' Washington said. ''It's supposed to prevent ulcers.''

''Are you suggesting I'm going to need it?'' Wohl asked with a smile.

''*Somebody* thinks that TV lady is going to be trouble,'' Washington said.

Wohl popped the antacid in his mouth, and then turned and walked out of Homicide.

SIX

When Sergeant Hobbs and Officer McFadden got to the Roundhouse, and McFadden started to open the passenger-side door, Hobbs touched his arm.

"Wait a minute," he said. He then got out of the car, walked to the passenger side, motioned for McFadden to get out, and when he had, put his hand on his arm, and then marched him into the building. It looked for all the world as if McFadden was in custody and being led into the Roundhouse, which is exactly what Hobbs had in mind.

The Roundhouse is a public building, but it is not open to the public to the degree, for example, that City Hall is. It is the nerve center of the police department, and while there are always a number of ordinary, decent, law-abiding citizens in the building, the overwhelming majority of private citizens in the Roundhouse are there as nonvoluntary guests of the police, or are relatives and friends of the nonvoluntary guests who have come to see what can be done about getting them out, either by posting bail, or in some other way.

There are almost always a number of people in this latter category standing just outside, or just inside, the door leading into the Roundhouse from the parking lot out back. Immediately inside the door is a small foyer. To the right a corridor leads to an area from which the friends and relatives of those arrested can watch preliminary arraignments before a magistrate, who either sets bail or orders the accused confined until trial.

To the left is a door leading to the main lobby of the building, which is not open to the general public. It is operated by a solenoid controlled by a police officer who sits behind a shatterproof plastic window directly across the corridor from the door to the parking lot.

Hobbs didn't want anyone with whom McFadden might now, or eventually, have a professional relationship to remember later having seen the large young man with the forehead band walking into the place and being passed without question, as if he was cop, into the main lobby.

Still holding on to Officer McFadden's arm, Hobbs flashed his badge at the corporal on duty behind the window, who took a good look at it, and then pushed the button operating the solenoid. The door lock buzzed as Hobbs reached it. He pushed it open, and went through it, and marched McFadden to the elevator doors.

There was a sign on the gray steel first-floor door reading CRIMINAL RECORDS, AUTHORIZED PERSONNEL ONLY. Hobbs pushed it open, and eventually the door opened. A corporal looked at Officer McFadden very dubiously.

"This is McFadden, Narcotics," Hobbs said. The room held half a dozen enormous gray rotary files, each twelve feet long. Electric motors rotated rows of files, thousands of them, each containing the arrest and criminal records of one individual who had at one time come to the official attention of the police. The files were tended by civilian employees, mostly women, under the supervision of sworn officers.

Hobbs saw the sergeant on duty, Salvatore V. DeConti,

a short, balding, plump, very natty man in his middle thirties, in a crisply starched shirt and perfectly creased uniform trousers, sitting at his desk. He saw that DeConti was unable to keep from examining, and finding wanting, the fat bearded large young man he had brought with him into records.

Amused, Hobbs walked McFadden over to him and introduced him: "Sergeant DeConti, this is Officer McFadden. He's identified the woman who shot Captain Moffitt."

It was an effort, but DeConti managed it, to offer his hand to the fat, bearded young man with the leather band around his forehead.

"How are you?" he said, then freed his hand, and called to the corporal. When he came over, he said, "Officer McFadden's got a name on the girl Captain Moffitt shot."

"I guess the fingerprint guy from Identification ought to be back from the medical examiner's about now with her prints," the corporal said. "What's the name?"

"Schmeltzer, Dorothy Ann," McFadden said. "And I got a name, Sergeant, for the guy who got away from the diner." He gestured with his hand, a circular movement near his head, indicating that he didn't actually *have* a name, for sure, but that he knew there was one floating around somewhere in his head. That he was, in other words, working intuitively.

"Florian will help you, if he can," Sergeant DeConti said.

"Gallagher, Grady, something Irish," McFadden said.

"There's only three or four thousand Gallaghers in there, I'm sure," Corporal Florian said. "But we can look."

"Help yourself to some coffee, Sergeant," DeConti said. Then, "Damned shame about Dutch."

"A rotten shame," Hobbs agreed. "Three kids." Then he looked at DeConti. "I'm sure McFadden is right," he said. "Lieutenant Pekach said he's smart, a good cop. Even if he doesn't look much like one."

"I'm just glad I never got an assignment like that,"

DeConti said. "Some of it has to rub off. The scum he has to be with, I mean."

Hobbs had the unkind thought that Sergeant DeConti would never be asked to undertake an undercover assignment unless it became necessary to infiltrate a group of hotel desk clerks, or maybe the Archdiocese of Philadelphia. If you put a white collar on DeConti, Hobbs thought, he could easily pass for a priest.

Across the room, McFadden, a look of satisfaction on his face, was writing on a yellow, lined pad. He ripped off a sheet and handed it to Corporal Florian. Then he walked across the room to Hobbs and DeConti.

"Gerald Vincent Gallagher," he announced. "I remembered the moment I saw her sheet. He got ripped off about six months ago by some Afro-American gentlemen, near the East Park Reservoir in Fairmount Park. They really did a job on him. She came to see him in the hospital."

"Good man, McFadden," DeConti said. "Florian's getting his record?"

"Yes, sir. Her family lives in Holmesburg," McFadden went on. "I went looking for her there one time. Her father runs a grocery store around Lincoln High School. Nice people."

"This ought to brighten their day," Hobbs said.

Corporal Florian walked over with a card, and handed it, a little uneasily, to McFadden. DeConti and Hobbs leaned over to get a look.

"That's him. He's just out on parole, too," McFadden said.

"He fits the description," Hobbs said, and then went on: "If you were Gerald Vincent Gallagher, McFadden, where do you think you would be right now?"

McFadden's heavily bearded face screwed up in thought.

"I don't think I'd have any money, since I didn't get to pull off the robbery," he said. "So I don't think I would be on a bus or train out of town. And I wouldn't go back where I lived, in case I had been recognized, so I would probably be holed up someplace, probably in North Philly, if I got that far. Maybe downtown. I can think of a couple of places.''

"Make up a list," Hobbs ordered.

"I'd sort of like to look for this guy myself, Sergeant," McFadden said.

Hobbs looked at him dubiously.

"I don't want to blow my cover, Sergeant," McFadden went on. "I could look for him without doing that."

"You can tell Lieutenant Pekach that I said that if he thinks you could be spared from your regular job for a while, that you could probably be useful to Detective Washington," Hobbs said. "*If* Washington wants you."

"Thank you," McFadden said. "I'll ask him as soon as I get back to the office."

"Jason Washington's got the job?" Sergeant DeConti asked.

"Uh-huh," Hobbs said. He picked up the telephone and dialed it.

"Detention Unit, Corporal Delzinski."

"This is Sergeant Hobbs, Homicide, Corporal. The next time a wagon from the Sixth District—"

"There's one just come in, Sergeant," Delzinski interrupted.

"As soon as they drop off their prisoner, send them up to Criminal Records," Hobbs said. "I've got a prisoner that has to be transported to Narcotics. They'll probably have to fumigate the wagon, afterward, but that can't be helped."

DeConti laughed.

"We have a lot of time and money invested in making you a credible turd, McFadden," Hobbs said. "I would hate to see it all wasted."

"I understand, sir," McFadden said. "Thank you."

A civilian employee from the photo lab, a very thin woman, walked up with three four-by-five photographs of Gerald Vincent Gallagher.

"I wiped them," she said. "But they're still wet. I don't know about putting them in an envelope."

"I'll just carry them the way they are," Hobbs said.

"McFadden, you make up your list. When the Sixth District wagon gets here, Sergeant DeConti will tell them to transport you to Narcotics. I'll send somebody up to get the list from you."

"Yes, sir," McFadden said.

"Thank you, Brother DeConti," Hobbs said. "It's always a pleasure doing business with you."

"I just hope you catch the bastard," DeConti said.

The Wackenhut Private Security officer did not raise the barrier when the blue Ford LTD nosed up to it, nor even when the driver tapped the horn. He let the bastard wait a minute, and then walked slowly over to the car.

"May I help you, sir?"

"Raise the barrier," Wohl said.

"Stockton Place is not a public thoroughfare, sir," the security officer said.

Wohl showed him his badge.

"What's going on, Inspector?" the security officer said.

"Nothing particular," Wohl said. "You want to raise that thing?"

Louise Dutton's old yellow Cadillac convertible, the roof now up, was parked three-quarters of the way down the cobblestone street.

When the barrier was raised, Wohl drove slowly down the street and pulled in behind the convertible. Wohl looked around curiously. He hadn't even known this place was here, although his office was less than a dozen blocks away.

Stockton Place looked, he thought, except for the cars on the street, as it must have looked two hundred years ago, when these buildings had been built.

He got out of the car, then crossed to the nearest doorway. There was no doorbell that he could see, and after a moment, he saw that the doorway was not intended to open; that it was a facade. He backed up, smiled more in amusement than embarrassment, and looked at the doorways to the right and left. There were doorbells beside the doorway on the left.

There were three of them, and one of them read DUT-TON.

He saw that the door was slightly ajar, and tried it, and then pushed it open.

There was a small lobby inside. To the right was a shiny mailbox, and more doorbell buttons, these accompanied by a telephone. Beside the mailboxes was a door with a large brass ''C'' fixed to it, and a holder for a name card. Jerome Nelson.

There were three identical doors against the other wall. They each had identifying signs on them: STAIRWAY, ELE-VATOR, SERVICE.

If ''C'' was the ground floor, Wohl reasoned, ''A'' would be the top floor. He opened the door marked ELE-VATOR and found an open elevator behind it. He pushed ''A''. A door closed silently, faint music started to play, and the elevator started upward. It stopped, and the door opened and the music stopped. There was another door in front of him, with a lock and a peephole, and a doorbell button. He pushed it and heard the faint ponging of chimes.

''Whoever that is, Jerome,'' Louise Dutton said, ''send them away.''

Jerome walked quickly and delicately to the elevator door, rose on his toes, and put his eye to the peephole. It was a handsome, rather well dressed, man.

Jerome pulled the door open.

''I'm very sorry,'' he said, ''but Miss Dutton is not receiving callers.''

''Please tell Miss Dutton that Peter Wohl would like to see her,'' Wohl said.

''Just one moment, please,'' Jerome said.

He walked into the apartment.

''It's a very good-looking man named Peter Wohl,'' he told Louise Dutton, loud enough for Wohl to hear him. A smile flickered on and off Wohl's face.

''He's a policeman,'' Louise said, and walked toward the door.

Louise Dutton was wearing a bathrobe, Wohl saw, and

then corrected himself, *a dressing gown,* and holding both a cigarette and a drink.

"Oh, you," she said. "Hi! Come on in."

"Good afternoon, Miss Dutton," Wohl said, politely.

She was half in the bag, Wohl decided. There was something erotic about the way she looked, he realized. Part of that was obviously because he could see her nipples holding the thin material of her dressing gown up like tent poles—it was probably silk, he decided—but there was more to it than that.

"I'm glad that you got home all right," Wohl said.

"Thank you for that," Louise said. "I was more upset than I realized, and I shouldn't have been driving."

"I just made her take a long soak in a hot tub," Jerome said. "And I prescribed a *stiff* drink." He put out his hand. "I'm Jerome Nelson, a friend of the family."

"I'm Inspector Peter Wohl," Wohl said, taking the hand. "How do you do, Mr. Nelson?"

"You certainly, if you don't mind me saying so, don't look like a policeman," Jerome Nelson said.

"That's nice, if you're a detective," Wohl said. "What would you say I *do* look like?"

Jerome laid a finger against his cheek, cocked his head, and studied Wohl.

"I just *don't know,*" he said. "Maybe a stockbroker. A *successful* stockbroker. I *love* your suit."

"Miss Dutton, they're ready for you at the Roundhouse," Wohl said.

"Meaning what?"

"Meaning, I'd like you to come down there with me. They want your statement, and I think they'll have some photographs to show you. And then I'll see that you're brought back here."

"Will whatever it is wait five minutes?" Louise said. "I want to see what Cohen's going to put on."

"I beg your pardon?" Wohl asked.

"It's time for 'Nine's News,' " she said.

"Oh," he said.

"Can I offer you a drink?" Jerome asked.

"Yes, thank you," Wohl said. "I'd like a drink. Scotch?"

"Absolutely," Jerome said, happily.

Louise opened the door of a maple cabinet, revealing a large color television screen. She turned it on and, still bent over it, so that Wohl had a clear view of her naked breast, looked at him as she waited for it to come on.

"The guy on 'Dragnet,' " Louise Dutton said, "Sergeant Joe Friday, would say, 'No ma'am, I'm on duty.' "

"I'm not Sergeant Friday," Wohl said, with a faint smile.

She's bombed, and unaware her dressing gown is open. Or is it the to-be-expected casualness about nudity of a hooker?

That's an interesting possibility. She's obviously not walking the streets asking men if they want a date, but I don't think she's making half enough money smiling on television to afford this place. Is she somebody's mistress, some middle-aged big shot's extracurricular activity, who was taking a bus driver's holiday with Dutch?

And who's Jerome? The friend of the family?

The picture suddenly came on, and the sound. Louise turned the volume up, and stepped back as Jerome touched Wohl's shoulder and handed him a squarish glass of whiskey.

The screen showed Louise Dutton's old convertible with a cop at the wheel leaving the Waikiki Diner parking lot.

A female voice said, "This is a special 'Nine's News' bulletin. A Philadelphia police captain gave his life this afternoon foiling a holdup. 'Nine's News' co-anchor Louise Dutton was an eyewitness. Full details on 'Nine's News' at six."

The Channel Nine logo came on the screen. A male voice said, "WCBL-TV, Channel 9, Philadelphia. It's six o'clock."

Another male voice said, as the "Nine's News" set appeared on the screen, " 'Nine's News' at six is next."

The "Nine's News" logo appeared on the screen, and then dissolved into a close-up shot of Barton Ellison, a tanned, handsome, craggy-faced former actor, who had abandoned the stage and screen for television journalism, primarily because he hadn't worked in over two years.

"Louise Dutton isn't here with me tonight," Barton Ellison said, in his deep, trained actor's voice, looking directly into the camera. "She wanted to be. But she was an eyewitness to the gun battle in which Philadelphia Highway Patrol Captain Richard C. Moffitt gave his life this afternoon. She knows the face of the bandit that is, at this moment, still free. Louise Dutton is under police protection. Full details, and exclusive 'Nine's News' film, after these messages."

There followed twenty seconds of Louise being escorted to her car at the Waikiki Diner, and of the car, with a policeman at the wheel, following a police car out of the parking lot. Then there was a smiling baby on the screen, as a disposable-diaper commercial began.

"That *sonofabitch!*" Louise Dutton exploded. She looked at Wohl. "I had nothing to do with that."

"I don't understand," Wohl said.

"I never told him I was under police protection," Louise said.

"Oh," Wohl said. He could not understand why she was upset. He took a sip of his scotch. He couldn't tell what brand it was, only that it was expensive.

The diaper commercial was followed by one for a new motion picture to be shown later that night for the very first time on television, and then for one for a linoleum floor wax which apparently had an aphrodisiacal effect on generally disinterested husbands.

Then Louise reappeared. She looked into the camera.

"Moments before he was fatally wounded," she said, "Police Captain Richard C. Moffitt said, 'Put the gun down, son. I don't want to have to kill you. I'm a police officer.'

"Moffitt was meeting with this reporter over coffee in

the Waikiki Diner in the sixty-five-hundred block of Roosevelt Boulevard early this afternoon. He was concerned with the image his beloved Highway Patrol has in some people's eyes . . . 'Carlucci's Commandos' is just one derogatory term for them.

"He had just started to explain what they do, and why, and how, when he spotted a pale-faced blond young man police have yet to identify holding a gun on the diner's cashier.

"Captain Moffitt was off duty, and in civilian clothing, but he was a policeman, and a robbery was in progress, and it was his duty to do something about it.

"There was a good thirty-second period, maybe longer, during which Captain Moffitt could have shot the bandit where he stood. But he decided to give the bandit a break, a chance to save his life: 'Put the gun down, son. I don't want to have to kill you.'

"That humanitarian gesture cost Richard C. Moffitt his life. And Moffitt's three children their father, and Moffitt's wife her husband.

"The bandit had an accomplice, a woman. She opened fire on Moffitt. Her bullets struck all over the interior of the diner. Except for one, which entered Richard C. Moffitt's chest.

"He returned fire then, and killed his assailant.

"And then, a look of wonderment on his face, he slumped against a wall, and slid down to the floor, killed in the line of duty.

"Police are looking for the pale-faced blond young man, who escaped during the gun battle. I don't think it will take them long to arrest him, and the moment they do, 'Nine's News' will let you know they have."

A formal portrait of Dutch Moffitt in uniform came on the screen.

"Captain Richard C. Moffitt," Louise said, softly, "thirty-six years old. Killed . . . shot down, cold-bloodedly murdered . . . in the line of duty.

"My name is Louise Dutton. Barton?"

She took three steps forward and turned the television off before Barton Ellison could respond. Peter Wohl took advantage of the visual opportunity offered.

"That was just beautiful," Jerome Nelson said, softly. "I wanted to cry."

I'll be goddamned, Peter Wohl thought, *so did I.*

He looked at Louise, and saw her eyes were teary.

"That bullshit about me being under police protection cheapened the whole thing," she said. "That cheap son-ofabitch!"

She looked at Wohl as if looking for a response.

He said, "That was quite touching, Miss Dutton."

"It won't do Dutch a whole fucking lot of good, will it? Or his wife and kids?" Louise said.

"Do you always swear that much?" Wohl asked, astounding himself. He rarely said anything he hadn't carefully considered first.

She smiled. "Only when I'm pissed off," she said, and walked out of the room.

"God only knows how long that will take," Jerome Nelson said. "Won't you sit down, Inspector?" He waved Wohl delicately into one of four identical white leather upholstered armchairs surrounding a coffee table that was a huge chunk of marble.

It did not, despite what Jerome Nelson said, take Louise Dutton long to get dressed. When she came back in the room Wohl stood up. She waved him back into his chair.

"If you don't mind," she said, "I'll finish my drink."

"Not at all," Wohl said.

She sat down in one across from them, and then reached for a cigarette. Wohl stole another glance down her neckline.

"What's your first name?" Louise Dutton asked, when she had slumped back into the chair.

"Peter," he said, wondering why she had asked.

"Tell me, Peter, does your wife know of this uncontrollable urge of yours to look down women's necklines?"

He felt his face redden.

"It's probably very dangerous," Louise went on. "The last time I felt sexual vibrations from a cop, somebody shot him."

With a very great effort, which he felt sure failed, Staff Inspector Peter Wohl picked up his glass and took a sip with as much savoir faire as he could muster.

The telephone was ringing when Peter Wohl walked into his apartment. He lived in West Philadelphia, on Montgomery Avenue, in a one-bedroom apartment over a four-car garage. It had once been the chauffeur's apartment when the large (sixteen-room) brownstone house on an acre and a half had been a single-family dwelling. There were now six apartments, described as "luxury," in the house, whose new owner, a corporation, restricted its tenants to those who had neither children nor domestic pets weighing more than twenty-five pounds.

Peter nodded and smiled at some of his fellow tenants, but he wasn't friendly with any of them. He had rebuffed friendly overtures for a number of reasons, among them the problems he saw in associating socially with bright young couples who smoked *cannabis sativa,* and probably ingested by one means or another other prohibited substances.

To bust, or not to bust, that is the question! Whether 'tis nobler to apprehend (which probably would result in a stern warning, plus a slap on the wrist) or look the other way.

Or, better yet, not to know about it, by politely rejecting invitations to drop by for a couple of drinks, and maybe some laughs, and who knows what else. They believed, he thought, what he had told them: that he worked for the city. They probably believed that he was a middle-level functionary in the Department of Public Property, or something like that. He was reasonably sure that his neighbors did not associate him with the fuzz, the pigs, or whatever pejorative term was being applied to the cops by the chicly liberal this week.

And then there was the matter of his having two of the four garages, which meant that some of his fellow tenants had to park their cars on the street, or in the driveway, or find another garage someplace else. He had been approached by three of his fellow tenants at different times to give up one of his two garages, if not for fairness, then for money.

He had politely rejected those overtures, too, which had been visibly disappointing and annoying to those asking.

The apartment looked as if it had been decorated by an expensive interior decorator. The walls were white; there was a shaggy white carpet; the furniture was stylish, lots of glass and white leather and chrome. He had been going with an interior decorator at the time he'd taken the apartment, and willing to acknowledge that he knew next to nothing about decorating. Dorothea had decorated it for him, free of charge, and got the furniture and carpet for him at her professional discount.

Dorothea was long gone, they having mutually agreed that the mature and civilized thing to do in their particular circumstance was to turn him in on a lawyer, and so was much of what she had called the *"unity of ambience."*

A men's club downtown had gone under, and auctioned off the furnishings. Peter had bought a small mahogany service bar; two red overstuffed leather armchairs with matching footstools; and a six-by-ten-foot oil painting of a voluptuous nude reclining on a couch that had for fifty odd years decorated the men's bar of the defunct club. That had replaced a nearly as large modern work of art on the living room wall. The artwork replaced had had a title *(!! Number Three.)*, but Peter had taken to referring to it as "The Smear," even before Love in Bloom had started to wither.

Dorothea, very pregnant, had come to see him, bringing the lawyer with her. The purpose of the visit was to see if Peter could "do anything" for a client of the lawyer, who was also a dear friend, who had a son found in possession of just over a pound of Acapulco Gold brand of *cannabis sativa.* Dorothea had been even more upset about the bar, the chairs, and the painting than she had been at his announcement that he couldn't be of help.

"You've *raped* the ambience, Peter," Dorothea had said. "If you want my opinion."

When Peter went into the bedroom, the red light was blinking on his telephone answering device. He snapped it off and picked up the telephone.

"Hello?"

"We're just going out for supper," Chief Inspector (Retired) August Wohl announced, without any preliminary greeting, in his deep, rasping voice, "and afterward, we're going to see Jeannie and Gertrude Moffitt. Your mother thought you might want to eat with us."

"I was over there earlier, Dad," Peter said. "Right after it happened."

"You were?" Chief Inspector Wohl sounded surprised.

"I went in on the call, Dad," Peter said.

"How come?"

"I was on Roosevelt Boulevard. I was the first senior guy on the scene. I just missed Jeannie at Nazareth Hospital, but then I saw her at the house."

"But that was on the job," August Wohl argued. "Tonight's for close friends. The wake's tomorrow. You and Dutch were friends."

"It won't look right, if you don't go to the house tonight." Mrs. Olga Wohl came on the extension. "We've known the Moffitts all our lives. And, tomorrow, at the wake, there will be so many people there . . ."

"I'll try to get by later, Mother," Peter said. "I'm going out to dinner."

"With who, if you don't mind my asking?"

He didn't reply.

"You hear anything, Peter?" Chief Inspector Wohl asked.

"The woman who shot Dutch is a junkie. They have an ID on her, and on the guy, another junkie, who was involved. I think they'll pick him up in a couple of days; I wouldn't be surprised if they already have him. My phone answerer is blinking. A Homicide detective named Jason Washington's got the job—''

"I know him," August Wohl interrupted.

"I asked him to keep me advised. As soon as I hear something, I'll let you know."

"Why should he keep you advised?" August Wohl asked.

"Because the commissioner, for the good of the department, has assigned me to charm the lady from TV."

"I saw the TV," Wohl's father said. "The blonde really was an eyewitness?"

"Yes, she was. She just made the identification, of the dead girl, and the guy who ran. Positive. I was there when she made it. The guy's name is Gerald Vincent Gallagher."

"White guy?"

"Yeah. The woman, too. Her name is Schmeltzer. Her father has a grocery store over by Lincoln High."

"Jesus, I know him," August Wohl said.

"Dad, I better see who called," Peter said.

"He's going to be at Marshutz & Sons, for the wake, I mean. They're going to lay him out in the Green Room; I talked to Gertrude Moffitt," Peter's mother said.

"I'll be at the wake, of course, Mother," Peter said.

"Peter," Chief Inspector Wohl, retired, said thoughtfully, "maybe it would be a good idea for you to wear your uniform to the funeral."

"What?" Peter asked, surprised. Staff inspectors almost never wore uniforms.

"There will be talk, if you're not at the house tonight—"

"You bet, there will be," Peter's mother interjected.

"People like to gossip," Chief Inspector Wohl went on. "Instead of letting them gossip about maybe why you didn't come to the house, let them gossip about you being in uniform."

"That sounds pretty devious, Dad."

"Either the house tonight, with his other close friends,

or the uniform at the wake,'' Chief Inspector Wohl said. ''A gesture of respect, one way or the other.''

''I don't know, Dad,'' Peter said.

''Do what you like,'' his father said, abruptly, and the line went dead.

He's mad. He offered advice and I rejected it. And he's probably right, too. You don't get to be a chief inspector unless you are a master practitioner of the secret rites of the police department.

There was only one recorded message on the telephone answerer tape:

''Dennis Coughlin, Peter. You've done one hell of a job with that TV woman. That was very touching, what she said on the TV. The commissioner saw it, too. I guess you know—Matt Lowenstein told me he saw you—that the commissioner wants you to stay on top of this. None of us wants anything embarrassing to anyone to happen. Call me, at the house, if necessary, when you learn something.''

While the tape was rewinding, Peter glanced at his watch.

''Damn!'' he said.

He tore off his jacket and his shoulder holster and started to unbutton his shirt. There was no time for a shower. He was late already. He went into the bathroom and splashed Jamaica Bay lime cologne from a bottle onto his hands, and then onto his face. He sniffed his underarms, wet his hands again, and mopped them under his arms.

He stripped to his shorts and socks, and then dressed quickly. He pulled on a pale blue turtleneck knit shirt, and then a darker blue pair of Daks trousers. He slipped his feet into loafers, put his arms through the straps of the shoulder holster, and then into a maroon blazer. He reached on a closet shelf for a snap-brim straw hat and put that on. He examined himself in the full-length mirrors that covered the sliding doors to the bedroom closet.

''My, don't you look splendid, you handsome devil, you!'' he said.

And then he ran down the stairs and put a key to the

padlock on one of the garage doors, and pulled them open. He went inside. There came the sound of a starter grinding, and then an engine caught.

A British racing green 1950 Jaguar XK-120 roadster emerged slowly and carefully from the garage. It looked new, rather than twenty-three years old. It had been a mess when Peter bought it, soon after he had been promoted to lieutenant. He'd since put a lot of money and a lot of time into it. Even his mother appreciated what he had done; it was now his "cute little sporty car" rather than "that disgraceful old junky rattletrap."

He drove at considerably in excess of the speed limit down Lancaster Avenue to Belmont, and then to the Pennsylvania Psychiatric Institute. Barbara Crowley, R.N., a tall, lithe young woman of, he guessed, twenty-six, twenty-seven, who wore her blond hair in a pageboy, was waiting for him, and smiled when the open convertible pulled up to her.

But she was pissed, he knew, both that he was late, and that he was driving the Jaguar. She contained her annoyance because she was trying as hard as he was to find someone.

"We're being sporty tonight, I see," Barbara said as she got in the car.

"I'm sorry I'm late," he said. "I will prove that, if you give me a chance."

"It's all right," she said.

Impulsively, and although he knew he wasn't, in the turtleneck, dressed for it, he decided on the Ristorante Alfredo. He could count, he thought, on having some snotty Wop waiter, six months out of a Neapolitan slum, look haughtily down his nose at him.

It started going bad before he got that far.

An acne-faced punk in the parking garage gave him trouble about parking the Jaguar himself. It had taken him, literally, a year to find an unblemished, rust-free right front fender for the XK-120, and no sooner had he got it on, and had, finally, the whole car lacquered (20 coats) prop-

erly than a parking valet who looked like this one's idiot
uncle scraped it along a concrete block wall.

He had since parked his car himself.

The scene annoyed Barbara further, although he re-
solved it with money, to get it over with.

SEVEN

When she saw that Peter Wohl was leading her to Ristorante Alfredo, Barbara Crowley protested.

"Peter, it's so expensive!"

She sounds like my mother, Peter thought.

"Well, I'll just stiff my ex-wife on her alimony," he said, as he opened the door to Ristorante Alfredo. "Tell her to have the kids get a job, too."

Barbara, visibly, did not think that was funny. There was no ex-wife and no kids, but it was not the sort of thing Barbara thought you should joke about, particularly when there was someone who could hear and might not understand. She hadn't thought it was funny the last time he'd made his little joke, and, to judge by her face, it had not improved with age.

The headwaiter was a tall, silver-haired man, who had heard.

"Have you a reservation, sir?" he asked.

"No, but it doesn't look like you have many, either,"

Peter said, waving in the general direction of the half-empty dining room.

The headwaiter looked toward the bar, where a stout man in his early thirties sat at the bar. He was wearing an expensive suit, and his black hair was expensively cut and arranged, almost successfully, to conceal a rapidly receding hairline.

His name was Ricco Baltazari, and the restaurant and bar licenses had been issued in his name. It was actually owned by a man named Vincenzo Savarese, who, for tax purposes, and because it's hard for a convicted felon to get a liquor license, had Baltazari stand in for him.

Ricco Baltazari had taken in the whole confrontation. There was nothing he would have liked better than to have the fucking cop thrown the fuck out—what a hell of a nerve, coming to a class joint like this with no tie—but instead, with barely visible moves of his massive head, he signaled that Wohl was to be given a table. It's always better to back away from a confrontation with a fucking cop, and this fucking cop was an inspector, and Mr. Savarese was in the back, having dinner with his wife and her sister, and it was better not to risk doing anything that would cause a disturbance.

Besides, he had seen in *Gentlemen's Quarterly* where turtlenecks were making a comeback. It wasn't like the fucking cop was wearing a fucking *shirt* and no necktie. A turtleneck was *different*.

"Spaghetti and meatballs?" Peter Wohl asked, when they had been shown to a table covered with crisp linen and an impressive array of crystal and silverware, and handed large menus. "Or maybe some lasagna? Or would you like me to slip the waiter a couple of bucks and have him sing 'Santa Lucia' while you make up your mind?"

Barbara didn't think that was witty, either.

"I don't know why you come to these places, if you really don't like them."

"The mob serves the best food in Philadelphia," Peter said. "I thought everybody knew that."

Barbara decided to let it drop.

"Well, everything on here looks good," she said, with a determined smile.

Wohl looked at her, rather than at the menu. He knew what he was going to eat: First some cherrystone clams, and then veal Marsala.

She is a good-looking girl. She's intelligent. She's got a good job. She even tolerates me, which means she probably understands me. On a scale of one to ten, she's an eight in bed. What I should do is marry her, and buy a house somewhere and start raising babies. But I don't want to.

She asked him what he was going to have, and he told her, and she said that sounded fine, she would have the same thing.

"Let's have a bottle of wine," Peter said, and opened the wine list and selected an Italian wine whose name he remembered. He pointed out the label to Barbara and asked if that was all right with her. It was fine with her.

Maybe what she needs to turn me on is a little streak of bitchiness, a little streak of not-so-tolerant-and-understanding.

He was nearly through the bottle of wine, and halfway through the veal Marsala, when he looked up and saw Vincenzo Savarese approaching the table.

Vincenzo Savarese was sixty-three years old. What was left of his hair was silver and combed straight back over his ears. His face bore marks of childhood acne. He was wearing a double-breasted brown pin-striped suit, and there was a diamond stickpin in his necktie. He was trailed by two almost identical women in black dresses, his wife and her sister.

Vincenzo Savarese's photo was mounted, very near the top, on the wall chart of known organized crime members the Philadelphia Police Department maintained in the Organized Crime unit.

"I don't mean to disturb your dinner, Inspector," Vincenzo Savarese said. "Keep your seat."

Wohl stood up, but said nothing.

"I just wanted to tell you we heard about what happened to Captain Moffitt, and we're sorry,'' Vincenzo Savarese said.

"My heart goes out to his mother," one of the women said.

Wohl wasn't absolutely sure whether it was Savarese's wife, or his sister-in-law. Looking at the woman, he said, "Thank you."

"I was on a retreat with Mrs. Moffitt, the mother," the woman went on. "At Blessed Sacrament."

Wohl nodded.

Savarese nodded, and took the woman's arm and led them out of the dining room.

"Who was that?" Barbara Crowley asked.

"His name is Vincenzo Savarese," Wohl said, evenly. "He owns this place."

"I thought you said the mob owns it."

"It does," Wohl said.

"Then why? Why did he do that?"

"He probably meant it, in his own perverse way," Wohl said. "He probably thought Dutch was a fellow man of honor. The mob is big on honor."

"I saw that on TV," Barbara said.

He looked at her.

"About Captain Moffitt. I wasn't going to bring it up unless you did," Barbara said. "But I suppose that's what's wrong, isn't it?"

"I didn't know anything was wrong," Wohl said.

"Have it your way, Peter," Barbara said.

"No, you tell me, what's wrong?"

"You're wearing a turtleneck sweater, and you're driving the Jaguar," she said. "You always do that when something went wrong at work; it's as if—as if it's a *symbol*, that you don't want to be a cop. At least then. And then you got into it with the kid who wanted to park your car, and then the headwaiter here . . ."

"That's very interesting," he said.

"Now, I'm sorry I said it," Barbara said.

"No, I mean it. I didn't know I was that transparent."

"I know you pretty well, Peter," she said.

"You want to know what's really bothering me?" Wohl asked.

"Only if you want to tell me," she said.

"My parents called, just before I went to pick you up," he said. "They told me I should go by Jeannie Moffitt's house tonight. Tonight's for close friends. Tomorrow, they'll have the wake. And they're right, of course. I should, but I didn't want to go, and I didn't."

"You were a friend of Dutch Moffitt's," Barbara said. "Why don't you want to go?"

"Did I tell you that I went in on the assist?"

"You were there?" she asked. She seemed more sympathetic than surprised.

He nodded. "I was a couple of blocks away. When I got there, Dutch was still slumped against the wall of the Waikiki Diner."

"You didn't tell me anything," Barbara said. It was, he decided, a statement of fact, rather than a reproof.

"There's an eyewitness, that woman from Channel Nine, Louise Dutton," Wohl said.

"I saw her," Barbara said. "When she was on TV talking about it."

"I think she had something going with Dutch," Wohl said. "I'll bet on it, as a matter of fact."

"Oh, my!" Barbara said. "And is it going to come out? Will his wife find out?"

"No, I don't think so," Wohl said. "The commissioner has assigned that splendid police officer, Staff Inspector Peter Wohl, to see that 'nothing awkward develops.' "

"You mean, the commissioner knows about Captain Moffitt and that woman?"

"Staff Inspector Peter Wohl, with the good of the department ever foremost in his mind, told him," Wohl said.

Barbara Crowley laid her hand on his.

"I probably shouldn't tell you this," she said. "But one of the main reasons I like you is that you are really a moral man, Peter. You really think about right and wrong."

"And all this time, I thought it was my Jaguar," he said.

"I hate your Jaguar," she said.

"The reason, more or less subconsciously, that I wore the turtleneck and drove the Jaguar, was that I can't go play the role of the bereaved close friend of the family wearing a turtleneck and driving the Jaguar."

"I thought that maybe it was because you didn't want to take me with you," Barbara said.

"You didn't want to go over there," Peter said.

"No, but you didn't know that," Barbara said. When he looked at her in surprise, she went on: "You could go home and change. I'll go over there with you, if you would like. If you think I would be welcome."

"Don't be silly, of course you'd be welcome," he said.

"People might get the idea, that if I went there with you, I was your girl friend."

"I don't think that's much of a secret, is it?" Peter said. "But I'm not really up to going there. I suppose this makes me a moral coward, but I don't want to look at Jeannie's face, or the kids'," he said. "But thank you, Barbara."

"What it makes you is honest," Barbara said, and laid her hand on his. Then she added, "We could go to my place."

Barbara lived in a three-room apartment on the top floor of one of the red-brick buildings at the hospital. It was roomy and comfortable.

She really thought the reason I wasn't going over to the house was because taking her there would be one more reluctant step on our slow, but inexorable march to the altar. I squirmed out of that, and now she is offering me comfort, in the way women have comforted men since they came home with dinosaur bites.

"What I think I will do is take you home, apologize for my lousy attitude—"

"Don't be silly, Peter," Barbara interrupted.

"And then go home and get my uniform out of the bag so that I will remember to get it pressed in the morning."

"Your uniform?"

"Dutch was killed in the line of duty," Peter said. "There will be, the day after tomorrow, a splendiferous ceremony at Saint Dominic's. I will be there, in uniform, which, my mother and dad hope, will be accepted as a gesture of my respect overwhelming my bad manners for not joining the other close friends at the house tonight.''

He saw a question forming in her eyes, but she didn't, after a just perceptible hesitation, ask it. Instead, she said, ''I don't think I've ever seen you in your uniform.''

''Very spiffy,'' he said. ''When I wear my uniform, I have to fight to preserve my virtue. It drives the girls wild.''

''I'll bet you look very nice in a uniform,'' Barbara said.

He looked for and found the waiter and waved him over and called for the check.

There would be no check, the waiter said. It was Mr. Savarese's pleasure.

Barbara insisted in going home in a cab. She wasn't mad, she assured him, but she was tired and he was tired, and they both had had bad days and a lot to do tomorrow, and a cab was easier, and made sense.

She kissed him quickly, and got in a cab and was gone. He went to the parking garage and reclaimed the Jaguar.

As soon as he got behind the wheel, Peter Wohl began to regret not having gone to her apartment with Barbara. For one thing, he had learned that turning down an offer of sexual favors was not a good way to maintain a good relationship with a female. *They* could have headaches, or for other reasons be temporarily out of action, but the privilege was not reciprocal. He had probably hurt her feelings, or angered her (even if she didn't let it show), or both, by leaving her. He was sorry to have done that, for Barbara was a good woman.

Less nobly, he realized that a piece of ass would probably be just what the doctor would order for what ailed him. Seeing Dutch slumped dead against the wall had affected him more than he liked to admit. And looking down Louise Dutton's dressing gown, even if she had caught him at it, and made an ass of him, had aroused him. Whatever else could or would be said about the TV lady, she really had a set of perfect teats.

He had been driving without thinking about where he was going. When he oriented himself, he saw he was on Market Street, west of the Schuylkill River, just past Thirtieth Street Station. That wasn't far from Barbara's place.

What the hell am I doing? I really don't want to see her any more tonight.

He was also, he realized, just a couple of blocks away from the Adelphia Hotel.

There was a bar off the lobby of the Adelphia Hotel, in which, from time to time, he had found females sitting who were amenable to a dalliance; often guests of the hotel who, he supposed, were more prone to fool around while in Philadelphia than they would back in Pittsburgh; and sometimes what he thought of as *Strawbridge & Clothier* women, the upper crust of Philadelphia and the Main Line, who, if the moon was right, could as easily be talked out of their fashionable clothing.

And even if there were no females, the bar was dark, and he was not known to the bartenders as a cop, and there was a guy who played the piano.

He would see what developed naturally. The worst possible scenario would be no available women. In which case, he would have a couple drinks and listen to the guy play the piano and then do what he probably should have done anyway, go home. He really did have to remember to get his uniform out of the zipper bag in the closet and get it pressed tomorrow.

His eyes had barely adjusted to the darkness of the bar when a male voice spoke in his ear.

"Can I buy you a drink?"

He turned to see who had made the offer. The face was familiar, but he couldn't immediately put a name, or an identification, to it.

"It is you, Inspector? I mean . . . you *are* Inspector Wohl, aren't you?"

It came together. Dutch's nephew. He had met the kid that afternoon, outside Dutch's house.

"Let me buy you one," Wohl said, smiling and offering his hand. "Matt Moffitt, right?"

"Matt Payne," the boy said. "I was adopted."

"Yeah, I heard something about that," Wohl said. "Sorry."

"No problem," Matt said.

The bartender appeared.

"I don't know what he wants," Wohl said, "but Johnnie Red and soda for me."

"The same," Matt said.

"You old enough?" the bartender challenged. "You got a driver's license?"

Matt handed it over. The bartender eyed it dubiously, then asked Matt for his birth date. Finally he shrugged, and went to make the drinks.

"They lose their licenses," Wohl said. "You can't blame them."

When the drinks came, Matt laid a twenty on the bar.

"Hey, I'll get these," Wohl said.

"My pleasure," Matt Payne said. He picked up his glass, raised it, and said, "Dutch."

"Dutch," Wohl repeated, and raised his glass.

"I just came from the Moffitts'," Matt said. "After that, I needed this."

"I was supposed to be there. But I got tied up," Wohl said. "I couldn't get away. I'll go by Marshutz & Sons, to the wake, tomorrow."

"It was pretty awful," Matt said.

"Why do you say that?" Wohl asked.

"The kids, for one thing, my cousins," Matt said. "Losing their father is really tough on them. And my grandmother was a flaming pain in the ass, for another. She was a real bitch toward my mother."

"What?" Wohl asked. "Why?"

"My grandmother thinks what my mother should have done when my father got killed was turn into a professional widow, like she is. Instead, she married my stepfather."

"What's wrong with that?"

"Out of the church," Matt said. "Mother married one of those heathen Protestant Episcopals. And then Mother converted herself, and took me with her. And then let my stepfather adopt me."

"German Catholic mothers of that generation have very positive ideas," Wohl said. "I know, I've got one of them. She and Gertrude Moffitt are old pals."

"You weren't at the house," Matt said, and Wohl wasn't sure if it was a question or a challenge.

"I also have a German Lutheran father," Wohl said, "who went along with her until he suspected, correctly, that a priest at Saint Joseph's Prep was trying to recruit me for the Jesuits. Then he pulled me out of Good Ol' Saint Joe's and moved me into Northeast High. She still has high hopes that I will meet some good Catholic girl, who will lead me back into the fold."

I wonder why I told him that?

"Then you do know," Matt said.

"The reason I didn't go to see Jeannie Moffitt tonight was because I didn't want to," Wohl said. "And I figured if Dutch is really looking down from his cloud, he would understand."

Matt chuckled. "You were pretty close?"

"I knew him pretty well, all our lives, but we weren't close. Dutch was Highway Patrol, and that's a way of life. They don't think anybody else really is a cop. Maybe Organized Crime, or Intelligence, but certainly not a staff inspector. I guess, really, that Dutch tolerated me. I'd been in the Highway Patrol, even if I later went wrong."

"You were there, where he was shot, I mean. I heard that."

"I was nearby when I heard the call. I responded."

"I don't understand what really happened," Matt said. "He didn't *know* he was shot?"

"The adrenaline was flowing," Wohl said. "The minute he went to work, his system was all charged up. I'm sure he knew he was hit, but I don't think he had any idea how bad."

"You ever been shot?" Matt asked.

"Yes," Wohl said, and changed the subject. "How come you're in here? As opposed to some saloon around the campus, for example?"

"I heard they're going to close it and tear it down," Matt said, "so I thought I'd come in for a drink for auld lang syne."

"They're going to tear it down? I hadn't heard that."

"They are, but that wasn't a straight answer," Matt said.

"Oh?"

"When I left the Moffitt house," Matt said, "I had two choices. My fraternity house, or a saloon near the fraternity house. There would be two kinds of people in both, those who felt sorry for me—"

"That's understandable," Wohl said.

"Not because of my uncle Dutch," Matt said. "They didn't know about that. Because I failed my precommissioning physical examination, and am now officially exempt from military service. I didn't want sympathy on one hand, and if one more of those sonsofbitches had told me how lucky I was, I think I would have punched him out."

"Why'd you flunk the physical? Did they tell you?"

"Something with my eyes. Probably, they said, I'll never have a moment's trouble with them, but on the other hand, the United States Marine Corps can't take the chance that something will."

"I guess I'm with those who think you were probably lucky," Wohl said. "I did a hitch in the army when I finished high school. *I* wasn't going to be a cop like my old man. So I joined the army and they made me an MP. You didn't miss anything."

"I wanted to go," Matt said. "My father was a marine. My real father."

"He was also a cop," Wohl said.

"I've been thinking about that, too," Matt said. "I've seen the ads in the papers."

"The reason those ads are in the paper is because they don't pay a starting-off police officer a living wage," Wohl said. "A guy just out of high school can go to work for

Budd, someplace like that, and make a lot more money. So they have to actively recruit to find a guy who meets the standards, and who really wants to be a cop, even if it means waiting for the city council to come across with long-overdue pay raises.''

''I don't need money,'' Matt said.

''Everybody needs money,'' Wohl said, surprised at the remark; it sounded stupid.

''I mean, I have more than enough,'' Matt said. ''When my father . . . I think of him as my father. My *real* father was killed before I was born. When my *stepfather* adopted me, he started investing the money my real father had left, the insurance money, the rest of it, for me. My father is a very clever guy. He turned it into a lot of money, and when I turned twenty-one, he handed it over to me.''

''What would he say if you joined the police department? What would your mother say?''

''Oh, they wouldn't like it at all,'' Matt said. ''My father wants me to go to law school. But I don't think they would say anything. I think he would sort of understand.''

The booze is talking, Peter Wohl decided. *The kid lost his uncle. His father got killed on the job. He just came from Dutch's house, where Denny Coughlin and my father, and maybe the commissioner and maybe even the mayor, plus a dozen other cops were standing around, half in the bag, recounting the heroic exploits of Dutch Moffitt. And this kid's father. In the morning, if he remembers this conversation, this kid will be embarrassed.*

I am not fall-down drunk, Peter Wohl thought, as he put the key in his apartment door. *If I were fall-down drunk, I would have tried to put the Jaguar in the garage. I am still sober enough to realize that I am too drunk to try to thread that narrow needle with the nose of the Jaguar.*

He had stayed at the bar in the Hotel Adelphia nightclub far longer than he had intended to stay, and he had far more to drink than he usually did. He had all of a sudden realized that he was drunk, shaken Matt Payne's hand, collected his change, reclaimed the Jaguar, and driven home.

A shrink would say that he had gotten drunk as a delayed reaction to seeing Dutch Moffitt slumped dead against the wall of the Waikiki Diner. So, for that matter, would his boss, Chief Inspector Dennis V. Coughlin. And so, he realized, would his father. His father had known he would not be at the wake, and why.

There was no way either Denny Coughlin or his father would hear about it. There had been no other cops in the Hotel Adelphia, and he had managed to get home without running over a covey of nuns or into a fire hydrant.

God, Peter Wohl thought, *takes care of fools and drunks, and I certainly qualify on both counts.*

The red light on his telephone answering machine was glowing a steady red. If there had been calls, it would have been blinking on and off.

He went into the kitchen, opened the refrigerator, and drank most of a twelve-ounce bottle of soda water from the neck, which produced a booming belch.

Then he went to his bedroom, and remembered (which pleased him) about getting his uniform out of the zipper bag so that he could have it pressed in the morning. He had just laid the bag on an upholstered chair and started to work the zipper when the phone rang.

He looked at his watch. It was almost two in the morning. Neither his mother nor Barbara would be calling at this hour; it was therefore safe to answer the phone.

He picked up the phone beside the bed.

"Wohl," he said.

"I hope I didn't wake you, Inspector." Wohl recognized the voice of Lieutenant Louis Natali of Homicide.

"I just walked in, Lou," Wohl said.

"Well, if you heard it over the radio, I'm sorry, but I thought you would want to know."

"I didn't have a radio," Wohl said. "What didn't I hear?"

He's calling to tell me they caught the little shit who killed Dutch; that was nice of him.

"I'll try to give it to you quick," Natali said. "Hobbs and I were down in the Third District . . . checking out a report that Gerald Vincent Gallagher had been seen. About one o'clock, we heard a radio call of a stabbing and hospital case at Six-C Stockton Place. A little while later, I called Homicide and found we had a job there. Lieutenant DelRaye is on the scene. The deceased is a guy named Jerome Nelson."

"Christ, I met him this afternoon," Wohl said. "Nice little . . ." He stopped himself and ended, "Guy."

"The female who called it in is your friend Louise Dutton."

"I'll be damned," Wohl said. "She lives upstairs."

"I was told she was hysterical and locked herself in her apartment. DelRaye just called for a wagon to transport her to Homicide. I think he's talking about taking her door if she doesn't come out."

"Jesus!"

"You didn't get this from me, Peter," Natali said.

"I owe you," Wohl said, broke the connection with his finger, and dialed from memory the number of the Homicide Division. A detective answered.

"This is Inspector Wohl," he said. "Lieutenant Del-Raye is at a homicide scene on Stockton Place. Please get word to him that I am en route, and he is not to, not to, take the door until I get there."

At 2:03 A.M., One-Ninety-Four, a patrol car assigned to the Nineteenth District, went on the air and reported that he was in pursuit of an English sports car proceeding eastward on Lancaster Avenue just past Girard Avenue at a high rate of speed.

At 2:05 A.M. One-Ninety-Four went back on the air:

"One-Ninety-Four. Disregard the pursuit. It was a Three-Six-Nine."

Three-Six-Nine is the radio code used to identify a police officer.

The officer in One-Ninety-Four was naturally curious why a man carrying the tin of a staff inspector was going hell for leather down Lancaster Avenue in an English sports car at two in the morning, but he had been on the job long enough to understand that patrol officers were wise not to ask staff inspectors what the hell they thought they were doing.

Stockton Place was crowded with police vehicles when Peter Wohl, holding his badge in one hand, weaved the Jaguar through them to the door of Number Six.

There were two cars from the Sixth District, what looked to Wohl to be three unmarked detective cars, the crime lab van, and a Sixth District wagon.

And the press was there, on foot behind the crime scene barriers, and on the roofs of two vans bearing television station logotypes.

Wohl had put his identification away when he'd passed the last uniform barring his way to Number Six Stockton Place, but he had to take it out again to get past another uniform keeping people out of the building itself.

"Where's Lieutenant DelRaye?" he asked.

"Ground-floor apartment," the uniform told him.

Jerome Nelson was lying on his stomach on an outsize bed in his mirrored bedroom. He was, save for a sleeveless undershirt, naked. There were more wounds than Wohl could conveniently count on his back, his buttocks and legs, and the bed was soaked with darkening blood. There was the sweet smell of blood in the air, competing with the smell of perfume.

Lieutenant Edward M. DelRaye, a large, balding man who showed vestiges of having been a very handsome man in his twenties and thirties, was standing with his arms folded on his chest, watching a photographer from the crime lab taking pictures of the body with a 35-mm camera.

"DelRaye," Wohl said, and DelRaye turned around and looked at him. He didn't say anything.

"Radio relay my message to you?" Wohl asked.

DelRaye nodded. "What's going on, Inspector?" he asked.

Edward M. DelRaye had been a detective when Peter Wohl had entered the academy. He had not liked Peter

Wohl from the time they had met, when Wohl had been a
plainclothes patrolman in Civil Disobedience. He had still
been a detective when Wohl made corporal, equivalent in
rank to a detective, and they'd had a couple of run-ins,
jurisdictional disputes, when Wohl had been a Highway
Patrol corporal and then sergeant. When Wohl had been
assigned to Internal Affairs, DelRaye had run off at the
mouth more than once about how nice it must be to have
a Chief Inspector for a father, who could arrange your
career for you, see that you got good jobs.

DelRaye had made sergeant about the time Peter Wohl
had made captain, and had only recently been promoted
to lieutenant, long after Wohl had become a staff inspector. He was a good detective, from what Wohl had heard,
and which seemed to be proved by his long-time assignment to Homicide, but he was also a loud-mouthed, crude
sonofabitch whom Wohl disliked, and whom he avoided
whenever possible.

"You want to tell me what you have, Lieutenant?" Wohl
said.

"Somebody carved up the fag," DelRaye said, jerking
his thumb toward the bed.

"I'm interested in the witness," Wohl said.

"Are you really, now?"

"Take it from the top, DelRaye," Wohl said, evenly,
but coldly.

"Well, in case you didn't know, her name is Louise
Dutton. The same one that was with Dutch Moffitt this
afternoon when he got blown away. She come home from
work about half past twelve, quarter to one, and found the
door, his door, open. So she went in, and found the faggot
in here, and called it in. I was up, so when the radio
notified us, I rolled on it. I heard what she had to say, and
told her I was going to take her to the Roundhouse for her
statement, and to let her look at some mug shots, and she
told me to go fuck myself, she wasn't going anywhere."

"You were, I'm sure, your usual tactful, charming self,
DelRaye," Wohl said.

"I don't like drunken women, and I especially don't like dirty-mouthed ones," DelRaye said.

"Then what happened?" Wohl asked.

"I turned around, and she was gone, and the Sixth District cop in the foyer, or the lobby, outside the apartment, said she went up in the elevator. So I went upstairs, and knocked on her door, and told her who I was, and she told me to go fuck myself again. Then I called for a wagon. I was going to have her door forced. She's acting like she could be the doer, Wohl."

That's bullshit, DelRaye. You know as well as I do she didn't do it. But there is now a Staff Inspector on the scene, who knows that while you can batter down the door of a suspect, you can't go around busting open witnesses' doors without a better reason than she told you to go fuck yourself.

"You really think she could be the doer, Lieutenant?" Wohl asked, dryly sarcastic, and then, without waiting for an answer, asked, "She's still upstairs? You didn't enter her apartment?"

"I got your message, Inspector," DelRaye said. "She can't go anywhere. I got two cops trying to talk sense to her through the door."

"I know her," Wohl said. "I'll try to talk to her."

"I know," DelRaye said. "When she's not screaming at me to go fuck myself, she's screaming that she demands to see Inspector Wohl."

"Really?" Wohl asked, surprised.

"Her exact words were, *'Get that sonofabitch down here!'*" DelRaye said. "Don't you think you ought to tell me what's going on with you and her?"

"I was in on the assist when Dutch Moffitt was shot," Wohl said. "When the commissioner heard that the eye-witness was Miss Dutton, and who she was, he decided it was in the best interest of the department to treat her with kid gloves, and since I was there, told me to take care of it."

"Something going on between her and Dutch? Is that what you're saying?"

"I'm saying that when a woman goes on television twice a day, it doesn't hurt to have her think kindly of the police department," Wohl said.

"Yeah, sure."

"And that's what I'm going to do now," Wohl said. "I'm going to go charm the hell out of her, if I can, and apologize for you, if it seemed to her you weren't as understanding as you could have been."

"Fuck understanding," DelRaye said. "My job is to catch the guys who done in the faggot."

"And my job is to do what the commissioner tells me to do," Wohl said. "I'm going to go talk to her. You make sure there's a car outside when, if, I bring her down the stairs. Get those TV people, and the other reporters, away from the door."

"How'm I going to do that, Inspector?" DelRaye asked sarcastically. "It's a public street."

"No, it's not Lieutenant," Wohl said. "It's a *private* street. Technically, anybody on Stockton Place who hasn't been invited is trespassing. Now get them away from the door, if you have to do it yourself."

"Yes, sir, Inspector," DelRaye said, his tone of voice leaving no question what he thought about the order, about Staff Inspector Peter Wohl, or Peter Wohl *being* a Staff Inspector.

EIGHT

Wohl walked out of Jerome Nelson's apartment and rode the elevator to the upper floor. There were two uniformed policemen there, a portly, red-faced man in his late thirties, and a pleasant-faced young man. He had his head against Louise Dutton's door and was trying, without success, to get her to talk back to him.

"What can I do for you?" the young one challenged when the elevator door opened.

"That's Inspector Wohl," the older one said.

"Hello," Peter said, and smiled. "I know Miss Dutton. I think I can get her to come out of there. Lieutenant DelRaye is going to move the press away, and have a car waiting downstairs. I'd like you guys to see that Miss Dutton gets in it without being hassled."

"Yes, sir," the young cop said.

"She's got a mouth, that one," the older one offered. "Even considering she's had too much to drink, and is upset by what she saw downstairs, you wouldn't think a woman would use language like that.''

''Haven't you heard? That's what women's lib is all about,'' Peter said. ''The right to cuss like a man.''

The younger cop shook his head and smiled at him.

He waited until they had gone down in the elevator, and then knocked on the door.

''Go the fuck away!'' Louise called angrily.

''Miss Dutton, it's Peter Wohl,'' he called.

There was no response for a long moment, and Peter was just about to raise his cigarette lighter to knock on the door when it opened to the width its burglar chain would permit; wide enough for Louise Dutton to look out and see Peter, and that he was alone.

Then it closed and he heard the chain rattle, and then the door opened completely.

''I wasn't sure you would come,'' she said, and pulled him into the apartment and closed the door again.

She was wearing a blue skirt and a high-ruffle-collared blouse. The body of the blouse was so thin as to be virtually transparent. Through it he could see quite clearly that she wore no slip, only a brassiere, and that the brassiere was no more substantial than the blouse; he could see her nipples.

Her eyes looked more frightened than drunk, he thought, and there was something about her it took him a moment to think he recognized, an aura of sexuality.

She looks horny, Peter Wohl thought.

''Here I am,'' Peter said.

She put a smile on her face; grew, he thought, determinedly bright.

''And what did Mrs. Wohl say when you were summoned from your bed at two in the morning, when the crazy lady from TV called for you?'' Louise Dutton asked.

I know what it is. She hasn't really been going around in a transparent shirt, baring her breasts. That skirt is part of a suit; there's a jacket, and when she wears that, only the ruffles show at the neck. That's what she wore when she was on TV.

"Nobody summoned me," Peter Wohl said. "I heard about it, and came. And the only Mrs. Wohl is my mother."

"They didn't send for you?" Louise asked, surprised. "Then why did you come?"

"I don't know," he said. "Why did you ask for me?"

"I'm scared, and a little drunk," she said.

"So'm I," he said. "A little drunk, I mean. There's nothing to be afraid of."

"*Bullshit!* Have you been downstairs? Did you see what those . . . *maniacs* . . . did to that poor, pathetic little man?"

"There's nothing for you to be afraid of," Peter said.

"The cops are here, right? My knight in shining armor has just ridden up in his prowl car?"

"Actually, I came in my Jaguar," Peter said. "My department car was in the garage and I wasn't sure I was sober enough to back it out."

"A *Jaguar?*" she asked, starting to giggle. "To go with that ridiculous turtleneck? I'll bet you even have got one of those silly little caps with the buttons in the front."

"I had one, but it blew off on the Schuylkill Expressway," he said.

She snorted, and then suddenly stopped. She looked at him, and bit her lower lip, and then she walked to him.

"*Goddamn,* I'm glad you're here," she said, and put her hand to his cheek. "Thank you."

And then, without either of them knowing exactly how it happened, he had his arms around her, and she was sobbing against his chest. He heard himself soothing her, and became aware that he was stroking her head, and that her arms were around him, holding him.

He could not remember, later, how long they had stayed like that. What he was to remember was that as he became aware of the warmth of her body against him, the pressure of her breasts against his abdomen, he had felt himself stirring. And when what had happened to him became evident to her, she pushed herself away from him.

"Well," she said, looking into his eyes, "this has been a bitch of a day, Peter Wohl, hasn't it? For both of us."

"I've had better," he said.

"What happens now?" Louise asked.

"There's a car waiting downstairs," Peter said. "It'll take you down to the Roundhouse, where you can make your statement, and then they'll type it up, and you can sign it, and then they'll bring you back here."

She looked at him, on the verge, he decided, of saying something, but not speaking.

"I'll go with you, if you'd like me to."

"I told that faded matinee idol everything I know," she said.

He chuckled, and she smiled back at him.

"I did the 'Nine's News' at eleven," Louise said. "And then I went with the producer for a drink. Okay, drinks. Three or four. Then I came home. I went into the lobby to check the mailbox. Jerome's door was open. I went in. I . . . saw what was in the bedroom. So I called the cops. That's all I know, Peter. And I told him."

"There's a procedure that has to be followed," Peter said. "The police department is a bureaucracy, Miss Dutton."

" 'Miss Dutton'?" she quoted mockingly. "A moment ago, I thought we were at least on a first-name basis."

"Louise," Peter said, aware that his face was flushing.

"I'll be damned," she said. "A blushing cop!"

"Jesus Christ!" Peter said. "Do you always think out loud?"

"No," she said. "For some mysterious reason, I seem to be a little upset right now. But thinking out loud, I don't seem to be the only one around here who's a little off balance. Do you always calm down hysterical witnesses that way, Inspector?"

"Jesus H. Christ!" Wohl said, shaking his head.

"Don't misunderstand me," she said. "That wasn't a complaint. I just wondered if it was standard bureaucratic procedure."

"You know better than that," Peter said.

"Get me out of here, Peter," Louise said, softly, entreatingly.

"Where do you want to go?"

"I'm not that far yet," she said. "All I know is that I don't want to run the gauntlet of my professional associates outside, and that I can't, *won't,* spend the night here. I'm *afraid,* Peter."

"I told you, there's nothing to be afraid of," he said. "And I sent two officers downstairs to make sure you weren't hassled when you get in the car."

"There's an Arch Street entrance to the garage," she said. "I don't think the press knows about it."

"But you'd have to get past them to get to the garage," he said.

"There a passage in the basement," she said. "A tunnel. And even if they were on Arch Street, I could get down on the seat, or on the floor in the back, and they wouldn't see me."

"Take your car, you mean?" he asked.

"Please, Peter," she said.

Why not? She's calmed down. You can't blame her for wanting to avoid those press and TV bastards. I'll take her someplace and buy her a cup of coffee and then I'll go with her to the Roundhouse.

"Okay," he said. "Get your jacket."

"My jacket?" she asked, surprised, and then looked down at herself. "Oh, Christ!" She crossed her arms over her breasts and looked at him. "I wasn't expecting visitors."

"I'll be damned," he said. "A blushing TV lady."

"Fuck you, Peter," she flared.

"Promises, promises," he heard himself blurt.

"You *bastard!*" she said, but she chuckled. She went farther into the apartment, and returned in a moment, shrugging into the jacket of her suit.

He waited until she had buttoned it, and then opened the door to the foyer. There was no one there. He pushed the elevator button, and he heard the faint whine of the electric motor. She stood very close to him, and her shoulder touched his. He put his arm around her shoulders.

"You're going to be all right, Louise," he said.

There was a uniform cop sitting on a wooden folding chair outside the elevator door in the basement. He got up quickly when he saw Wohl and Louise.

"I'm Inspector Wohl," Peter said. "I'm taking Miss Dutton out this way. Are you alone down here?"

"No, sir, a couple of guys are in the garage."

"Thank you," Peter said. He put his hand on Louise's arm and led her down the corridor. Halfway down the tunnel, she put a set of keys in his hand.

Two uniform cops walked quickly across the underground garage when they saw them. The eyes of one of them widened—a cop Wohl recognized, a bright guy named Aquila—when he recognized them.

"Hello, Inspector," Officer Aquila said.

"I'm going to take Miss Dutton out this way," Wohl said. "The press is all over the street."

"There's a couple of them outside, too," Aquila said. "But only a couple. You can probably get past them before they know what's happening. You want to use my car?"

"We'll take Miss Dutton's car," Wohl said. "When we're gone, would you tell Lieutenant DelRaye we've gone, and that I'm taking Miss Dutton to the Round-house?"

"Yes, sir," Office Aquila said. It was obvious that he approved of Wohl's tactics. He had certainly heard that DelRaye had sent for a wagon to haul a drunken and belligerent Louise Dutton off. This would be one more proof that Staff Inspector Peter Wohl knew how to turn an unpleasant situation into a manageable one.

They got in Louise's Cadillac.

"There's a thing in the floor that you run over, and the door opens," Louise said, and then, "What are you looking for?"

"How do you get the parking brake off?"

"It comes off automatically when you put it in gear," she said.

"Oh," he said.

As they approached the exit, she laid down on the seat with her head on his lap. The door opened as she said it would, and he drove through. A reporter and a couple of photographers moved toward the car, but without great interest. And then he was past them, heading up Arch Street.

"We're safe," Wohl said. "You can sit up."

She pushed herself erect.

"I am not going to the 'Roundhouse'!" Louise said. "Not tonight."

She had not moved away from him. When she spoke, he could feel and smell her warm breath.

"We can go somewhere and get a cup of coffee," Wohl said.

"Hey, Knight in Shining Armor, when I say something, I can't be talked out of it," Louise said.

"Where would you like to go, then?" Peter asked.

There was a perceptible pause before she replied.

"I don't want to go to a hotel," she said. "They smirk, when you check in without luggage. What would your mother say if you brought me home with you, Peter?"

"I don't live with my mother," he said, quickly.

"Oh, you don't? Then I guess you have an apartment?"

"I'm not so sure that would be a good idea," he said.

"I don't have designs on your body, if that's what you're thinking. I'm wide open to other suggestions."

"I'll make you some coffee," Peter said.

"I don't want coffee," she said.

"Okay, no coffee," Peter said.

Ten minutes later, as they drove up Lancaster Avenue, she said, "Where the hell do you live, in Pittsburgh?"

"It's not far."

"All of my life, my daddy told me, 'If you're ever in trouble, you call me, day or night,' so tonight, for the first time, after the matinee idol told me he was sending for a battering ram, I called him. And his wife told me he's in London."

"Your stepmother?"

"No, his wife," Louise Dutton said, as if annoyed at his denseness. He didn't press the question.

"But you came, didn't you?" Louise asked, rhetorically. "Even if you didn't know I'd sent for you?"

Peter Wohl couldn't think of a reply. She half turned on the seat and held on to his arm with both hands.

"Why did they do that to him? Keep stabbing him, I mean? My God, they *hacked* him!"

"That's not unusual with murders involving sexual deviates," Peter Wohl said. "There's often a viciousness, I guess is the word, in what they do to each other."

She shuddered.

"He was such a *nice* little man," she said. She sighed and shuddered, and added, "Bad things are supposed to come in threes. God, I hope that isn't true. I can't take anything else!"

"You're going to be all right," Peter said.

When they were inside the apartment, he turned the radio on, to WFLN-FM, the classical music station, and then smiled at her.

"I won't ask you if I can take your jacket," he said. "How do you like your coffee?"

"Made in the highlands of Scotland," she said.

"All right," he said. "I'll be right with you."

He went in the kitchen, got ice, and carried it to the bar. He took his jacket off without thinking about it, and made drinks. He carried them to her.

"Until tonight, I always thought there was something menacing about a man carrying a gun," she said. "Now I find it pleasantly reassuring."

"The theory is that a policeman is never really off duty," he said.

"Like Dutch?" she said.

"You want to talk about Dutch?" he asked.

"Quickly changing the subject," Louise said. "This is not what I would have expected, apartment-wise, for a policeman," she said, gesturing around the apartment. "Or even for Peter Wohl, private citizen."

"It was professionally decorated," he said. "I once had a girl friend who was an interior decorator."

"Had?"

"Had."

"Then I suppose it's safe to say I like the naked lady and the red leather chairs, but I think the white rug and most of the furniture looks like it belongs in a whorehouse."

He laughed delightedly.

She looked at her drink.

"I don't really want this," she said. "What I really would like is something to eat."

"How about a world-famous Peter Wohl Taylor ham and egg sandwich?"

"Hold the egg," Louise said.

He went into the kitchen and took a roll of Taylor ham from the refrigerator and put it on his cutting board and began to slice it.

He fried the Taylor ham, made toast, and spread it with Durkee's Dressing.

"Coffee?" he asked.

"Milk?" she asked.

"Milk," he replied. He put the sandwiches on plates, and set places at his tiny kitchen table, then filled two glasses with milk and put them on the table.

Louise ate hungrily, and nodded her head in thanks when he gave her half of his sandwich.

She drained her glass of milk, then wiped her lips with a gesture Peter thought was exquisitely feminine.

"Aren't you going to ask me about me and Dutch?"

"Dutch is dead," Peter said.

"I never slept with him," Louise said. "But I thought about it."

"You didn't have to tell me that," he said.

"No," she said, thoughtfully. "I didn't. I wonder why I did?"

"I'm your friendly father figure," he said, chuckling.

"The hell you are," she said. "Now what?"

"Now we see if we can find you a pair of pajamas or something—"

"Have you a spare T-shirt?"

"Sure, if that would do."

"And then we debate who gets the couch, right? And who gets the bed?"

"You get the bed," he said.

"Why are you being so nice to me?"

"I don't know," he said.

"No pass, Peter?" she asked, looking into his eyes.

"Not tonight," he said. "Maybe later."

He walked into his bedroom, took sheets and a blanket from a chest of drawers, carried them into the living room, and tossed them on the couch. Then he went back into the .bedroom, found a T-shirt and handed it to her, wondering what she would look like wearing it.

"I'll brush my teeth," he said. "And then the place is yours. I shower in the morning."

Brushing his teeth was not his major priority in the bathroom, with all he'd had to drink, and as he stood over the toilet trying to relieve his bladder as quietly as possible, the interesting fantasy that he would return to the bedroom and find her naked in his bed, smiling invitingly at him, ran through his head.

When he went back in the bedroom, she was fully dressed, and standing by the door, as if she wanted to close it, and lock it, after him as soon as possible.

"Good night," he said. "If you need anything, yell."

"Thank you," she said, almost formally.

As if, he thought, *I am the bellhop being rushed out of the hotel room.*

He heard the lock in the door slide home, and remembered that both Dorothea and Barbara were always careful to make sure the door was locked; as if they expected to have someone burst in and catch them screwing.

He took off his outer clothing, folded it neatly, and laid it on the armchairs.

Then he remembered that he had told the cop in the basement garage to tell Lieutenant DelRaye that he was taking her to the Roundhouse. He would have to do something about that.

He tiptoed around the living room in his underwear until he found the phone book. He had not called Homicide in so long that he had forgotten the number. He found the book, and then sat down on the leather couch and dialed the number. The leather was sticky against his skin and he wondered if it was dirty, or if that's the way leather was; he had never sat on his couch in his underwear before.

"Homicide, Detective Mulvaney."

"This is Inspector Wohl," Peter said.

"Yes, sir?"

"Would you please tell Lieutenant DelRaye that I will bring Miss Dutton there, to Homicide, at eight in the morning?"

"Yes, sir. Is there any place Lieutenant DelRaye can reach you?"

Wohl hung up, and then stood up, and started to spread sheets over the leather cushions.

The telephone rang. He watched it. On the third ring, there was a click, and he could faintly hear the recorded message: "You can leave a message for Peter Wohl after the beep."

The machine beeped.

"Inspector, this is Lieutenant DelRaye. Will you please call me as soon as you can? I'm at the Roundhouse."

It was evident from the tone of Lieutenant DelRaye's voice that he was more than a little annoyed, and that leaving a polite message had required some effort.

Peter finished making a bed of the couch, took off his shoes and socks, and lay down on it. He turned off the light, and went to sleep listening to the sound of the water running in his shower, his mind's eye filled with the images of Louise Dutton's body as she showered.

When Police Commissioner Taddeus Czernick, trailed by Sergeant Jank Jankowitz, walked briskly across the lobby of the Roundhouse toward the elevator, it was quarter past eight. He was surprised therefore to see Colonel J. Dunlop Mawson hurrying to catch up with him. He would have laid odds that Colonel J. Dunlop Mawson never cracked an eyelid before half past nine in the morning.

"How are you, Colonel?" Czernick said, smiling and offering his hand. "What gets you out of bed at this unholy hour?"

"Actually, Ted," J. Dunlop Mawson said, "I'm here to see you."

They were at the elevator; there was nothing Commissioner Czernick could do to keep Mawson from getting on with him.

"Colonel," Czernick said, smiling and touching Mawson's arm, "you have *really* caught me at a bad time."

"This is important, or else I wouldn't bother you," Mawson said.

"I just came from seeing Arthur Nelson," Commissioner Czernick said. "You heard what happened to his son?"

"Yes, indeed," Mawson said. "Tragic, shocking."

"I wanted to both offer my personal condolences," Commissioner Czernick said, and then interrupted himself, as the elevator door opened. "After you, Colonel."

They walked down the curving corridor together. There were smiles and murmurs of "Commissioner" from people in the corridor. They reached the commissioner's private door. Jankowitz quickly put a key to it, and opened it and held it open.

Commissioner Czernick looked at Mawson.

"I can give you two minutes, right now, Colonel," he said. "You understand the situation, I'm sure. Maybe later today? Or, better yet, what about lunch tomorrow? I'll even buy."

"Two minutes will be fine," Mawson said.

Czernick smiled. "Then come in. I'll really give you five," he said. "You can hardly drink a cup of coffee in two minutes. Black, right?"

"Thank you, black."

"Doughnut?"

"Please."

Commissioner Czernick nodded at Sergeant Jankowitz and he went to fetch the coffee.

"I have been retained to represent Miss Louise Dutton," Colonel J. Dunlop Mawson said.

"I don't understand," Czernick said. "You mean by WCBL-TV? Has something happened I haven't heard about?"

"Ted, that seems to be the most likely answer," Mawson said.

"Take it from the beginning," Czernick said. "The last I heard, we had arranged to have Miss Dutton taken home from the Waikiki Diner, so that she wouldn't have to drive. Later, as I understand it, we picked her up at her home, brought her here for the interview, and then took her home again."

"You didn't know she was the one who found young Nelson's body?" Mawson asked.

Jankowitz handed him a cup of coffee and two doughnuts on a saucer.

"Thank you," Mawson said.

"No, I didn't," Commissioner Czernick said. "Or if somebody told me, it went in one ear and out the other. At half past six this morning, they called me and told me what had happened to Arthur Nelson's boy. I went directly from my house to Arthur Nelson's place. I offered my condolences, and told him we would turn the earth upside down to find who did it. Then I came here. As soon as we're through, Colonel, I'm going to be briefed on what happened, and where the investigation is at this moment."

"Well, when that happens, I'm sure they'll tell you that Miss Louise Dutton was the one who found the body, and called the police," Mawson said.

"I don't know where we're going, Colonel. I don't understand your role in all this. Or why WCBL-TV is so concerned."

"I've been retained to represent Miss Dutton," Mawson said. "But not by WCBL. I've been told that the police intended to bring her here, to interview her—"

"Well, if she found Nelson's body, Colonel, that would be standard procedure, as I'm sure you know."

"No one seems to know where she is," Mawson said. "She's not at her apartment, and she's not here. And I've been getting sort of a runaround from the people in Homicide."

" 'A runaround'?" Czernick asked. "Come on, Colonel. We don't operate that way, and you know we don't."

"Well, then, where is she?" Mawson asked.

"I don't know, but I'll damned sure find out," Czernick said. He pulled one of the telephones on his desk to him and dialed a number from memory.

"Homicide, Lieutenant DelRaye."

"This is the commissioner, Lieutenant," Taddeus Czernick said. "I understand that Miss Louise Dutton is the citizen who reported finding Mr. Nelson's body."

"Yes, sir, that's true."

"Do you know where Miss Dutton is at this moment?"

"Yes, sir. She's here. Inspector Wohl just brought her in. We've just started to take her statement."

"Well, hold off on that a minute," Czernick said. "Miss Dutton's legal counsel, Colonel J. Dunlop Mawson, is here with me in my office. He wants to be present during any questioning of his client. He'll be right down."

"Yes, sir," DelRaye said.

Commissioner Czernick hung up and looked up at Colonel J. Dunlop Mawson.

"You heard that?" he asked, and Mawson nodded. "Not only is she right here in the building, but Staff Inspector Peter Wohl is with her. You know Wohl?"

Mawson shook his head no.

"Very bright, very young for his rank," Czernick said. "When I heard that Miss Dutton was a witness to Captain Moffitt's shooting, I asked Wohl to make sure that she was treated properly. We don't want WCBL-TV's anchor lady sore at the police department, Colonel. I'm sure that Wohl showed her every possible courtesy."

"Then where the hell has she been? Why haven't I been

able to see her, even find out where she is, until you got on the phone?''

"I'm sure she'll tell you where she's been," Czernick said. "There's been some crossed wire someplace, but whatever has been done, I'll bet you a dime to a doughnut, has been *in* your client's best interest, not against it.''

Mawson looked at him, and decided he was telling the truth.

"We still friends, Colonel?" Commissioner Czernick asked.

"Don't be silly," Mawson said. "Of course we are.''

"Then can I ask you a question?" Czernick asked, and went ahead without waiting for a response. "Why is Philadelphia's most distinguished practitioner of criminal law involved with the routine interview of a witness to a homicide?''

"Homicides," Mawson said. "Plural. Two cases of murder in the first degree.''

"Homicides," Commissioner Czernick agreed.

"Okay, Ted," Mawson said. "We're friends. At half past three this morning, I had a telephone call. From London. From Stanford Fortner Wells III.''

Commissioner Czernick shrugged. He didn't know the name.

"Wells Newspapers?" Mawson asked.

"Okay," Czernick said. "Sure.''

"He told me he had just been on the telephone to Jack Tone, of McNeel, Tone, Schwartzenberger and Cohan, and that Jack had been kind enough to describe me as the . . . what he said was 'the dean of the Philadelphia criminal bar.' ''

"That seems to be a fair description," Commissioner Czernick said, smiling. He was familiar with the Washington, D.C., law firm of McNeel, Tone, Schwartzenberger and Cohan. They were heavyweights, representing the largest of the *Fortune* 500 companies, their staff larded with former cabinet-level government officials.

"Mr. Wells said that he had just learned his daughter was in some kind of trouble with the police, and that he wanted me to take care of whatever it was, and get back to him. And he told me his daughter's name was Louise Dutton.''

''Well, that's interesting, isn't it?'' Czernick said. ''Dutton must be a TV name.''

''We're friends, Ted,'' Mawson said. ''That goes no farther than these office walls, right?''

''Positively,'' Commissioner Czernick said.

''Presuming your Inspector Wohl hasn't had her up at the House of Correction, working her over with a rubber hose, Ted,'' Mawson said, ''asking him to look after her was probably a very good idea.''

Commissioner Czernick laughed, heartily, and shook his head, and walked to Mawson and put his hand on his arm. ''Can you find Homicide all right, Colonel? Or would you like me to have Sergeant Jankowitz show you the way?''

''I can find it all right,'' Mawson said. ''Thank you for seeing me, Commissioner.''

''Anytime, Colonel,'' Czernick said. ''My door's always open to you. You know that.''

The moment Colonel J. Dunlop Mawson was out the door, Commissioner Czernick went to the telephone, dialed the Homicide number, and asked for Inspector Wohl.

When Wohl came on the line, Commissioner Czernick asked, ''Anything going on down there that you can't leave for five minutes?''

''No, sir.''

''Then will you please come up here, Peter?''

There are four interview rooms in the first-floor Round-house offices of the Homicide Division of the Philadelphia Police Department. They are small windowless cubicles furnished with a table and several chairs. One of the chairs is constructed of steel and is firmly bolted to the floor. There is a hole in the seat through which handcuffs can be locked, when a suspect is judged likely to require this kind of restraint.

There is a one-way mirror on one wall, through which

the interviewee and his interrogators can be observed without being seen. No real attempt is made to conceal its purpose. Very few people ever sit in an interview room who have not seen cop movies, or otherwise have acquired sometimes rather extensive knowledge of police interrogative techniques and equipment.

When Colonel J. Dunlop Mawson walked into Homicide, Miss Louise Dutton was in one of the interview rooms. Mawson recognized her from television. She was wearing a suit, with lace at the neck. She was better-looking than he remembered.

With her were three people, one of whom, Lieutenant DelRaye, Mawson had once had on the witness stand for a day and a half, enough time for them both to have acquired an enduring distaste for the other. There was a police stenographer, a gray-haired woman, and a young man in blue blazer and gray flannel slacks who looked like a successful automobile dealer, but who had to be, Mawson decided, Staff Inspector Wohl, "very bright; very young for his rank."

"Miss Dutton, I'm J. Dunlop Mawson," he said, and handed her his card. She glanced at it and handed it to Inspector Wohl, who looked at it, and handed it to Lieutenant DelRaye, who put it in his pocket.

"Lieutenant, I intended that for Miss Dutton," Mawson said.

"Sorry," DelRaye said, and retrieved the card and handed it to Louise.

"The station sent you, I suppose, Mr. Mawson?" Louise Dutton asked.

"Actually, it was your father," Mawson said.

"Okay," Louise Dutton said, obviously pleased. She looked at Inspector Wohl and smiled.

"Gentlemen, may I have a moment with my client?" Mawson asked.

"You're coming back?" Louise Dutton asked Inspector Wohl.

"Absolutely," Wohl said. "I'll just be a couple of minutes."

"Let's step out in the corridor a moment, Miss Dutton, shall we?" Mawson asked.

"What's wrong with here?"

"I meant alone," he said, gesturing at the one-way mirror. "And I wouldn't be at all surprised if there was a microphone in here that someone might inadvertently turn on."

She got up and followed him out of the room, and out of the Homicide office into the curved corridor. Mawson saw her eyes following Inspector Wohl as he walked down the corridor.

"How far did the interview get?" Mawson asked.

"Nowhere," she said. "The stenographer just got there."

"Good," he said. "I've been looking for you since four this morning, Miss Dutton. Where have they had you?"

"Since four?"

"Your father called from London at half past three," Mawson said.

"Okay," she said.

"I went to your apartment, and they said you had been taken here, and when I came here, no one seemed to know anything about you. Where did they have you?"

"What exactly are you going to do for me here and now, Mr. Mawson?" Louise replied.

"Well, I'll be present to advise you during their interview, of course. To protect your rights. You didn't answer my question, Miss Dutton?"

"You can't take the hint? That I didn't want to answer it? *They* didn't have me anywhere. Where I was, I don't think is any of your business."

"Your father is going to be curious, I'm sure of that."

"It's none of his business, either," Louise said.

"We seem to have somehow gotten off on the wrong foot, Miss Dutton," Mawson said. "I'm really sorry. Let's try to start again. I'm here to protect your interests, your rights. To defend you, in other words. I'm on your side."

"My side? The cops are the bad guys? You've got that wrong, Mr. Mawson. I'm on their side. I'll tell the cops anything they want to know. I want them to catch whoever butchered Jerome Nelson.''

''You misunderstand me,'' Mawson said.

''I want to be as helpful and cooperative as I can,'' Louise said. ''I just wasn't up to it last night . . . or early this morning, and that's what that flap was all about. But I've had some rest, and now I'm willing to do whatever they want me to.''

''What 'flap'?''

''There was some disagreement last night about when I was to come here,'' she said. ''But Inspector Wohl took care of that.''

''All I want to do, Miss Dutton, is protect your rights,'' Mawson said. ''I'd like to be there when they question you.''

''I can take care of my own rights,'' she said.

''Your father asked me to come here, Miss Dutton,'' Mawson said.

''Yeah, you said that,'' Louise said. She looked at him thoughtfully, obviously making up her mind. ''Okay. So long as you understand how I feel.''

''I understand,'' Mawson said. ''You were close to Mr. Nelson?''

She didn't respond immediately.

''He was a friend when I needed one,'' she said, finally.

Mawson nodded. ''Well, why don't we go back in there and get it over with?''

The door from the curving third-floor corridor to the commissioner's office opens onto a small anteroom, crowded with desks. The commissioner's private office is to the right; directly ahead is the commissioner's conference room, equipped with a long, rather ornate table. Its windows overlooked the just-completed Metropolitan Hospital on Race Street.

When Peter Wohl walked into the outer office, he saw the conference room was crowded with people. He recognized Deputy Commissioner Howell, Chief Inspector Dennis V. Coughlin, Captain Henry C. Quaire, com-

manding officer of the Homicide Bureau, Captain Charley
Gaft of the Civil Disobedience Squad, Captain Jack Mc-
Govern of the Second District, and Chief Inspector of De-
tectives Matt Lowenstein before someone closed the door.

"He's waiting for you, Inspector," Sergeant Jank
Jankowitz said, gesturing toward the commissioner's office
door.

"Thank you," Peter said, and walked to the open door
and put his head in.

"Come on in, Peter," Commissioner Czernick said.
"And close the door."

"Good morning, sir," Peter said.

"I've got a meeting waiting. This will have to be
quick," Czernick said. "I want to know what happened
with that TV girl from the time I asked you to keep a lid
on things. If something went wrong, start there."

"Nothing went wrong, sir," Peter said. "I had her taken
from the scene by two cops I borrowed from Jack Mc-
Govern. She went to WCBL, and the cops stayed with her
until she was finished. Then they took her home. I later
went to her apartment and brought her to Homicide." He
smiled, and went on: "Jason Washington put on his kindly
uncle suit, and the interview went very well. She told me
afterward she thought he was a really nice fellow."

Commissioner Czernick smiled, and went on: "But you
did get involved with what happened later? With the Nelson murder?"

"Yes, sir. I was on my way home from dinner—"

"Did you go by the Moffitt house? I didn't see you. I
saw your dad and mother."

"No, I didn't," Peter said. "I'm going to go to the
wake. I went and had dinner . . . damn!"

"Something wrong?"

"I had dinner in Alfredo's," Peter said. "Vincenzo Savarese came by the table, with his wife and sister, and
said he was sorry to hear about Dutch Moffitt, and left.
When I called for the bill, they told me he'd picked up the
tab. I forgot about that. I want to send a memo to Internal
Affairs."

"Who were you with?"

"A girl named Barbara Crowley. She's a nurse at the Psychiatric Institute."

"That's the girl you took to Herman Webb's retirement party?"

"Yes, sir."

"I admire your taste, Peter," Commissioner Czernick said. "She seems to be a very fine young woman."

"So my mother keeps telling me," Wohl said.

"You should listen to your mother," Czernick said, smiling.

"When I got home, I called Homicide to see if anything had happened, if they'd found Gerald Vincent Gallagher, and they told me what had happened at Stockton Place, and I figured I'd better go, and I did."

That, Peter thought, *wasn't the truth, the whole truth, and nothing but the truth, but it wasn't a lie. So why do I feel uncomfortable?*

"What happened there?"

"Can I go off the record?" Wohl asked.

The commissioner looked at him with surprise, thought that over, and then nodded.

"Lieutenant DelRaye had rolled on the job, and with his usual tact, he'd rubbed Louise Dutton the wrong way. When I got there, she was locked in her apartment, and DelRaye was about to take down her door. He had a wagon waiting to bring her over here."

"Jesus!" Czernick said. "So what happened?"

"I talked to her. She'd found the body, and was understandably pretty upset. She said she was not going to come over here, period. And she meant it. She asked me to take her out of there, and I did."

"Where did you take her?"

"To my place," Peter said. "She said she didn't want to go to a hotel. I'm sure she felt she would be recognized. Anyway, it was half past two in the morning, and it seemed like the thing to do."

"You better hope your girl friend doesn't find out," Czernick said.

"So I calmed her down, and gave her something to eat, and at eight o'clock, I brought her in. I just got to Homicide when you called down there."

"How do you think she feels about the police department?" Czernick asked.

"DelRaye aside, I think she likes us," Peter said.

"She going to file a complaint about DelRaye?" Czernick asked.

"No, sir."

"You see Colonel Mawson downstairs?"

"Yes, sir. I guess WCBL sent him over?"

"No," Czernick said. "The name Stanford Fortner Wells mean anything to you, Peter?"

Wohl shook his head no.

"Wells Newspapers?" Czernick pursued.

"Oh, yeah. Sure."

"He sent the colonel," Czernick said.

Peter suddenly recalled, very clearly, what he'd thought when he'd first seen Louise Dutton's apartment; that she couldn't afford it; that she might be a high-class hooker on the side, or some rich man's "good friend." That certainly would explain a lot.

"He's her father," Czernick went on. "So it seems the extra courtesies we have been giving Miss Dutton were the thing to do."

"She told me she had tried to call her father, but that he was out of the country," Peter said. "London, she said. She didn't tell me who he was."

He realized that he had just experienced an emotional shock, several emotions all at once. He was ashamed that he had been so willing to accept that Louise was someone's mistress, which would have neatly explained how she could afford that expensive apartment. His relief at learning that Stanford Wells was her father, not her lover, was startling. And immediately replaced with disappointment, even chagrin. Whatever slim chance there could be that something might develop between him and Louise had just been blown out of the water. The daughter of a newspaper empire was not about to even dally with a cop, much less move with him into a vine-covered cottage by the side of the road.

"Peter, I want you to stay with this," Commissioner Czernick said. "I'm going to tell J. Arthur Nelson that I've assigned you to oversee the case and that you'll report to him at least daily where the investigation is leading."

"Yes, sir," Peter said.

"Find out where things stand, and then you call him. Better yet, go see him."

"Yes, sir."

"Make sure that he understands what you're telling him is for him personally, not for the *Ledger*. Tell him as much as you think you can. I don't want the *Ledger* screaming about police ineptitude. And stay with the Dutton woman, too. I don't want the Philadelphia Police Department's federal grants cut because Stanford Fortner Wells III tells his politicians to cut them. Which I think he damned sure would have done if we had brought his daughter here handcuffed in the back of a wagon."

"Yes, sir," Peter said.

"That's it, Peter," Commissioner Czernick said. "Keep me advised."

NINE

Mr. and Mrs. Kevin McFadden, who lived in a row house on Fitzgerald Street, not far from Methodist Hospital in South Philadelphia, were not entirely pleased with their son Charles's choice of a career as a policeman. Kevin McFadden had been an employee of the Philadelphia Gas Works since he had left high school, and Mrs. McFadden (Agnes) had just naturally assumed that Charley would follow in his father's footsteps. By and large the gas works had treated Kevin McFadden all right for twenty-seven years, and when he turned sixty, he would have a nice pension, based on (by then) forty-one years of service to the company.

Mrs. Agnes McFadden could not understand why Charley, who his father had got on as a helper with the gas works after his graduation from Bishop Newman High School, had thrown that over to become a cop. Her primary concern was for her son's safety. Being a policeman was a dangerous job. Whenever she went in Charley's room and saw his gun and the boxes of ammunition for it, on the closet shelf, it made her shudder.

And it wasn't as if he would have been a helper forever. You can't start at the top, you have to work your way up. Kevin had worked his way up. He was now a lead foreman, and the money was good, and with his seniority, he got all of his weekends and most holidays off.

Kevin hadn't been a lot of a help, when Agnes McFadden had tried to talk Charley out of quitting the gas works and going on the cops. He had taken Charley's side, agreeing with him that a pension when you were forty-five was a hell of a lot better than a pension you got only when you were sixty, if you lived that long.

"Christ," he said, "Charley could retire at *forty-five years old,* still a young man, and go get another job, and every month there would be a check from the city for as long as he lived."

And he added that if Charley didn't want to work for the gas works, that was his business.

Mr. and Mrs. McFadden, however, were in agreement concerning Charley's duties within the police department. They didn't like that one damned bit, even if they tried (with not much success) to keep it to themselves.

He went around looking like a goddamned bum. Facts are facts. Agnes hadn't let Kevin go to work in clothes like that, even way back when he didn't have much seniority and was working underground. God only knew what people in the neighborhood thought Charley was doing for a living.

Not that he was around the neighborhood much. They hardly ever saw him, they couldn't remember the last time he had gone to church with them, and he never even went to Flo & Danny's Bar & Grill with his father anymore.

They understood, of course, when he told them he had been assigned to the Narcotics Squad, in a "plainclothes" assignment, and that the reason he dressed like a bum was you couldn't expect to catch drug guys unless you looked like them. It wasn't like arresting somebody for speeding. And they believed him when he said it was an opportunity, that if he did good, he could get promoted quickly, and that there was practically unlimited overtime right now.

So far as Agnes McFadden was concerned, overtime was fine, but there was also such a thing as too much of a good thing. Charley had had his own phone put in; and two, three, and sometimes even more nights a week, he would no sooner get home, usually at some ungodly hour after they had gone to bed, than it would ring, and it would be his partner calling; and she would hear him running down the stairs and slamming the front door (he'd been doing that since he was five years old) and then she would hear him starting up the battered old car—a Volkswagen— he drove and tearing off down the street.

Maybe, Agnes McFadden thought, if he was a *real* cop, and wore a uniform, and shaved, and had his hair cut; and rode around in a prowl car giving out tickets, going to accidents, and doing *real cop-type* things; it wouldn't be so bad; but she didn't like it at all, now, and if he wouldn't admit it, neither did his father.

Charley was twenty-five, and it was time for him to be thinking about getting married and starting a family. No decent girl would want to be seen with him in public, the way he looked (and sometimes smelled) and no girl in her right mind would marry somebody she couldn't count on to come home for supper, or who would jump out of bed in the middle of the night every time the phone rang. Not to mention being in constant danger of getting shot or stabbed or run over with a car by some nigger or spic or dago full of some kind of drug.

Officer Charles McFadden, who had been engaged in dipping a piece of toast into the yolk of his fried eggs, looked up at his father.

"Pop, ask me how many stars are in the sky?"

His father, who had been checking the basketball scores in the sports section of the *Philadelphia Daily News*, eyed him suspiciously, and took another forkful of his own eggs.

"It's not dirty," Charley McFadden said, reading his father's mind.

"Okay," Kevin McFadden said. "How many stars are in the sky?"

"All of them," Charley McFadden said, pleased with himself.

It took Kevin a moment, but finally he caught on, and laughed.

"Wiseass," he said.

"Chip off the old block," Charley said.

"I don't understand," Agnes McFadden said.

"The only place, Mom, stars is, is in the sky," Charley explained.

"Oh," she said, not quite sure why that was funny. "There's some more home fries in the pan, if you want some."

Charley had come in in the wee hours, and slept until, probably, he smelled the coffee and the bacon, and then come down. It was now quarter after nine.

"No, thanks, Mom," Charley said. "I got to get on my horse."

"You goin' somewhere?" Agnes McFadden asked when Charley stood up and carried his plate to the sink. "Here, give me that. Neither you or your father can be trusted around a sink with dishes."

"I got to change the oil in the car," Kevin McFadden said. "And I bought some stuff that's supposed to clean out the carburetor. Afterward, I thought maybe you and me could go to Flo and Danny's and hoist one."

"I can't, Pop," Charley said. "I got to go to work."

"You didn't get in until four this morning—" Agnes McFadden said.

"Three, Mom," Charley interrupted. "It was ten after three when I walked in the door."

"*Three* then," she granted. "And you got to go back? Your father has the day off, and it would be good for you to spend some time together. And fun, too. You go down to Flo and Danny's and when I finish cleaning up around here, I'll come down and have a glass of beer with the two of you."

"Mom, I got to go to work."

"Why?" Agnes McFadden flared. "What I would like to know is what's so important that it can't wait for a couple of hours, so that you can spend a little time with your family."

She was more hurt, Charley saw, than angry.

"Mom, you see on the TV where the police officer, Captain Moffitt, got shot?"

"Sure. Of course I did. What's that got to do with you?"

"There was two of them," Charley said. "Captain Moffitt shot one of them, and the other got away."

"I asked, so what's that got to do with you?"

"I think I know where I can catch him," Charley said.

"Mr. Big Shot," his mother said, heavily sarcastic. "There's eight thousand cops—I know 'cause I seen it in the newspaper—there's eight thousand cops, and you, you been on the force two years, and all you are is a patrolman, though you'd never know it to look at you, and *you're* going to catch him!"

Charley's face colored.

"Well, let me just tell *you* something, Mom, if you don't mind," he said, angrily. *"I'm* the officer who made the identification of the girl who shot Captain Moffitt, and those eight thousand cops you're talking about are *all* looking for a guy named Gerald Vincent Gallagher, because I was able to identify him as a known associate of the girl."

"No shit?" Kevin McFadden asked, impressed.

"Watch your tongue," Agnes McFadden snapped. "Just because you work in a sewer doesn't mean you have to sound like one!"

"You bet your ass," Charley said to his father. "And I got a pretty good idea where the slimy little bastard's liable to be!"

"I won't tolerate that kind of dirty talk from either one of you, I just won't put up with it," Agnes said.

"Agnes, shut up!" Kevin McFadden said. "Charley, you're not going to do anything dumb, are you? I mean, what the hell, why take a chance on anything if you don't have to?"

"What I'm going to do, Pop, is find him. If I can. Hang around where I think he might be, or will show up. If I see him, or if he shows up there, I'll get Hay-zus to go with me."

Officer Jesus Martinez, a twenty-three-year-old Puerto Rican, was Officer Charley McFadden's partner. He pronounced his Christian name as it was pronounced in Spanish, and Charley McFadden had taken to using that pronounciation when discussing him with his mother. Agnes McFadden had made it plain that she was uncomfortable with Jesus as somebody's first name. Hay-zus was all right. It was like Juan or Alberto or some other strange spic name.

"I wish *you* wore a uniform," Agnes McFadden said.

"Yeah, sure," Charley said. "Maybe be a traffic cop, right? So I can stand in the middle of the street downtown somewhere, and freeze to death in winter and boil my brains in the summer? Breathing diesel exhaust all the time?"

"It would be better than what you're doing," his mother said.

"Mom, you don't get promoted guarding school crossings," Charley said. "Or riding around some district in a car on the last out shift."

"I don't see you getting promoted," Agnes McFadden said.

"Leave him alone, Agnes," Kevin McFadden said. "He hasn't been with the cops long enough to get promoted."

"The detective's examination is next month, and I'm going to take it," Charley said. "And for your information, I think I'm going to pass it. If I can arrest this Gallagher punk, I *know* I'd make it."

"You're getting too big for your britches," Agnes McFadden replied, aware that she was angry and wondering why.

"Yeah? Yeah? My lieutenant, Lieutenant Pekach, you know how old *he* is? He's *thirty* years old, that's all how old he is. And he's a lieutenant, and he's eligible to take the captain's examination."

"That's young for a lieutenant," Kevin McFadden said. "I suppose they do all right on payday."

"You can do it," Charley said. "Pop, when I went to identify the girl who shot Captain Moffitt, down to the medical examiner's, where they were autopsying her, Lieutenant Pekach introduced me to Staff Inspector Wohl."

"Who's he? Am I supposed to know what that means?" Kevin McFadden asked.

"A staff inspector is higher than a captain," Charley explained. "All they do is the *important* investigations."

"So?" Agnes McFadden said.

"So, Mom, so here is this Staff Inspector Wohl, wearing a suit that must have cost him two hundred bucks, and driving this brand-new Ford LTD, and he ain't hardly any older than Lieutenant Pekach, that's what!"

"He must have pull, then," Agnes McFadden said. "He must know somebody."

"Ah, Jesus Christ, Mom!" Charley said, and stormed out of the kitchen.

"You shouldn't have said that, Agnes," Kevin McFadden said. "Charley's ambitious, there's nothing wrong with that."

The front door slammed, and a moment later, they could hear the whine of the Volkswagen starter.

"Talk to me about ambition," Agnes replied, "when they call up and tell you they're sorry, some bum shot him. Or stuck a knife in him."

Peter Wohl started the LTD and looked across the seat at Louise Dutton.

"You okay?" he asked.

"I'm fine," she said. "I *have* seen faster typists."

He chuckled. The typist who had typed up her statement had been a young black woman, obviously as new to the typewriter as she was determined to do a good, accurate, no strike-over, job.

"Where to now?" he asked.

"I've got to go to work, of course," Louise said. "But

I think I had better get my car, first. On the way, you can drop off your uniform."

"Not that I don't want your company," he said, "but I could drop you at the station, and we could get your car later. For that matter, I could bring it to the station."

"I thought about that," she said. "And decided that since you live in Timbuctoo, I'd rather get it now. On the long way back downtown, I'll have time to think, to come up with a credible reason why I was such a disgrace to journalism last night."

"Huh? Oh, you mean they expected you to come in and—what's the term?—*write up* what happened to Nelson?"

"Yes, they did," Louise said. "And when I didn't, I confirmed all of Leonard Cohen's male chauvinist theories about the emotional instability of female reporters. Real reporters, *men* reporters, don't get hysterical."

"You weren't hysterical," Peter said. "You were upset, but you had every right to be."

They were now passing City Hall, and heading out John F. Kennedy Boulevard, past the construction sites of what the developers said would be *Downtown Philadelphia Reborn.*

Louise turned and looked at him.

"You're a really nice guy, Peter Wohl," she said. "Anyone ever tell you that?"

"All the time," he said.

She laughed, and changed the subject: "When we get to your place, I have to go inside."

"Why?"

"Because my underwear was still wet, and I couldn't put it on," she said.

The logical conclusion to be drawn from that statement, Peter thought, *is that she is at this moment, underwearless. Phrased another way, she is naked under her dress.*

"You should have seen your face just now," Louise said.

"What are you talking about?" he asked.

"Your eyes grew wide," she said. "Does that turn you on, Peter Wohl? A woman not wearing underwear?"

"Get off my back," he flared.

"It does!" she said, delighted. "It does!"

He turned and glared at her. She wasn't fazed. She smiled at him.

He returned his attention to the road. Louise noticed that he was gripping the steering wheel so tightly that his knuckles were white.

They said nothing else to each other until they reached his apartment. He pulled the nose of the Ford against the garage door, turned off the ignition, handed her the apartment key, and laid his arm on the back of the seat.

"I would just run along," he said. "But I'm going to need my key back. I'll wait here."

"I'll throw it out the window," she said.

"Fine," he said.

She went up the stairs and he leaned on the fender of the Ford LTD. A minute or so later, he heard the window in his bathroom grate open. He turned and looked up at the window. All he could see was her head; she had to be kneeling on the toilet seat.

"Can you come up here a minute?" she said. "I've got a little trouble."

He went up the stairs and into the apartment.

Louise's head peered at him around his nearly closed bedroom door.

"What's the trouble?" he asked.

"I don't want to go to work," Louise said. "Not right now."

"Then don't go," he said. "Stay here as long as you like."

"You really are a very sweet guy, Peter," Louise said.

"You seem to be a little ambiguous about that," Peter said.

"You're sore about the way I teased you in the car, aren't you?"

"You enjoy humiliating people, go ahead," he said.

"I was just *teasing*," she said. "If I didn't *like* you, I wouldn't tease you."

"I understand," he said. "I don't think you're half as clever, or as sophisticated as you do, but I understand you."

"Oh, damn you," she said, and opened the door all the way. "You don't understand me at all."

She walked within six feet of him and stopped, and looked into his eyes.

"Come on, Peter," she said. "Loosen up."

"Is there anything else I can get you?" Peter asked.

Louise unbuttoned her jacket, and then shrugged out of it.

She raised her eyes to his.

"What do I have to do, Peter?" she asked, very softly. "Throw you on the white couch and rip your clothes off?"

Officer Charley McFadden pulled into a gas station and called Jesus Martinez and told him what he had in mind. Hay-zus's mother answered the phone and with obvious reluctance, after she told him Hay-zus was asleep, got him on the phone.

"You want to help me catch Gerald Vincent Gallagher?"

"I thought you were working with Homicide," Hay-zus said.

"The detective with the job let me very politely know that he didn't need my help, thank you very much."

There was a long pause.

"Where do you think he is?" Hay-zus asked.

"I want to look for him at the Bridge Street Terminal," McFadden said.

The Bridge Street Terminal, which is the end of the line for the Market Street Elevated, a major transfer point for people traveling to and from Center City and West Philadelphia.

"In other words, you don't have the first fucking idea where he is," Martinez said.

"I got a feeling, Hay-zus," Charley McFadden said.

Gerald Vincent Gallagher, Charley McFadden had reasoned, would have hidden someplace for a while. Then he would want to get out of the Northeast. He didn't have a car—few junkies did—but he would have the price of bus or subway fare, if he had to panhandle for it.

There was a long pause.

"Ah, shit," Jesus Martinez said. "I'll meet you there."

And then he hung up.

McFadden parked his Volkswagen fifty feet from the intersection of Frankford and Bridge Streets. He went to a candy store across the street and bought two large 7-Ups to go (lots of ice); two Hershey bars; two Mounds bars; two bags of Planter's peanuts; and a pack of Chesterfields.

He carried everything back to the Volkswagen, and arranged it and himself on and around the front seat. He slumped down on the seat, and lit a cigarette.

It was liable to be a long wait for Gerald Vincent Gallagher. And, of course, he might not show.

If he didn't show, McFadden decided, he would not put in for overtime. Nobody had told him to stake out the terminal.

But he might. And he would really like to catch the despicable shit, so he would wait.

He had been there ten minutes when a trackless trolley pulled in. A slight, dark, young-appearing man wearing blue jeans and a T-shirt got off. He looked around until he spotted the Volkswagen and then walked to it, and got in.

"I just thought," he said. "Since nobody told us to do this, we can't put in for overtime, right?"

"When we catch him, we can," McFadden said.

"I'll bet you believe in the Easter Bunny, too, huh?" Jesus Martinez said. Then he looked at the supplies McFadden had laid in. "No wonder you're fat," he said. "That shit's no good for you."

He reached for one of the 7-Ups, and they settled down to wait.

•   •   •

Mawson, Payne, Stockton, McAdoo & Lester maintained law offices on the eleventh floor of the Philadelphia Savings Fund Society Building on Market Street, east of Broad. It was convenient to both the federal courthouse and the financial district.

Colonel J. Dunlop Mawson and Brewster Cortland Payne II, the founding partners of the firm, occupied offices on either side of the Large Conference Room. They shared a secretary, Mrs. Irene Craig, a tall, dignified, silver-haired woman in her fifties. Mrs. Craig had two secretaries of her own, set up in an office off her own tastefully furnished office. Although she could, if necessary, type nearly one hundred words per minute on her state-of-the-art IBM typewriter, Mrs. Craig rarely typed anything on it except Memoranda of Incoming Calls.

Her function, she had once told her husband, was to serve as sort of a traffic cop, offering, and barring, entrance to the attention, either in person or on the phone, of her bosses. Their time was valuable, and it was her job to see that it was not wasted.

She was very good at her job, and although it was a secret between them, she brought home more money than did her husband, who worked for the Prudential Insurance Company.

When she came to work, at her ritual time of 8:45, fifteen minutes before the business day actually began, she was surprised to see the colonel's office door open. Colonel J. Dunlop Mawson rarely appeared before ten, or ten-thirty. She went into his office. He wasn't there, but there was evidence that he had been.

There were cigarettes in his ashtray; two cardboard coffee containers from the machine way down the hall by the typists' pool; and crumpled paper in his wastebasket. The colonel's leather-framed doodle pad was covered with triangles, stars, a setting sun, and a multidigit telephone number Mrs. Craig recognized from the prefix to be one in London, England.

Mrs. Craig retrieved the crumpled paper from the wastebasket, unfolded it, and read it. There were names

on it: *Louise Dutton, Lt. DelRaye, Insp. Wohl (Wall?)*,
and, underlined, *Stanford Fortner Wells III*. There was an
address, *6 Stockton Place*, and several telephone numbers,
none of which Mrs. Craig recognized. And then she remembered that Stanford Fortner Wells III had something
to do with newspapers; what, exactly, she couldn't recall.

She dumped the contents of the ashtray in the wastebasket, added the cardboard coffee containers, and then
carried it outside and dumped it in her own wastebasket.
Then she went to the smaller office where her assistants
worked and started the coffee machine. That was for her.
She liked a cup of coffee to begin the day, and sometimes
Mr. Payne came in wanting a cup.

Colonel J. Dunlop Mawson came in the office at ten
past nine, smiled at her, and asked if Mr. Payne was in.

"Not yet, any minute," she said.

"Let me know the minute he does, will you please?
And could you get me a cup of coffee?"

He went in his office, and as she went to fetch the coffee, she saw him go to the window of his office that gave
a view of Market Street down to the river and stand, with
his hands on his hips, as if he was mad at something,
looking out.

Brewster Cortland Payne II came into her office as she
was carrying a cup of coffee, with two envelopes of sac-
charin and a spoon on the saucer across it to the colonel's
office.

"Good morning," Brewster Payne said, with a nod and
a smile. He was a tall and thin, almost skinny, man wearing a single-breasted vested gray suit, a subdued necktie,
and black shoes. Yet there was something, an air of authority and wisdom, Mrs. Craig knew, that made people
look at him in a crowd. He looked, she thought, like what
a successful attorney should look like. Sometimes, especially when she was annoyed with him, the colonel didn't
look that way to her.

"Good morning," she said. "He asked me to let him
know the minute you came in." Brewster Payne's face
registered amused surprise.

"Do you think he is annoyed that I'm a little late?" he asked, and added: "I would be grateful for some coffee myself."

"Here," Mrs. Craig said, handing him the cup and saucer. "Tell him I'm getting his."

When she delivered the coffee, Brewster Payne was sprawled on the colonel's red leather couch, his long legs stretched out in front of him, balancing his coffee on his stomach. The colonel was standing beside his desk. When she handed him the coffee, he gave her an absent smile and set it down on the desk.

Mrs. Craig left, closing the door after her. There was someone new in the outer office.

"Hello, Matt," she said. She liked Matt Payne, thought that he was a really handsome, and more important, *nice* young man. She liked the way he smiled.

"Good morning, Mrs. Craig," he said, and then blurted: "Is there any chance I could see him this morning? He doesn't expect me, but . . ."

"He's in with the colonel," she said. "I don't know how long they'll be."

"I think this was a bad idea," Matt said.

"Don't be silly. Sit down, I'll get you some coffee."

"You're sure?"

"Positive."

He was enormously relieved, Mrs. Craig saw, and was glad that she had insisted that he stay, even though it would delay the morning's schedule by fifteen minutes or more. Fifteen minutes, plus however long the colonel and Mr. Payne were in the colonel's office.

Louise Dutton came out of the bathroom wearing Peter's bathrobe. It hung loosely on her but even in the dim light, he could see the imprint of her nipples. He thought she looked incredibly appealing.

She walked across the bedroom to the bed, looked down at Peter a moment, and then sat down on the bed.

"Well," she said. "Look who woke up."

"I wasn't asleep, Delilah," he said. "I watched you get out of bed."

"Delilah?"

"I never really thought she rendered Samson helpless by giving him a *haircut*," Peter said. "That was the edited-for-children version."

"You Samson"—she chuckled—"me Delilah?"

"And as soon as I get my strength back, I'll tear the temple down," Peter said. "Actually, what I have to do is face the dragon in his lair."

"Now I'm the dragon? The dragon lady?"

"I was referring to Chief Inspector Matt Lowenstein, our beloved chief of detectives," Wohl said. He reached to his right, away from her, and took his wristwatch from the bedside table. He glanced at it, strapped it on, and said, "I've got to see how the Nelson investigation is going, and then go see Arthur J. Nelson. I'm late now."

"Then why aren't you out of bed, getting dressed?" she asked.

He held his arms out, and she came into them. He kissed the top of her head.

She purred, "Nice."

"I wasn't sure you would like me to do that," he said, her face against his chest.

"Why not?"

"It's *after*," Peter said. "Women have been known to regret a moment of passion."

"I was afraid when I came back in here, you would be all dressed and ready to leave," she said. "Because it's *after*."

He laughed, and pulled his head back so that he could look at her face.

"Wham, bam, thank you, ma'am?" he asked.

"You're the type, Peter," she said.

"You like this better?"

"Much better," she said.

"Blow in my ear, and the world is yours," he said.

She giggled and kissed his chest.

"There's no small voice of reason in the back of your

mind sending up an alarm?'' she asked. '' 'What am I getting myself into with this crazy lady?' ''

"What the small voice of reason is asking is, 'What happens when she realizes what she's done? The TV Lady and the Cop?' ''

"That would seem to suggest there was more for you in what happened than one more notch on your gun,'' Louise said.

"If I wasn't afraid it would trigger one of your smartass replies, I would tell you it's never been that way for me before,'' Peter said.

She pushed herself into a sitting position and looked down at him.

"For me, either,'' she said. "I mean, really, I had to ask you.''

"Oh, come on,'' he said.

"Yes, I did,'' she said. "And that suggests the possibility that I'm queer for cops. What do they call those pathetic little girls who chase the bands around? 'Groupies'? Maybe I'm a cop groupie.''

"This is what I was afraid of,'' Peter said. "That you would start thinking.''

"Why shouldn't I think?''

"Because if you do, sure as Christ made little apples, you'll come up with some good excuse to cut it off between us.''

"Maybe that would be best, in the long run,'' she said.

"Not for me, it wouldn't,'' he said.

'' 'He said, with finality,' '' Louise said. "Why do you say that, Peter? So . . . With such finality?''

"I told you before, it was never that way for me, before,'' Peter said.

"You don't think that might be because you saw a friend of yours slumped dead against the wall of a diner yesterday afternoon? That sort of thing would tend, I would suppose, to excite the emotions. Or that I might be at a high emotional peak myself? I was there, too, not to mention poor little Jerome?''

"I don't give a damn what caused it, all I know is how

I feel about what happened," Peter said. "I gather this is not what they call a reciprocal emotion?"

"I didn't say that," Louise said quickly. "Jesus Christ, Peter, I didn't know you existed this time yesterday!" she said. "What do you expect from me?"

He shrugged.

She looked into his eyes for a long moment. "So where does that leave us? Where do we go from here?"

"How would you react to a suggestion that it's a little warm in here, and you would probably be more comfortable if you took the robe off?"

"I was hoping you would ask," she said.

"Where the hell have you been?" Leonard Cohen demanded of Louise Dutton when she walked into the WCBL-TV newsroom. "I called all over, looking for you."

"I was a little upset, Leonard," Louise said. "I can't imagine why. I mean, why should something unimportant like walking into a room and finding someone you knew and liked hacked up like . . . I can't think of a metaphor—hacked up?"

"It was a story, Lou," Cohen said.

She glared at him, her eyebrows raised in contempt, her eyes icy.

"It was pretty bad, huh?" he said, backing down.

"Yes, it was."

"What I would like to do, Lou," he said, "is open the news at six by having Barton interview you. Nothing formal, you understand; he would just turn to you and say something like, 'Mr. Nelson lived in your apartment building, didn't he, Louise?' and then you would come back with, 'Yes, and I found the body.' "

"Fuck you, Leonard," Louise said.

He just looked at her.

"For Christ's sake," she said. "The address has been in the papers . . ."

"And so has your name," he countered.

"I've seen the papers," she said. "There must be ten

Louise Duttons in the phone book, and none of the papers I saw made the connection between me and here. If it is made, every creepy-crawly in Philadelphia, including, probably, the animals who killed that poor little man, will come out of the woodwork looking for me."

"Why should that bother you? Aren't you under police protection?"

"What does that mean?"

"Just what it sounded like. I called the Homicide guy, DelRaye, Lieutenant DelRaye, when I couldn't find you, and he said that I would have to talk to Inspector Wohl, that Wohl was 'taking care of you.' "

"I am not under police protection," she said, evenly. "I'll tell you what I will do, Leonard. I'll look at what you have on tape, and if there's anything there that makes it worthwhile, I'll do a voice-over. But I am not going to chat pleasantly with Barton Ellison about it on camera."

"Okay," Leonard Cohen replied. "Thank you *ever* so much. Your dedication to journalism touches me deeply. Who's Wohl?"

"He's a cop. He's a friend of mine. He's a nice guy," Louise said.

"He's the youngest staff inspector in the police department," Cohen said. "He was also the youngest captain. His father is a retired chief inspector, which may or may not have had something to do with his being the youngest captain and staff inspector. What he usually does is investigate corruption in high places. He put the head of the plumber's local, two fairly important Mafiosi, *and* the director of the Housing Authority in the pokey just before you came to town."

She looked at him, her eyebrows raised again.

"Very bright young man," Cohen went on. "He normally doesn't schmooze people. I'm sure, you being a professional journalist and all, that you have considered the police department may have a reason for assigning an attractive young bachelor to schmooze you."

"You find him attractive, Leonard, is that what you're saying?" Louise asked innocently. "I'll have to tell him."

His lips tightened momentarily, but he didn't back off. "You're going to see him again, huh?"

"Oh, God, Leonard, I hope so," Louise said. "He's absolutely marvelous in the sack!" She waited until his eyes widened. "Put that in your file, too, why don't you?" she added, and then walked away.

TEN

Colonel J. Dunlop Mawson was sitting on the sill of a
wall of windows that provided a view of lower Market
Street, the Delaware River and the bridge to New Jersey.

"So, I went down to Homicide," he said, nearing the
end of his story, "and finally got to meet Miss Wells, also
known as Dutton."

"Where had she been?" Brewster Payne asked. Mawson had aroused his curiosity. Through the entire recital
of having been given a runaround by the police, and the
gory details of the brutal murder of Jerome Nelson, he had
not been able to guess why Mawson was telling it all to
him.

"She wouldn't tell me," Mawson said. "She's a very
feisty young woman, Brewster. I think she was on the edge
of telling me to butt out."

"How extraordinary," Payne said, dryly, "that she
would even consider refusing the services of 'Philadelphia's most distinguished practitioner of criminal law.' "

''I knew damned well I made a mistake telling you that,'' Mawson said. ''Now I'll never hear the end of it.''

''Probably not,'' Payne agreed.

''I have an interesting theory,'' Mawson said, ''that she spent the night with the cop.''

''Miss Dutton? And which cop would that be, Mawson?'' Payne asked.

''Inspector Wohl,'' Mawson said. ''He took her away from the apartment, and then he brought her in in the morning.''

''I thought, for a moment, that you were suggesting there was something romantic, or whatever, between them,'' Payne said.

''That's exactly what I'm suggesting,'' Mawson said. ''He's not what comes to mind when you say 'cop.' Or 'inspector.' For one thing he's young, and very bright, and well dressed . . . *polished* if you take my meaning.''

''Perhaps they're friends,'' Payne said. ''When he heard what had happened, he came to be a friend.''

''She doesn't look at him like he's a friend,'' Mawson insisted, ''and unless Czernick is still playing games with me, he didn't even know her until yesterday. According to Czernick, he assigned him to the Wells/Dutton girl to make sure she was treated with the appropriate kid gloves for a TV anchorwoman.''

''I don't know where you're going, I'm afraid,'' Payne said.

''Just file that away as a wild card,'' Mawson said. ''Let me finish.''

''Please do,'' Payne said.

''So, after she signed her statement, and she rode off into the sunrise with this Wohl fellow, I came here and put in a call to Wells in London. He wasn't there. But he left a message for me. Delivered with the snotty arrogance that only the English can manage. Mr. Wells is on board British Caledonian Airways Flight 419 to New York, and 'would be quite grateful if I could make myself available to him imm-ee-jut-ly on his arrival at Philadelphia.' ''

''Philadelphia?'' Payne asked, smiling. Mawson's mimicry of an upper-class British accent was quite good. "Does British Caledonian fly into here?"

"No, they don't. I asked the snotty Englishman the same question. He said, he 'raw-ther doubted it. What Mr. Wells has done is shed-yule a helicopter to meet the British Caledonian air-crawft in New York, don't you see? To take him from New York to Philadelphia.' "

Payne set his coffee cup on the end table beside the couch.

"You're really very good at that," he said, chuckling. "So you're going to meet him at the airport here?"

Mawson hesitated, started to reply, and then stopped.

"Okay," Brewster Payne said. "So that's the other question."

"I don't like being summoned like an errand boy," Mawson said. "But on the other hand, Stanford Fortner Wells is Wells Newspapers, and there—"

"Is a certain potential, for the future," Payne filled in for him. "If he had counsel in Philadelphia, he would have called them."

"Exactly."

"We could send one of our bright young men to the airport with a limousine," Payne said, "to take Mr. Wells either here, to see you, or to a suite which we have reserved for him in the . . . what about the Warwick? . . . where you will attend him the moment your very busy schedule—*shed-yule*—permits."

"Good show!" Mawson said. "Raw-ther! Quite! I knew I could count on you, old boy, in this sticky wicket."

Payne chuckled.

"You said 'the other question', Brewster," Mawson said.

"What, if anything, you should say to Mr. Wells about where his daughter was when you couldn't find her, and more specifically, how much, if at all, of your suspicions regarding Inspector Wall—"

"Wohl. Double-U Oh Aitch Ell," Mawson interrupted.

"*Wohl*," Payne went on. "And his possibly lewd and carnal relationship with his daughter."

"Okay. Tell me."

"Nothing, if you're asking my advice."

"I thought it might show how bright and clever we are to find that out so soon," Mawson said.

"No father, Mawson, wants to hear from a stranger that his daughter is not as innocent as he would like to believe she is."

Mawson laughed.

"You're right, Brewster," he said. He walked to the door and opened it. "Irene, would you ask Mr. Fengler to come over, please? And tell him to clear his schedule for the rest of the day? And then reserve a *good* suite at the Warwick, billing to us, for Mr. Stanford Fortner Wells? And finally, call that limousine service and have them send one over, to park in our garage? And tell them I would be very grateful if it was clean, and not just back from a funeral?"

"Yes, sir," she said, smiling.

"Hello, Matt," Mawson said. "How are you?"

"Morning, Colonel," Matt said. "I was hoping to see Dad."

"Having just solved all the world's problems, he's available for yours," Mawson said, and turned to Brewster Payne. "Matt's waiting for you."

"I'll be damned," Payne said, and got up from the couch. "I wonder what's on his mind?"

He had, in fact, been expecting to see Matt, or at least to have him telephone. He had heard from Matt's mother how awkward it had been at the Moffitt home, and later at the funeral home, making the senseless death of Matt's uncle even more difficult for him. He had half expected Matt to come out to Wallingford last night, and, disappointed that he hadn't, had considered calling him. In the end he had decided that it would be best if Matt came to him, as he felt sure he would, in his own good time.

He went in the outer office and resisted the temptation to put his arms around Matt.

"Well, good morning," he said.

"If I'm throwing your schedule in disarray, Dad—" Matt said.

"There's nothing on my schedule, is there, Irene?"

"Nothing that won't wait," she said.

"Go on in, Matt," Payne said, gesturing toward his office. "I've got to step down the corridor a moment, and then I'll be with you."

He waited until Matt was inside and then told Irene Craig that she was to hold all calls. "It's important. You heard about Captain Moffitt?"

"I didn't know what to say to him," she said. "So I said nothing."

"I think a word of condolence would be in order when he comes out," Payne said, and then went in his office and closed the door.

Matt was sitting on the edge of an antique cherrywood chair, resting his elbows on his knees.

"I'm very sorry about your uncle Dick, Matt," Brewster Payne said. "He was a fine man, and I know how close you were. Aside from that, I have no comforting words. It was senseless, brutal, unspeakable."

Matt looked at him, started to say something, changed his mind, and said something else: "I just joined the police department."

My God! He's not joking!

"That was rather sudden, wasn't it?" Brewster Payne said. "What about the Marine Corps? I thought you were under a four-year obligation to them?"

"I busted the physical," Matt said. "The marines don't want me."

"When did that happen?"

"A week or so ago," Matt said. "My fault. When I went to the naval hospital, the doctor asked me why didn't I take the flight physical, I never knew when I might want to try for flight school. So I took it, and the eye examination was more thorough than it would have been for a grunt commission, and they found it."

"Found what?"

"It had some Latin name, of course," Matt said. "And

it will probably never bother me, but the United States Marine Corps can't take any chances. I'm out."

"You didn't say anything," Brewster Payne said.

"I'm not exactly proud of being a 4-F," Matt said. "I just . . . didn't want to."

"Perhaps the army or the air force wouldn't be so particular," Brewster Payne said.

"It doesn't work that way, Dad," Matt said. "I already have a brand-new 4-F draft card."

"Think that through, Matt," Brewster Payne said. "You should be embarrassed, or ashamed, only of things over which you have control. There is no reason at all that you should feel in any way diminished by this."

"I'll get over it," Matt said.

"It is not really a good reason to act impulsively," Brewster Payne said.

"Nor, he hesitates to add, but is thinking, is the fact that Uncle Dick got himself shot a really good reason to act impulsively; for example, joining the police force."

"The defense rests," Brewster Payne said, softly.

"Actually, I was thinking about it before Uncle Dick was killed," Matt said. "From the time I busted the physical. The first thing I thought was that it was too late to apply for law school."

"Not necessarily," Brewster Payne said. "There is always an exception to the rule, Matt."

"And then, with sudden clarity, I realized that I didn't *want* to go to law school," Matt went on. "Not right away, anyway. Not in the fall. And then I saw the ads in the newspaper, heard them on the radio . . . the police department, if not the Marine Corps, is looking for a few good men."

"I've noticed the advertisements," Brewster Payne said. "And they aroused my curiosity to the point where I asked about them. The reason they are actively recruiting people is that the salary is quite low—"

"Thanks to you," Matt said, "that really isn't a problem for me."

"Yes, I suppose that's true," Payne said.

"I went out and got drunk with a cop last night."

"After you left the Moffitts', you mean? I thought maybe you would come home."

"I wanted to be alone, so I went to the bar in the Hotel Adelphia. It's a great place to be alone."

"And there you met the policeman? And he talked you into the police?"

"No. I'd met him that afternoon before. At Uncle Dick's house. Mr. Coughlin introduced us. Staff Inspector Wohl. He was wounded, too. He was a friend of Uncle Dick's, and he was there . . . at the Waikiki Diner. I think he was probably in the Adelphia bar to be alone, too. I spoke to him at the bar."

"Wohl?" Brewster Payne parroted.

"Peter Wohl," Matt said. "You know him?"

"I think I've heard the colonel mention him," Payne said. "Younger man? The word the colonel used was 'polished.' "

"He would fit in with your bright young men," Matt said. "If that's what you mean."

"I don't know how you manage to make 'bright young men' sound like a pejorative," Brewster Payne said, "but you do."

"I know why you like them," Matt said. "Imitation is the most sincere form of flattery. If you started chewing tobacco this morning, they'd all be chawin' 'n' spitting by noon."

Payne chuckled. "Is it that bad?"

"Yes, it is," Matt said.

"You said you drank with Inspector Wohl?"

"Yeah. He's a very nice guy."

"And you discussed your joining the police department?"

"Briefly," Matt said. "I am sure I gave him the impression I was drunk, or stupid, or burning with a childish desire to avenge Uncle Dutch. Or all of the above."

"But you're still thinking about it?" Payne asked, and then went on without waiting for a reply. "It would be a very important decision, Matt. Deserving of a good deal of careful thought. Pluses and minuses. Long-term ramifications . . .''

He stopped when he saw the look on Matt's face.

"I have joined the police department," Matt said. *"Fait accompli,* or nearly so."

"How did you manage to do that, since last night? You can't just walk in and join, can you? Or can you?"

"I got to bed about two last night," Matt said. "And at half past five this morning, I was wide awake. So I went for a long walk. At five minutes after eight, I found myself downtown, in front of Wanamaker's. And I was hungry. There's a place in Suburban Station that serves absolutely awful hot dogs and really terrible 'orange drink' twenty-four hours a day. Just what I had to have, so I cut through City Hall, and that was my undoing."

"I don't understand," Payne said.

"The cops have a little recruiting booth set up there," Matt said, "presumably to catch the going-to-work crowd. So I saw it, and figured what the hell, it wouldn't hurt to get some real information. Five minutes later, I was upstairs in City Hall, taking the examination."

"That quickly?"

"I was a live one," Matt said. "Anyway, there are several requirements to get in the police department. From what I saw, aside from not having a police record, the most important is having resided within the city limits for a year. I passed that with flying colors, since I gave the Deke house as my address for my new driver's license, and that was more than a year ago. Next came the examination itself, with which I had some difficulty, since I had to answer serious posers like how many eggs would I have if I divided a dozen eggs by six. But I got through that, too. At eleven, I'm supposed to be in the Municipal Services Building, across from City Hall, for a physical, and, I think, some kind of an interview with a shrink."

"That's all there is to it?"

"Well, they took my fingerprints, and are going to check me out with the FBI, and there's some kind of background investigation they'll conduct here, but for all practical purposes, yes, that's it.''

"I wonder how your mother is going to react to this?''

"I don't know,'' Matt said.

"She lost a husband who was a policeman,'' Brewster Payne said. "That's going to be on her mind.''

Matt grunted.

"I want to do it, Dad, at least to try it.''

"You've considered, of course, that you might not like it? I don't know what they do with rookie policemen, of course, but I would suspect it's like anything else, that you start out doing the unpleasant things.''

"I didn't really want to go in the marines, Dad,'' Matt said. "Not until after they told me they didn't want me, anyway. It was just something you did, like go to college. But I really *want* to be a cop.''

Brewster Payne cocked his head thoughtfully and made a grunting noise.

"Well, I don't like it, and I won't be a hypocrite and say I do,'' Brewster Payne said.

"I didn't think you would,'' Matt said. "I sort of hoped you would understand.''

"The terms are not mutually exclusive,'' Payne said. "I do understand, and I don't like it. Would you like to hear what I really think?''

"Please.''

"I think that you will become a police officer, and because this is your nature, you will do the very best you can. And I think in . . . say a year . . . that you will conclude you don't really want to spend the rest of your life that way. If that happens, and you do decide to go to law school, or do something entirely different—''

"Then it wouldn't be wasted, is that what you mean?'' Matt interrupted.

"I was about to say the year would be *very valuable* to you,'' Brewster Payne said. "Now that I think about it, far more valuable than a year in Europe, which was a carrot I was considering dangling in front of your nose to talk you out of this.''

"That's a very tempting carrot," Matt said.

"The offer remains open," Payne said. "But to tell you the truth, I would be disappointed in you if you took it. It remains open because of your mother."

"Yeah," Matt said, exhaling.

"And also for my benefit," Brewster Payne said. "When your brothers and sister come to me, and they will, crying 'Dad, how could you let him do that?' I will be able to respond that I did my best to talk you out of it, even including a bribe of a year in Europe."

"I hadn't even thought about them," Matt said.

"I suggest you had better. You can count, I'm sure, on your sister trying to reason with you, and when that fails, screaming and breaking things."

Matt chuckled.

"I will advance the proposition, which I happen to believe, that what you're doing is both understandable, and with a little bit of luck, might turn out to be a very profitable thing for you to do."

"Thank you," Matt said.

Brewster Payne stood up and offered his hand to Matt.

Matt started to take it, but stopped. They looked at each other, and then Brewster Payne opened his arms, and Matt stepped into them, and they hugged each other.

"Dad, you're great," Matt said.

"I know," Brewster Payne said. He thought, *I don't care who his father was; this is my own, beloved, son.*

When Peter Wohl walked into Homicide, Detective Jason Washington signaled that Captain Henry C. Quaire, commanding officer of the Homicide Division, was in his office and wordlessly asked if he should tell him Wohl was outside.

Wohl shook his head, no, and mimed drinking a cup of coffee. Washington went to a Mr. Coffee machine, poured coffee, and then, still without speaking, made gestures asking Wohl if he wanted cream or sugar. Wohl shook his head again, no, and Washington carried the coffee to him.

Wohl nodded his thanks, and Washington bowed solemnly.

"We should paint our faces white," Wohl said, chuckling, "and set up on the sidewalk."

"Well, we'd probably make more money doing that than we do on the job," Washington said. "Mimes probably take more home in their begging baskets every day than we do in a week."

Wohl chuckled, and then asked, "Who's in there with him?"

"Mitell," Washington said. "You hear about that job? The old Italian guy?"

Wohl shook his head no.

"Well, he died. We just found out—Mitell told me as he went in that he just got the medical examiner's report—of natural causes. But his wife was broke, and didn't have enough money to bury him the way she thought he was entitled to be buried. So she dragged him into the basement, wrapped him in Saran Wrap, and waited for the money to come in. That was three months ago. A guy from the gas works smelled him, and called the cops."

"Jesus Christ!" Wohl said.

"The old lady can't understand why everybody's so upset," Washington said. "After all, it was *her* basement and *her* husband."

"Oh, God." Wohl laughed, and Washington joined him, and then Washington said what had just popped into Wohl's mind.

"Why are we laughing?"

"Otherwise, we'd go crazy," Wohl said.

"How did I do with the TV lady?" Washington asked.

"She told me she thought you were a very nice man, Jason," Wohl said.

"I thought she was a very nice lady," Washington said. "She looks even better in real life than she does on the tube."

"I don't suppose anything has happened?" Wohl asked.

"Gerald Vincent Gallagher's under a rock someplace,"

Washington said. "He'll have to come out sooner or later. I'll let you know the minute I get anything."

"Who's got the Nelson job?" Wohl asked.

"Tony Harris," Washington said. "Know him?"

Wohl nodded.

Detective Jason Washington thought that he was far better off, the turn of the wheel, so to speak, than was Detective Tony Harris, to whom the wheel had given the faggot hacking job.

The same special conditions prevailed, the close supervision from above, though for different reasons. The special interest in the Moffitt job came because Dutch was a cop, and it came from within the department. If Dutch hadn't been a cop, and the TV lady hadn't been there when he got shot, the press wouldn't really have given a damn. It would have been a thirty-second story on the local TV news, and the story would probably have been buried in the back pages of the newspapers.

But the Nelson job had everything in it that would keep it on the TV and in the newspapers for a long time. For one thing, it was gory. Whoever had done in Nelson had been over the edge; they'd really chopped up the poor sonofabitch. That in itself would have been enough to make a big story about it; the public likes to read about "brutal murders." But Nelson was rich, the son of a big shot. He lived in a luxurious apartment. And there was the (interesting coincidence) tie-in with the TV lady. She'd found the body, and since everybody figured they knew her from the TV, it was as if someone they knew personally had found it.

And so far, they didn't know who did it. Everybody could take a vicarious chill from the idea of having somebody break into an apartment and chop somebody up with knives. And if it came out that Jerome Nelson was homosexual, that would make it an even bigger story. Jason Washington didn't think it would come out (the father owned a newspaper and a TV station, and it seemed logical that out of respect for him, the other newspapers and TV stations would soft-pedal that); but if it did, what the papers would have was sexual perversion as well as a brutal murder among the aristocracy, and they would milk that for all they could get out of it.

But that wasn't Tony Harris's real problem, as Jason Washington saw it. Harris's real problem was his sergeant, Bill Chedister, who spent most of his time with his nose up Lieutenant Ed DelRaye's ass, and, more important, DelRaye himself. So far as Washington was concerned, DelRaye was an ignorant loudmouth, who was going to take the credit for whatever Tony Harris did right, and see that Harris got the blame for the investigation not going as fast as the brass thought it should go.

Washington thought that what happened between DelRaye and the TV woman was dumb, for a number of reasons, starting with the basic one that you learn more from witnesses if you don't piss them off. Threatening to break down her door and calling for a wagon to haul her to the Roundhouse was even dumber.

In a way, Washington was sorry that Peter Wohl had shown up and calmed things down. DelRaye thus escaped the wrath that would have been dumped on him by everybody from the commissioner down for getting the TV station justifiably pissed off at the cops.

Washington also thought that it was interesting that DelRaye had let it get around that Wohl had been "half-drunk" when he had shown up. Jason Washington had known Wohl ten, fifteen years, and he had never seen him drunk in all that time. But accusing Wohl of having been drunk was just the sort of thing a prick like DelRaye would do, especially if he himself had been. And if DelRaye had been drunk, that would explain his pissing off the TV woman.

Washington admired Wohl, for a number of reasons. He liked the way he dressed, for one thing, but, far more important, he thought Wohl was smart. Jason Washington habitually studied the promotion lists, not only to see who was on them, but to see who had done well. Peter Wohl had been second on his sergeant's list, first on his lieutenant's list, third on his captain's list, and first again on the staff inspector's list. That was proof enough that Wohl was about as smart a cop as they came, but also that he had kept his party politics in order, which sometimes wasn't easy for someone who was an absolutely straight arrow, as Washington believed Wohl to be.

Peter Wohl was Jason Washington's idea of what a good senior police officer should be; there was no question that Wohl (and quickly, because the senior ranks of the Department would soon be thinned out by retirement) would rise to chief inspector, and probably even higher.

As Wohl put his coffee cup to his lips, Captain Quaire's office door opened. Detective Mitell, a slight, wiry young man, came out, and Quaire, a stocky, muscular man of about forty, appeared in it. He spotted Wohl.

"Good morning, Inspector," he said. "I expect you want to see me?"

"When you get a free minute, Henry," Wohl said.

"Let me get a cup of coffee," Captain Quaire said, "and I'll be right with you."

Wohl waited until Quaire had carried his coffee mug into his office and then followed him in. Quaire put his mug on his desk, and then went to the door and closed it.

"I was told you would be around, Peter," he said, waving toward a battered chair. "But before we start that, let me thank you for last night."

"Thank me for what last night?" Wohl asked.

"I understand a situation developed on the Nelson job that could have been awkward."

"Where'd you hear that?"

Quaire didn't reply directly.

"My cousin Paul's with the Crime Lab. He was there," he said. "I had a word with Lieutenant DelRaye. I tried to make the point that knocking down witnesses' doors and hauling them away in a wagon is not what we of the modern enlightened law-enforcement community think of as good public relations."

Wohl chuckled, relieved that Quaire had heard about the incident from his own sources; after telling the commissioner what he had told him was off the record, he would have been disappointed if the commissioner had gone right to DelRaye's commanding officer with it.

"The lady was a little upset, but nothing got out of control."

"Was he drunk, Peter?"

I wonder if he got that, too, from his cousin Paul? And is Cousin Paul a snitch, or did Quaire tell him to keep his eye on DelRaye?

"No, I don't think so," Wohl replied, and added a moment later, "No, I'm sure he wasn't."

But I was. How hypocritical I am, in that circumstance. I wonder if anybody saw it, and turned me in?

"Okay," Quaire said. "That's good enough for me, Peter. Now what can I do for you to keep the commissioner off *your* back and Chief Lowenstein off mine?"

"Lowenstein said something to you about me? You said you expected me?" Wohl asked.

"Lowenstein said, quote, by order of the commissioner, you would be keeping an eye on things," Quaire said.

"Only as a spectator," Wohl said. "I'm to finesse both Miss Dutton and Mr. Nelson. I'm to keep Nelson up to date on how that job is going, and to make sure Miss Dutton is treated with all the courtesy an ordinary citizen of Philadelphia, who also happens to be on TV twice a day, can expect."

Quaire smiled. "That, the girl, might be very interesting," he said. "She's a looker, Peter. Nelson may be difficult. He's supposed to be a real sonofabitch."

"Do you think the Commissioner would rather have him mad at Peter Wohl than at Ted Czernick?" Wohl said. "I fell into this, Henry. I responded to the call at the Waikiki. My bad luck, I was on Roosevelt Boulevard."

"Well, what do you need?"

"I'm going from here to see Nelson," Wohl said. "I'd like to talk to the detective who has the job."

"Sure."

"If it's all right with you, Henry, I'd like to ask him to tell me when they need Miss Dutton in here. I don't want anybody saying, 'Get in the car, honey.' "

"Tony Harris got the Nelson job," Quaire said.

"I heard. Good man, from what I hear," Wohl said.

"Tony Harris is at the Nelson apartment," Quaire said. "You want me to get him in here?"

"I really have to talk to him before I see Nelson. Maybe the thing for me to do is meet him over there."

"You want to do that, I'll call him and tell him to wait for you."

"Please, Henry," Wohl said.

Staff Inspector Peter Wohl's first reaction when he saw Detective Anthony C. Harris was anger.

Tony Harris was in his early thirties, a slight and wiry man already starting to bald, the smooth youthful skin on his face already starting to crease and line. He was wearing a shirt and tie, and a sports coat and slacks that had probably come from the racks of some discount clothier several years before.

It was a pleasant spring day and Detective Harris had elected to wait for Inspector Wohl outside the crime scene, which had already begun to stink sickeningly of blood, on the street. Specifically, when Wohl passed through the Stockton Place barrier, Harris was sitting on the hood of Wohl's Jaguar XK-120, which was parked, top down, where he had left it last night.

There were twenty coats of hand-rubbed lacquer on the XK-120's hood, applied, one coat at a time, with a laborious rubdown between each coat, by Peter Wohl himself. *Only an ignorant asshole, with no appreciation of the finer things of life, would plant his gritty ass on twenty coats of hand-rubbed lacquer.*

Wohl screeched to a stop by the Jaguar, leaned across the seat, rolled down the window, and returned Tony Harris's pleasant smile by snapping, "Get your ass off my hood!"

Then he drove twenty feet farther down the cobblestoned street and stopped the LTD.

Looking a little sheepish, Harris walked to the LTD as Wohl got out.

"Jesus Christ, Tony!" Wohl fumed, still angry. "There's twenty coats of lacquer on there!"

"Sorry," Harris mumbled. "I didn't think."

"Obviously," Wohl said.

Wohl's anger died as quickly as it had flared. Tony Harris looked beat and worn down. Without consciously calling it up from his memory, what Wohl knew about Harris came into his mind. First came the important impression he had filed away, which was that Harris was a good cop, more important, one of the brighter Homicide detectives. Then he remembered hearing that after nine years of marriage and four kids, Mrs. Harris had caught Tony straying from the marital bed and run him before a judge who had awarded her both ears and the tail.

If I were Tony Harris, Peter Wohl thought, *who has to put in sixty, sixty-five hours a week to make enough money to pay child support with enough left over to pay for an "efficiency" apartment for myself, and some staff inspector, no older than I am, pulls rank and jumps my ass for scratching the precious paint on his precious sports car, I would be pissed. And rightly so.*

"Hell, Tony, I'm sorry," Wohl said, offering his hand. "But I painted that sonofabitch by myself. All twenty coats."

"I was wrong," Harris said. "I just wasn't thinking. Or I wasn't thinking about a paint job."

"I guess what I was really pissed about was my own stupidity," Wohl said. "I know better than using my own car on the job. Right after I saw you, I asked myself, 'Christ, what if it had rained last night?' "

"You took that TV woman out through the basement in her own car?" Harris asked.

"Yeah."

"It took DelRaye some time to figure that out," Harris said. "Talk about pissed."

"Well, I'm sorry he was," Wohl said. "But it was a vicious circle, the more pissed he got at her, the more pissed she got at him. I had to break it, and that seemed to be the best way to do it. The whole department would have paid for it for a long time.''

"I think maybe he was pissed because he knew his ass was showing," Harris said. "You can't push a dame like that around. She file a complaint?''

"No," Wohl said.

Harris shrugged.

"Did Captain Quaire say anything to you about me?" Wohl asked.

"He said it came from upstairs that you were to be in on it," Harris said.

"I've been temporarily transferred to the Charm Squad," Wohl said. "I'm to keep Miss Dutton happy, and to report daily to Mr. Nelson's father on the progress of your investigation."

Harris chuckled.

"What have you got, Tony?"

"He was a fag, I guess you know?"

"I met him," Wohl said.

"I want to talk to his boyfriend," Harris said. "We're looking for him. Very large black guy, big enough, strong enough, to cut up Nelson the way he was. His name, we think, is Pierre St. Maury. His birth certificate probably says John Jones, but that's what he called himself."

"You think he's the doer?"

"That's where I am now," Harris said. "The rent-a-cops told me that he spent the night here a lot; drove Nelson's car—cars—and probably had a key. There are no signs of forcible entry. And there's a burglar alarm. One of Nelson's cars is missing. A *Jaguar,* by the way, Inspector," Harris said, a naughty look in his eyes. "I put the Jag in NCIC."

The FBI's National Crime Information Center operated a massive computer listing details of crimes nationwide. If the Jaguar was found somewhere, or even stopped for a traffic violation, the information that it was connected with a crime in Philadelphia would be immediately available to the police officers involved.

"Screw you, Tony," Wohl said, and laughed.

"A new one," Harris went on. "An 'XJ6'?"

"Four-door sedan," Wohl furnished. "A work of art. Twenty-five, thirty thousand dollars."

Harris's face registered surprise at the price.

"Police radio is broadcasting the description every half hour," he went on. "I also ordered a subsector search. Nelson's other car is a Ford Fairlane convertible. That's in the garage."

"Lover's quarrel?" Wohl asked.

Harris held both palms upward in front of him, and made a gesture, like a scale in balance.

"Maybe," he said. "That would explain what he did to the victim. I think we have the weapons. They used one of those Chinese knives, you know, looks like a cleaver, but sharp as a razor?"

Wohl nodded.

"And another knife, a regular one, a butcher knife with a bone handle, which is probably what he used to stab him."

"You said 'maybe,' Tony," Wohl said.

"I'm just guessing, Inspector," Harris said.

"Go ahead," Wohl said.

"There was a lot of stuff stolen, or I think so. There's no jewelry to speak of in the apartment . . . some ordinary cuff links, tie clasps, but nothing worth any money. The victim wore rings, they're gone, we know that. No money in the wallet, or anywhere else that anybody could find. He probably had a watch, or watches, and there's none in there. And there was marks on the bedside table, probably a portable TV, that's gone."

"Leading up to what?"

"When two homosexuals get into something like this, they usually don't steal anything, too. I mean, not the boyfriend. They work off the anger and run. So maybe it wasn't the boyfriend."

"Or the boyfriend might be a cold-blooded sonofabitch," Wohl said.

"Yeah," Harris said, and made the balancing gestures again. "We got people looking for Mr. St. Maury," he went on. "And for the Jaguar. We're trying to find if he had any jewelry that was good enough to be insured, which would give us a description. Captain Quaire said you were going to see his father?"

"I'm going there as soon as I leave here," Wohl said. "I'll ask."

"I'd like to talk to him, too," Harris said.

"I think I'd better see him alone," Wohl thought out loud. "I'll tell him you'll want to see him. Maybe he can come up with some kind of a list of jewelry, expensive stuff in the apartment."

"You'll get the list?"

"No. I'll ask him to get it for you. This is your job, Tony. I'm not going to stick my nose in where it doesn't belong."

Harris nodded.

"But I would like to look around the apartment," Wohl said. "So when I see him, I'll know what I'm talking about."

"Sure," Harris said. He started toward the door. "I'm really sorry, Inspector, about sitting on your car."

"Forget it," Wohl said.

ELEVEN

The building housing the Philadelphia *Ledger* and the studios of WGHA-TV and WGHA-FM was on Market Street, near the Thirtieth Street Station, and built, Wohl recalled as he drove up to it, about the same time. It wasn't quite the marble Greek palace the Thirtieth Street Station was, but it was a large and imposing building.

He had been in it once before, as a freshman at St. Joseph's Prep, on a field trip. As he walked up to the entrance, he remembered that very clearly, a busload of boisterous boys, horsing around, getting whacked with a finger behind the ear by the priests when their decorum didn't meet the standards of Young Catholic Gentlemen.

There was a rent-a-cop standing by the revolving door, a receptionist behind a marble counter in the marble-floored lobby, and two more rent-a-cops standing behind her.

Wohl gave her his business card. It carried the seal of the City of Philadelphia in the upper left-hand corner, the legend POLICE DEPARTMENT CITY OF PHILADELPHIA in the lower left, and in the center his name, and below that, in slightly smaller letters, STAFF INSPECTOR. In the lower right-hand corner, it said INTERNAL SECURITY DIVISION FRANKLIN SQUARE and listed two telephone numbers.

It was an impressive card, and usually opened doors to wherever he wanted to go very quickly.

It made absolutely no impression on the receptionist in the Ledger Building.

"Do you have an appointment with Mr. Nelson, sir?" she asked, with massive condescension.

"I believe Mr. Nelson expects me," Wohl said.

She smiled thinly at him and dialed a number.

"There's a Mr. Wohl at Reception who says Mr. Nelson expects him."

There was a pause, then a reply, and she hung up the telephone.

"I'm sorry, sir, but you don't seem to be on Mr. Nelson's appointment schedule," the receptionist said. "He's a very busy man, as I'm sure—"

"Call whoever that was back and tell her *Inspector* Wohl, of the police department," Peter Wohl interrupted her.

She thought that over a moment, and finally shrugged and dialed the phone again.

This time, there was a longer pause before she hung up. She took a clipboard from a drawer, and a plastic-coated "Visitor" badge.

"Sign on the first blank line, please," she said, and turned to one of the rent-a-cops. "Take this gentleman to the tenth floor, please."

There was another entrance foyer when the elevator door was opened, behind a massive mahogany desk, and for a moment, Wohl thought he was going to have to go through the whole routine again, but a door opened, and a well-dressed, slim, gray-haired woman came through it and smiled at him.

"I'm Mr. Nelson's secretary, Inspector," she said. "Will you come this way, please?"

The rent-a-cop slipped into a chair beside the elevator door.

"I'm sorry about that downstairs," the woman said, smiling at him over her shoulder. "I think maybe you should have told her you were from the police."

"No problem," Peter said. It would accomplish nothing to tell her he'd given her his card with that information all over it.

Arthur J. Nelson's outer office, his secretary's office, was furnished with gleaming antiques, a Persian carpet, an oil portrait of President Theodore Roosevelt, and a startlingly lifelike stuffed carcass of a tiger, very skillfully mounted, so that, snarling, it appeared ready to pounce.

"He'll be with you just as soon as he can," his secretary said. "May I offer you a cup of coffee?"

"Thank you, no," Peter said, and then his mouth ran away with him. "I like your pussycat."

"Mr. Nelson took that when he was just out of college," she said, and pointed to a framed photograph on the wall. Wohl went and looked at it. It was of a young man, in sweat-soaked khakis, cradling his rifle in his arm, and resting his foot on a dead tiger, presumably the one now stuffed and mounted.

"Bengal," the secretary said—"That's a Bengal tiger."

"Very impressive," Wohl said.

He examined the tiger, idly curious about how they actually mounted and stuffed something like this.

What's inside? A wooden frame? A wire one? A plaster casting? Is that red tongue the real thing, preserved somehow? Or what?

Then he walked across the room and looked through the curtained windows. He could see the roof of Thirtieth Street Station, its classic Greek lines from that angle diluted somewhat by air-conditioning machinery and a surprising forest of radio antennae. He could see the Schuylkill River, with the expressway on this side and the boat houses on the far bank.

The left of the paneled double doors to Arthur J. Nelson's office opened, and four men filed out. They all seemed determined to smile, Wohl thought idly, and then he thought they had probably just had their asses eaten out.

A handsome man wearing a blue blazer and gray trousers appeared in the door. He was much older, of course, than the young man in the tiger photograph, and heavier, and there was now a perfectly trimmed, snow-white mustache on his lip, but Wohl had no doubt that it was Arthur J. Nelson.

Formidable, Wohl thought.

Arthur J. Nelson studied Wohl for a moment, carefully.

"Sorry to keep you waiting, Inspector," he said. "Won't you please come in?"

He waited at the door for Wohl and put out his hand. It was firm.

"Thank you for seeing me, Mr. Nelson," Wohl said. "May I offer my condolences?"

"Yes, you can, and that's very kind of you," Nelson said, as he led Wohl into his office. "But frankly, what I would prefer is a report that you found proof positive who the animal was who killed my son, and that he resisted arrest and is no longer among the living."

Wohl was taken momentarily aback.

What the hell. Any father would feel that way. This man is accustomed to saying exactly what he's thinking.

"I'm about to have a drink," Nelson said. "Will you join me? Or is that against the rules?"

"I'd like a drink," Peter said. "Thank you."

"I drink single-malt scotch with a touch of water," Nelson said. "But there is, of course, anything else."

"That would be fine, sir," Peter said.

Nelson went to a bar set into the bookcases lining one wall of his office. Peter looked around the room. A second wall was glass, offering the same view of the Schuylkill he had seen outside. The other walls were covered with mounted animal heads and photographs of Arthur J. Nelson with various distinguished and/or famous people, including the sitting president of the United States. There was one of Nelson with the governor of Pennsylvania, but not, Peter noticed, one of His Honor the Mayor Carlucci.

Nelson crossed the room to where Peter stood and handed him a squat, octagonal crystal glass. There was no ice.

"Some people don't like it," Nelson said. "Take a sip. If you don't like it, say so."

Wohl sipped. It was heavy, but pleasant.

"Very nice," he said. "I like it. Thank you."

"I was shooting stag in Scotland, what, ten years ago. The gillie drank it. I asked him, and he told me about it. Now I have them ship it to me. All the scotch you get here, you know, is a blend."

"It's nice," Peter said.

"Here's to vigilante justice, Inspector," Nelson said.

"I'm not sure I can drink to that, sir," Peter said.

"You can't, but I can," Nelson said. "I didn't mean to put you on a spot."

"If I wasn't here officially," Peter said, "maybe I would."

"If you had lost your only son, Inspector, like I lost mine, you *certainly* would. When something like this happens, terms like 'justice' and 'due process' seem abstract. What you want is vengeance."

"I was about to say I know how you feel," Peter said. "But of course, I don't. I can't. All I can say is that we'll do everything humanly possible to find whoever took your son's life."

"If I ask a straight question, will I get a straight answer?"

"I'll try, sir."

"How do you cops handle it psychologically when you do catch somebody you *know* is guilty of doing something horrible, obscene, unhuman like this, only to see him walk out of a courtroom a free man because of some minor point of law, or some bleeding heart on the bench?"

"The whole thing is a system, sir," Peter said, after a moment. "The police, catching the doer, the perpetrator, are only part of the system. We do the best we can. It's not our fault when another part of the system fails to do what it should."

"I have every confidence that you'll find whoever it was who hacked my son to death," Nelson said. "And then we both know what will happen. It will, after a long while, get into a courtroom, where some asshole of a lawyer will try every trick in the business to get him off. And if he doesn't, if the jury finds him guilty, and the judge has the balls to sentence him to the electric chair, he'll appeal, for ten years or so, and the odds are some yellow-livered sonofabitch of a governor will commute his sentence to life. I'm sure you know what it costs to keep a man in jail. About twice what it costs to send a kid to an Ivy League college. The taxpayers will provide this animal with three meals a day, and a warm place to sleep for the rest of his life."

Wohl didn't reply. Nelson drained his drink and walked to the bar to make another, then returned.

"Have you ever been involved in the arrest of someone who did something really terrible, something like what happened to my son?"

"Yes, sir."

"And were you tempted to put a .38 between his eyes right then and there, to save the taxpayers the cost of a trial, and/or lifelong imprisonment?"

"No, sir."

"Why not?"

"Straight answer?" Peter asked. Nelson nodded. "I could say because you realize that you would lower yourself to his level," Peter said, "but the truth is that you don't do it because it would cost you. They investigate all shootings, and—"

"Vigilante justice," Nelson interrupted, raising his glass. "Right now, it seems like a splendid idea to me."

He is not suggesting that I go out and shoot whoever killed his son. He is in shock, as well as grief, and as a newspaperman, he knows the way the system works, and now that he's going to be involved with the system himself, doesn't like it at all.

"It gets out of hand almost immediately," Peter said.

"Yes, of course," Nelson said. "Please excuse me, Inspector, for subjecting you to this. I probably should not have come to work, in my mental condition. But the alternative was sitting at home, looking out the window . . ."

"I understand perfectly, sir," Peter said.

"Have there been any developments?" Nelson asked.

"I came here directly from Stockton Place," Peter said, "where I spoke to the detective to whom the case has been assigned—"

"I thought it had been assigned to you," Nelson interrupted.

"No, sir," Peter said. "Detective Harris of the Homicide Division has been assigned to the case."

"Then what's your role in this? Ted Czernick led me to believe that you would be in charge."

"Commissioner Czernick has asked me to keep him advised, to keep you advised, and to make sure that Detective Harris has all the assistance he asks for," Wohl said.

"I was pleased," Nelson interrupted again. "I checked you out. You're in Internal Security, that sounds important whatever it means, and you're the man who caught the Honorable Mr. Housing Director Weaver and that Friend of Labor, J. Francis Donleavy, with both of their hands in the municipal cookie jar. And now you're telling me you're not on the case . . ."

"Sir, what it means is that Commissioner Czernick assigned the best available *Homicide* detective to the case. That's a special skill, sir. Harris is better equipped than I am to conduct the investigation—"

"That's why he's a detective, right, and you're an inspector?"

"And then the commissioner called me in and told me to drop whatever else I was doing, so that I could keep both you and him advised of developments, and so that I could provide Detective Harris with whatever help he needs," Wohl plunged on doggedly.

Arthur J. Nelson looked at Wohl suspiciously for a moment.

"I had the other idea," he said, finally. "All right, so what has Mr. Harris come up with so far?"

"Harris believes that a number of valuables have been stolen from the apartment, Mr. Nelson."

"He figured that out himself, did he?" Nelson said, angrily sarcastic. "What other reason could there possibly be than a robbery? My son came home and found his apartment being burglarized, and the burglar killed him. All I can say is that, thank God, his girl friend wasn't with him. Or she would be dead, too."

Girl friend? Jesus!

"Detective Harris, who will want to talk to you himself, Mr. Nelson, asked me if you could come up with a list of valuables, jewelry, that sort of thing, that were in the apartment."

"I'll have my secretary get in touch with the insurance company," Nelson said. "There must be an inventory around someplace."

"Your son's car, one of them, the Jaguar, is missing from the garage."

"Well, by now, it's either on a boat to Mexico, or gone through a dismantler's," Nelson snapped. "All you're going to find is the license plate, if you find that."

"Sometimes we get lucky," Peter said. "We're looking for it, of course, here and all up and down the Eastern Seaboard."

"I suppose you've asked his girl friend? It's unlikely, but possible that she might have it. Or for that matter, that it might be in the dealer's garage."

"You mentioned his girl friend a moment ago, Mr. Nelson," Wohl said, carefully, suspecting he was on thin ice. "Can you give me her name?"

"Dutton, Louise Dutton," Nelson said. "You *are* aware that she found Jerry? That she went into his bedroom, and found him like that?"

"I wasn't aware of a relationship between them, Mr.

Nelson," Peter said. "But I do know that Miss Dutton does not have Mr. Nelson's car."

"Miss Dutton is a prominent television personality," Nelson said. "It would not be good for her public image were it to become widely know that she and her gentleman friend lived in the same apartment building. I would have thought, however, that you would have been able to put two and two together."

Jesus Christ! Does he expect me to believe that? Does he believe it himself?

He looked at Nelson's face, and then understood: *He knows what his son was, and he probably knows that I know. I have just been given the official cover story. Arthur J. Nelson wants the fact that his son was homosexual swept under the rug. For his own ego, or maybe, even more likely, because there's a mother around. What the hell, my father would do the same thing.*

"Insofar as the *Ledger* is concerned," Nelson said, meeting Wohl's eyes, "every effort will be made to spare Miss Dutton any embarrassment. I can only hope my competition will be as understanding."

He obviously feels he can get to Louise, somehow, and get her to stand still for being identified as Jerome's girl friend. Well, why not? "Scratch my back and I'll scratch yours" works at all echelons.

"I understand, sir," Peter said.

"Thank you for coming to see me, Inspector," Arthur J. Nelson said, putting out his hand. "When I see Ted Czernick, I will tell him how much I appreciate your courtesy and understanding."

The translation of which is "Do what you're told, or I'll lower the boom on you."

Peter Wohl called Detective Tony Harris from a pay phone in the lobby of the Ledger Building and told him that Arthur J. Nelson's secretary was going to come up with a list of jewelry and other valuables that probably had been in the apartment, and that it would probably be ready by the time Harris could come to the Ledger Building.

And then he told Harris what Nelson had said about Louise Dutton being Jerome Nelson's girl friend, and warned him not to get into Jerome's sexual preference if there was any way it could be avoided. Somewhat surprising Wohl, Harris didn't seem surprised.

"Thanks for the warning," he said. "I can handle that."

"He also suggested that by now the Jaguar has been stripped," Wohl said.

"Could well be. They haven't found it yet, and Jaguars are pretty easy to spot; there aren't that many of them. Either stripped, or on a dock in New York or Baltimore waiting to get loaded on a boat for South America. I think we should keep looking."

Wohl did not mention to Harris Nelson's toast to vigilante justice, or his remark about what he really wanted to hear was that the doer had been killed resisting arrest. It was, more than likely, just talk.

When he hung up, he considered, and decided against, reporting to Commissioner Czernick about his meeting with Nelson. He really didn't have anything important to say.

Instead, he found the number in the phone book, dropped a dime in the slot, and called WCBL-TV.

He had nearly as much trouble getting Louise on the line as he had getting in to see Arthur J. Nelson, but finally her voice came over the line.

"Dutton."

Peter could hear voices and sounds in the background. Wherever she was, it wasn't a private office.

"Hi," Peter said.

"Hi," she breathed happily. "I hoped you would call!"

"You all right?"

"Ginger-peachy, now," she said. "What are you doing?"

"I just left Arthur J. Nelson," he said.

"Rough?"

"He told me you were Jerome's girl friend," Peter said.

"Oh, the poor man!" she said. "You didn't say anything?"

"No."

"So?"

"So?" he parroted.

"So why did you call?"

"I dunno," he said.

"What are you going to do now?" she asked.

"I've got to go by my office, and then figure out some way to get my car from where it's parked in front of your house," he said.

"I forgot about that," she said. "Why don't you pick me up here after I do the news at six? I could drive it to your place, or wherever."

"Where would I meet you?"

"Come on in," Louise said. "I'll tell them at reception."

"Okay," he said. "Thank you."

"Don't be silly," she said, and then added, "Peter, don't forget to pick up your uniform at the cleaners."

"Okay," he said, and chuckled, and the line went dead.

He realized, as he hung the telephone up, that he was smiling. More than that, he was very happy. There was something very touching, very intimate, in her concern that he not forget to pick up his uniform. Then he thought that if he had called Barbara Crowley and *she* had reminded him of it, he would have been annoyed.

Is this what being in love is like?

He went out of his way to get the uniform before he drove downtown, so that he really would not forget it.

He had not been at his desk in his office three minutes when Chief Inspector Dennis V. Coughlin slipped into the chair beside it.

"Jeannie was asking where you were last night, Peter," Coughlin said. "At the house."

"I wasn't up to it," Peter said. "And you know what happened later."

"You feel up to being a pallbearer?" Coughlin asked, evenly.

"If Jeannie wants me to, sure," Peter said.

"That's what I told her," Coughlin said. "Be at Marshutz & Sons about half past nine. The funeral's at eleven."

"I'll be there," Peter said. "Chief, my dad suggested I wear my uniform."

Chief Inspector Coughlin thought that over a moment.

"What did you decide about it?"

"Until I heard about being a pallbearer, I was going to wear it."

"I think it would nice, Peter, if we carried Dutch to his rest in uniform," Chief Inspector Coughlin said. "I'll call the wife and make sure mine's pressed."

Officer Anthony F. Caragiola, who was headed for the job on the four-to-midnight watch, glanced at his wristwatch, and walked into Gene & Jerry's Restaurant & Sandwiches across the street from the Bridge Street Terminal. There would be time for a cup of coffee and a sweet roll before he climbed the stairs to catch the elevated and go to work.

Officer Caragiola, who wore the white cap of the Traffic Division, had been a policeman for eleven years, and was now thirty-four years old. He was a large and swarthy man, whose skin showed the ravages of being outside day after day in heat and cold, rain and shine.

He eased his bulk onto one of the round stools at the counter, waved his fingers in greeting at the waitress, a stout, blond woman, and helped himself to a sweet roll from the glass case. He had lived three blocks away, now with his wife and four kids, for most of his life. When there was a problem at Gene & Jerry's, if one of the waitresses took sick, or one of the cooks, and his wife, Maria, could get somebody to watch the kids, she came and filled in.

The waitress put a china mug of coffee and three half-and-half containers in front of him.

"So how's it going?"

"Can't complain," Officer Caragiola said. "Yourself?"

She shrugged and smiled and walked away. Tony Caragiola carefully opened the three tubs of half-and-half and carefully poured them into his coffee, and then stirred it.

He heard a hissing noise, and looked at the black swinging doors leading to the kitchen. Gene was standing there, wiggling her fingers at him. Gene was Eugenia Santalvaria, a stout, black-haired woman in her fifties who had six months before buried her husband, Gerimino, after thirty-three years of marriage.

Caragiola slipped off the stool and, carrying his coffee with him, stepped behind the counter and walked to the doors to the kitchen.

"Tony, maybe it's something, maybe it ain't," Gene Santalvaria said, in English, and then switched to Italian. There were two bums outside, a big fat slob and a little guy that looked like a spic, she told him. They had been there for hours, sitting in an old Volkswagen. Maybe they were going to stick up the check-cashing place down the block, or maybe they were selling dope or something; every once in a while, one of them got out of the car and went up the stairs to the elevated, and then a couple of minutes later came back down the stairs and got back in the car. She didn't want to call the district, 'cause maybe it wasn't nothing, but since he had come in, she thought it was better she tell him.

"I'll have a look," Officer Caragiola said.

He left the kitchen and walked to the front of the restaurant and, sipping on his coffee, looked for a Volkswagen. There was two guys in it, one of them, a big fat slob with one of them hippie bands around his forehead, behind the wheel, slumped down in the seat as if he was asleep. And then the passenger door opened, and a little guy—she was right, he looked like a spic—got out and looked for traffic, and then walked across the street to the stairs to the elevated. Looked like a mean little fucker.

Officer Caragiola set his coffee on the counter and walked quickly out of Gene & Jerry's, and across the street, and up the stairs after him.

He got to the platform just as a train arrived. Everybody

on the platform got on it but the little spic. He acted as if he was waiting for somebody who might have ridden the elevated to the end of the line and just stayed on. If he did that, he would just go back downtown. If somebody like that was either buying or selling dope, that would be the way to do it.

Officer Caragiola ducked behind a stairwell so the little spic couldn't see him, and waited. People started coming up the stairs, filling up the platform, and then a train arrived from downtown and left, and then five minutes later reappeared on the downtown track. Everybody on the platform got on the train but the little spic.

Tony Caragiola came out from behind the stairwell and walked over to the little spic.

"Speak to you a minute, buddy?" he said.

"What about?"

Tony saw that the little spic was pissed. He probably knew all the civil rights laws about cops not being supposed to ask questions without reasonable cause.

"You want to tell me what you and your friend in the Volkswagen are doing?"

"Narcotics," the little spic said. "I'd rather not show you my I.D. Not here."

"Who's your lieutenant?" Tony asked.

"Lieutenant Pekach."

It was a name Officer Caragiola did not recognize.

"I think you better show me your ID," he said.

"Shit," the little spic said. He reached in his back pocket and came out with a plastic identity card. "Okay?" he said.

"The lady in the restaurant said you were acting suspicious," Tony Caragiola said.

"Yeah, I'll bet."

Officer Jesus Martinez put his ID back in his pocket and walked down the stairs. Officer Anthony Caragiola walked twenty feet behind him. He went back in Gene & Jerry's and told Gene everything was all right, not to worry about it. Then he went back across the street and climbed the stairs to catch the elevated to go to work.

Officer Martinez got back into the Volkswagen. He glowered for a full minute at Officer Charley McFadden, who was asleep and snoring. Then he jabbed him, hard, with his fingers, in his ribs. McFadden sat up, a look of confusion on his face.

"What's up?"

"I thought you would like to know, asshole, that the lady in the restaurant called the cops on us. Said we look suspicious."

At quarter to five, Peter Wohl drove to Marshutz & Sons. As he walked up the wide steps to the Victorian-style building, the Moffitts—Jean, the kids, and Dutch's mother—came out.

Jean Moffitt was wearing a black dress and a hat with a veil. The kids were in suits. Gertrude Moffitt was in a black dress and hat, but no veil.

"Hello, Peter," Jean Moffitt said, and offered a gloved hand.

"Jeannie," Peter said.

"You know Mother Moffitt, don't you?"

"Yes, of course," Peter said. "Good afternoon, Mrs. Moffitt."

"We're going out for a bite to eat," Gertrude Moffitt said. "Before people start coming after work."

"I'm very sorry, Mrs. Moffitt, about Dick," Peter said.

"His close personal friends, some of who I didn't even know," Gertrude Moffitt went on, "were at the house last night."

It was a rebuke.

"I'm sorry I couldn't come by last night, Jeannie," Peter said.

"Your mother explained," Jeannie Moffitt said. "Did Denny Coughlin ask you?"

"About being a pallbearer?" Peter asked, and when she nodded, went on: "Yes, and I'm honored."

"Dennis Coughlin was a sergeant when he carried my John, God rest his soul, to his grave," Gertrude Moffitt said. "And now, as a chief inspector, he'll be doing the same for my Richard."

"Mother, would you please put the kids in the car?" Jean Moffitt said. "I want a word with Inspector Wohl."

That earned Jeannie a dirty look from Mother Moffitt, but it didn't seem to faze her. She returned the older woman's look, staring her down until she led the boys down the stairs.

"Tell me about the TV lady, Peter," Jeannie Moffitt said.

"I beg your pardon?"

"Isn't that why you didn't come by the house last night? You were afraid I'd ask you?"

"I don't know what you're talking about, Jeannie," Wohl said.

"I'm talking about Louise Dutton of Channel Nine," she said. "Was there something between her and Dutch? I have to know."

"Where did you hear that?"

"It's going around," she said. "I heard it."

"Well, you heard wrong," Peter said.

"You sound pretty sure," Jeannie Moffitt accused sarcastically.

"I know for sure," Peter said.

"Peter, don't lie to me," Jeannie said.

"Louise Dutton and me, as my mother would put it, if she knew, and doesn't, are 'keeping company,' " Wohl said. "That's how I know."

Her eyes widened in surprise.

"Really?" she said, and he knew she believed him.

"Not for public consumption," Peter said. "The gossips got their facts wrong. Wrong cop."

"I thought you were seeing that nurse, what's her name, Barbara—"

"Crowley," Peter furnished. "I was."

"Your mother doesn't know?"

"And, for the time being, I would like to keep it that way," Peter said.

She looked in his eyes, and then stood on her toes and kissed his cheek.

"Oh, I'm glad I ran into you," she said.

"Dutch liked being married to you, Jeannie," Wohl said.

"Oh, God, I hope so," she said.

She turned and ran down the stairs.

Wohl entered the funeral home. The corridors were crowded with people, a third of the men in uniform. And, Peter thought, two-thirds of the men in civilian clothing were cops, too.

He waited in line, signed the guest book, and then made his way to the Green Room.

Dutch's casket was nearly hidden by flowers, and there was a uniformed Highway Patrolman standing at parade rest at each end of the coffin. Wohl waited in line again, until it was his turn to drop to his knees at the prie-dieu in front of the casket.

Without thinking about it, he crossed himself. Dutch was in uniform. *He looks,* Wohl thought, *as if he just came from the barber's.*

And then he had another irreverent thought: *I just covered your ass again, Dutch. One last time.*

And then, surprising him, his throat grew very tight, and he felt his eyes start to tear.

He stayed there, with his head bent, until he was sure he was in control of himself, and then got up.

TWELVE

Karl August Fenstermacher had immigrated to the United States in 1837, at the age of two. His father had indentured himself for a period of four years to Fritz W. Diehl, who had gone to the United States from the same village, Mochsdorf, in the Kingdom of Bavaria, twenty years previously. Mr. Diehl had entered the sausage business in Philadelphia, and prospered to the point where he needed good reliable help. His brother Adolph, back in Mochsdorf, had recommended Johann Fenstermacher to him, and the deal was struck:

Diehl would provide passage money for Fenstermacher and his wife and three children, provide living quarters for them over the shop, and see that they were clothed and fed. At the end of four years, provided Fenstermacher proved to be a faithful, hardworking employee, he would either offer young Fenstermacher a position with the firm, or give him one hundred dollars, so that he could make his way in life somewhere else.

At the end of two years, instead of the called-for four, Fritz released Johann Fenstermacher from his indenture, coinciding with the opening of Fritz's stall (Fritz Diehl Fine Wurstware & Fresh Meats) at the Twelfth Street Market. In 1860, when Diehl opened an abbatoir just outside the city limits, the firm was Diehl & Fenstermacher, Meat Purveyors to the Trade. Both men believed that God had been as good to them as he could be.

They were wrong. The Civil War came, and with it a limitless demand for smoked and tinned meats and hides. They became wealthy. Fritz Diehl took a North German Lloyd steamer from Philadelphia to Bremen, and went back to Mochsdorf, where he presented St. Johann's Lutheran Church with a stained glass window. He died of a stroke in Mochsdorf ten days before the window was to be officially consecrated.

His widow elected to remain in Germany. From that day until her death, Johann Fenstermacher scrupulously sent her half the profits from the firm, although, after several years, he changed the name to J. Fenstermacher & Sons. The name was retained on the Old Man's death, just before the Spanish-American War, by Karl Fenstermacher, who bought out his brother's interest, and formed J. Fenstermacher & Sons, Incorporated.

He turned over the business to his son Fritz in 1910, when he was seventy-five. He lived six more years. In early 1916, when it was clear that his father was failing, Fritz Fenstermacher went to Francisco Scalamandre, whose firm was to stonecutting in Philadelphia what J. Fenstermacher & Sons, Inc., was to the meat trade, and ordered the construction of a suitable monument where his mother and father could lie together for eternity.

It was erected in Cedar Hill Cemetery on Cheltenham Avenue in Northeast Philadelphia, of the finest Barre, Vermont, granite. Mr. Scalamandre's elder son Guigliemo himself sculpted the ten-foot-tall statue of the Angel Gabriel, arms spread, which was mounted on the roof of the tomb, and personally supervised the installation of both the stained glass windows and the solid bronze doors.

Karl Fenstermacher was laid to his last rest there on December 11, 1916, in a snowstorm. His wife followed him in death, and into the tomb, eight months later.

They lay there together, undisturbed, in bronze caskets in a marble tomb behind the solid bronze doors until several months before the shooting in the Waikiki Diner, when Gerald Vincent Gallagher, running away from both the police and an Afro-American dealer in heroin found himself leaning against the solid bronze doors.

It wasn't safe to leave the cemetery yet, Gerald Vincent Gallagher had decided; then both the cops and the jigaboo were really after his ass, but unless he could get inside somewhere, out of the fucking wind and snow, he was going to freeze to fucking death.

Gerald Vincent Gallagher had managed, without much effort at all, to pick the solid bronze lock mechanism on the solid brass door with a sharpened screwdriver he just happened to have with him; and he had spent the next four hours sitting, shivering but not freezing, and out of the snow, on top of Karl Fenstermacher's tomb.

The next time he went back to Cedar Hill Cemetery, he was prepared. He had cans of Sterno with him, and a dozen big, thick, white, pure beeswax candles he had lifted from St. George's Greek Orthodox Church. Both burned without smoke, and it was amazing how much heat that jelly alcohol, or whatever the fuck it was, made.

And the first thing Gerald Vincent Gallagher had thought when he ran out of the Waikiki Diner was that if he could only make it out to the fucking cemetery, he would be all right. It was not the first, or the fifth, time he had run from the cops and hidden in the cemetery until things cooled off.

When he was in Karl and Maria Fenstermacher's mausoleum, and the fear was mostly gone, and he got his breath back, and he had time to think things over, the first thing he thought was that when he got together with Dorothy Ann again, he really should kick the dumb bitch's ass. All she was supposed to do was stay outside and look out for the cops. Now she'd really gotten their ass in a crack. All the charge would have been was robbery. There was nothing like that on his record. Any public defender with half the brains he was born with could have plea-bargained that down to something that would have meant no more than a year in Holmesburg Prison, and with a little bit of luck, maybe even probation.

But the minute she had fired that fucking gun, she had really got them in fucking trouble. About the dumbest fucking thing she could have done was take a shot at a cop. That made it attempted murder, and the goddamned cops would pull every string they could to get them sent before Judge Mitchell "Hanging Mitch" Roberts, who thought that taking a poke, much less a shot, at a cop was worse than blowing up the Vatican with the pope in it.

Thank Christ, she had missed. The last thing he saw when he ran through the Waikiki Diner was the cop, or the detective, whatever the sonofabitch was, was him shooting Dorothy Ann. If she had hit the sonofabitch, that would be the goddamned end. He would be an old man before they let him out.

Another thought entered his mind. Maybe the cop had hit her and killed her when he shot back. It would serve the dumb bitch right, and if she was dead, she couldn't identify him. The cashier had been scared shitless; she wouldn't be able to remember him, much less identify him. The best thing that could have happened was that both Dorothy Ann and the cop was both dead. Then nobody could identify him.

The trouble with that was there was *another* fucking law that said if anybody got killed during a robbery, or some other felony, even somebody doing the robbery, it was just as if they had shot him theirselves. So if the cop had killed Dorothy Ann, they could hang a murder rap on him.

In the times he had been in the mausoleum before (almost for a way to pass the time), Gerald Vincent Gallagher had taken his screwdriver and worked on the lead that held the little pieces of stained glass in place, so that he could remove a little piece of glass and have a look around. There was stained glass in all four walls of the place.

He hadn't been in the mausoleum half an hour before he saw, through the hole where he'd taken a piece of stained glass out, a police car driving slowly through Cedar Hill Cemetery. Not just a police car, but a Highway Patrol car, he could tell that because there was two cops in it, and regular cop cars had only one cop in them. Those Highway Patrol cops was real mean motherfuckers, who would as soon shoot you as not.

He told himself that there was really nothing to worry about, that it wasn't the first time a cop car had driven through the cemetery looking for him, and they wouldn't find him this time any more than they had before. They were thinking he might be hiding behind a tombstone, or a tree, or something. They wouldn't think he was inside one of the marble houses, or whatever the fuck they were called. They would drive through once, or maybe twice, or maybe a couple of cop cars would drive through. But they would give up sooner or later.

Everybody would give up sooner or later. This wasn't the only robbery that had happened in Philadelphia. There would be other robberies and auto accidents on Roosevelt Boulevard and Frankford Avenue, or some guy beating up on his wife, and they would go put their noses into that and ease off on looking for him.

The thing to do was sit tight until they did ease off, and then get the fuck out of town. He had money, 380 bucks. The reason they had stuck up the Waikiki Diner in the first place was to come up with another lousy 120 bucks. The connection had shit, good shit, but he wanted 500 bucks, and wasn't about to trust them for the 120 they was short, until they sold enough of it on the street to pay him back.

If the cocksucker had only been reasonable, none of this would have happened!

Gerald Vincent Gallagher began to suspect, although he tried not to think about it, that he was really in the deep shit when not only did more cop cars, Highway Patrol and regular District ones, keep driving through the cemetery, but cops on foot came walking through. That had never happened before.

There was no place he could run to, so he put the little pieces of stained glass back into the holes, and sat down on the floor with his back against the wall and just hoped no one would come looking for him inside.

It grew dark, and that made things a little better, but he decided that the best thing to do was play it cool, and not light one of the Greek candles. If there was a cop looking, he would maybe see the light.

He took off his jacket and made a pillow of it, and lay down on the floor of the mausoleum and went to sleep.

Sometime in the middle of the night, he woke up, and looked out, and saw headlights coming into the cemetery. Then the car stopped and the headlights went out. A couple of minutes later, while he was still figuring out what the first car was doing, there were more headlights, and another car drove in. He saw that the first car was a cop car, and now he could see they were both cop cars. And a few minutes after that, a third cop car came in and parked beside the other two.

And then he understood what was going on. *The cops were fucking off, that's what they were doing! They were supposed to be out patrolling the streets, looking for crooks, and instead they were in the goddamned cemetery, taking a fucking nap!*

Gerald Vincent Gallagher was outraged at this blatant example of dereliction of duty.

In the morning, he woke up hungry, but it would be a goddamned fool thing to do to try to leave just yet, so he just waited. At noon, there was a funeral about a hundred yards away. Actually, they started getting ready for the funeral a little after eight, digging the hole, and then lowering a concrete vault in it, and then putting the phony grass over the pile of dirt they'd taken out of the hole, and then putting up a tent, and the whatever it was called they used to lower the casket into the hole.

Gerald Vincent Gallagher had never seen anything like that before, and it was interesting, and it helped to pass the time. So did the funeral. It was some kind of cockamamie Protestant funeral, and the minister prayed a lot, and loud, and then when that was finally over, everybody who had come to the funeral just stayed around the hole, kissing and shaking hands, and talking and smiling, like they was at a party, instead of a funeral.

Finally, they left, and the people from the funeral home put some kind of a lever into the machine with the casket sitting on it, and the casket started dropping into the hole. When it was all the way in, they unhitched one end of the green web belts that had held the casket up, and pulled them free from under the casket.

A truck appeared and they put the machine on it, and then the folding chairs, and then took down the tent and loaded that on, and finally picked up the phony grass and put that on the truck. Then that truck left, and the one that had lowered the concrete vault into the hole appeared again. A guy got out and mixed cement or something in a plastic bucket, and then got into the hole with the bucket and a trowel and spread the cement on the bottom of the vault. Then they lowered the lid on the vault, jumped up and down on the lid, and then they left.

Next came a couple of old men from the cemetery who shoveled the dirt into the hole, wetting it down with a hose so that it would all go back in, and finally putting the real grass on top of that and watering *that* down. There was still a lot of dirt left over, and Gerald Vincent Gallagher supposed they would come back and cart that off some-where.

By then it was four o'clock, and he was fucking *starved!*

He was just about to leave the mausoleum when a car drove up, and three people got out. It looked to him like a father and his two sons. They walked over to the grave and the old man stood there for a minute and started to cry. Then the younger ones started to cry. Finally, the younger ones put their arms around the older one, the one who was probably the father, and led him back to the car and drove off.

Gerald Vincent Gallagher waited until he was sure they wouldn't change their minds and come back, and looked carefully in all four directions to make sure there wasn't a cop car making another slow trip through Cedar Hill, and then, after first carefully replacing all the stained glass, and bending the lead over it so the wind wouldn't blow it out, quickly opened the bronze doors, grunting with the effort, grunted again as he pushed them closed, and then started walking to the narrow macadam road that led to the exit.

He passed the grave he had watched filled. There were what he guessed must be a thousand bucks' worth of flowers on it, and around it, just waiting to rot. He thought that was a hell of a lot of money to be just thrown away like that.

Five minutes later he was at the Bridge & Pratt Streets Terminal. A clock in a store window said ten minutes after five. This had worked out okay. The terminal, and the subway itself, would be crowded with people coming from work, or going downtown. He could hide in the crowd. He would be careful, when the train pulled into the station, to look for any cop that might be on it, and make sure he didn't get on that car.

Then he would ride downtown to Market Street, walk underground to the Suburban Station, and ride from there to Thirtieth Street Station. There he would buy a ticket on the Pennsylvania Railroad to Baltimore. He would find out when it left, and then go to the men's crapper, where he would stay until it was time for the train to leave. Then a quick trip up to the platform, onto the train, and he would be home free.

In Baltimore, he knew a couple of connections, if they were still in business, and he could get a little something to straighten him out. He was getting a little edgy, that way, and that would be the first thing to do, get himself straightened out. And then he would decide what to do next.

He walked past a place called Tates, where the smell of pizza made his stomach turn. He stopped and went to the window and ordered a slice of pizza and a Coke. When the Coke came, he drank it down. He hadn't realized he had been that thirsty.

"Do that again," he said, pushing the container toward the kid behind the counter, and laying another dollar bill on the counter. There was a newsstand right beside Tates called—somebody thought he was a fucking wit—Your Newsstand.

Gerald Vincent Gallagher drank some of the second Coke, then set the container down on the top of a garbage can and, taking a bite of the pizza, stepped to a newspaper rack offering the *Philadelphia Daily News,* to get a quick look at the headline, maybe there would be something about the Waikiki Diner in it.

There was. There were two photographs on the front page. One was of some cop in uniform, and the other was of Gerald Vincent Gallagher. The headline, in great big letters, asked, "COP KILLER?"

Under the photographs was a story that began, *"A massive citywide search is on for Gerald Vincent Gallagher, suspected of being the bandit who got away when Police Captain Richard C. Moffitt was shot to death in the Waikiki Diner yesterday."*

Gerald Vincent Gallagher's stomach tied in a painful knot. He felt a cold chill, and as if the hair on his neck was crawling. He spit out the piece of pizza he had been chewing, and carefully laid the piece in his hand on the garbage can beside the Coke container.

Then he started walking past Your Newsstand. At the end of the building was a glass door leading to a bingo parlor upstairs, and then the covered stairs to the subway platform.

Gerald Vincent Gallagher looked at the door and saw in it a reflection of the street. And something caught his eye. A big, fat sonofabitch was looking right at him as he came running across the street. The fat guy looked familiar and for a moment, Gerald Vincent Gallagher thought he was a guy he had done business with, but then the fat guy sort of kneeled down, and jerked up his pants leg, and pulled a gun from an ankle holster.

Then, as he started running again, he shouted, "Hold it right there, Gallagher, or I'll blow your ass away!"

Fuck him, Gerald Vincent Gallagher thought. *That fucking narc isn't going to shoot that gun with all these people around!*

He ran up the stairs toward the subway platform. With a little bit of luck, there would be a train there and he could get on it, and away.

The Bridge & Pratt Streets Terminal is the end of the line for the subway. The tracks are elevated, above Frankford Avenue, and widen as they reach the station. There is a center passenger platform, with stairs leading down to the lower level of the terminal, between the tracks, and a second passenger platform, to the right of the center platform. That way, passengers can exit incoming from downtown trains through doors on both sides of the car. Passengers heading downtown all have to board trains from the center platform.

After incoming trains from downtown Philadelphia offload their passengers from the right (in direction of movement) track, they move several hundred yards farther on, where they stop, the crews move to the rear end of the train (which now becomes the front end), and move back, now on the left track, to the station, where they pick up downtown-bound passengers.

The lower level of the terminal contains ticket booths, and two stairwells, one descending to the ground on either side of Frankford Avenue.

When Officer Charley McFadden spotted Gerald Vincent Gallagher shoving pizza in his face in front of Your Newsstand, he was sitting in his Volkswagen, which was parked in front of Gene & Jerry's Restaurant & Sandwiches on Pratt Street, fifty feet to the north of Frankford Avenue.

Officer Jesus Martinez was inside Gene & Jerry's sitting at the counter eating a ham and cheese sandwich, no mayonnaise or mustard or butter, just the ham and cheese and maybe a little piece of lettuce on whole wheat bread.

He had his mouth full of ham and cheese when he saw Charley erupt from the Volkswagen.

He swore, in Spanish, and spit out the sandwich, and jumped up and ran toward the door. As soon as he was through it, he dropped to his knees and drew his pistol from his ankle holster.

He had not seen Gerald Vincent Gallagher, but he knew that Charley McFadden must have seen him, for Charley, moving with speed remarkable for his bulk, was now headed up the stairs to the subway station.

Two cars and a truck, going like the hammers of hell, delayed Officer Martinez's passage across Pratt Street by thirty seconds. By the time he made it across, Charley McFadden was nowhere in sight. All he could see was people with wide eyes wondering what the fuck was going on.

"Police! Police!" Officer Martinez shouted as he forced his way through a crowd of people trying to leave the station.

He jumped over the turnstile, and then was forced to make a choice between stairs leading to the tracks for trains arriving *from* downtown and tracks for trains *headed* downtown. Deciding that it would be far more likely that McFadden and whoever it was he was chasing—almost certainly, Gerald Vincent Gallagher—would be on the downtown platform, he ran up those stairs.

Officer McFadden, who had lost sight of Gerald Vincent Gallagher as he ran up the stairs from Pratt Street, had made the same decision. Already starting to puff a little, he ran onto the platform. A downtown train had just pulled into the station; the platform was crowded with people in the process of boarding it.

Holding his pistol at the level of his head, muzzle pointed toward the sky, Charley McFadden ran down the train looking for Gallagher. He had reached the last car, and hadn't seen him, and had just about decided the little fucker was on the train, that he had missed him, and would have to start at the first car and work his way back through it when he did see him.

Gallagher was in the middle of the tracks, the other

tracks, the incoming from downtown tracks. As Mc-
Fadden ran to the side of the center platform, Gerald Vincent Gallagher boosted himself up on the platform on the
far side.

It had been his intention to run back down the stairs
and get onto Frankford Avenue, where he could lose himself in the crowd. The narc, Gerald Vincent Gallagher
reasoned, would not dare use his pistol because of all the
fucking people on the lower level of the terminal and on
Frankford Avenue.

But Gallagher had spotted him, and there was no way
he could run back toward the station, because there were
no people on that platform, and the goddamned narc would
feel free to shoot at him. He turned, instead, and ran down
the platform in the other direction, to the end, and jumped
over a yellow painted barrier with a sign on it reading
DANGER! KEEP OFF!

Beyond the barrier was a narrow workman's walkway.
It ran as far as the next station, but Gerald Vincent Gallagher wasn't planning on running that far, just maybe
two, three, blocks where he knew there was a stairway,
more of a ladder, really, he could climb down to Frankford
Avenue.

He looked over his shoulder and saw that the fucking
narc was doing what he had done, crossing the tracks and
then boosting himself up onto the passenger platform. The
big fat sonofabitch had trouble hauling all that lard onto
the platform, and for a moment, the way the fucking narc
was flailing around with his legs trying to get up on the
platform, Gerald Vincent Gallagher thought he might get
lucky and the narc's legs would touch the third rail, and
the cocksucker would fry himself.

But that didn't happen.

Officer McFadden got first to his knees, and then stood
up. Holding his pistol in both hands, he took aim at Gerald
Vincent Gallagher.

But he didn't pull the trigger. Heaving and panting the
way he was, there was little chance that he could hit the

little sonofabitch as far away as he was, and Christ only
knew where the bullet would go after he fired. Probably
get some nun between the eyes.

"You little sonofabitch! I'm going to get your ass!" he
screamed in fury, and started racing after him again.

Officer Jesus Martinez reached the center platform at
this time. He knew from the direction people were looking
where the action was, and ran down the center platform
to the end.

He saw Officer McFadden first, and then, fifty, sixty
yards ahead of him, a slight white male that almost certainly had to be Gerald Vincent Gallagher. They were running, carefully, along the walkway next to the rail.

The reason they were running carefully was that the
walkway was over the third rail. The walkway was built
of short lengths, about five feet long, of prefabricated
pieces. Some of them, the real old ones, were heavy
wooden planking. Some of the newer ones were pierced
steel, and the most modern were of exposed aggregate
cement. They provided a precarious perch in any event,
and they were not designed to be foot-racing paths.

Officer Martinez made another snap decision. There was
no way he could catch up with them, and even to try would
mean that he would have to jump down and cross the
tracks, and risk electrocuting himself on the third rail. But
he could catch the departing train, ride to the next station,
and then start walking back. That would put Gerald Vincent Gallagher between them.

He ran for the train and jumped inside, just as the doors
closed.

He scared hell, with his pistol drawn, out of the people
on the car, and they backed away from him as if he was
on fire.

"I'm a police officer," he said, not very loudly because
he was out of breath. "Nothing to worry about."

When the train passed Charley McFadden and Gerald
Vincent Gallagher, they were both still running very carefully, watching their feet.

Jesus Christ, Charley, shoot the sonofabitch!

The same thought had occurred to Charley McFadden at just about that moment, and even as he ran, he wondered why he didn't stop running, drop to his knees, and, using a two-handed hold, try to put Gerald Vincent Gallagher down.

There were several reasons, and they all came to him. For one thing, he wasn't at all sure that he could hit him. For another, he was worried about where the bullet, the bullets, plural, would go if he missed. People lived close to the tracks here. He didn't want to kill one of them.

And then he realized the real reason. He didn't *want* to kill Gerald Vincent Gallagher. The little shit might deserve it, and it might mean that Officer Charley McFadden didn't have the balls to be a cop, but the facts were that Gerald Vincent Gallagher didn't have a gun—if he had, the little shit would have used it, he had nothing to lose from a second charge of murder—and wasn't posing, right now, any real threat to anybody but himself, running down the tracks like this.

Hay-zus must have figured out what was going on by now, and got on the radio and called for help. In a couple of minutes, there would be cops responding from all over. All he had to do was keep Gerald Vincent Gallagher in sight, and keep him from hurting himself or somebody else, and everything would be all right.

Eighteen hundred and fifty-three feet (as was later measured with great care) south of the Bridge & Pratt Streets Terminal, Gerald Vincent Gallagher realized that he could not run another ten feet. His chest hurt so much he wanted to cry from the pain. And that big, fat, fucking narc was still on his tail.

Gerald Vincent Gallagher stopped running, and turned around and grabbed the railing beside the walkway, and dropped to his knees.

"I give up," he said. "For Christ's sake, don't shoot me!"

Officer Charley McFadden could understand what he said, even the way he said it puffing and out of breath.

Unable to speak himself, he walked up the walkway, heaving with the exertion.

And then he raised his arm, the left one, without the pistol, and pointed down the track, and tried to find his voice. What he wanted to say was "Watch out, there's a train coming!"

He couldn't find his voice, but Gerald Vincent Gallagher took his meaning. He looked over his shoulder at the approaching train. And tried to get to his feet, so that he would be able to hold on to the railing good and tight as the train passed.

And he slipped.

And he fell onto the tracks.

And he put his hand out as a reflex motion, to break his fall, and his wrist found the third rail and Gerald Vincent Gallagher fried.

And then the train came, and all four cars rolled over him.

When Officer Jesus Martinez came down the walkway, he found Officer Charley McFadden bent over the railing, sick white in the face, and covered with vomitus.

Michael J. "Mickey" O'Hara had worked, at one time or another, for all the newspapers in Philadelphia, and had ventured as far afield as New York City and Washington, D.C.

He was an "old-time" reporter, and even something of a legend, although he was just past forty. He looked older than forty. Mickey liked a drop of the grape whenever he could get his hands on one, and that was the usual reason his employment had been terminated; for in his cups Mickey O'Hara was prone not only to describing the character flaws and ancestry of his superiors in picaresque profanity worthy of a cavalry sergeant, but also, depending on the imagined level of provocation and the amount of alcohol in his system, to punch them out.

But on the other hand, Mickey O'Hara was, when off the sauce, one hell of a reporter. He had what some believe to be the genetic Irish talent for storytelling. He could breathe life into a story that otherwise really wouldn't deserve repeating. He was also a master practitioner of his craft, which was journalism generally and the police beat specifically. His car was equipped with a very elaborate shortwave receiver permitting Mickey to listen in to police communications.

Mickey had come to know a lot of cops in twenty years, and although he was technically not a member of either organization, if there was an affair of the Emerald Society or the Fraternal Order of Police and Mickey O'Hara was not there, people wondered, with concern, if he was sick or something.

Mickey liked most cops and most cops liked Mickey. Mickey, however, considered few cops above the grade of sergeant as *cops*. The cant of the law-enforcement community gets in the way here. All policemen are police officers, which means they are executing an office for the government.

There is a rank structure in the police department, paralleling that of the army, even to the insignia of rank. So far as Mickey was concerned, anybody in the rank of lieutenant or higher (a *white-shirt*) was not really a cop, but a brass hat, a member of the establishment. There were exceptions to this, of course. Mickey was very fond of Chief Inspector Matt Lowenstein, for example, and had used his considerable influence with the managing editor to see that when Lowenstein's boys were bar mitzvahed, those socioreligious events had been prominently featured in the paper.

And he had liked Dutch Moffitt. There were a few others, a captain here, a lieutenant there, whom Mickey liked, even including Staff Inspector Peter Wohl, but by and large he considered anyone who wore a white shirt with his uniform to be much like the officers he had known and actively disliked in the army.

He liked the guys—the ordinary patrolmen and the corporals and detectives and sergeants—on the street, and they liked him. He got their pictures in the paper, with their names spelled right, and he never violated a confidence.

Mickey O'Hara had just gone to work when he heard the call, *"man with a gun at the El terminal at Frankford and Pratt."* That is to say, he had just left Mulvaney's Tap Room at Tabor and Rising Sun avenues, where he had had two beers and nobly refused the offer of a third, and gotten in his car to drive downtown, where he planned to begin the day by dropping by the Ninth District police station.

Almost immediately, there were other calls. Another Fifteenth District car was ordered to the Margaret-Orthodox Station, which was the next station, headed downtown, from Bridge and Pratt Streets, and then right after that came an *"assist officer"* call, and then a warning that plainclothes officers were on the scene. Finally, there was a call for the rescue squad and the fire department.

Mickey O'Hara decided that whatever was happening between the Pratt & Bridge Streets Terminal and the Margaret-Orthodox Station might be worthy of his professional attention.

He went down to Roosevelt Boulevard, turned left, and entered the center lane. He drove fast, but not recklessly, weaving skillfully through traffic, cursing and being cursed in turn by the drivers of more slowly moving vehicles. He went around the bend at Friends' Hospital, slipped into the outside lane, and made a right turn, through a red light, onto Bridge Street.

When Mickey O'Hara got to the Bridge & Pratt Streets Terminal, he found a crowd of people who were being kept from going up the stairs to the El station by four or five cops under the supervision of a sergeant.

He caught the eye of the sergeant, winked, and shrugged his shoulders in a "what's up?" gesture.

A moment later, the sergeant shouldered his way through the crowd.

"Undercover Narcotics guy spotted the kid who shot Dutch Moffitt," the sergeant said instead of a greeting when they shook hands. "He took off down the tracks, with the undercover chasing him, and fell off the walkway, fried himself on the third rail, and then got himself run over by a train.''

''Jesus!'' Mickey O'Hara said.

''They're still up there,'' the sergeant said.

''Is there anyway I can get up there?'' Mickey asked.

''Watch out for the third rail, Mick,'' the sergeant said.

THIRTEEN

Ward V. Fengler, who had three months before been named a partner of Mawson, Payne, Stockton, McAdoo & Lester (there were seventeen partners, in addition to the five senior partners), pushed open the glass door from the Butler Aviation waiting room at Philadelphia International Airport and walked onto the tarmac as the Bell Ranger helicopter touched down.

Fengler was very tall and very thin and, at thirty-two, already evidencing male pattern baldness. He had spent most of the day, from ten o'clock onward, waiting around the airport for Mr. Wells.

Stanford Fortner Wells III got out of the helicopter, and then turned to reach for his luggage. He was a small man, intense, graying, superbly tailored. The temple piece of a set of horn-rimmed glasses hung outside the pocket of his glen plaid suit.

"Mr. Wells, I'm Ward Fengler of Mawson, Payne,

Stockton, McAdoo and Lester,'' Fengler said. ''Colonel Mawson asked me to meet you.''

Wells examined him quickly but carefully and put out his hand.

''Sorry to have kept you waiting like this,'' he said. ''First, we had to land in Newfoundland, and then when we got to New York, the goddamned airport, I suppose predictably, was stacked to heaven's basement.''

''I hope you had a good flight,'' Fengler said.

''I hate airplanes,'' Wells said, matter-of-factly.

''We have a car,'' Fengler said. ''And Colonel Mawson has put you up in the Warwick. I hope that's all right.''

''Fine,'' Wells said. ''Has Mawson talked to Kruger?''

''I don't know, sir.''

''The reason I asked is that someone is to meet me at the Warwick.''

''I don't know anything about that, sir.''

''Then maybe something is finally breaking right,'' Wells said. ''The Warwick's fine.''

The only thing Stanford Fortner Wells III said on the ride downtown was to make the announcement that he used to come to Philadelphia when he was at Princeton.

''And I went from Philadelphia to Princeton,'' Fengler said.

Wells grunted, and smiled.

When they reached the hotel, Wells got quickly out of the limousine and hurried across the sidewalk, up the stairs, and through the door to the lobby. Fengler scurried after him.

There was a television monitor mounted on the wall above the receptionist's desk at WCBL-TV when Peter Wohl walked in. ''Nine's News'' at six was on, and Louise Dutton was looking right into the camera.

My God, she's good-looking!

''May I help you?'' the receptionist asked.

''My name is Wohl,'' Peter said. ''I'm here to see Miss Dutton.''

The receptionist smiled at him, and picked up a light blue telephone.

"Sharon," she said. "Inspector Wohl is here." Then she looked at Wohl. "She'll be right with you, Inspector."

Sharon turned out to be a startlingly good-looking young woman, with dark eyes and long dark hair, and a marvelous set of knockers. Her smile was dazzling.

"Right this way, Inspector," she said, offering her hand. "I'm Sharon Feldman."

She led him into the building, down a corridor, and through a door marked STUDIO C. It was crowded with people and cameras, and what he supposed were sets, one of which was used for "Nine's News." He was surprised when Louise saw him and waved happily at him, understanding only after a moment that she was not at the moment being telecast, or televised, or whatever they called it.

Sharon Feldman led him through another door, and he found himself in a control room.

"There's coffee, Inspector," Sharon Feldman said. "Help yourself. See you!"

"Roll the Wonder Bread," an intense young woman in horn-rimmed glasses, sitting in the rear of two rows of chairs behind a control console said; and Peter saw, on one of a dozen monitors, one marked AIR, the beginning of a Wonder Bread commercial.

"Funny," a man said to Peter Wohl, "you don't look like a cop."

Peter looked at him icily.

"Leonard Cohen," the man said. "I'm the news director."

"Good for you," Peter said.

"No offense, Wohl," Cohen said. "But you really don't, you know, look like what the word 'cop' calls to mind."

"You don't look much like Walter Cronkite yourself," Peter said.

"I don't make as much money, either," Cohen said, disarmingly.

"Neither, I suppose, does the president of the United States," Wohl said.

"At least that we know about," Cohen said. "Did you catch the guy who got away from the Waikiki Diner?"

"Not as far as I know," Peter said.

"But you will?"

"I think so," Peter said. "It's a question of time."

"What about the party or parties unknown who hacked up the fairy?"

"What fairy is that?"

"Come on," Cohen said. "Nelson."

"Was he a fairy?" Peter asked, innocently.

"Wasn't he?"

"I didn't know him that well," Peter said. "Did you?"

Cohen smiled at Wohl approvingly.

"Maybe the princess has met her match," he said. "I knew there had to be some kind of an attraction."

"Leonard, for Christ's sake, will you shut up?" the intense young woman snapped, and then, "Two, you're out of focus, for Christ's sake!"

Cohen shrugged.

"Good night, Louise," Barton Ellison said to Louise Dutton.

"See you at eleven, Barton," Louise said, "when we should have film of the fire at the Navy Yard."

"It should be spectacular," Barton Ellison replied. "A real four-alarm blaze."

"Roll the logo," the intense young woman said.

Through the plate-glass window, Peter saw a man step behind Louise. She took something from her ear and handed it to him, and then stood up. Then she unclipped what he realized after a moment must be a microphone, and tugged at a cord, pulling it down and out of her sleeve.

Then she walked across the studio to the control room, entered it, walked up to him, said "Hi!"; stood on her toes, and kissed him quickly on the lips.

The intense young woman applauded.

"You're just jealous, that's all," Louise said.

"You got it, baby," the intense young woman said.
"Has he got a friend?"

Louise chuckled, and then took Peter's arm and led him
out of the control, through another door, and into a corridor.

"Since we'll be at my place," she said, "and I want to
change anyway, I can wipe this crap off there." She
touched the heavy makeup on her face. "Where are you
parked?"

"Out in front," he said.

She looked at him in surprise.

"Right in front?" she asked. He nodded.

She started to say something, and then laughed. She
had, Peter thought, absolutely perfect teeth.

"I was about to say, 'My God, the cops will tow your
car away,' " she said. "But I guess not, huh?"

"There are fringe benefits in my line of work," he said.
"Not many, but some."

"How do they know it's a cop car?"

"Most of the time, they can tell by the kind of car, or
they see the radio," he replied. "Or you just have the
ticket canceled. But if you have a car like mine, with the
radio in the glove compartment, and you don't want it
towed away, you put a little sign on the dash. Or sometimes on the seat."

"Can you get me a sign?"

"No."

"Fink," she said, and took his arm and led him out of
the building through the lobby.

At Stockton Place, he parked the LTD behind the Jaguar
and walked with her into the foyer of Number Six.

There was an eight-by-ten-inch white cardboard sign on
the door of Apartment A. Red letters spelled out, POLICE
DEPARTMENT, CITY OF PHILADELPHIA. CRIME SCENE. DO
NOT ENTER.

Louise looked at Peter but didn't say anything. But when
the elevator door opened and he started to follow her in,
she put up her hand to stop him.

''You wait down here,'' she said. ''What I have on my mind now is dinner.''

''That's all?''

''Dinner first,'' she said. ''No. Car first, then dinner. Then who knows?''

''I'm easy to please,'' Peter said. ''I'll settle for that.''

He walked back out onto the street and to the Jaguar, and examined the hood where Tony Harris had sat on it.

Louise came down much sooner than he expected her to. She had removed all her makeup and changed into a sweater and pleated skirt.

''That was quick,'' he said.

''It was also a mistake,'' Louise said, and got behind the wheel of the Jaguar.

''What?''

''I'll tell you later,'' she said. Then she said, ''Kind of low to the ground, isn't it?''

''I guess,'' Peter said.

''Well, first I need the keys,'' she said, and as he fished for them, added, ''and then you can explain how that little stick works, and we'll be off.''

''What little stick?''

''That one,'' she said, pointing to the gearshift, ''with all the numbers on it.''

''You do know how to drive a car with a clutch and gearshift?''

''Actually, no,'' she said. ''But I'm willing to learn.''

''Oh, God!''

''Just teasing, Peter,'' Louise said. ''You really love this car, don't you?''

''You're the first person to ever drive it since I rebuilt it,'' he said.

''I'm flattered,'' she said. ''Want to race to your house?''

''No,'' he said, smiling and shaking his head.

''Chicken.'' She started the engine, put it in gear, and made a U-turn.

He quickly got in the LTD and followed her, which

proved difficult. She drove fast and skillfully, and the Jaguar was more nimble in traffic than the LTD.

On Lancaster Avenue, just before it was time to turn off, she put her arm up and vigorously signaled for him to pass her, to lead her. She smiled at him as he did so, and his heart jumped.

At the apartment, as he was taking his uniform from the backseat to carry it upstairs, she came to him, and put her arms around him from the back.

"How would you feel about an indecent proposal?" she asked.

"Come into my parlor, said the spider to the fly," he said.

"What I was thinking was that you would put the uniform back in your car, and go upstairs and pack a few little things in a bag for tomorrow," Louise said.

He freed himself and turned to look at her.

"When I was in my place, alone . . ." Louise said. "Remember what I said about a mistake? I was frightened. I don't want to be alone there, tonight."

"You could stay here," he said.

"I thought about that," she said. "But I have to do the eleven o'clock news, which means I would have to come all the way out here again. *Please*, Peter." Then she smiled, and offered, "I'll blow in your ear."

"Sure, why not?" Peter said. *Sure, why not? Jesus, the most beautiful girl you have ever known asks you to spend the night and you say "Sure, why not?"*

"It won't take me a minute," he said. "You want to come up?"

"No," she said. "You're obviously the kind of man who would take advantage of an innocent girl like me."

He went in the apartment, put underwear and a white uniform shirt, his uniform cap, and his toilet things in a bag. Then, as an afterthought, he added his good bathrobe (a gift from his mother, which he seldom wore) and bottle of cologne in with it.

When he went back downstairs, she was behind the wheel of the Jaguar.

"The idea was to leave this car here," he said.

"We'll come back before we go downtown," she said. "What I want to do is go out in the country with the wind blowing my hair and eat in some romantic country inn."

"Where are you going to find one of those?"

"How about a Burger King?" she said. "Get in, Peter."

He got in beside her, and she drove off, spinning the wheels as she made a sweeping turn.

She headed out of town, driving, he decided, too fast.

"Take it easy," he said.

"If you don't complain about my driving," she said, "I won't say anything about you looking hungrily at my knees."

He felt his face color.

"My God!" he said.

She pulled her skirt farther up her legs.

"Better?" she asked.

As Stanford F. Wells III crossed the marble-floored, high-ceilinged, tastefully furnished lobby of the Warwick Hotel toward the reception desk, two men rose from a couch and intercepted him.

"How are you, boss?" the older of them said. He was short and stocky, with a very full head of curly pepper-and-salt hair.

"Who's minding the store, Kurt?" Wells asked, smiling, obviously pleased to see Kurt Kruger.

"Well, since I was here, I thought I'd wait and say hello and then go home," Kurt Kruger said. "Stan, this is Richard Dye. He's on the *Chronicle*. He used to work for the *Ledger* here. I thought he could be helpful, and he was. He's one hell of a leg man."

Wells gave the younger man his hand.

"This is Mr. Fengler," Wells said, "of Mawson, Payne, Stockton, McAdoo and Lester. Are we going to need all of them? Or just one or two?"

Kruger chuckled. "We probably won't need any of them," he said. "No offense, Mr. Fengler, but it's not nearly as bad—a legal problem, anyway—as I was afraid it would be when you called."

"My wife said she sounded very frightened on the telephone," Wells challenged.

"There's a reason for that," Kruger said. "But I think you can relax. Why don't we get out of the lobby? I got a suite for you."

"So did Mr. Fengler," Wells said. "I guess that means I have two. Let's hope there's whiskey in one of them."

When they got to the suite, Stanford Fortner Wells III disappeared into the bathroom and emerged ten minutes later pink from a shower and wearing only a towel.

"I now feel a lot better," he said, as he poured whiskey into a glass and added a very little water. "I offer the philosophical observation that not only did God not intend man to fly, but that whoever designed the crappers on airplanes should be forced to use them himself through all eternity."

There were polite "the boss is always witty" chuckles, and then Wells turned to Richard Dye.

"Okay, Dick, what have you come up with?"

Dye took a small notebook from his pocket, and glanced at it.

"Miss Dutton . . . or should I call her 'Miss Wells'?"

"Her name is Dutton," Wells said, matter-of-factly. "I already had a wife when I met Louise's mother."

Ward V. Fengler hoped that his surprise at that announcement didn't register on his face.

"Miss Dutton was interviewing a cop, a captain named Richard Moffitt, in a diner on Roosevelt Boulevard. Are you familiar with the diners in Philly, Mr. Wells?"

"Yeah."

"This was a big one, with a bigger restaurant than a counter, if you follow me." Wells nodded. "They were in the restaurant. The cop, who was the commanding officer of the Highway Patrol . . . you know about them?"

Wells thought that over and shook his head no.

"They patrol the highways, but there's more. They're sort of an elite force, and they use them in high-crime areas. They wear uniforms like they were still riding motorcycles. Some people call them 'Carlucci's Commandos.' "

"Carlucci being the mayor?" Wells asked. Dye nodded. "I get the picture," Wells said.

"Well, apparently what happened was that somebody tried to stick up the diner. The cop saw it, and tried to stop it, and there were two robbers, one of them a girl. She let fly at him with a .22 pistol, and hit him. He got his gun out and blew her away. From what I heard, he didn't even know he was shot until he dropped dead."

"I don't understand that," Wells said.

"According to my source—who is a police reporter named Mickey O'Hara—the bullet severed an artery, and he bled to death internally."

"Right in front of my daughter?"

"Yes, sir, she was right there."

"That's awful," Wells said.

"If I didn't mention this, the guy who was doing the stickup got away in the confusion. They're still looking for him."

"Do they know who he is?"

Dye dropped his eyes to his notebook.

"The guy's name is Gerald Vincent Gallagher, white male, twenty-four. The girl who shot the cop was a junkie—so is Gallagher, by the way—named Dorothy Ann Schmeltzer. High-class folks, both of them."

"Go on," Wells said.

"Of course, every cop in Philadelphia was there in two minutes," Dye went on. "One of them was smart enough to figure out who Miss Dutton was—"

"Got a name?"

"Wohl," Dye said. "He's a staff inspector. According to O'Hara he's one of the brighter ones. He's the youngest staff inspector; he just sent the city housing director to the slammer, him and a union big shot—"

Wells made a "go on" gesture with his hands, and then took underwear from a suitcase and pulled a T-shirt over his head.

"So Wohl treated her very well. He sent her home in a police car, and had another cop drive her car," Dye went on. "Half, O'Hara said, because she's on the tube, and half because he's a nice guy. So she went to work, and did the news at six, and again at eleven, and then she went out and had a couple of drinks with the news director, a guy named Leonard Cohen, and a couple of other people. Then she went home. The door to the apartment on the ground floor—I was there, she had to walk past it to get to the elevator—was open, and she went in, and found Jerome Nelson in his bedroom. Party or parties unknown had hacked him up with a Chinese cleaver."

"What's a Chinese cleaver?" Wells asked.

"Looks like a regular cleaver, but it's thinner, and sharper," Dye explained.

Wells, in the act of buttoning a shirt, nodded.

"What was my daughter's relationship with the murdered man?" Wells asked. "I mean, why did she walk into his apartment?"

"They were friends, I guess. He was a nice little guy. Funny."

"There was nothing between them?"

"He was homosexual, Mr. Wells," Dye said.

"I see," Wells said.

"And, Stan," Kurt Kruger said, evenly, "he's—he *was*—Arthur Nelson's son."

"Poor Arthur," Wells said. "He knew?"

"I don't see how he couldn't know," Dye said.

"And I suppose that's all over the front pages, too?"

"No," Dye said. "Not so far. Professional courtesy, I suppose."

"Interesting question, Kurt," Wells said, thoughtfully. "What would we have done? Shown the same 'professional courtesy'?"

"I don't know," Kruger said. "Was his . . . sexual inclination . . . germane to the story?"

"Was it?"

"Nobody knows yet," Kruger said. "Until it comes out, my inclination would be not to mention the homosexuality. If it comes out there is a connection, then I think I'd have to print it. One definition of news is that's it's anything people would be interested to hear.''

"Another, some cynics have said,'' Wells said dryly, ''is that news is what the publisher says it is. That's one more argument against having only one newspaper in a town.''

"Would you print it, Stan?'' Kruger asked.

"That's what I have all those high-priced editors for,'' Wells said. ''To make painful decisions like that.'' He paused. ''I'd go with what you said, Kurt. If it's just a sidebar, don't use it. If it's germane, I think you would have to.''

Kruger grunted.

"Go on, Dick,'' Wells said to Richard Dye.

"Miss We— Miss Dutton—''

"Try 'your daughter,' Dick,'' Wells said, adding, ''if there's some confusion in your mind.''

"Your daughter called the cops. They came, including the Homicide lieutenant on duty, a real horse's ass named DelRaye. They had words.''

"About what?''

"He told her she had to go to the Roundhouse—the police headquarters, downtown—and she said she had told him everything she knew, and wasn't going anywhere. Then she went upstairs to her apartment. DelRaye told her unless she came out, he was going to knock the door down, and have her taken to the Roundhouse in a paddy wagon.''

"Why do I have the feeling you're tactfully leaving something out, Dick? I want all of it.''

"Okay,'' Dye said, meeting his eyes. ''She'd had a couple of drinks. Maybe a couple too many. And she used a couple of choice words on DelRaye.''

"You have a quote?''

" 'Go fuck yourself,' '' Dye quoted.

"Did she really?'' Wells said. ''How to win friends and influence people.''

"So she must have called Inspector Wohl, and he showed up, and got her away from the apartment through the basement,'' Dye said. ''In the morning, he brought her to the Roundhouse. There was a lawyer, Colonel Mawson, waiting for her there.''

''She must have called me while she was in the apartment waiting for the good cop to show up,'' Wells said. ''Either my wife couldn't tell Louise was drinking, or didn't want to say anything. She said she was afraid.''

''I saw pictures of the murdered guy, Mr. Wells. Enough to make you throw up. She had every reason to be frightened.''

''Where was she from the time—what was the time?—the good cop took her away from the apartment, and the time he brought her to the police station?''

''After one in the morning,'' Dye said. ''He probably took her to a girl friend's house, or something.''

''Or boyfriend's house?'' Wells said. ''You are a good leg man, Dick. What did you turn up about a boyfriend?''

''No one in particular,'' Dye said. ''Couple of guys, none of whom seem to have been involved.''

''Mr. Wells,'' Ward V. Fengler said, ''if I may interject, Colonel Mawson asked Miss Dutton where she had been all night, and she declined to tell him.''

''That spells boyfriend,'' Wells said. ''And, maybe guessing I would show up here, she didn't want me to know she'd spent the night with him. Now my curiosity's aroused. Can you get me some more on that subject, Dick?''

''I'll give it a shot, sir,'' Dye said.

''Has she gone back to work?'' Wells asked, and then, looking at his watch, answered his own question. ''The best way to find that out is to look at the tube, isn't it?''

It was six-fifteen. As Stanford Fortner Wells III finished dressing, he watched his daughter do her telecast.

''She's tough,'' he said, admiringly.

''I'd forgotten how pretty she was,'' Kurt Kruger said.

''That, too.'' Wells chuckled. ''Okay. I'm going to see her. Mr. Fengler, there's no point that I can see in taking any more of your time. I'd like to keep the car, if I may, and I would be grateful if you would get in touch with

Colonel Mawson and tell him I'll be in touch in the morning."

"I'm at your disposal, Mr. Wells, if you think I could be of any assistance," Fengler said.

"I can handle it, I think, from here on in. If I need some help, I've got Mawson's number, office and home. Thank you for all your courtesy."

Fengler knew that he had been dismissed.

"I'd like to have dinner with you, Kurt, but that's not going to be possible. Thank you. Again."

"Aw, hell, Stan."

"You, Dick, I would like you to stick around. I may need a leg man to do more than find out who my daughter has been seeing. You came, I hope, prepared to stay a couple of days?"

"Yes, sir," Dye said.

"Whose suite is this?" Wells asked.

Fengler and Kruger looked at each other and shrugged, and smiled.

"Well, find out. And then see if you can turn the other one in on a room for Dick," Wells said. "Make sure he stays here in the hotel, in any case."

Then he walked quickly among them, shook their hands, and left the suite.

There was a Ford pulling away from the front door of WCBL-TV when the limousine arrived. The limousine took that place.

Wells walked up to the receptionist.

"My name is Stanford Wells," he said. "I would like to see Miss Louise Dutton."

The name Stanford Wells meant nothing whatever to the receptionist, but she thought that the nicely dressed man standing before her didn't look like a kook.

"Does Miss Dutton expect you?" she asked with a smile.

"No, but I bet if you tell her her father is out here, she'll come out and get me."

"Oh, I'm so sorry," the receptionist said. "You *just*

missed her! I'm surprised you didn't see her. She just this
minute left.''

"Do you have any idea where she went?''

"No,'' the receptionist said. "But she was with Inspector Wohl, if that's any help.''

"Thank you very much,'' Stanford Fortner Wells III
said, and went out and got back in the limousine. He fished
in his pockets and then swore.

"Something wrong, sir?'' the chauffeur asked.

"Take me back to the hotel. I left my daughter's address
on the goddamned dresser.''

Mickey O'Hara sat virtually motionless for three minutes before the computer terminal on his desk in the city
room of the *Philadelphia Bulletin*. The only thing that
moved was his tongue behind his lower lip.

Then, all of a sudden, his bushy eyebrows rose, his eyes
lit up, his lips reflected satisfaction, and his fingers began
to fly over the keys. He had been searching for his lead,
and he had found it.

SLUG: Fried Thug

By Michael J. O'Hara

Gerald Vincent Gallagher, 24, was electrocuted and dis-
membered at 4:28 this afternoon, ending a massive,
citywide, twenty-four-hour manhunt by eight thousand
Philadelphia policemen.

Gallagher, of a West Lindley Avenue address, had been
sought by police on murder charges since he eluded
capture following a foiled robbery at the Waikiki Diner
on Roosevelt Boulevard yesterday afternoon. Highway
Patrol Captain Richard C. "Dutch" Moffitt happened
to be in the restaurant, in civilian clothes, with WCBL-
TV Anchorwoman Louise Dutton. Police say Captain
Moffitt was shot to death in a gun battle with Dorothy

Ann Schmeltzer, whom police say was Gallagher's accomplice, when he attempted to arrest Gallagher.

At 4:24 p.m. Charles McFadden, a 22-year-old Narcotics plainclothesman, spotted Gallagher, at the Bridge & Pratt Streets Terminal in Northeast Philadelphia. Gallagher attempted escape by running down a narrow workman's platform alongside the elevated tracks toward the Margaret-Orthodox Station. Just as McFadden caught up with him, he slipped, fell to the tracks, touched the third rail; and moments later was run over by four cars of a northbound elevated train.

Mickey O'Hara stopped typing, looked at the screen, and read what he had written. The thoughtful look came back on his face. He typed MORETOCOME MORETOCOME, then punched the SEND key.

Then he stood up and walked across the city room to the city editor's desk, and then stepped behind it. When the city editor was finished with what he was doing, he looked up and over his shoulder at Mickey O'Hara.

"Punch up 'fried thug,' " Mickey said.

The city editor did so, by pressing keys on one of his terminals that called up the story from the central computer memory and displayed it on his monitor.

As the city editor read Mickey's first 'graphs, O'Hara leaned over and dialed the number of the photo lab.

"Bobby, this is Mickey. Did they come out?"

"Nice," the city editor said. "How much more is there?"

"How much space can I have?"

"Pictures?"

"Two good ones for sure," Mickey said. "I got a lovely shot of the severed head."

"I mean ones we can print, Mickey," the city editor said. He pointed to the telephone in Mickey's hand. "That the lab?" Mickey nodded, and the city editor gestured for the phone. "Print one of each, right away," he said, and hung up.

"I asked how much space I can have," Mickey O'Hara said.

"Everybody else was there, I guess?"

"Nobody else has pictures of the cop," Mickey said. "For that matter, of the tracks when anything was still going on."

"And you're sure this is the guy?"

"One of the Fifteenth District cops recognized the head," Mickey said.

"Give me a thousand, twelve hundred words," the city editor said. "Things are a little slow. Nothing but wars."

Mickey O'Hara nodded and walked back to his desk and sat down before the computer terminal. He pushed the COMPOSE key, and typed,

SLUG: Fried Thug
By Michael J. O'Hara
Add One

Sergeant Tom Lenihan stepped into the doorway of the office of Chief Inspector Dennis V. Coughlin, who commanded the Special Investigations Bureau, and stood waiting until he had Coughlin's attention.

"What is it, Tom?"

"They just got Gerald Vincent Gallagher, Chief," Lenihan said.

"Good," Coughlin said. "Where? How?"

"Lieutenant Pekach just phoned," Lenihan said. "Two of his guys—one of them that young plainclothes guy who identified the girl—went looking for him on their own. They spotted him at the Bridge Street Terminal. He ran. Officer McFadden chased him down the elevated tracks. Gallagher slipped, fell onto the third rail, and then a train ran over him."

Denny Coughlin's face froze. His eyes were on Lenihan, but Lenihan knew that he wasn't seeing him, that he was thinking.

Dennis V. Coughlin was only one of eleven chief inspectors of the Police Department of the City of Philadelphia. But it could be argued that he was first among equals. Under his command (among others) were the Narcotics Unit; the Vice Unit; the Internal Affairs Division; the Staff Investigation Unit; and the Organized Crime Intelligence Unit.

The other ten chief inspectors reported to either the deputy commissioner (Operations) or the deputy commissioner (Administration), who reported to the first deputy commissioner, who reported to the commissioner. Denny Coughlin reported directly to the first deputy commissioner.

Phrased very simply, there were only two people in the department who could tell Denny Coughlin what to do, or ask him what he was doing: the first deputy commissioner and the commissioner himself. On the other hand, without any arrogance at all, Denny Coughlin believed that what happened anywhere in the police department was his business.

"Tom, is Inspector Kegley out there?"

"Yes, sir, I think so."

"Would you tell him, please, unless there is a good reason he can't, I would like him to find out exactly what happened?"

"Yes, sir."

"I mean right now, Tom," Coughlin said. "He doesn't have to give me a white paper, just get the information to me." Coughlin looked at his watch. "I'll be at Dutch's wake, say from six o'clock until it's over. Are you going over there with me?"

"Yes, sir," Lenihan said, and departed.

Two minutes later, Lenihan was back.

"Inspector Kegley's on his way, sir. He said he'd see you at Marshutz & Sons," he reported.

"Good, Tom. Thank you," Coughlin said. Staff Inspector George Kegley had come up through the Detective Bureau, and had done some time in Homicide. He was a quiet, phlegmatic, soft-eyed man who missed very little once he turned his attention to something. If there was something not quite right about the pursuit and death of Gerald Vincent Gallagher, Kegley would soon sniff it out.

Coughlin returned his attention to the file on his desk. It was a report from Internal Affairs involving two officers of the Northwest Police Division. There had been a party. Officer A had paid uncalled-for personal attention to Mrs. B. Mrs. B had not, in Officer B's (her husband's) judgment, declined the attention with the proper outraged indignation. She had, in fact, seemed to like it. Whereupon Officer B had belted his wife in the chops, and taken off after Officer A, pistol drawn, threatening to kill the sonofabitch. No real harm had been done, but the whole matter was now official, and something would have to be done.

"I don't want to deal with this now," Dennis V. Coughlin said, although there was no one in his office to hear him.

He stood up, took his pistol from his left desk drawer, slipped it into his holster, and walked out of his office.

"Come on, Tom," he said to Sergeant Lenihan, "let's go."

FOURTEEN

Patrick Coughlin, a second-generation Irish-American (his father had been born in Philadelphia three months after his parents had immigrated from County Kildare in 1896) had spent his working life as a truck diver, and had been determined that his son Dennis would have the benefits of a college education.

But in 1946, despite an excellent record at Roman Catholic High School, Dennis V. Coughlin had been suspended from LaSalle College for academic inadequacy after his second semester. He had been on academic probation after the first semester.

Once Denny Coughlin had flunked out of LaSalle, life at home had been difficult, and he had enlisted in the navy for four years, in exchange for a navy promise to train him as an electronics technician. He was no more successful in the navy electronics school than he had been at LaSalle, and the navy found itself wondering what to do with a

251

very large young man for the forty-two months remaining on his enlistment.

Shortly after reporting aboard the aircraft carrier U.S.S. *Coral Sea* as an engineman striker, the *Coral Sea*'s master at arms had offered him a chance to become what was in effect a shipboard policeman. That had far more appeal than long days in the hot and greasy bowels of the ship, and Denny jumped at it.

It wasn't what he thought it would be, marching into waterfront bars and hauling drunken sailors back to the ship, after beating them on the head with a nightstick. There was some of that, to be sure, and once or twice Denny Coughlin did have to use his nightstick. But not often. A sailor had to be both foolhardy as well as drunk to take on someone the size of Coughlin. And Denny learned that a kind word of understanding and reason was almost always more effective than the nightstick.

He found, too, that often the sailors were the aggrieved party to a dispute, that the saloonkeepers were in the wrong. And he found that he could deal with the saloonkeepers as well as he could with sailors. He sensed, long before he could put it into words, that the cowboys really had used the right word. He was a *peace* officer, and he was good at it.

After eighteen months of sea duty aboard the *Coral Sea*, he was assigned as a shore patrolman attached to the U.S. Naval Hospital, Philadelphia. He worked with the Philadelphia police, and came to the attention of several senior officers, who saw in him just what the department was looking for in its recruits: a large, healthy, bright, pleasant hometown boy with an imposing presence. The police department was suggested to him as a suitable civilian career when his navy hitch was up. With his navy veteran's preference, he had no trouble with the civil service exam. Once that was out of the way, Captain Francis X. Halloran had a word with the Honorable Lawrence Sheen, M.C., and shortly after that Bosun's Mate Third Class Dennis V. Coughlin was honorably discharged from the U.S. Navy

for the convenience of the government to accept essential
civilian employment—law enforcement.

Three weeks after taking off his navy blues, Dennis V.
Coughlin reported to the police academy for training.

On his first day there, he met John X. Moffitt, just back
from a three-year hitch in the marines. They were of an
age, they had much in common, and they became buddies.
When they graduated from the academy, they were both
assigned downtown, Denny Coughlin to the Ninth District, Jack Moffitt to the Sixth. Without much trouble, they
managed to have their duty schedules coincide, so they
spent their off-duty time together, drinking beer and chasing girls, except for Tuesday nights, when Jack Moffitt
went to meetings of the marine corps reserve.

He needed the money, Jack Moffitt argued, and there
wasn't going to be a war anyway; Denny should join up
too. Denny did not. Jack was called back to the Marines
on seventy-two-hours' notice, a week after they had both
learned they had passed the detective's exam, in August
1950.

Jack was back in just over a year, medically retired as
a staff sergeant for wounds received in the vicinity of
Hangun-Ri, North Korea, where he also earned the Silver
Star. He went back to work in the West Detective Divi-
sion; Denny Coughlin was then in the Central Detective
Division.

But things weren't the same between them, primarily
because of Patricia Stevens, whom Jack had met when she
went with the girls from Saint Agnes's to entertain the
boys in the navy hospital. Denny was best man at their
wedding, and Patty used to have him to supper a lot, and
she helped the both of them prepare for the sergeant's examination.

A month after Jack Moffitt died of gunshot wounds suf-
fered in the line of duty, a month before Matt was born,
Denny Coughlin had made a rare visit to his parish rectory, for a private conversation with Monsignor Finn. It
took some time before Finn realized what Denny Coughlin

really wanted to talk about, and it was not his immortal soul.

"You don't want to marry the girl, Denny," Monsignor Finn said, "because you feel sorry for her, or because she's your friend's wife; nor even to take care of the baby when it comes. And you sure don't want her to marry you because she needs someone to support her and the baby. Now you'll notice that I didn't say you don't want to marry the girl. What I'm saying to you is, have a little patience. Time heals. And it wouldn't surprise me at all if Patty Moffitt saw in you the same things she saw in Jack, God rest his soul. But you want to be sure, son. Marriage is forever. You don't want to be jumping into it. What I'm saying is just keep being what you are, a good friend, until Patty gets over both her grief and the baby. Then if you still feel the same way . . ."

Dennis V. Coughlin had still felt the same way six months later, and a year later, but before he could bring himself to say anything, Patty Moffitt had gone to work, trying to work her way up to be a legal secretary, and then she'd taken Matt for a walk in his stroller, and she'd run into Brewster Cortland Payne II taking his motherless kids for a walk, and then it had been too late.

Chief Inspector Dennis V. Coughlin had been at Dutch Moffitt's wake at the Marshutz & Sons Funeral Home for about an hour when he saw Matt Payne, standing alone, and called him over. He shook his hand, and then put his arm around his shoulders.

"I'd like you to meet these fellows, Matt," he said. "Gentlemen, this is Matt Payne, Dutch's nephew."

Matt was introduced to two chief inspectors, three inspectors, two captains, and a corporal who had gone through the academy with Dutch Moffitt and was being tolerated by the brass for being a little drunk, and just a shade too friendly.

"When you get a moment, Uncle Denny, could I talk to you?"

"You bet you can," Denny Coughlin said. "Excuse us, fellows." He took Matt's arm and led him far down a wide corridor in the funeral home. Finally, they found an empty corner.

"I joined the police department," Matt announced.

"How's that again?"

"I said I'm going to be a policeman," Matt repeated.

"And when did this happen?"

"Today."

"I'll be damned," Dennis V. Coughlin said. "Let me get adjusted to that, Matt."

"So far only my dad knows," Matt said.

"Your dad is dead," Coughlin said, and was immediately contrite. "Ah, Christ, why did I say that? I'm proud to claim Brewster Payne as a friend, and you couldn't have had a better father."

"I understand," Matt said. "I have trouble with my real father, too. Keeping them separate, I mean."

"Matt, I'm going to say something to you and I don't want you to take offense, son, but I have to say it—"

"I flunked the marine corps physical," Matt said. "I was thinking about becoming a cop before Uncle Dick was killed."

"If you flunked the marine corps physical, what makes you think you can pass the police department physical?"

"I passed it," Matt said. "And I even had a talk with the shrink. Today."

"Jesus, Mary, and Joseph! What's your mother going to say?"

"Why am I getting the feeling that you're a long way from yelling '*Whoopee, good for you!*'?"

"Because I'm not entirely sure it's a good idea, for you, or the department," Coughlin said, evenly.

"Why not?"

"I don't know," Coughlin said. "Gut feeling, maybe. Or maybe because I buried your father, and we're about to bury your uncle. Or maybe I'm afraid your mother will think I talked you into it."

"My father, my *adoptive* father, understands," Matt said.

"Then he's one up on me," Coughlin said. "Matt,

you're not doing this because of what you think the police are like, from watching them on TV, are you?"

"No, I'm not," Matt said, simply.

"But you will admit that you have no idea what you're getting into?"

"I was going into the marines, and I had no idea what I was getting into there, either."

Sergeant Tom Lenihan and Staff Inspector George Kegley appeared in the corridor, waiting for Coughlin's attention. Coughlin saw them, and motioned them over.

"You met Sergeant Lenihan yesterday," Coughlin said. "And this is Staff Inspector Kegley. George, this is Matt Payne. He's Dutch's nephew."   .

They all shook hands.

"What have you got, George?" Coughlin asked.

Kegley seemed momentarily surprised that Coughlin was asking for a report to be delivered before what he thought of as a "civilian relative," but he delivered a concise, but thorough report of what had transpired at the Bridge & Pratt Streets Terminal, including the details of Gerald Vincent Gallagher's death and dismemberment.

"Did they get in touch with Peter Wohl?" Coughlin asked. "Matt Lowenstein said they wanted him to get an identification of Gallagher as the man in the diner from that TV woman."

"Nobody seems to know where either of them are, Chief," Kegley said.

Coughlin snorted, and then his face stiffened in thought.

"Thank you, George," Coughlin said. "I appreciate this. Tom, get the car, we're going for a ride."

"Yes, sir," Sergeant Lenihan said.

"You're coming," Dennis Coughlin said to Matt Payne.

"Are you all right, Matthew?" Chief Inspector Dennis V. Coughlin asked when Sergeant Tom Lenihan had eased the Oldsmobile up on the curb before the row house on Fitzgerald Street in South Philadelphia.

Matt had thrown up at the medical examiner's, not when Coughlin expected him to, when they pulled the sheet off

the remains of Gerald Vincent Gallagher, but several minutes later, outside, just before they got back into the Oldsmobile. Tom Lenihan had disappeared at that point for a
couple of minutes, and Coughlin wasn't sure if he had
done that to spare Matt embarrassment, or whether Lenihan had gone behind a row of cars to throw up himself.

"I'm all right," Matt said.

His face was white.

"Sure?"

"I'm fine, thank you," Matt said, firmly.

"You want me to come along, Chief?" Lenihan asked.

"I think maybe you better," Coughlin said, and opened
the door.

The door to the McFadden house had a doorbell, an
old-fashioned, cast-iron device mounted in the center of
the door. You twisted it, and it rang. Coughlin remembered one just like it on the door of the row house where
he had grown up. Somebody, he thought, had probably
made a million making those bells; there was one on just
about every row house in Philly.

Agnes McFadden opened the door, and looked at them
in surprise as Coughlin whipped off his snap-brimmed
straw hat.

" 'Evening, ma'am," he said. "I'm Chief Inspector
Coughlin. I'd like to see Officer McFadden, if that would
be convenient."

"What?" Agnes McFadden said.

"We'd like to see Charley, if we can," Lenihan said.
"I'm Sergeant Lenihan and this is Chief Inspector Coughlin."

"He's in the kitchen, with his lieutenant," she said.
"Lieutenant Pekach. And Mr. McFadden."

"Could we see him, do you think?" Coughlin asked.

"Sure, of course, I don't know what I was thinking of,
please come in."

They followed her down a dark corridor to the kitchen,
where the three men sat at the kitchen table. There was a
bottle of Seagram's 7-Crown and quart bottles of Coke and
beer on the table.

Pekach's eyes widened when he saw them. He started to get up.

"Keep your seat, David," Coughlin said.

Officer Charley McFadden, who was sitting slumped straight out in the chair, supporting a Kraft cheese glass of liquor on his stomach, finally realized that something was happening. He looked at the three strangers in his kitchen without recognition.

Coughlin crossed the small room to him with his hand extended.

"McFadden, I apologize for barging into your home like this, but I wanted to congratulate you personally on a job well done. I'm sure your parents are very proud of you. The police department is."

Matt saw that McFadden had no idea who was shaking his hand.

Charley's father put that in words. "Who're you?" he asked.

"Mr. McFadden," Lieutenant Pekach said, "this is Chief Inspector Coughlin. And that's Sergeant Lenihan. I'm afraid I don't know the other gentleman."

"My name is Matthew Payne," Matt said, putting out his hand.

"Matt is . . . Captain Moffitt was Matt's uncle," Coughlin said.

"I'm sorry about your uncle," Charley McFadden said. Then he realized that he should be standing, and got up. He looked at Coughlin. "You're Chief Inspector Coughlin," he said, but there was a question, or disbelief, in his voice.

"That's right," Coughlin said.

"Could I offer you gentlemen a little something to drink?" Mrs. McFadden asked.

"All I got, I'm afraid, is the Seagram's Seven," Mr. McFadden said.

"Well, we're all off duty," Coughlin said. "I think a little Seagram's Seven would go down very nicely."

More cheese glasses were produced, and filled three-quarters full of whiskey.

"I'm afraid the house is a terrible mess," Agnes McFadden said.

"Looks fine to me," Dennis Coughlin said. He raised his glass. "To Officer McFadden, of whom we're all very proud."

"I didn't want that to happen to him," Charley McFadden said, very slowly. "Jesus Christ, that shouldn't happen to anybody."

"Charley," Coughlin said, firmly. "What happened to Gallagher, he brought on himself."

Charley looked at him, and finally said, "Yes, sir."

"Lieutenant Pekach, may I see you a moment?" Coughlin said, and signaled Matt to come along.

They went to the vestibule.

"Where's his partner?" Coughlin asked.

"He was here, Chief. His doctor gave him something to calm him down, and it didn't mix with the booze. I sent him home."

"McFadden on anything?"

"No, sir." Pekach said. "He's got a thing about pills. He won't even take an aspirin."

"How long are you going to stay?"

"As long as necessary," Pekach said. "The booze will get to him, sooner or later."

"Had you planned to write him up?"

"A commendation?" Pekach asked. "I hadn't thought about that. But yes, sure."

"Not only 'at great risk to his life,' " Coughlin said. "But 'exercising great restraint,' et cetera, et cetera. You follow me?"

"Yes, sir."

"This is going to be all over the papers," Coughlin said. "George Kegley tells me that Mickey O'Hara was even up on the elevated tracks. What's that going to do to McFadden on the streets?"

"Well, he won't be much use, not what he's been doing," Pekach said.

"I'll find something else for him to do." Coughlin said. "When you're that age, working plainclothes, and they put you back in a uniform, you think you did something wrong. I don't want that to happen.''

"I'll find something for him, Chief," Pekach said.

When they went back in the kitchen, Officer McFadden was being nauseous in the sink. Coughlin put out his hand and stopped Matt from going in, then gestured for Sergeant Lenihan to come along with them.

When they were in the car, moving north on South Broad Street, Coughlin reached forward and touched Matt Payne's shoulder. Matt turned and looked at him.

"Still think you want to be a cop, Matt?" he asked.

"I was just wondering how I would react in a situation like that," Matt said, softly.

"And?"

"I don't know," Matt said. "I was wondering. But to answer your question, yes, I still want to be a cop."

Coughlin made a grunting noise.

"Tom," he ordered, "when you get to a phone, call Pekach and tell him I want that boy and his partner at the funeral tomorrow. And then find out who's in charge of the seating arrangements and make sure they have seats in Saint Dominic's."

"Uniform or plainclothes?"

Coughlin thought that over a moment. "Uniforms," he said. "I think uniforms. Tell Pekach to make sure they get haircuts and are cleaned up."

"I've got to check my machine," Peter said, when he and Louise had returned from dinner and put the Jaguar into the garage. "It won't take a minute."

"I'll go with you," she said, and caught his hand and held it as they walked up the stairs. Inside the apartment, as he snapped on the lights, he saw that she was standing very close, looking at him.

She wants to be kissed, he realized. *Jesus, that's nice.*

But when he put his arms around her, and she pressed her body against his, and he tried to kiss her, she averted her face.

"I've got some Lavoris," Peter said.

She chuckled.

"No," she said. "That's not it. But I'll be on the air at eleven, and I don't want everybody in the Delaware Valley thinking, 'That dame looks like she just got out of bed.' "

"You really think it shows?" he asked, smelling her hair.

"Once might not," she said. "But we seem to have a certain tendency to keep going back for seconds."

"God, you feel good," Peter said, giving in to an urge to hug her tightly.

"Duty calls," Louise said, freeing herself. "Yours and mine. See what your machine says."

There were a number of messages.

Barbara Crowley had called.

"Peter, your mother called and asked me if I was going to the wake. I told her that I expected to hear from you. Please call me. I'll go over there with you, if you want me to."

And Detective Jason Washington had called:

"This is Jason Washington, Inspector," his recorded voice reported tinnily. "It's five-thirty. In a manner of speaking, we have Gerald Vincent Gallagher. McFadden, the kid from Narcotics who identified the girl, went looking for him, and found him at the Bridge Street Terminal. The reason I say 'in a manner of speaking' is that Gallagher got himself run over by a subway train. After he hit the third rail. Hell of a mess. McFadden knew Gallagher, of course, and so did a couple of guys from the Fifteenth District. But under the circumstances, I think, and so does Lieutenant Natali, that they'll probably want Miss Dutton to identify the body as that of the man she saw in the Waikiki. They just took the body to the medical examiner's. Do you think you could get in touch with her, and take her down there around seven, seven-thirty? I'd appreciate it if you could call me. I'll either be here at the office, or at the M.E.'s, or maybe home. Thank you."

And Lieutenant Louis Natali had called:

"Inspector, this is Lou Natali. Jason Washington said he called and left a message on your machine about an hour ago. It's now quarter to seven. Anyway, it's now official. Captain Quaire requests that you get in touch with Miss Dutton, and bring her by the M.E.'s to identify Gallagher as the guy she saw in the diner. You better warn her he's in pieces. The wheels cut his head off, intact, I mean. I'll try to have them cover the rest of him with a sheet, but it's pretty rough. And would you call me, please, when you get this? Thank you.''

And Chief Inspector Matt Lowenstein had called:

''Peter, what the hell is going on? I need that woman to identify Gallagher. Nobody seems to know where you are, so I called the TV station. I was going to very politely ask her if I could take her to the M.E.'s myself, and they tell me they don't know where she is, only that she left there with you. Jesus, it's half past eight, and I've got to get over to Marshutz & Sons for the damned wake.''

That message ended abruptly. Peter was quite sure that Chief Inspector of Detectives Matt Lowenstein had glanced at his watch toward the end, seen the time, thought out loud, and then slammed the phone down.

The machine reached the end of the recorded messages and started to rewind.

''What was that all about?'' Louise asked.

''Well, apparently an undercover cop spotted—''

''Who was she?'' Louise interrupted.

It took him a moment to frame his reply.

''Three days ago, I would have said she was my girl friend,'' he said.

''Nice girl?''

''Very nice,'' he said. ''Her name is Barbara Crowley, and she's a psychiatric nurse.''

''That must come in handy,'' Louise said.

''Everybody who knows us, except one, thinks that Barbara and I make a lovely couple and should get married,'' Peter said.

''Who's the dissenter? Her father?''

''Me,'' Peter said. ''She's a nice girl, but I don't love her.''

''As of when?''

"As of always," Peter said. "I never felt that way about her."

"What way is that?"

"The way I feel about you," Peter said.

"I suppose it has occurred to you that about the only thing we have going for us is that we screw good?"

"That's a good starting place," Peter said. "We can build on that."

She met his eyes for a long moment, then said: "I'm not going to go look at a headless corpse tonight."

"Okay," he said. "But you will have to eventually."

"What if I just refuse?"

"You don't want to do that," Peter said.

"What if I do?"

"They'll get a court order. If you refuse the order, they'll hold you in contempt, put you in the House of Correction until you change your mind. You wouldn't like it in the House of Correction. They're really not your kind of people."

She just looked at him.

"I'll call Jason Washington and tell him to meet us at the medical examiner's tomorrow morning. Say, eight o'clock," Peter said.

"I've got to work in the morning," she said.

"We'll go there before you go to work," Peter said, and then added: "I thought you told me you went to work at two o'clock?"

"I usually do," she said. "But tomorrow, I've got to cover a funeral."

"You didn't tell me that," he said.

"It's my story," she said. "I was there when it started, remember?"

He nodded. They looked at each other without speaking for a moment.

"Why are you looking at me that way?" Louise asked. "What are you thinking?"

"That you are incredibly beautiful, and that I love you," Peter said.

"I know," she said. "I mean, that you love me. And I

think that scares me more than going to go look at a headless body . . . or a bodyless head.''

"Why does it scare you?"

"I'm afraid I'll wake up," she said. "Or, maybe, that
I won't."

"I don't think I follow that," he said.

"I think we better get out of here," she said. "Before
we wind up in the playroom again."

"Let me call Washington," Peter said.

"Call him from my apartment," she said. "What we're
going to do is go there, whereupon I will pick up my car
and go to work. You will go to my apartment."

"Is that what I *will* do?" he asked, smiling.

"Uh-huh," she said. "Where you will do the dishes,
and dust, and then make yourself pretty for me when I
come home tired from work."

"If you're going to be tired, you can do your own
dishes."

"I won't be that tired, Peter, if that's what you're thinking, and I'm sure you are."

"I don't mind waiting around the studio for you," he
said.

"But I do. I saw you looking at Sharon's boobs. And,
although I know I shouldn't tell you this, I saw the way
she was looking at you."

"That sounds jealous, I hope."

"Let's go, Peter," she said, and walked to the door.

Mickey O'Hara sat at the bar in the Holiday Inn at
Fourth and Arch streets, sipping on his third John Jamison's.

It had happened to him often enough for him to recognize what was happening. He was doing something a
reporter should not do any more than a doctor or a lawyer, letting the troubles of people he was dealing with professionally get to him personally. And it had happened to
him often enough for him to know that he was dealing
with it in exactly the worst possible way, with a double
John Jamison's straight up and a beer on the side.

He had started out feeling sorry for the young under-cover Narcotics cop, Charley McFadden. The McFadden kid had gone out to play the Lone Ranger, even to the faithful brown companion Hay-zus whateverthefuck his name was, at his side. He was going to bring the bad man to justice. Then he would kiss his horse and ride off into the sunset.

But it hadn't happened that way. He had not been able to get the bad man to repent and come quietly by shooting a pistol out of his hand with a silver bullet.

The bad man had first been fried and then chopped into pieces, and at that point he had stopped being a bad man and become another guy from Philadelphia, one of the kids down the block, another Charley McFadden. Gerald Vincent Gallagher had died with his eyes open, and when his head had finished rolling around between the tracks it had come to rest against a tie, looking upward. When Charley McFadden looked down at the tracks, Gerald Vincent Gallagher had looked right back at him.

There hadn't been much blood. The stainless steel wheels of subway cars get so hot that as they roll over throats and limbs, severing them neatly, they also cauter-ize them. What Charley McFadden saw was Gerald Vincent Gallagher's head, and parts of his arms and legs and his torso, as if they were parts of some enormous plastic doll somebody had pulled apart and then had thrown down between the tracks.

And then as Charley McFadden was shamed before God, his parish priests, and all the good priests at Bishop New-man High School, and his mother, of course, for violating the "thou shalt not kill" commandment, the cavalry came riding up, late as usual, and he was shamed before them.

Big strong tough 225-pound plainclothes Narc tossing his cookies like a fucking fourteen-year-old because he did what all the other cops would have loved to do, fry the fucking cop killer, and saving the city the expense of a trial in the process.

By the time he ordered his third double John Jamison's with a beer on the side, Mickey O'Hara had begun to consider the tragedy of the life of Gerald Vincent Gallagher, deceased. How did a nice Irish Catholic boy wind up a junkie, on the run after a bungled stickup? What about *his* poor, heartbroken, good, mass-every-morning mother? What had she done to deserve, or produce, a miserable shit like Gerald Vincent Gallagher?

Mickey O'Hara was deep in his fourth double John Jamison's with a beer on the side and even deeper into a philosophical exploration of the injustice of life and man's inhumanity to man when he sensed someone slipping onto the stool beside him at the bar, and turned to look, and found himself faced with Lieutenant Edward M. DelRaye of the Homicide Division of the Philadelphia Police Department.

"Well, as I live and breathe," Lieutenant DelRaye said, "if it isn't Mrs. O'Hara's little boy Mickey."

"Hello, DelRaye," Mickey said.

Lieutenant DelRaye was not one of Mickey O'Hara's favorite police officers.

"Give my friend another of what he's having," DelRaye said to the bartender.

Mickey O'Hara had his first unkind thought: *I could be the last of the big spenders myself, if I put the drinks I bought people on a tab I had no intention of paying.*

"And what have you been up to, dressed to kill as you are?" Mickey asked.

"I was to the wake," DelRaye said. "I'm surprised you're not there."

"I paid my respects," Mickey said. "I liked Dutch."

"You heard we got the turd who got away from the diner?"

Mickey O'Hara nodded. And had his second unkind thought: We? We got the turd? *In a pig's ass, we did. A nice lad named Charley McFadden got him, and is sick about getting him, and you didn't have a fucking thing to do with it, Ed DelRaye. Not that it's out of character for you to take credit for something the boys on the street did.*

"So I heard," Mickey replied. "You were in on that, were you?"

''I made my little contribution,'' DelRaye said.

''Is that so?''

''A plainclothesman from Narcotics actually ran him down; I'm trying to think of his name—''

''How are you doing with the Nelson murder?'' Mickey O'Hara asked, as his John Jamison's with beer on the side was delivered.

''You wouldn't believe how many nigger faggots there are in Philly,'' DelRaye said.

''What's that got to do with anything?''

''Off the record, Mickey?'' DelRaye asked.

''No,'' Mickey said. ''Let's keep this on the record, Ed. Or change the subject.''

''I think we better change the subject, then,'' DelRaye said. He raised his glass. ''Mud in your eye.''

''I'm working on that story, is what it is,'' Mickey said. ''And if we go off the record, and you tell me something, and then I find it out on my own and use it, then you would be pissed, and I wouldn't blame you. You understand?''

''Sure, I understand perfectly. I was just trying to be helpful.''

''I know that, and I appreciate it,'' Mickey said. ''And I know what kind of pressure there must be on you to come up with something, his father being who he is and all.''

''You better believe it,'' DelRaye said.

''What can you tell me about Nelson and the TV lady?'' Mickey asked. ''On the record, Ed.''

''Well, she came home from work, half in the bag, and walked in and found him,'' DelRaye said.

''She was his girl friend?''

DelRaye snorted derisively.

''I take it that's a no?''

''That's neither a no or anything else, if we're still on the record,'' DelRaye said.

''I could, I suppose, call you an 'unnamed senior police officer involved in the investigation,' '' Mickey offered.

"I wouldn't want you quoting me as saying Nelson was a faggot," DelRaye said. "Because I didn't say that."

"Jesus Christ, was he?"

"If we're still on the record, no comment," DelRaye said. "We're still on the record?"

"Yeah. Sorry," Mickey O'Hara said, and then went for the jugular. "If I asked you, on the record, but as an 'unnamed senior police officer involved in the investigation' if you are looking for a Negro homosexual for questioning in the Nelson murder investigation, what would you say?"

"You're not going to use my name?"

"Scout's honor."

"Then I would say 'that's true.' "

"And if I asked you how come you can't find him, what would you say?"

"There are a number of suspects, and we believe that the name we have, Pierre St. Maury—"

"Who's he?"

"He's the one we want to question most. He lived with Nelson. We don't think that's his real name."

"Colored guy?"

"Big black guy. That description fits a lot of people in Philadelphia. It fits a lot of people who call themselves 'gay.' But we'll get him."

"But he's not the only one you're looking for?"

"There are others who meet the same description. The rent-a-cops on Stockton Place told us that Nelson had a lot of large black men friends."

"And you think one of them did it?"

"When people like that do each other in, they usually do it with a vengeance," DelRaye said.

"The way Nelson was done in, you mean?"

DelRaye did not reply. He suspected that he had gone too far.

"Mickey," he said, "I'm getting a little uncomfortable with this. Let's get off it, huh?"

"Sure," Mickey O'Hara said. "I got to get out of here anyway."

• • •

Ten minutes later, Mickey O'Hara walked back into the city room, walked with elaborate erectness to his desk, where he sat down at his computer terminal, belched, and pushed the COMPOSE button.

SLUG: Fairy Axman?

By Michael J. O'Hara

According to a senior police officer involved in the investigation of the brutal murder of Jerome Nelson, a "large black male," in his twenties, going by the name of Pierre St. Maury, and who reportedly shared the luxurious apartment at 6 Stockton Place, is being sought for questioning.

The police official, who spoke with this reporter only on condition of anonymity, said that it was believed the name Pierre St. Maury was assumed, and suggested this was common practice among what he described as Philadelphia's "large 'gay' black community."

Mickey stopped typing, found a cigarette and lit it, and then read what he had written.

Then he typed, "Do you have the balls to run this, or am I wasting my time?"

Then he moved the cursor to the top of the story and entered FLASH FLASH. This would cause a red light to blink on the city editor's monitor, informing him there was a story, either from the wire services, or from a reporter in the newsroom, that he considered important enough to demand the city editor's immediate attention. Then he pushed the SEND key.

Less than a minute later, the city editor crossed the city room to Mickey's desk.

"Jesus, Mickey," he said.

"Yes, or no?"

"I don't suppose you want to tell me who the cop who gave you this is?"

"I always protect my sources," Mickey said, and burped.

"It's for real?"

"The gentleman in question is a horse's ass, but he knows what he's talking about."

"The cops will know who talked to you," the city editor said.

"That thought had run through my mind," Mickey O'Hara said.

"You're going to put his ass in a crack," the city editor said.

"I have the strength of ten because in my heart, I'm pure," Mickey O'Hara said. "I made it perfectly clear that we were on the record."

"It will be tough on Mr. Nelson," the city editor said.

"Would we give a shit if he didn't own the *Ledger*?" Mickey countered.

The city editor exhaled audibly.

"This'll give you two by-lines on the front page," he said.

"Modesty is not my strong suit," Mickey said. "Yes, or no?"

"Go ahead, O'Hara," the city editor said.

FIFTEEN

It had been the intention of Lieutenant Robert McGrory, commanding officer of Troop G (Atlantic City) of the New Jersey State Police, to take off early, say a little after eight, which would have put him in Philly a little after nine-thirty, in plenty of time to go by the Marshutz & Sons Funeral Home for Dutch Moffitt's wake.

But that hadn't proved possible. One of his troopers, in pursuit of a speeder on U.S. 9, had blown a tire and slammed into a culvert. It wasn't as bad as it could have been; he could have killed himself, and the way the car looked it was really surprising he hadn't. But all he had was a broken arm, a dislocated shoulder, and some bad cuts on his face. But by the time he had that all sorted out (the trooper's wife was eight-and-a-half months gone, and had gotten hysterical when he went by the house to tell her and to take her to the hospital, and he had been afraid that she was going to have the kid right there and then) it was almost nine.

271

By then, the other senior officers going to Captain Dutch Moffitt's funeral had not elected to wait for him; a major and two captains could not be expected to wait for a lieutenant. Major Bill Knotts left word at the barracks for Lieutenant McGrory that Sergeant Alfred Mant (who was coming from Troop D, in Toms River, bringing people from there and further north) had been directed to swing by Atlantic City and wait at the Troop G Barracks for McGrory, however long it took for him to get free.

The senior state police officers in Knotts's car were all large men. They all had small suitcases; and they were, of course, in uniform, with all the regalia. The trunk of Knotts's Ford carried the usual assortment of special equipment, and there was no room in it for two of the three suitcases; they had to be carried in the backseat. When they were all finally in it, the Ford was crowded and sat low on its springs.

"I think you'd probably make better time on Three Twenty-two," Knotts said, as he settled into the front seat, beside Captain Gerry Kozniski, who was driving.

"Whatever you say, Major," Captain Kozniski said, aware that he had just been given authority, within reason, to "make good time" between Atlantic City and Philadelphia. There were two major routes, 322 and 30, between the two cities. U.S. 30 was four-laned nearly all the way, from Atlantic City to Interstate 295, just outside Camden. Only some sections of U.S. 322 were four-laned. Consequently, 30 got most of the traffic; there would be little traffic on 322 and it would be safer to drive faster on that road.

Captain Kozniski hit sixty-five, and then seventy, and then seventy-five. The Ford seemed to find its cruising speed just under eighty. They would still be late, but unless something happened, they could still at least put in an appearance at the wake.

"Word is," Captain Kozniski said, "that Bob McGrory's going to be a pallbearer."

"Yeah. Mrs. Moffitt asked for him," Knotts said.

"Dutch Moffitt and he went way back. They went to the FBI National Academy together."

He did not add, wondering why he didn't, that the Moffitts and McGrorys, having made friends at the FBI Academy in Quantico, had kept it up. They visited each other, the Moffitts and their kids staying at the McGrory house in Absecon for the beach in the summer, and the McGrorys and their house apes staying with the Moffitts in Philly for, for example, the Mummers' parades, or just because they wanted to go visit.

The wives got on well. Lieutenant Bob McGrory had told Knotts he had heard from his weeping wife that Dutch had stopped a bullet before he heard officially. Dutch's Jeannie had called McGrory's Mary-Ellen the minute she got back from the hospital. Mary-Ellen had parked the kids with her mother and gone right to Philly.

"I met him a couple of times," Captain Stu Simons, riding alone in the backseat, said. "VIP protection details, stuff like that. He was a nice guy. It's a fucking shame, what happened to him."

"You said it," Bill Knotts said.

"They catch him yet, the one that got away?"

"I think so," Captain Simons said. "I think I heard something. They canceled the GRM (General Radio Message) for him."

"I didn't hear anything," Knotts said. "It was a busy night."

"I hope they fry the sonofabitch," Captain Kozniski said.

"Don't hold your breath," Captain Simons said. "He'll get some bleeding-heart lawyer to defend him, and they'll wind up suing Moffitt's estate for violation of the bastard's civil rights."

Major Bill Knotts suddenly shifted very quickly on his seat, and looked out the window.

Captain Kozniski looked at him curiously.

"That shouldn't be there," Knotts said, aloud, but as if to himself.

"Whatever it was, I missed it," Captain Kozniski said.

"There was a Jaguar back there, on a dirt road."

"Somebody taking a piss," Captain Kozniski said.

"Or getting a little," Simons said.

"You want me to call it in, Major?" Captain Kozniski said.

"We're here," Knotts said simply.

Captain Kozniski eased slowly off on the accelerator, and when the car had slowed to sixty, began tapping the brakes. The highway was divided here by a median, and he looked for a place to cross it. The Ford bottomed out as they bounced across the median.

"Jesus Christ, Gerry!" Simons called out. "All we need is to wipe the muffler off!"

Captain Kozniski ignored him. "Where was it, Major?" he asked.

"Farther down," Knotts said. "Where the hell are we? Anybody notice?"

"We're three, four miles east of State Fifty-four," Captain Kozniski replied with certainty.

It took them five minutes to find the car, and then another two minutes to find another place to cross the median again.

"Stay on the shoulder," Knotts ordered, as they approached the dirt road.

Captain Kozniski stopped the car, and Knotts got out. Kozniski followed him, and then Simons. There was the sudden glare of a flashlight, and then Simons walked back to the car and got in the front seat and turned on the radio.

Knotts, carefully keeping out of the grass-free part of the road so as not to disturb tire tracks, approached the car, which was stopped, headed away from the highway, in the middle of the road.

"Give me a flashlight, please," he said, and put his hand out. Kozniski handed him his flashlight. Knotts flashed the light inside the car. It was empty. He moved the beam of the light very slowly around the front of the car.

"Major!" Captain Simons called. "It's a hit on the

NCIC computer. NCIC says it was reported stolen in Philadelphia.''

"Bingo," Captain Kozniski said.

"Get on the radio, please, Stu," Knotts said, "and have a car meet us here. And see if Philadelphia has any more on it."

"There was another car," Kozniski said. "You can see where they turned around." He used his flashlight as a pointer.

"If it was a couple of kids who 'borrowed' it, and then had second thoughts," Knotts said, "why get rid of it out here in the sticks?"

Kozniski went to the bumper and carefully examined it with his flashlight.

"It wasn't pushed in here, either," he said. "That rubber stuff on the bumper doesn't have a mark on it. I mean, I was thinking maybe it broke down, and they had to leave it."

"If they were going to dismantle it, there wouldn't be anything left by now but the license plate," Knotts said.

Captain Simons walked up to them.

"If the driver is apprehended," he said, formally, "he is to be held for questioning about a homicide."

"Double bingo," Captain Kozniski said. "You telepathic, Major?"

"Absolutely," Major Bill Knotts said. "You mean you didn't know?"

He walked to the Ford, switched the radio frequency to the statewide frequency, established communication with state police headquarters in Trenton; and, after identifying himself and reporting they had located a car NCIC said was hot, and which the Philadelphia police were interested in for a homicide investigation, asked for the dispatch of the state police mobile crime lab van.

"And first thing in the morning, I think we had better get enough people out here to have a good look at the woods," he said. "In the meantime, I'll need somebody to guard the site. I pulled a car off patrol, but I'd like to get him released as soon as possible."

They all got back in the Ford and waited for the patrol car to come to the scene.

Captain Kozniski, without really being aware he had done it, switched on the radar. A minute or so later, it came to life, and a car headed for Atlantic City came down the highway twenty-five miles an hour faster than the posted limit.

"You want to ticket him, Major?" Kozniski asked.

"God no, if we pulled him over and a major and two captains got out of the car, we'd give him a heart attack," Knotts said.

The car was filled with chuckles and laughter.

Two minutes later, Kozniski saw in his rearview mirror the flashing lights on top of a patrol car.

"Here comes the car," he said. Knotts got out of the Ford, explained the situation to the trooper, and then got back in.

He looked at his watch as Kozniski got the Ford moving.

"Christ, we're going to be late for the wake," he said. "You better step on it, Gerry."

The Wackenhut rent-a-cop on the Arch Street entrance to the Stockton Place underground garage stooped over and looked into the Ford LTD. Recognizing Louise Dutton, he smiled, went back to his little cubicle, and pushed the button raising the barrier.

Once inside the garage, Peter Wohl parked the LTD beside her yellow Cadillac convertible, and they got out.

She met him at the back of the LTD.

"If you find the time, dear, you might do the ironing," Louise said as she dropped the keys to her apartment in his hand. "But don't wear yourself out."

"What I think I'll do is call Sharon," Peter said.

"You bastard!" she said, and kissed him quickly and got in her Cadillac convertible.

He waited until she had driven out of the underground garage and then walked through the tunnel to the elevators. The call button for the elevator required a key to function, and he had to work his way through half a dozen before he found the right one. And then he had trouble getting into the apartment itself.

He felt strange, once he was inside and had snapped on the lights, and wasn't sure if he was uncomfortable or excited. There was something very personal, very intimate, in being here alone. He took off his jacket and threw it on an overstuffed chair, and then changed his mind and hung it in a closet by the door. There were two fur coats in there, a long one, and one so short it was almost a cape.

That reminded him that his uniform and other things were still in the LTD, so he retraced his steps and carried them up. He carried everything into the bedroom. The bedroom smelled of Louise. There was a display of perfume bottles on her dressing table and he walked to them and squirted a bulb, and then it really smelled like her.

He found the bathroom, voided his bladder, and then took a good look around. The bathtub looked like a small black marble swimming pool. He wondered if it contained a Jacuzzi, and looked for controls, but found none.

What he needed, he decided, was a drink. He went back in the living room and opened doors and found her liquor supply. He carried a bottle of scotch into the kitchen and found ice cubes and made himself a drink. Then he said aloud, "You goddamned voyeur, Wohl," and went back in the bedroom and opened the drawers of her dresser, one at a time. He found the array of underwear erotic; but a rather diligent—one might say professional—search of the premises failed to come up with a photograph or any other evidence, of any other male, young, old, handsome, ugly, or otherwise.

He was pleased. He went to make himself another drink, and then changed his mind. This was a momentous occasion; the most beautiful girl in the world, the love, finally, of his life, was going to welcome him into her bed, and the worst thing he could arrange would be for him to be shit-faced when she came home. No more booze.

Christ! Washington!

Five minutes later, he had relayed the information to Detective Jason Washington that he would have Miss Louise Dutton at the medical examiner's office at eight o'clock the following morning.

Champagne! Why didn't I think of that before? I'll have a couple of bottles on ice when she walks in the door.

He put his coat back on and went out in search of champagne. He bought three bottles, instead of two, and two plastic bags of ice, and returned to the apartment. He couldn't find a champagne bucket, so he put the champagne and the ice in the kitchen sink and covered it with a dishcloth. That raised the question of champagne glasses, and a further diligent search came up with some, which apparently had not been washed for years. He washed and rinsed two of them and then polished them with a paper towel.

He was ready. But she would not be here for an hour, an hour and fifteen minutes.

An idea, so ridiculous and absurd on its face that he laughed out loud, popped into his mind.

What the hell, why not?

He went into the bathroom and turned the taps on to fill the marble swimming pool. He saw a glass container with BUBBLE BATH printed on it. If half a cupful of detergent was the proper amount to use for a washerful of dirty clothes, that measure would probably work for a bubble bath. He poured what he estimated to be a half cupful into the tub.

Next, he looked for and found a razor. He examined it carefully. It was a ladies' razor, with a gold-plated head, and a long, pink, curved handle. But the working part of it, the gold-plated device, seemed to be identical to a regular razor. He decided it would do.

He took the cover from the bed, folded it neatly, and then turned a corner of the sheet and blanket down, and finally returned to the bathroom. The swimming pool was now overflowing with bubbles. There were more bubbles than he would have imagined possible.

There was nothing to do about it now, obviously, so he

slipped into the water. There were so many bubbles that he had to push them away from his mouth with his hand.

There's room in here for both of us. I wonder how she would react to that suggestion?

There came the sound of a door opening against a lock chain.

Oh, Christ, she came home early! And I put the god-damned chain on the goddamned door!

He erupted from the swimming pool, called "Wait a minute, I'll be right there!" and dried himself hastily. He grabbed his bathrobe from where he had left it on the bed, and ran through the apartment to the door.

"Sorry," he said, as he pushed the door closed so that he could unfasten the chain lock. "I was taking a god-damned bath."

He pulled the door open.

He found himself looking at a smallish, dapper, intense, middle-aged man.

"I'll just bet," Stanford Fortner Wells III said, "that your name is Peter Wohl."

Louise Dutton let herself into her apartment, and then turned to fasten the dead-bolt lock and door chain.

"Peter, don't tell me you're asleep," she called, and then walked into her living room, where she found her father and Staff Inspector Peter Wohl standing by the couches and coffee table. There were glasses; a bottle of scotch; a cheap glass bowl half-full of ice; and an open box of Ritz crackers on the table. They were both smoking cigars.

"Hello, baby," her father said.

"Oh, *God!*" Louise said.

"You called," Stanford Fortner Wells III said, "and I came."

"So I see," Louise said, and then ran across the room to him, and threw herself in his arms. "Oh, Daddy!"

When she let him go, she took a handkerchief from her purse and blew her nose loudly in it.

She looked at Peter. "Is my mascara running?"

He shook his head no.

She walked to him, and took the glass from his hand and took a large swallow.

"Peter and I have been having a pleasant chat," Wells said.

"I'll bet you have," Louise said, as she handed the glass back. She pointed to the bowl of ice. "What's with that?"

"It's a bowl, with ice in it," Peter said.

"What do you think that is?" she said, pointing to a large, square heavy crystal bowl on a sideboard.

Both Peter and her father shrugged.

"That's an ice bowl," she said. "I paid two hundred dollars for it. Where did you get that one?"

"Under the sink in the kitchen," her father said.

"That figures," she said. She went to the crystal bowl, moved it to the coffee table, dumped the ice from the cheap bowl into it, and then carried it into the kitchen. She returned in a moment with a small silver bowl full of cashews and a glass.

"Where were they?" her father asked. "All we could find was the crackers."

"In the kitchen," she said. She made herself a drink and then looked at them. "Gentlemen, be seated," she said.

They sat down, Wells on the couch, Peter Wohl in an armchair.

"Well," Louise said. "Now that we're all here, what should we talk about?"

Wohl and her father chuckled.

"I thought the standard scenario in a situation like this was that the father was supposed to thrash the boyfriend within an inch of his life," Louise said. "What happened, Daddy, did you see his gun?"

"No," Wells said. "I just decided that a man who takes bubble baths can't be all bad."

"Bubble baths?" Louise asked.

"Oh, shit," Peter said.

"When he answered the door, he had bubbles in his

ears, all over his head," Wells said. "You really don't want to thrash a man with bubbles on him."

Peter, grimacing, laughed deep in his throat. Wells grinned at him.

They like each other, Louise realized, and it pleased her.

"Tell me about the champagne in the sink," Louise said.

Her father threw up his hands, signaling his innocence about that.

"I'm a scotch drinker, myself," he said.

"Ooooh," Louise cooed, "champagne for little ol' me, Peter?"

"At the time, it seemed like a splendid idea," Peter said.

"That was before he answered the door," Wells said.

"Surprise! Surprise!" Peter said.

The two men laughed.

"You should have seen his face," Wells said.

"How long have you been here, in Philadelphia, I mean?" Louise asked.

"Since late this afternoon," Wells said. "I just missed you at WCBL."

The telephone rang.

"I wonder who that can be?" Louise said. "Oh, God! My mother?"

"For your sake, Peter, I hope not," Wells said.

"Jesus!" Wohl said, as Louise went to the telephone.

"Hello?" Louise said to the telephone. Then her face stiffened. "How did you get this number? Who is this?"

Then she offered the telephone to Wohl.

"Lieutenant DelRaye for you, *Inspector Wohl,*" she said, just a little nastily.

As Wohl got up and crossed the room, Wells asked, "DelRaye? Is that the cop you had trouble with?"

"Yes, indeed," Louise said.

"This is Peter Wohl," Wohl said to the telephone. Then he listened, asked a few cryptic questions, then finally said, "Thank you, Lieutenant. If anything else comes up, I'll either be at this number or at home."

He hung up.

" 'I'll either be at this number or at home,' " Louise parroted. "What did you do, Peter, thumbtack my number, my *unlisted* number, to the bulletin board?"

"I don't even know your number," Peter said, just a little sharply. "He must have gotten it from Jason Washington."

"What did he want?" Louise asked quickly. She had seen her father's eyebrows raise in surprise to learn that Peter didn't know her number.

"They found Jerome Nelson's car," Wohl said. "Actually, a New Jersey state trooper major found it as he was driving here for Dutch's wake. In the middle of New Jersey, on a dirt road off U.S. Three Twenty-two."

"What does that mean?" Wells asked.

"One of Nelson's cars, a Jaguar, was missing from the garage downstairs," Peter said. "It's possible that the doer took it."

"The *'doer'?*" Wells asked.

"Whoever chopped him up," Wohl said.

"I love your delicate choice of language," Louise said. "Really, Peter!"

"Does finding the car mean anything?" Wells asked.

"Only, so far, to reinforce the theory that the doer took it. As opposed to an ordinary, run-of-the-mill car thief," Wohl said. "The New Jersey State Police sent their mobile crime lab to where they found the car, and, in the morning, they'll search the area. With a little luck, they may turn up something."

"Such as?" Wells pursued.

Wohl threw his hands up. "You never know."

"Why do you look so worried, Peter?" Louise asked.

"Do I look worried?" he asked, and then went on before anyone could reply: "I'm trying to make up my mind whether or not I should call Arthur Nelson. Now, I mean, rather than in the morning."

"Why would you call him?" Wells asked.

"Commissioner Czernick has assigned me to stroke him," Peter said. "To keep him abreast of where the investigation is going."

"Until just now, I thought they liked you on the police department," Wells said. "How did you get stuck with that?"

"He can be difficult," Peter said, chuckling. "You know him?"

"Sure," Wells said. "Which is not the same thing as saying he's a friend of mine."

"He's not willing to face the facts about his son," Peter said. "I don't know whether he expected me to believe it or not, but he suggested very strongly that Louise was his son's girl friend."

"Obviously not knowing about you and Louise," Wells said.

"Nobody, with your exception, knows about Louise and me," Wohl said.

"The two of you have developed the infuriating habit of talking about me as if I'm not here," Louise said.

"Sorry," her father said. "Are you going to call him—now, I mean?"

"Yeah," Peter said. "I think I'd better."

"I was going to suggest that," Wells said. "Better to have him annoyed by a late-night call than sore that you didn't tell him something as soon as you could."

They like each other, Louise thought again. *Because they think alike? Because they* are *alike? Is that what's going on with me and Peter? That I like him because he's so much like my father? Even more so than Dutch?*

Peter dialed information and asked for Arthur J. Nelson's residence number. There was a reply, and then he said, obviously annoyed, "Thank you."

He sensed Louise's eyes on him, and met hers for a moment, and then smiled mischievously.

"He's got an unlisted number, too."

He dialed another number, identified himself as Inspector Wohl, and asked for a residence phone number for Arthur J. Nelson.

He wrote the number down, and put his finger on the telephone switch.

"That's it?" Louise asked. "You can get an unlisted number from the phone company that easily?"

"That wasn't the information operator," Wohl said, as he dialed the telephone. "I was talking to the detective on duty in Intelligence. The phone company won't pass out numbers."

There was the faint sound of a telephone ringing.

"Mr. Arthur J. Nelson, please," he said. "This is Inspector Peter Wohl of the Philadelphia Police Department."

Neither Louise nor her father could hear both sides of the conversation, but it was evident that the call was not going well. The proof came when Peter exhaled audibly and shook his head after he hung up.

"Arthur was being his usual, obnoxious self, I gather?" Wells asked.

"He wanted to know precisely where the car was found, where it is. I told him I didn't know. He made it plain he didn't believe me. I was on the verge of telling him that if I knew, I wouldn't tell him. I don't want a dozen members of the goddamned press mucking around by the car until the lab people are through with it."

"Thank you very much, you goddamned policeman," Louise said.

"You're welcome," Peter said, and Wells laughed.

"God*damn* you, Peter!"

"*I* didn't teach her to swear like that," Wells said. "She learn that from you?"

"I'd hate to tell you what she said to Lieutenant Del-Raye," Peter said.

"I know what she said," Wells said. "If she was a little younger, I'd wash her mouth out with soap."

"I may get to that," Peter said.

"What the hell is it with you two?" Louise demanded. "A mutual-admiration society? A mutual-male-chauvinist-admiration society?"

"Could be," Wells said. "I don't know how he feels about me, baby, but I like Peter very much."

Louise saw happiness and perhaps relief in Peter's eyes. Their eyes met for a moment.

"Then can I have him, Daddy?" Louise said, in a credible mimicry of a small girl's voice. "I promise to feed him, and housebreak him, and walk him, and all that stuff. Please, Daddy?"

Wohl chuckled. Wells grew serious.

"I think he'd have even more trouble housebreaking you than you would him," he said. "You come from very different kennels. My unsolicited advice—to both of you—is to take full advantage of the trial period."

"I thought you said you liked him," Louise said, trying, and not quite succeeding, to sound light and bright.

"I do. But you were talking about marriage, and I think that would be a lousy idea."

"But if we love each other?" Louise asked, now almost plaintively.

"I have long believed that if it were as difficult to get married as it is to get divorced, society would be a hell of a lot better off," Wells said.

"You're speaking from personal experience, no doubt?" Louise flared.

"Cheap shot, baby," Wells said, getting up. "I've had a long day. I'm going to bed. I'll see you tomorrow before I go."

"Don't go, Daddy," Louise said. "I'm sorry. I didn't mean what I said."

"Sure, you did. And I don't blame you. But just for the record, if I had married your mother, that would have been even a greater mistake than marrying the one I did. I don't expect you to pay a bit of attention to what I've said, but I felt obliged to say it anyway."

He crossed the room to Peter Wohl and put out his hand.

"It was good to meet you, Peter," he said. "And I meant what I said, I do like you. Having said that, be warned that I'm going to do everything I can to keep her from marrying you."

"Fair enough," Peter said.

"You understand why, I think," Wells said.

"Yes, sir," Peter said. "I think I do."

"And you think I'm wrong?"

"I don't know, Mr. Wells," Peter Wohl said.

Wells snorted, looked into Wohl's eyes for a moment, and then turned to his daughter.

"Breakfast? Could you come to the Warwick at say, nine?"

"No," she said.

"Come on, baby," he said.

"I have a busy schedule tomorrow," she said. "I begin the day at eight by looking at a severed head, and then at ten, I have to go to a funeral. It would have to be in the afternoon. Can you stay that long?"

"I'll stay as long as necessary," he said. "We are going to have a very serious conversation, baby, you and I."

"Can I drop you at your hotel, Mr. Wells?" Peter asked. "It's on my way."

"Come on, Peter," Wells said. "Don't ruin a fine first impression by being a hypocrite now. Anyway, there's a limo waiting for me."

He kissed Louise's cheek, waved at Wohl, and walked out of the apartment.

SIXTEEN

Arthur J. Nelson did not like pills. There were several reasons for this, starting with a gut feeling that there was something basically wrong with chemically fooling around with the natural functions of the body, but primarily it was because he had seen what pills had done to his wife.

Sally was always bitching about his drinking, and maybe there was a little something to that; maybe every once in a while he *did* take a couple of belts that he really didn't need; but the truth was that, so far as *intoxication* was concerned, she had been floating around on a chemical cloud for years.

It had been going on for years. Sally had been nervous when he married her, and once a month, before that time of the month, she had been like a coiled spring, just waiting for a small excuse to blow up. She'd started taking pills then, a little something to help her cope. That had worked, and when she'd gotten pregnant, the need for them had seemed to pass.

But even before she'd had Jerome, she'd started on pills again, to calm her down. Tranquilizers, they called them. Then, after Jerome was born, when he was still a baby, she'd kept taking them whenever, as she put it, things just *"made her want to scream."*

She hadn't taken them steadily then, just when there was some kind of stress. Over the years, it had just slipped up on her. There seemed to be more and more stress, which she coped with by popping a couple of whatever the latest miracle of medicine was.

In the last five years, it had really gotten worse. Jerome had had a lot to do with that. It had been bad when he was still living at home, and had grown worse when he'd moved out. It had gotten so bad that he'd finally put her in Menninger's, where they put a name to it, "chemical dependency," and had weaned her from what she was taking and put her on something else, which was supposed to be harmless.

Maybe it was, but Sally hadn't given it a real try. The minute she got back to Philadelphia, she'd changed doctors again, finding a new one who would prescribe whatever she had been taking in the first place that helped her cope. The real result of her five months in Menninger's was that she was now on two kinds of pills, instead of just one.

Now, probably, three kinds of pills. What she had been taking, plus a new bottle of tiny oblong blue ones provided by the doctors when she'd gone over the edge when he'd had to tell her what happened to Jerome.

They would, the doctor said, help her cope. And the doctor added, it would probably be a good idea if Arthur Nelson took a couple of them before going to bed. It would help him sleep.

No fucking way. He had no intention of turning himself into a zombie, walking around in a daze smiling at nothing. Not so long as there was liquor, specifically cognac. Booze might be bad for you, but all it left you with was a hangover in the morning. And he had read somewhere that cognac was different from say, scotch. They made scotch from grain, and cognac was made from wine. It was different chemically, and it understandably affected people differently than whiskey did.

Arthur J. Nelson had come to believe that if he didn't make a pig of himself, if he didn't gulp it down, if he just sipped slowly at a glass of cognac, or put half a shot in his coffee, it was possible to reach a sort of equilibrium. The right amount of cognac in his system served to deaden the pain, to keep him from painful thought, but not to make him drunk. He could still think clearly, was still very much aware of what was going on. The only thing he had to do, he believed, was exercise the necessary willpower, and resist the temptation to pour another glass before it was really safe to do so. And there was no question in his mind that he had, in the last twenty-four hours, been doing just that. A lesser man would have broken down and wept, or gotten falling-down drunk, or both, and he had done neither.

When Staff Inspector Peter Wohl had telephoned, Arthur J. Nelson had been a third of the way through a bottle of Hennessey V.S.O.P., one delicate sip at a time, except of course for the couple of hookers he had splashed into his coffee.

And he took a pretty good sip, draining the snifter, when he hung up after talking to Staff Inspector Peter Wohl, that miserable arrogant sonofabitch.

He poured the snifter a third full, and then, carrying it with him, walked upstairs from his den to his bedroom on the second floor. He quietly opened the door and walked in.

Sally was in the bed, flat on her back, asleep. She looked, he thought, old and tired and pale. Although he hated what the fucking pills had done to her, he was glad, for her sake, that she had them now. And then she snored. It was amazing, he thought, how noisily she snored. It sounded as if she were a 250-pound man, and he supposed she didn't weigh 100 pounds, if that much.

He remembered the first time he had seen her naked, held her naked in his arms. She had been so small and delicate he had been afraid that he was going to break her. And he remembered when she was large with Jerome. That had been almost impossible to believe, even looking right at it.

A tear ran down his cheek, and he brushed at it, forgetting that that hand held the snifter. He spilled a couple of drops on his shirt, and swore, loud enough for it to get through to Sally, who sort of groaned.

He held himself motionless for a moment, until her regular, slow, heavy breathing pattern returned. Then he left the room as carefully and quietly as he entered it.

He stood at the top of the stairs. He was hungry. He hadn't eaten. The house had been full of people, and although Mrs. Dawberg, the housekeeper, had seen to it that there had been a large buffet of cold cuts, he just hadn't gotten around to eating.

And now all the help was in bed, and he hated to get them out of bed in any case; and especially now, when they would need all the rest they could get to get ready for tomorrow, when the house, all day, would be like goddamn Suburban Station at half past five.

He walked down the wide staircase, wondering if he really wanted to go into the kitchen and fix himself an egg sandwich or something. He went back in his den and drained what was left in the snifter after he—Jesus, what a dumb thing to do!!!—had spilled it on his shirt, and then poured a little more in.

To hell with going in the kitchen, he decided. *What I'll do is just get in a car and go find a fast-food joint.*

The idea had a sudden appeal. He realized that what he really wanted was junk food. Hamburgers and french fries. Not what they served these days in McDonald's or Burger King, but the little tiny ones they used to sell for a dime, the kind they sort of steamed on the grill over chopped onions. In those white tile buildings with no booths, just round-seat stools by a counter, where everything was stainless steel. He could practically smell the damned things.

He had a little trouble finding where they kept the keys

to the cars. He supposed they took them from the ignition last thing when they locked up for the night. He finally found a rack of keys in a little cupboard in the pantry off the garage. They were all in little numbered leather cases, except the key to the Rolls, which had a Rolls insignia on it.

Which was which?

He didn't want to take the Rolls. He was going to go to a hamburger joint and sit on a round stool and eat cheap little hamburgers and french fries, and you don't take a Rolls-Royce to do that.

He took one key and worked his way through a Cadillac coupe and a Buick station wagon before it worked in the ignition switch of an Oldsmobile sedan he didn't remember ever having seen before. He remembered vaguely that Sally had said something about having to get Mrs. Dawberg a new car, and that he'd told her to go ahead and do it.

He thought he remembered a White Palace or a Crystal Palace or whatever the hell they called those joints about a mile away, but when he got there, there was a Sunoco gas station, so he drove on. When he stopped at a red light, he decided it had been some time since he'd last had a little sip, and pulled the cork from the Hennessey bottle and took a little nip.

Thirty minutes later, not having found what he wanted, he decided to hell with it. What he would do was go by the *Ledger*. It wouldn't be a cheap little White Palace hamburger, but the cafeteria operated twenty-four hours a day, and he could at least get a hamburger, or something else. And it was always a good idea to drop in unannounced on the city room. Keep them on their toes.

He drove to the back of the building and pulled the nose of the Oldsmobile in against a loading dock, and took another little sip. He could hardly walk into the city room carrying a bottle of cognac, and there was no telling how long he would be in there.

There was a tap on his window, and he looked out and saw a security officer frowning at him. With some difficulty, Arthur J. Nelson managed to find the window switch and lower the window.

"Hey, buddy," the security officer said, "you can't park there."

"Let me tell *you* something, *buddy,*" Arthur J. Nelson said. "I own this goddamned newspaper and I can park any goddamned place I please!"

The security officer's eyes widened, and then there was recognition.

"Sorry, Mr. Nelson, I didn't recognize you."

"Goddamned right," Arthur Nelson said, and got out of the car. "Keep up the good work!" he called after the retreating security officer.

He entered the building and walked down the tile-lined corridor to the elevator bank. Windows opened on the presses in the basement. They were still, although he saw pressmen standing around. He glanced at his watch.

It was not quite one A.M. The first (One Star) edition started rolling at two-fifteen. Christ alone knew what it was costing him to have all those pressmen standing around for an hour or more with their fingers up their asses at $19.50 an hour. He'd have to look into that. Goddamned unions would bankrupt you if you didn't keep your eye on them.

He got in the elevator and rode it up to the fifth, editorial, floor, and went into the city room.

He felt eyes on him as he walked across the room to the city desk.

Well, why the hell not? I don't come in here at this time nearly often enough.

There were half a dozen men and two women at the city desk. The city editor got to his feet when he saw him.

"Good evening, Mr. Nelson," he said. "How are you, sir?"

"How the hell do you think I am?" Nelson snapped.

"I'd like to offer my condolences, sir," the city editor said.

"Very kind of you," Arthur Nelson said, automatically,

and then he remembered that goddamned cop, whatsis-name, *Wohl.*

"I've got something for you," Nelson said. "The cops have found my son's car. It was stolen from the garage at his apartment when . . . it was stolen from his apart-ment."

"Yes, sir?"

"You haven't heard about it?"

"No, sir."

"Well, I'm telling you," Nelson said. "And they're giving me the goddamned runaround. Somewhere in Jer-sey is where they found it. Some Jersey state trooper found it, but he wouldn't tell me where."

"I'm sure we could find out, sir," the city editor said. "If that's what you're suggesting."

"Goddamn right," Nelson said. "Get somebody on it. It's news, wouldn't you say?"

"Yes, sir, of course it is. I'll get right on it."

"I think that would be a good idea," Nelson said.

"I was about to go to Composing, Mr. Nelson," the city editor said. "We're just about pasted up. Would you like to go with me?"

"Why not?" Nelson said. "Have you got somebody around here you could send to the cafeteria for me?"

"What would you like?"

"I'd like a hamburger and french fries," Nelson said. "Hamburger with onions. Fried, not raw. And a cup of black coffee."

"Coming right up," the city editor said.

Nelson walked across the city room to Composing. The *Ledger* had, the year before, gone to a cold-type process, replacing the Linotype system. The upcoming One Star edition was spread out on slanting boards, in "camera-ready" form. Here and there, compositors were pasting up.

Nelson went to the front page. The lead story, under the headline "Man Sought In Police Murder Killed Elud-ing Capture" caught his eye, and he read it with interest.

If all the goddamned cops in the goddamned city hadn't

*all been looking for that guy, they probably could have
caught the bastards who killed my Jerome. They don't give
a shit about me, or any other ordinary citizen, but when
one of their own gets it, that's a horse of a different color.
That sonofabitch Wohl wouldn't even tell me where Jerome's car was found.*

The city editor appeared.

"Now that the cops have found that pathetic sonofabitch," Arthur J. Nelson said, "maybe, just maybe, they'll
have time to look for the murderer of my son."

"Yes, sir," the city editor said, uncomfortably. "Mr.
Nelson, I think you better have a look at this."

He thrust the Early Bird edition of the *Bulletin* at him.

"What's this?" Nelson said. And then his eye fell on
the headline, "Police Seek 'Gay' Black Lover In Nelson
Murder" and the story below it by Michael J. O'Hara.

"I thought O'Hara worked for us," Arthur J. Nelson
said, very calmly.

"We had to let him go about eighteen months ago,"
the city editor said.

"Oh?" Arthur J. Nelson asked.

"Yes, sir. He had a bottle problem," the city editor
said.

"And a nice sense of revenge, wouldn't you say?" Nelson said. He didn't wait for a reply. He turned and walked
down the line of paste-ups until he found the editorial
page.

He pointed to it. "Hold this," he said. "There will be
a new editorial."

"Sir?"

"I'm not going to let the goddamned cops get away with
this," Arthur J. Nelson said. "Not on your goddamned
life."

Louise Dutton slipped out of her robe, draped it over
the water closet, and then slid open the glass door to her
shower stall. She giggled at what she saw.

"What the hell are you doing?" she asked.

Peter Wohl, who had been shaving with Louise's pink,

long-handled ladies' razor, heard her voice, but not what she had said, and opened his eyes and looked at her.

"What?"

"What are you doing?"

"Shaving."

"In the shower? With your eyes closed?"

"Why not?"

"You look ridiculous doing that," she said.

"On the other hand," he said, leering at her nakedness, "you look great. Why don't you step into my office and we can fool around a little?"

"There's not room for the both of us in there," she said.

"That would depend on how close we stood," he said.

"Hurry up, Peter," she said, and closed the door.

She wiped the condensation from the mirror and bent forward to examine her face closely. She looked into the reflection of her eyes. She felt a sense of sadness, and wondered why.

Peter came out of the shower.

"I left it running," he said, as he reached for a towel.

Louise gave in to the impulse and wrapped her arms around him, resting her face on his back.

"The offer to fool around is still open," Peter said.

"What's this?" she asked, tracing what looked like a dimple on his back.

"Nothing," he said.

"What *is* it, Peter?" she demanded.

"It's what they call an entrance wound," he said.

"You were *shot?*" she asked, letting him go, and then turning him around so she could look into his face.

"Years ago," he said.

"You're not old enough for it to be 'years ago,' " she said. "Tell me!"

"Not much to tell," he said. "I was working the Ninth District as a patrolman, and a lady called the cops and said her husband was drunk and violent and beating her and the kids up; and when I got there, he was, so I put the cuffs on him, and as I was putting him in the backseat of the car, she shot me.''

''Why?''

''She wanted the cops to make her husband stop beating up on her,'' Peter said, ''but *arresting* the love of her life and father of her children was something else.''

''She could have killed you,'' Louise said.

''I think that's what she had in mind,'' Peter said.

''Did you shoot her?'' Louise asked.

''I don't even remember getting shot . . . I remember what felt like somebody whacking me with a baseball bat, and the next thing I know, I'm being wheeled into a hospital emergency room.''

''How long were you in the hospital?''

''About two weeks.''

''But you're all right? I mean, there was no permanent damage?''

''All the important parts are working just fine,'' Peter said. He moved his midsection six inches closer to Louise to demonstrate. ''See?''

''Why, you dirty old man, you!'' Louise said, and turned and went into the shower.

When she came out of the shower, she could smell both frying bacon and coffee, and smiled.

Peter Wohl, she thought, *the compleat lover, as skilled in the kitchen as the bedroom.*

Then she went into her bedroom, and saw that he had left his uniform tunic, and his uniform cap, and his gun, on the bed.

She walked to the bed and picked up the hat first and looked at it, and the insignia on it, and then laid it down again. Then she leaned on the bed and examined the badge pinned to the uniform tunic. And finally, she looked at the gun.

It was in a shoulder holster, of leather and stretch elastic that showed signs of much use. The elastic was wrinkled, and the leather sweat-stained and creased. She tugged the pistol loose and held it up to the level of her face by holding the grip between her thumb and index finger.

It was not a new pistol. The finish had been worn through to the white metal beneath at the muzzle and at the front of the cylinder. The little diamonds of the checkering on the grips were worn smooth. She sniffed it, and smelled the oil.

It's a tool, she thought, *like a carpenter's hammer, or a mechanic's wrench. It's the tool he carries to work. The difference is that the function of his tool is to shoot people, not drive nails or fix engines.*

She put the pistol back into the holster, and then wiped her hands on the sheet.

Then she got dressed.

He had made bacon and eggs. He was mopping the remaining yolk from his plate with an English muffin; her eggs and bacon were waiting for her.

"Your eggs are probably cold," Peter said.

"I had to take a shower," she said, a shade snappishly.

"Not for me you didn't," he said. "You smelled great to me."

"Don't be silly," she snapped, and this time the snappishness registered.

"Coffee?" he asked, a little coldly.

"Please," she said.

He went to the stove and returned with a pot.

"Did you ever kill anyone, Peter?"

His eyebrows went up.

"Did you?"

"Yes," he said. "Lovely subject for breakfast conversation."

"Why?"

"Because I think otherwise he would have shot me," Peter said. "Lovely weather we've been having, isn't it?"

"An interesting scenario popped into my mind in the bedroom," Louise said.

"That happens to me all the time," he said. "You really thought of something we haven't done?"

He smiled, and she knew he was pleased that he thought she had changed the subject, but she knew she couldn't stop now.

"There I am, sitting in my rocking chair, knitting little booties, in our little rose-covered cottage by the side of the road," Louise said, "while our three adorable children . . . You get the picture."

"Sounds fine to me," Peter said.

"And the doorbell rings, and I go to answer it, and there stands Hizzoner the Mayor Carlucci. 'Sorry, Mrs. Wohl,' Hizzoner says. 'But your fine husband, the late Inspector Wohl, was just shot by an angry housewife. Or was it a bandit? Doesn't really matter. He's dead. Gone to that Great Roundhouse in the Sky.' "

It took Peter a moment to reply, but finally he said, "Are you always this cheerful in the morning?"

"Only when I'm on my way to see a severed head while en route to a funeral," Louise said. "But I'm serious, Peter."

"Then I'll answer you seriously," he said. "I *am* a Staff Inspector. I don't respond to calls. Supervisors supervise. The guys on the street are the ones that have to deal with the public. That's for openers. And most police officers who do their twenty years on the street never fire their pistols except on the range."

"That's why you carry a gun all the time, right?" Louise countered.

"I can't remember the last time I took it out of the holster except to clean it," Peter said.

"I can," Louise said. "The very first time I saw you, Peter, you were jumping out of a car with your gun in your hand."

"That was an anomaly," Peter said. "Dutch getting shot was an anomaly. He's probably the first captain who fired his weapon in the line of duty in twenty years."

"That may be, but Dutch got shot," Louise said. "Got shot and killed. And there you were, with your gun in your hand, rushing to the gun battle at the OK Corral."

"What did you think when you saw me getting out of my car?"

" 'Where did that good-looking man come from?' "

"How about 'Thank God, it's the cops'?" Peter asked, softly.

She met his eyes for a long moment.

"Touché," she said, finally.

"That's what I do, baby," Peter said. "I'm a cop. And I'm good at what I do. And, actuarially speaking, I'm in probably no more of a risky occupation than a, hell, I don't know, an airline pilot or a stockbroker."

"Tell that to Mrs. Moffitt," Louise said.

"Eat your eggs before they get cold, baby," Peter said.

"I don't think so," she said, pushing the plate away. "I think I would rather get something to eat *after* I look at the head."

"I'm sorry, but that is necessary," Peter said.

"Peter, I don't know if I could spend the rest of my life wondering if I'm going to be a widow by the end of the day," Louise said.

"You're exaggerating the risk," he said.

"Is it graven on stone somewhere that you have to spend the rest of your life as a cop?"

"It's what I do, Louise. And I like it."

"I was afraid you'd say that," she said, and got to her feet. "Go put on your policeman's suit, and take me to see the severed head," she said.

"We can talk this out," Peter said.

"I think everything that can be said on the subject has been said," Louise said. "It was what Daddy was talking about when he said the idea of us getting married was a lousy one."

"Come on, baby," Peter said. "I understand why you're upset, but—"

"Just shut up, Peter," Louise said. "Just please shut up."

Antonio V. "Big Tony" Amarazzo, proprietor of Tony's Barbershop, stood behind the barber chair, swinging it from side to side so that the man in the chair could admire his handiwork. He had given the large man under the striped bib his very first haircut, twenty years before, the day before he started kindergarten.

Officer Charles McFadden looked into the mirror. The mirror was partly covered by the front page of the Four Star Edition of the *Bulletin,* with his picture on it, which had been taped to the mirror below the legend (lettered with shoe whitener) "OUR NEIGHBORHOOD HERO CHARLEY MCFADDEN."

"Looks fine, Mr. Amarazzo," Charley said. "Thank you."

" *'Mister* Amarazzo'?" Big Tony replied. "You sore at me or what? We haven't been friends since God only knows how long?"

Charley, who could not think of a response, smiled at Big Tony's reflection in the mirror.

"And now we're gonna give you a shave that'll turn your chin into a baby's bottom," Big Tony said.

"Oh, I don't want a shave," Charley protested.

"You can't go to Saint Dominic's needing a shave," Big Tony said, as he pushed Charley back in the chair and draped his face in a hot towel, "and don't worry, it's on the house. My privilege."

Ninety seconds later, as Charley wondered how long (he had never had a barbershop shave before) Big Tony was going to keep the towels on his face, someone else came into the barbershop.

"You know who's in the chair, under the towels?" Charley heard Big Tony say. "Charley McFadden, that's who. You seen the *Bulletin?*"

"I seen it," an unfamiliar voice said. "I'll be god-damned."

Charley had folded his hands over his stomach. He was startled when his right hand was picked up, and vigorously shaken by two hands.

"Good for you, Charley," the voice said. "I was just telling the wife, when we seen the paper, that if there was more cops like you, and more shitasses killed like the one you killed, Philly'd be a hell of a lot better off. We're all proud of you, boy."

"I knew all along," Charley heard Big Tony say, "that Charley was a cop. I couldn't say anything, of course."

When Big Tony pulled the hot towel off, and started to lather Charley's face, there were three other men from the neighborhood standing behind the chair, waiting to shake his hand.

It was a pleasant spring morning, and the Payne family was having breakfast outside, on a flagstone patio. The whole family, for the first time in a long time, was all home at once. Foster J. Payne, twenty-five, who looked very much like his father, had come home from Cambridge, where he had just completed his second year at Harvard Law; and Amelia Alice "Amy" Payne, twenty-seven, who had three years before—the youngest in her Johns Hopkins class—earned the right to append "M.D." after her name, had just completed her residency in psychiatry at the Louisiana State University Medical Center, and had come home to find a place for herself in Philadelphia. Brewster C. Payne III, eighteen, who had just graduated from Episcopal Academy, had commuted to school; but he was, after spending the summer in Europe (his graduation present), going to Dartmouth; and Patricia Payne was very aware that the nest would then be forever empty.

Amy was petite and intense, not a pretty girl, but an attractive, natural one. In judging his children intellectually (and of course, privately) Brewster Payne had rated his daughter first, then Matt, then Foster, and finally Brewster, who was known as "B.C." Just as privately, Patricia Payne had done the same thing, with the same result, except that she had rated B.C. ahead of Foster.

Amy was very smart, perhaps even brilliant. She had been astonishingly precocious, and as astonishingly determined from the time she had been a little girl. Patricia worried that it might cause her trouble when she married, until she learned to adapt to her husband, or perhaps to the more general principle that it is sometimes far wiser to keep your mouth shut than to persist in trying to correct someone else's erroneous notions.

Matt was bright. He had never had any trouble in school, and there had been at least a dozen letters from teachers and headmasters saying essentially the same thing, that if he applied himself, he could be an A student. He never applied himself (Patricia was convinced he had never done an hour's honest homework in his life) and he had never been an A student.

Foster was, but Foster had to work at it. By definition, Foster was the only student among the three of them. Amy rarely had to crack a book, Matt was never willing to, and Foster seldom had his nose out of one. B.C. had been a 3.5 average student at Episcopal without ever having brought a book home from school.

The patio was furnished with a long, wrought-iron, mottled-glass-topped table, with eight cushioned wrought-iron chairs. Two smaller matching tables sat against the fieldstone, slate-topped patio wall. Two electric frying pans had been set up on one of them, and it also held a bowl of eggs and a plate with bacon and Taylor ham. The other held an electric percolator, a pitcher of milk, a toaster, bread and muffins, and a pitcher of orange juice.

Patricia Payne had decided, when the kids were growing up, that the solution to everybody's sauntering down to breakfast in their own good time was, rather than shouted entreaties and threats up the kitchen stairwell, a cafeteria-style buffet. The kids came down when they wanted, and cooked their own eggs. In the old days, too, there had been two newspapers, which at least partially solved the question of who got what section when.

There was something bittersweet about today's breakfast, Patricia thought: fond memories of breakfasts past, pleasure that everyone was once again having breakfast together again, and a disquieting fear that today, or at least the next week or so, might be the very last time it would happen.

"That's absolute *bullshit!*" Matthew Payne said, furiously.

Everybody looked at him. He was on the right side of the far end of the table, bent over a folded copy of the *Ledger*.

"Matt!" Patricia Payne said.

"Did you see this?" Matt asked, rhetorically.

"Actually, no," Brewster Payne said, dryly. "When I came down, all that was left of the paper was the real estate ads."

"Tell us what the goddamn liberals have done this time, Matty," Amy said.

"You watch your language, too, *Doctor*," Patricia Payne said.

Matt got up and walked down the table to Brewster Payne and laid the editorial page on the table before him. He pointed.

" 'No Room In Philadelphia For Vigilante Justice'," Matt quoted. "Just read that garbage!"

Brewster Payne read the editorial, then pushed the paper to his wife.

"Maybe they know something you don't, Matt," he said.

"I met that cop yesterday," Matt said.

"You met him?" Amy said.

"Denny Coughlin took me to meet him," Matt said. "First he took me to the medical examiner's and showed me the body, and then he took me to South Philadelphia to meet the cop."

"Why did he do that?" Amy asked.

"He shares your opinion, *Doctor*, that I shouldn't join the police," Matt said. "He was trying to scare me off."

"I suppose even a policeman can spot obvious insanity when he sees it," Amy said.

"Amy!" Patricia Payne said.

Foster Payne got up and stood behind Patricia Payne and read the editorial.

"Whoever wrote this," he said, "is one careful step the safe side of libel," he said.

"It's bullshit," Matt said. "It's . . . vicious. I saw that cop. He was damned near in shock. He was so shook up he didn't even know who Denny Coughlin was. He's a nice, simple Irish Catholic guy who could no more throw somebody in front of an elevated train than Mom could."

"But it doesn't *say* that, Matthew," Foster Payne explained patiently. "It doesn't *say* he pushed that man onto the tracks. What it *says* is that that allegation has been raised, and that having been raised, the city has a clear duty to investigate. Historically, police have overreacted when one of their own has been harmed."

Matthew glared at him; said, with infinite disgust, "Oh, Jesus!" and then looked at Brewster Payne. "Now that Harvard Law has been heard from, Dad, what do you say?"

"I don't really know enough about what really happened to make a judgment," Brewster Payne said. "But I think it reasonable to suggest that Arthur J. Nelson, having lost his son the way he did, is not very happy with the police."

"Daddy, you saw where the police are looking for the Nelson boy's homosexual lover?" Amy asked. "His *Negro* homosexual lover?"

"Oh, no!" Patricia Payne said. "How awful!"

"No, I didn't," Brewster Payne said. "But if that's true, that would lend a little weight to my argument, wouldn't it?"

"You're not suggesting, Brew, that Mr. Nelson would allow something like that to be published; something untrue, as Matt says it is, simply to . . . get back at the police."

"Welcome to the real world, Mother," Amy said.

SEVENTEEN

Jason Washington was waiting for them at the medical examiner's office. His expressive face showed both surprise and, Peter Wohl thought, just a touch of amusement when he saw that Wohl was in uniform.

"Good morning, Miss Dutton," Washington said. "I'm sorry to have to put you through this."

"It's all right," Louise said.

"They're installing a closed-circuit television system, to make this sort of identification a little easier on people," Washington said. "But it's not working yet."

"I can come back in a month," Louise said.

They chuckled. Washington smiled at Wohl.

"And may I say, Inspector, how spiffy you look today?" he said.

"I'm going to be a pallbearer," Wohl said.

"Can we get on with this?" Louise asked.

"Yes, ma'am," Washington said. "Miss Dutton, I'm going to take you inside, and show you some remains. I will then ask you if you have ever seen that individual, and if so, where, when, and the circumstances.''

"All right," Louise said.

"You want me to come with you?" Peter asked.

"Only if you want to," Louise said.

Louise stepped back involuntarily when Jason Washington lifted the sheet covering the remains of Gerald Vincent Gallagher, but she did not faint, nor did she become nauseous. When Peter Wohl tried to steady her by putting his hands on her arms, she shook free impatiently.

"I don't know his name," she said, levelly. "But I have seen that man before. In the Waikiki Diner. He's the man who was holding the diner up when Captain Moffitt tried to stop him."

"There is no question in your mind?" Washington asked.

"For some reason, it stuck in my mind," Louise said, sarcastically, and then turned and walked quickly out of the room.

Wohl caught up with her.

"You all right?" he asked.

"I'm fine," she said.

"You want a cup of coffee? Something else?"

"No, thank you," she said.

"You want to go get some breakfast?"

"No, thank you."

"You have to eat, Louise," Wohl said.

"He said, ever practical," she said, mockingly.

"You do," he said.

"All right, then," she said.

They went to a small restaurant crowded with office workers on the way to work. They were the subject of a good deal of curiosity. People recognized Louise, Wohl realized. They might not be able to recognize her as the TV lady, but they knew they had seen her someplace.

She ate French toast and bacon, but said very little.

"I have the feeling that I've done something wrong," Peter said.

"Don't be silly," she said.

As they walked back to his car, they passed a Traffic Division cop, who saluted Peter, who, not expecting it, returned it somewhat awkwardly. Then he noticed that the cop was wearing the mourning band over his badge. He had completely forgotten about that. The mourning bands were sliced from the elastic cloth around the bottom of old uniform caps. He didn't have an old uniform cap. He had no idea what had happened to either his old regular patrolman's cap, or the crushed-crown cap he had worn as a Highway Patrol sergeant. And there never had been cause to replace his senior officer's cap; he hadn't worn it twenty times.

He wondered if someone would have one at Marshutz & Sons, predicting that someone like him would show up without one. And if that didn't happen, what he would do about it.

He drove Louise back to Stockton Place and pulled to the curb before Number Six.

"What about later?" he asked.

"What about later?" she parroted.

"When am I going to see you?"

"I have to work, and then I have to see my father, and then I have to go back to work. I'll call you."

"Don't call me, I'll call you?"

"Don't press me, Peter," she said, and got out of the car. And then she walked around the front and to his window and motioned for him to lower it. She bent down and kissed him. It started as a quick kiss, but it quickly became intimate.

Not passionate, he thought, *intimate.*

"That may not have been smart," Louise said, looking into his eyes for a moment, and then walking quickly into the building, not looking back.

Intimate, Peter Wohl thought, *and a little sad, as in a farewell kiss.*

He looked at her closed door for a moment, and then made a U-turn on the cobblestones, and drove away.

He had headed, without thinking, for Marshutz & Sons, but changed his mind and instead drove to the Roundhouse. There might have been another development, something turned up around Jerome Nelson's car, maybe, or something else. If there was something concrete, maybe it would placate Arthur J. Nelson. His orders had been to stroke him, not antagonize him.

And somewhere in the Roundhouse he could probably find someone who could give him a mourning band; he didn't want to take the chance that he could get one at the funeral home.

He went directly to Homicide.

Captain Henry C. Quaire was sitting on one of the desks, talking on the telephone, and seemed to expect him; when he saw Wohl he pointed to one of the rooms adjacent to one of the interrogation rooms. Then he covered the phone with his hand and said, "Be right with you."

Wohl nodded and went into the room. Through the one-way mirror, he could see three people in the interrogation room. One was Detective Tony Harris. There was another man, a tall, rather aesthetic-looking black man in his twenties or thirties whom Wohl didn't recognize but who, to judge by the handcuffs hanging over his belt in the small of his back, was a detective. The third man was a very large, very black, visibly uncomfortable man handcuffed to the interrogation chair. He fit the description of Pierre St. Maury.

As Peter reached for the switch that would activate the microphone hidden in the light fixture, and permit him to hear what was being said, Captain Quaire came into the room. Peter took his hand away from the switch.

"What's going on?" Peter asked. "Is that Pierre St. Maury?"

"No," Quaire said. "His name is Kostmayer. But Porterfield thought he was, and brought him in."

"Porterfield is the other guy?"

Quaire nodded and grunted. "Narcotics. Good cop. He's high on the detective's list and wants to come over here when he gets promoted."

"So what's going on?"

"This guy was so upset that Porterfield thought he was

Maury that Porterfield thinks he knows something about the Nelson job.''

''Does he?'' Wohl asked.

''We are about to find out,'' Quaire said, throwing the microphone switch. ''He already gave us Mr. Pierre St. Maury's real name—Errol F. Watson—and address. I already sent people to see if they can pick him up at home.''

Wohl watched the interrogation for fifteen minutes. Admiringly. Tony Harris and Porterfield worked well together, as if they had done so before. He wondered if they had. They pulled one little thing at a time from Kostmayer, sometimes sternly calling him by his last name, sometimes, kindly, calling him ''Peter,'' one picking up the questioning when the other stopped.

It was slow. Kostmayer was reluctant to talk. It was obvious he was more afraid of other people than his own troubles with the law.

''What have you got on him?'' Wohl asked.

''Couple of minor arrests,'' Quaire said. ''He's a male prostitute. The usual stuff. Possession of controlled substances. Rolling people.''

Kostmayer finally said something interesting.

''Well, I heard *this*,'' he said, seemingly on the edge of tears. ''I only *heard* it; I don't know if it's *true* or not.''

''We understand, Peter,'' Tony Harris said, kindly. ''What did you hear?''

''Well, there was talk, and you know people just talk, that a certain two men who knew Pierre, and knew that he was, you know, *friends,* with Jerome Nelson, were going to get the key to the apartment—you know, the Nelson apartment—from him.''

''Why were they going to do that, Peter?'' Tony Harris asked.

''What certain two people, Kostmayer?'' Detective Porterfield demanded.

''Well, they were, you know, going to *take* things,'' Kostmayer said.

''What were their names, Kostmayer?'' Porterfield said,

walking to him and lowering his face to his. "I'm losing my patience with you."

"I don't know their names," Kostmayer said.

He's lying, Peter Wohl thought, at the exact moment Porterfield put that thought in words: "Bullshit!"

Wohl looked at Quaire, who had his lower lip protruding thoughtfully.

Then Wohl looked at his watch.

"Hell, I have to get out of here," he said. "I'm due at Marshutz & Sons in fifteen minutes."

"You going to be a pallbearer? Is that why you're wearing your uniform?"

"Yeah. And Henry, I need a mourning strip for my badge. Where can I get one?"

"I've got one," Quaire said, taking Wohl's arm and leading him to his office. There, he took a small piece of black elastic hatband material from an envelope and stretched it over Wohl's badge.

"I appreciate it, Henry. I'll get it back to you."

"Why don't you?" Quaire said. "Then the next time, God forbid, we need one, you'll know where to find one."

Wohl nodded.

"I'll let you know whatever else they find out, Peter," Quaire said.

"As soon as you get it, please. Even at Dutch's funeral."

"Sure," Quaire said.

Wohl shook Quaire's hand and left.

Brewster Cortland Payne II had had some difficulty persuading Amy, Foster, and B.C. to attend the funeral of Captain Richard C. Moffitt.

Amy had caved in more quickly, when her father told her that her mother felt the loss more than she was showing, and that while she wouldn't ask, would really appreciate having another female along.

Foster and B.C. were a little more difficult. When Brewster Payne raised the subject, he saw his sons were desperately searching for a reason not to go.

Finally, B.C. protested, truthfully, that he had "seen the man only once or twice in my life."

"He was your brother's uncle, Brew," Brewster Payne said, "and your mother's brother-in-law."

"You know," Foster said, thoughtfully, "the only time I ever think that Mother isn't my—what's the word?— *natural* mother is when something like this comes up."

"I'm sure she would accept that as a compliment," Brewster Payne said.

"Or that Matt isn't really my brother," Foster went on. "I presume you did try to talk him out of this becoming-a-policeman nonsense?"

"First things first," Brewster Payne said. "Matt is your brother, de facto and de jure, and I'm sure you won't say anything about something like that to him."

"Of course not," Foster said.

"I already told him," B.C. said, "that I thought he was nuts."

Out of the mouth of the babe, Brewster C. Payne thought. He said: "To answer your second question, no, I didn't really try to talk Matt out of becoming a police-man. For one thing, I learned of it after the fact, and for another, he's your mother's son, and as you have learned there are times when neither of them can be dissuaded from what they want to do. And, finally, son, I don't agree that it's nonsense. I told him, and I believe, that it can be a very valuable learning experience for him."

"Amy says that he was psychologically castrated when he failed the marine corps physical, and is becoming a policeman to prove his manhood," B.C. said.

"She talks to you like that? When I was a boy—"

"All the girls you knew were virgins who didn't even know what 'castrated' meant," Foster said, laughing. "But Amy has a point, and she's really concerned."

"I don't think I quite understand," Brewster Payne said.

"What if Matt can't make it as a policeman? He really doesn't know what he's letting himself in for. What if he fails? Double castration, so to speak."

"I have confidence that Matt can do anything he sets

his mind to do," Brewster Payne said. "And I'm beginning to wonder if sending your sister to medical school was such a good idea. I'm afraid that we can expect henceforth that she will ascribe a Freudian motive to everything any one of us does, from entering a tennis tournament to getting married."

Patricia and Amelia Payne came down the wide staircase from the second floor. They were dressed almost identically, in simple black dresses, strings of pearls, black hats, and gloves.

Brewster Payne had what he thought a moment later was an unkind thought. He wondered how many men were lucky enough to have wives who were better looking than their daughters.

"Where's Matt?" Patricia Payne asked.

The two men shrugged.

Amelia Payne turned and shouted up the stairs.

"Matty, for God's sake, will you come?"

"Keep your goddamned pants on, Amy," Matt's voice replied.

"It is such a joy for a father to see what refined and well-mannered children he has raised," Brewster C. Payne II said.

Matt came down the stairs two at a time, a moment later, shrugging into a jacket; his tie, untied, hanging loosely around his neck. He looked, Brewster Payne thought, about eighteen years old. And he wondered if Matt really understood what he was getting into with the police, if he could indeed cope with it.

"Since there's so many of us," Patricia said, "I guess we had better go in the station wagon."

"I asked Newt to get the black car out," Brewster Payne said, meeting his wife's eyes. "And to drive us."

"Oh, Brew!" she said.

"I considered the station wagon," Brewster Payne said. "And finally decided the black car was the best solution to the problem."

"What problem?" Matt asked.

"How to avoid anything that could possibly upset your grandmother," Patricia Payne said. "All right, Brew. If you think so, then let's go."

They collected Foster and B.C. from the patio, and then filed outside. Newt, the handyman, who was rarely seen in anything but ancient paint-splattered clothing, was standing, freshly shaved and dressed in a suit, and holding a gray chauffeur's cap in his hand by the open rear door of a black Cadillac Fleetwood.

When Peter Wohl reached the Marshutz & Sons Funeral Home, there were six Highway Patrol motorcycles in the driveway, their riders standing together. Behind them was Chief Inspector Dennis V. Coughlin's Oldsmobile. Behind that was a Cadillac limousine with a "FUNERAL" flag on its right fender, then a Cadillac hearse, then finally two Ford Highway Patrol cars.

When Peter drove in, Sergeant Tom Lenihan, Denny Coughlin's aide, got out of the Olds and held up his hand for Peter to stop.

"They're waiting for you inside, Inspector," he said. "Park your car. After the funeral, there will be cars to bring you all back here."

Peter parked the car behind the building beside other police cars, marked and unmarked, and a few privately owned cars, and then walked into the funeral home. The corridor was crowded with uniformed police officers, one of them a New Jersey state trooper lieutenant in a blue-and-gray uniform. Wohl wondered who he was.

As he walked toward them, Wohl saw that the Blue Room, where Dutch had been laid out for the wake, and which had been full of flowers, was now virtually empty except for the casket itself, which was now closed, and covered with an American flag.

"We were getting worried about you, Peter," Chief Inspector Dennis V. Coughlin said to him. "The Moffitts left just a couple of minutes ago. I think Jeannie maybe expected you to be here when they closed the coffin."

"I took Miss Dutton to identify Gallagher," Peter replied. "And I just left Homicide. Vice turned up a suspect who seems to know something about why Nelson was killed."

"I thought maybe you'd run into the commissioner," Coughlin said.

He's pissed that I'm late. Well, to hell with it. I couldn't help it.

"Was the commissioner looking for me?" Peter asked.

"I think you could say that, yes," Coughlin said, sarcastically.

"Chief, I'm missing something here," Wohl said. "If I've held things up here, I'm really sorry."

Coughlin looked at him for a long moment.

"You really don't know what I'm talking about, do you?"

"No, sir."

"You haven't seen the *Ledger?* Nobody's shown it to you? Said anything about it?"

"The *Ledger?* No, sir."

"When was the last time you saw Mickey O'Hara? Or talked to him?"

"I saw him a week, ten days ago," Peter said, after some thought. "I ran into him in Wanamaker's."

"Not in the last two, three days? You haven't seen him, or talked to him?"

"No, sir," Peter said, and then started to ask, "Chief—"

"Now that we're all here," an impeccably suited representative of Marshutz & Sons interrupted him, "I'd like to say a few words about what we're all going to do taking our part in the ceremonies."

"You ride from here to Saint Dominic's with me," Chief Inspector Coughlin ordered, earning himself a look of annoyance from the funeral director.

"With one exception," the man from Marshutz began, "pallbearer positions will reflect the rank of the pallbearer. Chief Inspector Coughlin will be at the right front of the casket, with Staff Inspector Wohl on the left. Immediately behind Chief Inspector Coughlin, the one exception I mentioned, will be Lieutenant McGrory of the New Jersey State Police. From then on, left, right, left, right, positions are assigned by rank. I have had a list typed up . . ."

Patrol cars from the Seventh District were on hand to block intersections between Marshutz & Sons and Saint Dominic's Roman Catholic Church.

When Dutch Moffitt's flag-draped casket had been rolled into the hearse, Dennis Coughlin and Peter Wohl walked forward to Coughlin's Oldsmobile. The Highway Patrol motorcycle men kicked their machines into life and turned on the flashing lights. Then, very slowly, the small convoy pulled away from the funeral home.

The officers from the Seventh District cars saluted as the hearse rolled past them.

"Tom, have you got the *Ledger* up there with you?" Denny Coughlin asked, from the backseat of the Oldsmobile.

"Yes, sir. And the *Bulletin.*"

"Pass them back to Inspector Wohl, would you please, Tom? He hasn't seen them."

When Sergeant Lenihan held the papers up, Wohl leaned forward and took them.

"You never saw any of that before, Peter?" Coughlin asked, when Wohl had read Mickey O'Hara's story in the *Bulletin* and the editorial in the *Ledger.*

"No, sir," Peter said. "Is there anything to it? Did Gallagher get pushed in front of the train?"

"No, and there are witnesses who saw the whole thing," Coughlin said. "Unfortunately, they are one cop— Martinez, McFadden's partner—and the engineer of the elevated train. Both of whom could be expected to lie to protect a cop."

"Then what the hell is the *Ledger* printing crap like that for?"

"Commissioner Czernick believes it is because Staff Inspector Peter Wohl first had diarrhea of the mouth—that's a direct quote, Peter—when speaking with Mr. Michael J. O'Hara—''

"I haven't spoken to Mickey O'Hara—"

"Let me finish, Peter," Coughlin interrupted. "First you had diarrhea of the mouth with Mr. O'Hara, and then you compounded your—another direct quote—incredible stupidity—by antagonizing Arthur J. Nelson, when you were under orders to charm him. Anything to that?"

"Once again, I haven't seen Mickey O'Hara, or talked to him, in ten days, maybe more."

"But maybe you did piss off Arthur J. Nelson?"

"I called him late last night to tell him the Jaguar had been found. He asked me where, and I told him— truthfully—that I didn't know. He was a little sore about that, but I don't think *antagonize* is the word."

"You didn't—and for God's sake tell me if you did— make any cracks about homosexuality, 'your son the fag,' something like that?"

"Sir, I don't deserve that," Peter said.

"That's how it looks to the commissioner, Peter," Coughlin said. "And to the mayor, which is worse. He's going to run again, of course, and when he does, he wants the *Ledger* to support him."

Peter looked out the window. They were still some distance from Saint Dominic's but the street was lined with parked police cars.

Dutch, Peter thought, *is going to be buried in style.*

"Chief," Peter said, "all I can do is repeat what I said. I haven't seen, or spoken to, Mickey O'Hara for more than a week. And I didn't say anything to Arthur Nelson that I shouldn't have."

Coughlin grunted.

"For Christ's sake, I even kept my mouth shut when he tried to tell me his son was Louise's boyfriend."

"'Louise's boyfriend'?" Coughlin parroted. "When did you get on a first-name basis with her?"

Peter turned and met Coughlin's eyes.

"We've become friends, Chief," he said. "Maybe a little more."

"You didn't say anything to her about the Nelson boy being queer, did you? Could that have got back to Nelson?"

"She knew about him," Peter said. "I met him in her apartment."

"When was that?"

"When I went there to bring her to the Roundhouse," Peter said. "The day Dutch was killed."

Out the side window, Peter saw that the lines of police cars were now double-parked. When he looked through the windshield, he could see they were approaching Saint Dominic's. There was a lot of activity there, although the funeral mass wouldn't start for nearly an hour.

"All I know, Peter," Coughlin said, "is that right now, you're in the deep shit. You may be—and I think you are—lily white, but the problem is going to be to convince Czernick and the mayor. Right now, you're at the top of their shit list."

The small convoy drove past the church, and then into the church cemetery, and through the cemetery back to the church, finally stopping beside a side door. The pall-bearers got out of the limousine and went to the hearse. Coughlin and Wohl joined them, and took Dutch Moffitt's casket from the hearse and carried it through the side door into the church. Under the direction of the man from Marshutz & Sons, they set it up in the aisle.

The ornate, Victorian-style church already held a number of people. Peter saw Jeannie Moffitt and Dutch's kids and Dutch's mother, and three rows behind them his own mother and father. Ushers—policemen—were escorting more people down the aisles.

"About—face," Chief Inspector Dennis V. Coughlin ordered softly, and the pallbearers standing beside the casket turned around. "For-ward, march," Coughlin said, and they marched back toward the altar, and then turned left, leaving Saint Dominic's as they had entered it. They would reenter the church as the mass started, as part of the processional, and take places in the first row of pews on the left.

The nave of the church was full of flowers.

Peter wondered how much they had all cost, and whether there wasn't something really sinful in all that money being spent on flowers.

Newt Gladstone pulled the Payne Cadillac to the curb in front of Saint Dominic's. A young police officer with a mourning band crossing his badge opened the door, and Brewster, Patricia, and Foster Payne got out of the backseat as Amy and Matt got out of the front.

The young policeman leaned in the open front door.

"Take the first right," he ordered Newt. "Someone there will assign you a place in the procession."

Patricia Payne took Matt's arm and they walked up the short walk to the church door. Both sides of the flagstone walk were lined with policemen.

A lieutenant standing near the door with a clipboard in his hands approached them.

"May I have your invitations, please?" he asked.

"We don't have any invitations," Matt said.

"Our name is Payne," Patricia said. "This is my son, Matthew. He is Captain Moffitt's nephew."

"Yes, ma'am," the lieutenant said. "Family."

He flipped sheets of paper on his clipboard, and ran his fingers down a list of typewritten names. His face grew troubled.

"Ma'am," he said, uncomfortably, "I've only got one Payne on my list."

"Then your list is wrong," Matt said, bluntly.

"Let me see," Patricia said, and looked at the clipboard. Her name was not on the list headed "FAMILY—Pews 2 through 6, Right Side." Nor were Brewster's, or Foster's, or B.C.'s, or Amy's. Just Matt's.

"Well, no problem," Patricia said. "Matt, you go sit with your Aunt Jean and your grandmother, and we'll sit somewhere else."

"You're as much family as I am," Matt said.

"No, Matt, not really," Patricia Payne said.

"Is there some problem?" Brewster Payne asked, as he stepped closer.

"No," Patricia said. "They just have Matt sitting with the Moffitts. We'll sit somewhere else."

The lieutenant looked even more uncomfortable.

"Ma'am, I'm afraid that all the seats are reserved."

"What does that mean?" Patricia asked, calmly.

"Ma'am, they're reserved for people with invitations," he said.

"Mother," Amy said. "Let's just go!"

"Perhaps that would be best, Pat," Brewster Payne said.

"Be quiet, the both of you," Patricia snapped. "Lieutenant, is Chief Inspector Coughlin around here somewhere?"

"Yes, ma'am," the lieutenant said. "He's a pallbearer. I'm sure he's here somewhere."

"Get him," Patricia said, flatly.

"Ma'am?"

"I said, go get him, tell him I'm here and I want to see him," Patricia said, her voice raised just a little.

"Pat . . ." Brewster said.

"Brewster, shut up!" Patricia said. "Do what I say, Lieutenant. Matt, I told you to go inside and sit with your Aunt Jean."

"Do what she says, Matt," Brewster Payne ordered.

Matt looked at him, then shrugged, and went inside.

"Would you please stand to the side?" the lieutenant said. "I'm afraid we're holding things up."

"This is humiliating," Amy said, softly.

The lieutenant caught the eye of a sergeant, and motioned him over.

"See if you can find Chief Coughlin," the lieutenant ordered. "Tell him that a Mrs. Payne wants to see him, here."

Four other mourners filed into Saint Dominic's after giving their invitations to the lieutenant.

Then two stout, gray-haired women, dressed completely in black, with black lace shawls over their heads, walked slowly up the flagstones, accompanied by an expensively dressed muscular young man with long, elaborately combed hair.

"May I have your invitations, please?" the lieutenant asked politely.

"No invitations," the muscular young man said. "Friends of the family. This is Mrs. Turpino, and this is Mrs. Savarese."

The lieutenant now took a good look at the expensively dressed young man.

"And you're Angelo Turpino, right?"

"That's right, Lieutenant," Turpino said. "I saw Captain Moffitt just minutes before this terrible thing happened, and I've come to pay my last respects."

The lieutenant, with an almost visible effort to keep control of himself, went through the sheets on his clipboard.

"You're on here," he said. "Won't you please go inside? Tell the usher 'friends of the family.' "

"Thank you very much," Angelo Turpino said. He took the women's arms. "Come on, Mama," he said. He led them into Saint Dominic's.

The sergeant whom the lieutenant had sent after Chief Inspector Coughlin came back. "He'll be right here, Lieutenant," he said. "He's on the phone."

The lieutenant nodded.

"Was that who I thought it was just going in?" the sergeant asked.

"That was Angelo Turpino," the lieutenant said. "And his mother. And a Mrs. Savarese. 'Friends of the family.' "

"Probably Vincenzo's wife," the sergeant said. "They was on the list?"

"Yes, they were," the lieutenant said.

"I'll be damned," the sergeant said.

"*Mother,*" Amy Payne, who had heard all this, and who was fully aware that Vincenzo Savarese was almost universally recognized to be the head of the mob in Philadelphia, exploded, "I refuse to stand here and see you humiliated like this . . ."

Chief Inspector Dennis V. Coughlin came around the corner of the church. He kissed Patricia as he offered his hand to Brewster Payne.

"What can I do for you, darling?" he asked.

"You can get us into the church," Patricia Payne said. "I am not on the family list, nor do we have invitations."

"My God!" Coughlin said, and turned to the lieutenant, who handed him his clipboard.

"You keep that," Coughlin said. "And you personally usher the Paynes inside and seat them wherever they want to sit."

"Yes, sir. Chief . . ."

"Just do it, Lieutenant," Coughlin said. "Brewster, I'm sorry . . ."

"We know what happened, Dennis," Brewster Payne said. "Thank you for your courtesy."

The pallbearers waited to be summoned behind Saint Dominic's, in a small grassy area between the church and the fence of the church cemetery.

Wohl took the opportunity to speak to the Jersey trooper lieutenant.

"I'm Peter Wohl," he said, walking up to him and extending his hand.

"Bob McGrory," the lieutenant said. "I heard Dutch talk about you."

"All bad?"

"He said you had all the makings of a good Highway Patrolman, and then went bad and took the examination for lieutenant."

"Dutch really liked Highway," Wohl said. "And they liked him. One of his sergeants rolled on the 'assist officer' call, found out that Dutch was involved, and called in every Highway Patrol car in the city."

"Dutch was a good guy. Goddamned shame, this," McGrory said.

"Yeah," Wohl agreed. "Mind if I ask you something else?"

"Go ahead."

"We've got a homicide. Son of a very important man. His car, a Jaguar, turned up missing. Then I heard they found it in Jersey. You know anything about that?"

"Major Knotts found it," McGrory said. "On his way over here last night. It was on a dirt road off Three Twenty-two."

"Do you know if they turned up anything? Besides the car?" Wohl asked.

"Knotts told me that when they got the NCIC hit, and then heard from you guys, he ordered the mobile crime lab in. And they were supposed to have people out there this morning, when it was light, to have a look around the area."

"You usually do that when you find a hot car?"

"No, but the word was 'homicide,' " McGrory said. Then he added, "Inspector, if they found anything interesting, I'm sure they would have passed it on to you. And probably to me, too. I mean, they knew Dutch and I were close."

"Yeah, I'm sure they would have," Wohl said, and started to say something else when someone spoke his name.

He turned and saw Sergeant Jankowitz, Commissioner Czernick's aide.

"Hello, Jank," Wohl said. "This is Lieutenant Mc-Grory. Sergeant Jankowitz, Commissioner Czernick's indispensable right-hand man."

The two shook hands.

"Inspector Wohl," Jankowitz said, formally, "Commissioner Czernick would like to see you in his office at two this afternoon."

"Okay," Wohl said. "I'll be there."

Jankowitz started to say something, then changed his mind. He smiled, nodded at McGrory, and walked away.

Watching him go, Wohl's eyes focused on the street. He saw a roped-off area in which a number of television camera crew trucks were parked. And he saw Louise. She was standing on a truck, and looking at the area through binoculars. When they seemed to be pointed in his direction,

he raised his hand to shoulder level and waved. He wondered if she saw him.

A hand touched his shoulder. He turned and saw his
father. And then his mother and Barbara Crowley.

"Hello, Dad," Peter said. "Lieutenant McGrory, this
is my father, Chief Inspector Wohl, Retired. And my
mother, and Miss Crowley."

Barbara surprised him by kissing him.

"When we heard you were going to be a pallbearer,"
Peter's mother said, "I asked Barbara if she wanted to
come. Gertrude Moffitt, before she knew you were going
to be a pallbearer, told me she'd given us three family
seats, and since you wouldn't need one now, I asked Barbara. I mean she's almost family, you know what I mean."

"That was a good idea," Peter said.

"Got a minute, Peter?" Chief Inspector August Wohl,
Retired, said, and took Peter's arm and led him out of
hearing.

"You're in trouble," Peter's father said. "You want to
tell me about it?"

"I'm not in trouble, Dad," Peter said. "I didn't do
anything wrong."

"What's that got to do with being in trouble? The word
is around that both the Polack and the mayor are after your
scalp."

"They think I talked to Mickey O'Hara and said something I shouldn't. I haven't seen O'Hara in ten days. I
don't know who ran off at the mouth, but it wasn't me.
And I can't help it if Nelson is pissed at me. I didn't say
anything to him, either, that I shouldn't."

"The mayor will throw you to the fish if he thinks he
will get the *Ledger* off his back. And so will the Polack.
You better get this straightened out, Peter, and quick."

There was a burst of organ music from Saint Dominic's.
The man from Marshutz & Sons began to collect the pallbearers.

When he was formed in ranks beside Chief Inspector
Dennis V. Coughlin, Staff Inspector Peter Wohl glanced
at the street again, at the TV trucks. He saw Louise again,

and was sure that she was looking at him, and that she had seen Barbara kiss him.

She was waving her hand slowly back and forth, as if she knew he was watching her, and wanted to wave good-bye.

EIGHTEEN

One of their own had died in the line of duty, and police officers from virtually every police department in a one-hundred-mile circle around Philadelphia had come to honor him. They had come in uniform, and driving their patrol cars, and the result was a monumental traffic jam, despite the best efforts of more than twenty Philadelphia Traffic Division officers to maintain order.

When Chief Inspector Dennis V. Coughlin and Staff Inspector Peter Wohl made their careful way down the brownstone steps of Saint Dominic's Church (Dutch Moffitt's casket was surprisingly heavy) toward the hearse waiting at the curb, there were three lines of cars, parked bumper to bumper, prepared to escort Captain Moffitt to his last resting place.

Their path to the curb was lined with Highway Patrol officers, saluting. There was an additional formation of policemen on the street, and the police band, and the color guard. To the right, behind barriers, was the press. Peter looked for, but did not see, Louise Dutton.

Both Peter and Dennis Coughlin grunted with the effort as they raised the end of the casket to the level of the hearse bed, and set it gently on the chrome-plated rollers in the floor. They pushed it inside, and a man from Marshutz & Sons flipped levers that would keep it from moving on the way to the cemetery.

The hearse would be preceded now by the limousine of the archbishop of Philadelphia and his entourage of lesser clerics, including Dutch's parish priest, the rector of Saint Dominic's, and the police chaplain. Ahead of the hearse was a police car carrying a captain of the Traffic Division, sort of an en route command car. And out in front were twenty Highway Patrol motorcycles.

Next came Dennis V. Coughlin's Oldsmobile, with the limousine carrying the rest of the pallbearers behind it. Then came the flower cars. There had been so many flowers that the available supply of flower cars in Philadelphia and Camden had been exhausted. It had been decided that half a dozen vans would be loaded with flowers and sent to Holy Sepulchre Cemetery ahead of the procession, both to cut down the length of the line of flower cars, and so that there would be flowers in place when the procession got there.

The flower vans would travel with other vehicles, mostly buses, preceding the funeral procession, the band, the honor guard, the firing squad, and the police officers who would line the path the pallbearers would take from the cemetery road to the grave site.

Behind the flower cars in the funeral procession were the limousines carrying the family, followed by the mayor's Cadillac, two cars full of official dignitaries, and then the police commissioner's car, and those of chief inspectors. Next came the cars of "official" friends (those on the invitation list), then the cars of other friends, and finally the cars of the police officers who had come to pay their respects.

It would take a long time just to load the family, dignitaries, and official friends. As soon as the last official-friends car had been loaded, the procession would start to move away from the church.

"Tom," Chief Inspector Coughlin ordered from the backseat of the Oldsmobile, "anything on the radio?"

"I'll check, sir," Sergeant Lenihan said. He took the microphone from the glove compartment.

"C-Charlie One," he said.

"C-Charlie One," radio replied.

"We're at Saint Dominic's, about to leave for Holy Sepulchre," Lenihan said. "Anything for us?"

"Nothing, C-Charlie One," radio said.

"Check for me, please, Tom," Wohl said. "Seventeen."

"Anything for Isaac Seventeen?" Lenihan said.

"Yes, wait a minute. They were trying to reach him a couple of minutes ago."

Wohl leaned forward on the seat to better hear the speaker.

"Isaac Seventeen is to contact Homicide," the radio said.

"Thank you," Lenihan said.

"There's a phone over there," Coughlin said, pointing to a pay phone on the wall of a florist's shop across the street. "You've got time."

Peter trotted to the phone, fed it a dime, and called Homicide.

"This is Inspector Wohl," he said, when a Homicide detective answered.

"Oh, yeah, Inspector. Wait just a second." There was a pause, and then the detective, obviously reading a note, went on: "The New Jersey state police have advised us of the discovery of a murder victim meeting the description of Pierre St. Maury, also known as Errol F. Watson. The body was found near the recovered stolen Jaguar automobile. The identification is not confirmed. Photographs and fingerprints of St. Maury are being sent to New Jersey. Got that?"

"Read it again," Wohl asked, and when it had been,

said, "If there's anything else in the next hour or so, I'm with C-Charlie One."

He hung up without waiting for a reply and ran back to Chief Inspector Coughlin's Oldsmobile.

"They found—the Jersey state troopers—found a body that's probably St. Maury near Nelson's car," he reported.

"Interesting," Coughlin said.

"The suspect they had in Homicide said there was talk on the street that two guys were going to get the key to Nelson's apartment from his boyfriend," Wohl said. "To see what they could steal."

There was no response from Coughlin except a grunt.

The Oldsmobile started to move.

As they passed the cordoned-off area for the press, Wohl saw Louise. She was talking into a microphone, not on camera, but as if she were taking notes.

Or, Peter thought, *she didn't want to see me.*

More than three hundred police cars formed the tail of Captain Richard C. Moffitt's funeral procession. They all had their flashing lights turned on. By the time the last visiting mourner dropped his gearshift lever in "D" and started moving, the head of the procession was well over a mile and a half ahead of him.

The long line of limousines and flower cars and police cars followed the hearse and His Eminence the Archbishop down Torresdale Avenue to Rhawn Street, out Rhawn to Oxford Avenue, turned right onto Hasbrook, right again onto Central Avenue, and then down Central to Tookany Creek Parkway, and then down the parkway to Cheltenham Avenue, and then out Cheltenham to the main entrance to Holy Sepulchre Cemetery at Cheltenham and Easton Road.

Each intersection along the route was blocked for the procession, and it stayed blocked until the last car (another Philadelphia Traffic Division car) had passed. Then the officers blocking that intersection jumped in their cars (or later, in Cheltenham Township, on their motorcycles) and raced alongside, and past, the slow-moving procession to block another intersection.

Dennis V. Coughlin lit a cigar in the backseat of the Oldsmobile almost as soon as they started moving, and sat puffing thoughtfully on it, slumped down in the seat.

He didn't say a word until the fence of Holy Sepulchre Cemetery could be seen, in other words for over half an hour. Then he reached forward and stubbed out the cigar in the ashtray on the back of the front seat.

"Peter, as I understand this," he said, "we put Dutch on whatever they call that thing that lowers the casket into the hole. Then we march off and take up position far enough away from the head of the casket to make room for the archbishop and the other priests."

"Yes, sir," Peter agreed.

"From the time we get there, we don't have anything else to do, right? I mean, when it's all over, we'll walk by and say something to Jeannie and Gertrude Moffitt, but there's nothing else we have to do as pallbearers, right?"

"I think that's right, Chief," Peter said.

"The minute we get there, Peter, I mean when we march away from the gravesite, and are standing there, you take off."

"Sir?"

"You take off. You go to the first patrol car that can move, and you tell them to take you back to Marshutz & Sons. Then you get in your car, whose radio is out of service, and you go home and you throw some stuff in a bag, and you go to Jersey in connection with the murder of the suspect in the Nelson killing. And you stay there, Peter, until I tell you to come home."

"Commissioner Czernick sent Sergeant Jankowitz to tell me the commissioner wants me in his office at two this afternoon," Peter said.

"I'll handle Czernick," Coughlin said. "You do what I tell you, Peter. If nothing else, I can buy you some time for him to cool down. Sometimes, Czernick lets his temper get in the way of his common sense. Once he's done something dumb, like swearing to put you in uniform, assigned to Night Command, permanently, on the 'last out' shift—''

"My God, is it that bad?" Peter said.

"If Carlucci loses the election, the new mayor will want a new police commissioner," Coughlin said. "If the *Ledger* doesn't support Carlucci, he may lose the election. You're expendable, Peter. What I was saying was that once Czernick has done something dumb, and then realized it was a mistake, he's got too hard a head to admit he was wrong. And he doesn't have to really worry about the cops lining up behind you for getting screwed. *I* think you're a good cop. Hell, I *know* you're a good cop. But there are a lot of forty-five- and fifty-year-old lieutenants and captains around who think the reason *they* didn't get promoted when *you* did is because *their* father wasn't a chief inspector."

"I won't resign," Peter said. "Night Command, back in uniform . . . no matter what."

"Come on, Peter," Coughlin said. "You didn't come on the job last week. You know what they can do to somebody—civil service be damned—when they want to get rid of him. If you can put up with going back in uniform and Night Command, he'll think of something else."

Peter didn't reply.

"It would probably help some if you could catch whoever hacked up the Nelson boy and shot his boyfriend," Coughlin said.

They were in the cemetery now, winding slowly down access roads. He could see Dutch Moffitt's gravesite. Highway Patrolmen were already lined up on both sides of the path down which they would carry Dutch's casket.

Jesus, Peter thought. *Maybe that was my mistake. Maybe I should have just stayed in Highway, and rode around on a motorcycle, and been happy to make Lieutenant at forty-five. That way there wouldn't have been any of this goddamned politics.*

But then he realized he was wrong.

There's always politics. In Highway, it's who gets a new motorcycle and who doesn't. Who gets to do interesting things, or who rides up and down Interstate 95 in the rain, ticketing speeders. Same crap. Just a different level.

"Thank you, Chief," Peter said. "I appreciate the vote of confidence."

"I owe your father one," Chief Inspector Dennis V. Coughlin said, matter-of-factly. "He saved my ass, one time."

"Hello?"

Peter's heart jumped at the sound of her voice.

"Hi," he said.

"I thought it might be you," she said.

"You don't seem thrilled to hear my voice," Peter said.

"I don't get very many calls at midnight," she said, ignoring his reply.

"It took me that long to get up my courage to call," he said.

"Where are you, home? Or out on the streets, protecting the public?"

"I'm in Atlantic City," he said.

"What are you doing there?"

"Working on the Nelson job," he said.

"At two o'clock this afternoon, I had a call from WCTS-TV, Channel Four, Chicago," Louise said. "They want me to co-anchor their evening news show."

"Oh?"

"They want me so bad that they will give me twenty thousand a year more than I'm making now, and they will buy out my contract here," Louise said. "That may be because I am very good, and have the proper experience, and it may be because my father owns WCTS-TV."

"What are you going to do?"

"I'd like to talk to you about that," she said. "Preferably in a public place. I don't want to be prone to argue."

He didn't reply.

"That was a joke," she said. "A clever double entendre on the word 'prone.' "

"I've heard it before," Peter said.

"But if you promise to just talk, you could come here. How long will it take you to drive from Atlantic City?"

"I can't come," Peter said.

"Why not?" she asked.

"I just can't, Louise."

"Your girl friend down there with you? Taking the sea air? I saw her kiss you this morning."

"No," he said. "I told you I'm working."

"At midnight?"

"I can't come back to Philadelphia right now," he said.

"Somebody told your girl friend about me? She's looking for you with a meat cleaver?" She heard what she said. "That was really first-class lousy taste, wasn't it? I'm upset, Peter."

"Why?"

"My father is a very persuasive man," she said. "And then he topped his hour and a half of damned-near-irrefutable arguments why you and I could never build anything permanent with that lovely WCTS-TV carrot. And seeing good ol' whatsername kiss you didn't help much, either. I think it would be a very good idea if you came here, as soon as you could, and offered some very convincing counter arguments."

"Would you be happy with the carrot? Knowing it was a carrot?"

"I think the news director at WCTS-TV will be very pleasantly surprised to find out how good I am. Since I have been shoved down his throat, he expects some simpering moron. And I'm not, Peter. I'm good. And Chicago is one step from New York, and the networks."

"Is that what you want? New York and the networks?"

"I don't know right now what I want, except that I want to talk to you," she said.

"I can't come tonight, Louise," Peter said.

"Why not? I can't seem to get an answer to that question."

"I'm in trouble with the department," Peter said.

"What kind of trouble?"

"Political trouble."

"Any chance they'll fire you, I hope, I hope?"

"Thanks a lot," he said.

"Sorry, I forgot how important being a policeman is to you," she said, sarcastically.

There was a long pause.

"We're fighting, and saying things we won't be able to take back," she said. "That's not what I wanted."

"I love you," Peter said.

"One of the interesting thoughts my father offered was that people tend to confuse love with lust. Lust comes quickly and eventually burns itself out. Love has to be built, slowly."

"Okay," Peter said. "I lust you, and I'm willing to work on the other thing."

She laughed, but stopped abruptly.

"I don't know why I'm laughing," she said. "I'm not sure whether I should cry or break things, but I know I shouldn't be laughing. I want you to come here, Peter. I want to look at you when we're talking."

"I can't come," he said. "I'm sorry."

"When can you come?"

"I don't know," he said. "Three, four days, maybe."

"Why not now?" Louise demanded plaintively.

"Because I'm liable to lose my job if I come back right now."

There was a long pause. When Louise finally spoke, her voice was calm.

"You know what you just said, of course? That your goddamned job is more important in your life than me."

"Don't be silly, Louise," Peter said.

"No, I won't," she said. "Not anymore."

The phone went dead in his ear.

When he dialed again, he got her answering device. He tried it three more times and then gave up.

When he tried to call her at WCBL-TV the next day, she was either not in, or could not be called to the telephone, and would he care to leave a message?

• • •

Staff Inspector Peter Wohl paid lip service to the notion
that he was in Atlantic City working on the Nelson homicide job. He went to the hospital where the autopsy on
Errol F. Watson, also known as Pierre St. Maury, was
performed, and looked at the corpse, and read the coro-
ner's report. Errol F. Watson had died of destruction of
brain tissue caused by three projectiles, believed to be .32
caliber, of the type commonly associated with caliber .32
Colt semiautomatic pistols.

That didn't mean he had been shot with a Colt. There
were a hundred kinds of pistols that fired the .32 ACP
cartridge. No fired cartridge cases had been found, despite
what Wohl believed had been a very thorough search of
the area where the body had been found. They had found
blood and bone and brain tissue.

Very probably, whoever had shot Errol F. Watson also
known as Pierre St. Maury had marched him away from
the Jaguar, and then shot him in the back of the head. And
then twice more, at closer range. God only knew what had
happened to the ejected cartridge cases. If they had been
ejected. There were some revolvers (which do not eject
fired cases), chambered for .32 ACP. Whatever the pistol
was, it was almost certainly already sinking into the sandy
ocean floor off Atlantic City, or into the muck of a New
Jersey swamp, and the chances of recovering it were practically nil.

He also spent most of a day at the state trooper garage,
watching, with professional admiration, the lab techni-
cians working on the Jaguar. They knew their business,
and they lifted fingerprints and took soil samples and did
all the clever things citizens have grown to expect by
watching cop stories on television.

Lieutenant Bob McGrory, who had taken him to the
garage, picked him up after work there and then insisted he come home with him for supper. He had been
at first reluctant and uncomfortable, but McGrory's
wife, Mary-Ellen, made him feel welcome, and Mc-
Grory produced a bottle of really good scotch, and

they sat around killing that, and telling Dutch
Moffitt stories, and Peter's mouth finally loosened, and
he told McGrory why he really had been sent to Atlantic City.

He left then, aware that he was a little drunk, and not
wanting to confide in Bob McGrory the painful details of
his romance with Miss Louise Dutton.

On his arrival in Atlantic City, in a fey mood, he had
taken a room in the Chalfonte-Haddon Hall, a thousand-
room landmark on the boardwalk, rather than in a smaller
hotel or a motel. He had told himself that he would endure
his time in purgatory at least in luxury.

It was, he decided, *faded grandeur* rather than *luxury*.
But it did have a bar, and he stopped there for a nightcap
before he went to his room. He had just had another one-
way conversation with Louise Dutton's answering machine, the machine doing all the talking, when there was
a knock at his door.

"Hi," she said. "I saw you downstairs in the bar, and
thought you might like a little company."

He laughed.

"What's so funny?"

"I'm a cop," he said.

"Oh, *shit!*"

He watched her flee down the corridor, and then, smiling, closed the door and walked across the room to his
bed.

The phone rang.

*Please, God, let that be Louise! Virtue is supposed to
be its own reward.*

"Did I wake you up?" Lieutenant Bob McGrory asked.

"No problem, I had to answer the phone anyway," Wohl
said, pleased with his wit.

"I just had a call from a friend of mine on the Atlantic
City vice squad," McGrory said. "Two gentlemen were
in an establishment called the Black Banana earlier this
evening. They paid for their drinks with a Visa credit card
issued to Jerome Nelson. The manager called it in. I un-

derstand he needs a friend—several friends—in the police department right now.''

"The Black Banana?" Wohl asked. "If it's what it sounds like, we've got one of those in Philly."

"Maybe it's a franchise," McGrory said, chuckling.

"They still there?"

"No. The cops are checking the hotels and motels. They have what may be a name from the manager of the Black Banana, and they're also checking to see if anyone is registered as Jerome Nelson. They have a stakeout at the Banana, too.''

"Interesting," Peter said.

"I told my friend I'd call him back and tell him if you wanted to be waked up if they find them.''

"Oh, yes," Peter Wohl said. "Thank you, Bob.''

On his fifth day in Atlantic City, when Peter Wohl walked into the state trooper barracks, Lieutenant Robert McGrory told him that he had just that moment hung up from talking with Chief Inspector Dennis V. Coughlin.

" 'Almost all is forgiven, come home' is the message, Peter," Lieutenant McGrory said.

"Thank you," Peter said. "Thanks for everything.''

"Any time. You going right back?"

"Yeah," Peter said. "My girl friend's probably finally given up on me.''

"The one at the church? Very nice.''

"Her, too," Peter said.

There was a Mayflower moving van parked on the cobblestone street before Six Stockton Place.

It is altogether fitting and proper, Peter Wohl thought, *that I should arrive here at the exact moment they are carrying out Louise's bed.*

But he got out of the LTD anyway, and walked into the building and rode up in the elevator. The door to Louise's apartment was open, and he walked in.

There were two men standing with a packing list.

"Where are you taking this stuff?" Peter asked.

"What's it to you?"

"I'm a police officer," Peter said, and took out his ID.

The man handed him a clipboard with forms on it. The household furnishings listed below were to be shipped to 2710 Lake Shore Drive, Chicago, Illinois, Apartment 1705.

"Thank you," Peter said.

"Something wrong?"

"Nothing at all," Peter said, and left the apartment and got in the LTD and drove to the Roundhouse.

He parked the car and went in and headed for the elevators, then turned and went to the receptionist's desk.

"Let me have that phone, will you please?" Peter asked.

He knew the number of WCBL-TV by memory now.

They told him they were sorry, Miss Louise Dutton was no longer connected with WCBL-TV.

He pushed the phone back to the officer on duty and walked toward the elevators.

When the door opened, Commissioner Taddeus Czernick and Sergeant Jankowitz got out. Jankowitz's eyes widened when he saw Wohl.

"Good afternoon, Commissioner," Peter said.

"Got a minute, Peter?" Czernick said, and took Wohl's arm and led him to one side.

"I think I owe you an apology," Czernick said.

"Sir?"

"I should have known you weren't the one with diarrhea of the mouth," Czernick said.

"No apology is necessary, Commissioner," Peter said.

Czernick met his eyes for a moment, and nodded.

"Well, I suppose you're ready to go back to your regular duties, aren't you, Peter?"

"Yes, sir."

"Give my regards to your dad, when you see him," Czernick said. He smiled at Peter, patted his shoulder, and walked away.

Peter got on the elevator and rode up to Chief Inspector Dennis V. Coughlin's office.

"Well, good afternoon, Inspector," Sergeant Tom Lenihan said, smiling broadly at him. "How nice to see you. I'll tell the chief you're here."

Dennis V. Coughlin greeted him by saying, "I was hoping you would walk in here about now. You can buy me lunch. You owe me one, I figure."

"Yes, sir. No argument about that."

They went, with Tom Lenihan, to Bookbinder's Restaurant. Coughlin ate a dozen cherrystone clams and drank a bottle of beer before he got into the meat of what he wanted to say.

"Commissioner Czernick happened to run into Mickey O'Hara," Coughlin said. "And the subject somehow turned to the story Mickey wrote quoting an unnamed senior police officer to the effect that we were looking for a Negro homosexual in connection with the Nelson murder."

"You set that up, didn't you, Chief?" Peter said.

"Mickey wouldn't tell him who the unnamed police officer was, but he did tell him, swearing by all that's holy, that it wasn't you."

"And the commissioner believed him?"

"I think so. I'd stay out of his way for a while, if I were you."

"I ran into him getting on the elevator in the Roundhouse," Peter said.

"And?"

"He apologized, I said none was necessary, and then he said he thought I would be happy to be getting back to my regular duties, and that I should give his regards to my dad."

"Okay," Coughlin said. "Even better than I would have hoped."

"I'm off the hook, then?"

"You weren't listening. I said that if I were you, I'd stay out of his sight for a while."

"Yes, sir."

"Since it wasn't you, who had the big mouth? That

wasn't hard to figure out. DelRaye. So DelRaye has been transferred from Homicide to the Twenty-Second District—in uniform—and he can kiss away, for good, his chances, not that there were many, to make captain. And then, I understand, Hizzoner the Mayor called Mr. Nelson, and told him what had happened, that he had found out who had the big mouth, and taken care of him, and that, proving our dedication to finding the murderers of his son, we sent you to Atlantic City where you did in fact assist the local police in apprehending the men we are sure are the murderers of his son, and couldn't we be friends again? Whereupon, Mr. Nelson let the mayor have it. I have it on reliable information that they said some very unpleasant things to each other."

"Oh, Christ!"

"I don't know what that will do to the mayor in the election, but right now he thinks that Nelson is crazy. I mean, really. He thinks Nelson is out of his mind, which gets you off the hook with him. I mean, it's you and him against the crazy man at the *Ledger*."

Wohl's eyebrows rose thoughtfully, but he didn't say anything.

Coughlin looked around for the waitress, found her, and ordered another beer and broiled swordfish.

"Same for me, please," Wohl said.

"I think I'll have some steamers," Lenihan said. "I'm trying to lose a little weight."

"That little bowl of melted butter will sure help, Tom," Coughlin said, and then turned to Peter. "Your friend Miss Dutton has left town."

"I know."

"That going to bother you, Peter?" Coughlin asked.

"Yeah," Peter said. "Yeah, it will. How did you know about that?"

Coughlin chuckled, but didn't answer.

"You'll get over it," Coughlin said. "It happens to everybody, and everybody gets over it, sooner or later."

"How late is later?" Peter asked.

"Find some nice girl, a nurse, for example, and take

her out. You'd be surprised how quickly some things pass when there's a nice girl around.''

Staff Inspector Peter Wohl didn't reply. But he picked up his beer glass and raised it to Chief Inspector Dennis V. Coughlin. He smiled, and then took a deep sip.